The Penguin Book of

IRISH VERSE

INTRODUCED AND EDITED BY
BRENDAN KENNELLY

SECOND EDITION

PENGUIN BOOKS

For
Harriet, Maurice
and Hallie Ōg

PENGUIN BOOKS

Published by the Penguin Group
Penguin Books Ltd, 27 Wrights Lane, London W8 5TZ, England
Penguin Books USA Inc., 375 Hudson Street, New York, New York 10014, USA
Penguin Books Australia Ltd, Ringwood, Victoria, Australia
Penguin Books Canada Ltd, 10 Alcorn Avenue, Toronto, Ontario, Canada M4V 3B2
Penguin Books (NZ) Ltd, 182–190 Wairau Road, Auckland 10, New Zealand

Penguin Books Ltd, Registered Offices: Harmondsworth, Middlesex, England

First published 1970
Second edition 1981
9 10

Printed in England by Clays Ltd, St Ives plc
Set in Monotype Garamond

CONTENTS

CONTENTS

PART TWO: Anglo-Irish

worth as 'the most perfect of our age', dealing with events in Irish history and scenes of Irish landscape. He also wrote a historical drama, *Mary Tudor*, published in 1847.

CHARLES WOLFE (1791–1823). A graduate of Trinity College, Dublin. 'The Burial of Sir John Moore' was published anonymously in 1817 and was attributed, among others, to Moore and Byron. It was later discovered to be Wolfe's.

JEREMIAH JOSEPH CALLANAN (1795–1829). Born in Cork; died in Lisbon, Portugal. While a student at Trinity College, he won two prizes for poetry. He may be considered a pioneer in translating Irish poetry into English. He also collected some of the legends and folklore of the Irish countryside.

GEORGE DARLEY (1795–1846). After leaving Trinity College, he went to London, where he wrote for the theatre, compiled textbooks on mathematics and became a well-known critic. A friend of Lamb and Carlyle. His incurable stammer may be one reason for the eloquent flow of his poetry. Even at this stage, Darley has not been given proper critical recognition. *Selected Poems of George Darley* (1979), edited by Anne Ridler, is an excellent introduction to this poet.

EUGENE O'CURRY (1796–1862). Best known as a Gaelic scholar. Did wonderful work in cataloguing old manuscripts. Professor of Irish History and Archaeology at the Catholic University, Dublin. His *Lectures on the Manuscript Materials of Ancient Irish History* were published in 1861.

JAMES CLARENCE MANGAN (1803–49). Born and died in Dublin. Though not formally educated, he mastered several languages. When he was fifteen, he began to work in a scrivener's office and continued this work for seven years. Later he worked in the library at Trinity College. Addicted to drugs and alcohol, he spent the last years of his life in a state of degrading poverty. Starved and exhausted, he died of

CONTENTS

CONTENTS

SAMUEL FERGUSON (1810–86). Born in Belfast; died in Dublin. Educated at Trinity College. Called to the Irish Bar in 1838, and to the Inner Bar in 1859. In 1867 he became first Deputy Keeper of the Records of Ireland. Travelled on the Continent in 1845–6. Was an expert on archaeology, art, history and architecture. Knighthood conferred on him in 1878. President of the Royal Irish Academy in 1881. A poet of indefatigable industry and stamina, and a thoroughly admirable man. See *The Poems of Samuel Ferguson*, edited by Padraic Colum (Allen Figgis, Dublin, 1963).

AUBREY DE VERE (1814–1902). A hard-working poet but a bit stuffy. Intimate friend of Carlyle, Tennyson and Wordsworth. A prolific writer.

THOMAS DAVIS (1814–45). Founded the newspaper, *The Nation*, in 1842, with John Blake Dillon and Charles Gavin Duffy. A leader of the Young Ireland political party. His *Poems* and *Literary and Historical Essays* were published in 1846.

WILLIAM McBURNEY (dates unknown). A contributor to *The Nation*, founded by Thomas Davis.

ARTHUR G. GEOGHEGAN (1810–89). Born in Dublin; died in London. Lived in England for thirty years.

CONTENTS

CONTENTS

CONTENTS

CONTENTS

Dublin. His *Collected Works* appeared in 1918. See also *The Best of Pearse* (Mercier Press, 1967); *Short Stories of Padraic Pearse* (Mercier Press, 1968); and *The 1916 Poets* (Allen Figgis, Dublin, 1963; 1980).

JOSEPH PLUNKETT (1887–1916). Executed, Easter 1916. Strong mystical strain in his poetry. See *The Poems of Joseph Mary Plunkett*, 1916; also *The 1916 Poets* (Allen Figgis, Dublin, 1963; 1980).

FRANCIS LEDWIDGE (1891–1917). Born in County Meath. Killed in action in Flanders, 31 July 1917. Lord Dunsany helped to make him known as a poet. His *Complete Poems* has gone through many editions.

PART THREE: Yeats and After

W. B. YEATS (1865–1939). Yeats always tried to 'hammer his thoughts into a unity', and his works should be read as a whole. See especially his *Collected Poems* (first edition 1933 and numerous reprints thereafter); *Collected Plays* (1953); *Mythologies* (1959); *Autobiographies* (1961); *Explorations* (1962); and *Essays and Introductions* (1961).

GEORGE RUSSELL (AE) (1867–1935). Poet, painter, mystic. Helped to found the Irish Agricultural Cooperative Movement. Referred to by W. R. Rodgers as 'the Sophocles of Dublin'. See *Homeward: Songs by the Way* (1894); *Collected*

CONTENTS

Poems (1913); *House of the Titans* (1934). A mystic with a good deal of commonsense.

OLIVER ST JOHN GOGARTY (1878–1957). A fine lyric poet who appears as Buck Mulligan in *Ulysses*. Famous talker and wit. See his *Collected Poems* (1954). A lively biography by Ulick O'Connor appeared in 1964.

JOSEPH CAMPBELL (1879–1944). Born in Belfast. Director of Studies at Fordham University, New York, but returned to Ireland, where he died. An early experimenter with Imagism. See *The Mountainy Singer* (1909), *Irishry* (1913), *Earth of Cualann* (1917) and *Complete Poems* (1963).

SEAMAS O'SULLIVAN (1879–1958). His best work deals with Dublin, its half-lit backstreets and alleyways. Founded the *Dublin Magazine* in 1923 and edited it until he died in 1958. His *Collected Poems* appeared in 1940.

PADRAIC COLUM (1881–1972). A very prolific poet. A pioneer in the Abbey Theatre tradition of realistic drama and a good novelist. See *The Poet's Circuits: Collected Poems of Ireland* (1960); *The Flying Swans* (1957), a novel; and *Three Plays* (1963).

JAMES JOYCE (1882–1941). One of the finest modern novelists. Has had enormous influence on younger writers. 'Gas from a Burner' is from *Pomes Penyeach* (Paris, 1932; Faber 1966). It is interesting to compare Joyce's satire with that of Swift. Both writers are fierce, lucid masters of the art.

JAMES STEPHENS (1882–1950). A writer of great charm. His *Crock of Gold* is a classic. Among his poems, *Insurrections* (1909), *Songs from the Clay* (1915), *Strict Joy* (1931), and *Kings and the Moon* (1938) are very attractive. His *Collected Poems*, first published in 1926, is still in print. There is a popular image of Stephens as an effervescent leprechaun.

In fact, he knew a great deal of suffering and was totally devoted to his art.

AUSTIN CLARKE (1896–1974). Poet, novelist, dramatist, and critic. *Collected Poems* published in 1974.

MONK GIBBON (1896–). Born in Dublin. Educated at St Columba's College, Dublin, and Keble College, Oxford. Won the Silver Medal for Poetry at the Tailteann Games, 1928. Member of the Irish Academy of Letters. Publications include *The Tremulous String* (1926); *For Daws to Peck At* (1929); *Seventeen Sonnets* (1932); and *This Insubstantial Pageant* (*Collected Poems*, 1951). Prose works include *The Seals* (1935), *Mount Ida* (1948) and *Inglorious Soldier* (1968). Is a thoughtful, prolific writer of both verse and prose. Lives in Sandycove, Dublin.

F. R. HIGGINS (1896–1941). An accomplished lyric poet who influenced and was influenced by Yeats. Published books include *Island Blood* (1925) and *The Gap of Brightness* (1940). A director of the Abbey Theatre from 1935 to 1941. His early death cut short a promising career as a poet.

R. N. D. WILSON (1899–1953).

PATRICK MACDONOGH (1902–61). His single substantial collection is *One Landscape Still* (1958) and it shows MacDonogh's fine sense of drama and rhythm. Experimented successfully with the rhythm-patterns of Gaelic poetry. At his best, a very moving lyric poet.

EWART MILNE (1903–). Has been a schoolteacher, sailor, and labourer. Of his many volumes of poetry, *A Garland for the Green* (1962) best shows his merits and defects as a poet. Some poems are marred by prosaic rhythms, but his best work is dramatic, richly imaged and direct.

CONTENTS

1968. His best work is marked by a hard, vigorous lyricism. He describes himself as 'an Irishman of Planter stock, by profession an art gallery man, politically a man of the Left'. Has edited the poems of William Allingham.

CONTENTS

CONTENTS

CONTENTS

CONTENTS

and *Dublin Magazine* since 1952. His first collection is due shortly from Profile Press.

JAMES SIMMONS (1933–). Born in Londonderry, educated at Leeds University. Taught for five years at Friends' School, Lisburn, where he began to write his own songs and sing them on radio and television. Won a Gregory Award for poetry. Is now lecturing in the English Department of the New University of Ulster, Coleraine. His best verse is marked by strong rhythms and verbal gusto. See *Selected Poems* (1978).

JAMES LIDDY (1934–). Born in Clare. An address on James Joyce, *Esau, My Kingdom for a Drink*, was published on Bloomsday 1962. Other publications include *In a Blue Smoke* (1964) and *Blue Mountain* (1968).

RIVERS CAREW (1935–). Educated at Trinity College, Dublin. Publications include *Figures out of Mist* (with Timothy Brownlow) (1966), as well as poems in a variety of periodicals and magazines.

JAMES McAULEY (1935–). His urbane, fastidious tone emerges in *A New Address* (1965). Has also written strong satire on the complacency of contemporary Ireland. Lives in America.

DESMOND O'GRADY (1935–). His works include *Chords And Orchestrations* (1956); *Reilly* (1961); *The Dark Edge of Europe* (1967); *Separations* (1973); *The Headgear Of The Tribe: New and Selected Poems* (1979).

BRENDAN KENNELLY (1936–). Published work includes *Dream Of A Black Fox* (1968); *Selected Poems* (1969); *Salvation, The Stranger* (1972); *The Voices* (1973); *Islandman* (1977); *A Small Light* (1979).

CONTENTS

CONTENTS

CONTENTS

INTRODUCTION

1

IN this anthology I try to give an idea of the origins and development of the Irish poetic tradition. I want to trace its growth, to show its tough capacity for survival despite long silences and methodical oppression, and to indicate the directions in which I believe it is likely to develop. Some critics may argue that I am in fact talking about two traditions in poetry; the early native Gaelic and the later Anglo-Irish. There is something to be said for this, but I personally believe that both Gaelic and Anglo-Irish combine to create a distinctively Irish tradition. It is on the basis of that belief that I have compiled this anthology.

2

Legends, myths, themes, rhythms and ideas are not like political parties and social groups. They do not thrive on an identity based on a sense of separateness; they fertilize and enrich each other constantly and deliberately in order to create new legends, myths, themes, rhythms and ideas. 'Thus far shalt thou go, and no farther' may be wise words in the mouth of a politician, but in the mouth of a poet they are death. An outstanding example of the fertilizing influence of one mode of thought and expression on another is the way in which Yeats took the dust-covered figures of Cuchulain, Conchubar, Maeve and others and proved how totally adequate these products of an ancient mythology were to express the immense complexity of life in the twentieth century. Yeats's achievement alone would justify the fusion of Gaelic and Anglo-Irish into a single, sturdy tradition. It is simply another example of his capacity to discover unity where so many before and after him have perceived and perpetuated discord and division. Today it is clear that although history nearly always sundered Irish from Anglo-Irish, the imagination has nearly always brought them closer together so that now, in retrospect, the cultures they both produced may be seen as a compact imaginative unity. Ideally, I would like to have included poems in Irish in this anthology, but since *The Penguin Book of Irish Verse* is aimed essentially at readers of English, this was impractical, if not impossible. Translation is at all times a poor substitute for the original, but where a translation from the Irish is good, it is also a completely new, autonomous poem in English and is therefore an immediate and enduring part of the tradition I am describing. In presenting what I believe are the best examples of early Irish poetry, I have relied heavily on the translations of Frank O'Connor which have been put at my disposal by the grace and kindness of his wife, Harriet. O'Connor is Ireland's Ezra Pound: he has made available in English some of the finest poems in early, middle and later Gaelic. Although he is best known as a writer of short stories, O'Connor was always and essentially a poet whose work of translation from the Irish was not a matter of spasmodic interest but of lifelong devotion. In his books, *The Wild Bird's Nest*, *Kings, Lords and Commons* and *The Little Monasteries*, O'Connor has left behind a body of work which will grow in importance and significance with time. Ireland has been fortunate in her translators; Kuno Meyer, Douglas Hyde and Lady Gregory have all done magnificent work. Today that work is being continued by poets such as Thomas Kinsella, John Montague, Seán Lucy and Desmond O'Grady, and by such distinguished scholars as Professor James Carney. But on the whole I have elected to allow early Ireland to speak through O'Connor's mouth. And what a singing, eloquent mouth it is!

If I had to generalize about all Irish poetry and say what single quality strikes me most from *The Deer's Cry*, attributed to Saint Patrick, to *The Great Hunger* by Patrick Kavanagh (available in Penguin, *Longer Contemporary Poems*), I would say that a hard, simple, virile, rhetorical clarity is its most memorable characteristic. The Irish mind has never taken kindly to obscurity. It delights in simple, direct, lively expression. Among the virtues of early Irish poetry are accurate observation and precise diction. Those early poets said exactly what they meant, and meant (for the most part) exactly what they said. They never bothered with Celtic

Twilight or Pre-Raphaelite ornament. They cut to the bone in a hard, accurate idiom. One of the finest early poems is *The Old Woman of Beare*. Its difficulty springs not from any inherent obscurity in the verse but from the fact that much of the poetry occurred in prose texts and since this poem has lost its prose framework there are certain references which remain puzzling. In spite of this the poem is an extremely moving lament for lost youth and a haunting outcry against the brutal but inevitable ravages of time:

> The Old Woman of Beare am I
> Who once was beautiful.
> Now all I know is how to die.
> I'll do it well.
>
> Look at my skin
> Stretched tight on the bone.
> Where kings have pressed their lips,
> The pain, the pain.
>
> I don't hate the men
> Who swore the truth was in their lies.
> One thing alone I hate –
> Women's eyes.
>
> The young sun
> Gives its youth to everyone,
> Touching everything with gold.
> In me, the cold.

Two other strongly characteristic features of early Irish poetry are its passionate love of nature and its religious intensity. Frequently, these two qualities merge with each other and the result is an exultant spirituality springing from a delight in the natural world:

> I hear the stag's belling
>   Over the valley's steepness;
> No music on earth
>   Can move me like its sweetness.
>
> Christ, Christ hear me!
>   Christ, Christ of Thy meekness!
> Christ, Christ love me!
>   Sever me not from Thy sweetness!

Again, I am struck by the similarity between this early poem and Patrick Kavanagh's *The Great Hunger* where the suspicious peasants, who are usually content to ignore the beauties of the natural world and to treat the supernatural with a blend of scepticism and cunning, occasionally experience a fusion of both, similar to that expressed by the speaker in the early Irish poem. The spanning centuries merely emphasize the similarity:

> Yet sometimes when the sun comes through a gap
> These men know God the Father in a tree:
> The Holy Spirit is the rising sap
> And Christ will be the green leaves that will come
> At Easter from the sealed and guarded tomb.

In a nation's tradition poets who have never heard of each other are brothers.

3

History happens in time, and like time, it cures and kills, kills and cures. In any survey of Irish poetry, however brief, history keeps breaking in like the uninvited guest whose rude intrusion is redeemed by his stimulating contribution. English rule in Ireland went a long way towards destroying the Irish language, and, therefore, writing in Irish; but the language never died completely, and in fact is still alive. It is fair to say, however, that the Battle of Kinsale in 1601 brought to an end the glorious native tradition in the literature of Ireland. (In the twentieth century there have been many encouraging signs of a renaissance. Today, a new body of impressive literature in Irish is being produced by a number of hard-working poets, novelists and dramatists. History smiles, and tradition revives.) It is important also to remember that Ireland was singularly untouched by the Renaissance in Europe; her poets never drank from that particular well of inspiration. If, in this anthology, I appear to give relatively short shrift to medieval Irish poetry, it is not because I am unimpressed by its urbane tone, courtly spirit and formal correctness, but because I am eager to present the wonderful lament for Art O'Leary by his wife Eileen, and Brian Merriman's *The Midnight Court*. Before that, however, mention should be made of the literature of Fionn and the Fianna, an essentially popular literature which is forbiddingly vast in quantity. The best work in it is *Agallamh Na Seanórach*, an epic wrangle between St Patrick and the pagan heroes Oisin and Caoilte. Being popular, the poems are in attractive, if obvious, ballad rhythms. Irish poets have always tended to use ballad rhythms, and this anthology includes examples from the nineteenth and twentieth centuries. The earlier Fenian poems are represented by *The Praise of Fionn, Oisin* and *Caoilte*.

The English broke the Treaty of Limerick in 1691 and Catholic Ireland became enslaved. The signs and effects of that slavery can be seen in the poetry of Egan O'Rahilly, who saw the new Anglo-Irish gentry replacing the old Irish aristocracy. Several of the poems included here show O'Rahilly's agonized sense of the break-up of the native order, and his profound disgust at the dominance of the 'English upstart'. O'Rahilly is a great poet, largely because there is pure passion in his lines which are a heart-broken and heart-breaking outcry against injustice and disintegration. Almost any one of O'Rahilly's poems contains this passion. Look, for example, at *On the Death of William Gould*. This is not simply a lament for an Irish nobleman; it is an elegy for Irish generosity:

> All over Ireland – why this chill?
>   Why this foul mist?
> Why the crying birds?
>   Why do the heavens mutter
>   Such wrathful words?
>
> Why this blow to a poet?
>   Why do the Feale and Shannon tremble?
> Why does the wild sky spill
>   Such venomous rain
>   On plain and hill?
>
> What has put song in chains
>   And nobles in bonds?
> Why do God's own bold
>   Servants and prophets
>   Walk shocked and appalled?

The cause of their grief
Is that fair William Gould
Has died in France.
Christ! No wonder this pall
Darkens the land.

Giver of horses and cloaks,
Of silver and gold,
Silk, wine, meat, bread;
This giver, this generous giver
Is dead.

(*translated by Brendan Kennelly*)

The two great Irish poems of the eighteenth century are, as I have said, *The Midnight Court* and *The Lament for Art O'Leary*. They both spring out of history, but the difference between them is the difference between the tragic and the comic vision. Both Merryman and Eileen O'Leary are aware of the frightful legacy of that history of enslavement. Merryman transforms it into uproarious, bawdy comedy while Eileen O'Leary's tragic lamentation frequently reaches a high pitch of visionary intensity. Of the two, I prefer Merryman's poem. Like all good comic writing, it is essentially serious. Written in couplets that Pope would have been proud to acknowledge, the poem soars into fantastic laughter at the inhibitions, at once terrible and ludicrous, of Irish puritanism, that dark force which has infuriated so many Irish writers and inspired so much Irish writing. Frank O'Connor's translation of Merryman's poem is, to my mind, the best we have. When it first appeared, it was banned – an ironical proof that early twentieth-century Ireland was as repressive as that eighteenth-century society which produced Merryman's frustrated and furiously articulate women. Its profound insight into human nature in general and Irish character in particular, its compassionate laughter and humanity, its lively dialogue and brilliant technique, make it a monument in Irish poetry. Some critics claim that it is a monument *to* Irish poetry, at once a climax and an epitaph. On the contrary, it points the way into a great deal of modern Irish writing, into the clumsy beginnings of a revival, into its gathering momentum and full flowering. Merryman is not simply a poet to be read again and again. He is a poet to be loved for his comic spirit, his artistic integrity, his gay inspiration.

4

If the eighteenth century was dominated by Merryman, O'Rahilly and Eileen O'Leary, the two leading poets of the nineteenth century are James Clarence Mangan and Sir Samuel Ferguson. Mangan is the better poet – more inspired, more passionate – but the importance of Ferguson's contribution to Irish poetry cannot be over-emphasized. It was Ferguson, more than any other single poet, who proved that the old mythology was an almost infinite source of inspiration. In 1834, when Ferguson was twenty-four, nineteen of his translations from the Irish were published in the *Dublin University Magazine*. These translations, mainly love poems, show Ferguson's technical competence and variety, his liking for vigorous rhythms, and his ability to capture the essence of the original. Many years later, Yeats wrote that Ferguson was 'consumed with one absorbing purpose, the purpose to create an Irish school of literature, and overshadowed by one masterful enthusiasm, an enthusiasm for all Gaelic and Irish things'. This passion was the driving-force behind Ferguson's life as a poet and it made him place all his faith in the mythology of his own land. The bulk of his poetry is heroic, though he also produced some fine lyrics. Edward Dowden, the well-known Shakespearean critic, said of him:

What distinguishes Ferguson as a poet and gives him a place apart is that he – and, I think, he alone among Victorian poets – possessed in a high degree the genius for epic poetry. He was indeed an epic poet, born out of due season.

Ferguson's attempt to write a national epic resulted in the huge poem, *Congal*, published in 1872, founded on John O'Donovan's translation of *Cath Muighe Rath* (the Battle of Moyra) which appeared in 1843. Ferguson spent almost thirty years writing *Congal* though in the meantime he wrote many other poems of a strongly heroic character. These poems, entitled *Lays of the Western Gael*, were published in 1865.

The theme of *Congal* is the conflict between paganism and Christianity in early Ireland. It is not ultimately a great epic poem. There are far too many long sections of dull writing, including tedious digressions, boring speeches and inflated descriptive passages. Worse again, Ferguson knew in his heart that Christianity had to win. So it does. Ferguson's heart, however, lies not with the triumphant Christians but with the defeated pagans. The poem suffers from the poet's divided sympathy. Taking these criticisms into account, *Congal* is still an impressive work; but it proved that Ireland has no Milton. A better poem is *Conary*, which tells the story of a king's downfall in taut, precise language. Perhaps the most remarkable thing in the poem is the restraint with which Ferguson evokes a terrifying supernatural world, in the frightening light of which a great man's destiny is spun to its tragic end. It is the work of a rich, disciplined imagination. Because of their length, I have not been able to include *Congal* and *Conary*, but my brief comments on these poems may help the reader to appreciate better the poems by which I have represented this solid, moving and enjoyable poet. To the end Ferguson kept his ideals, knowing full well that his likeliest reward was that, in his own day at least, he would be largely ignored. He wrote:

At present, the cultured criticism of the day is averse to the Irish subject in any form, and the uncultured will not have it save in that form of helotism in which I at least will not present it.

Other poets such as Aubrey de Vere and John Todhunter followed Ferguson and used Irish mythology to create new poetry. Yeats openly admitted his admiration for him; and other poets including James Stephens, George Russell (AE), and the early Austin Clarke owe something to Ferguson. In *Mesgedra*, one of his longer heroic poems, Ferguson succinctly stated his aim as a poet:

> the man aspires
> To link his present with his country's past,
> And live anew in knowledge of his sires.

In linking Irish poetry with the country's heroic past, Ferguson showed the way into the future.

If there is a single quality which characterizes Ferguson both as man and poet, it is his unshakeable solidity. He is at all times firm and stable. The very opposite is true of James Clarence Mangan, the most exciting poet in nineteenth-century Ireland. Very few poets have been more chaotic, more consistently lost than this colourful, eccentric Dubliner who was occasionally driven to madness, frequently afflicted by illness, and always bedevilled by poverty. Mangan seems almost a prototype of the *poète maudit*, a lonely figure permanently dogged by misfortune. The first chapter of his recently published *Autobiography* gives us a clue to his torment:

> In my boyhood I was haunted by an indescribable feeling of something terrible. It was as though I stood in the vicinity of some tremendous danger, to which my apprehensions could give neither form nor outline. What it was I knew not; but it seemed to include many kinds of pain and bitterness – baffled hopes – and memories full of remorse.

This fear entered Mangan's soul and gave him the most astounding energy. He was a haunted man and he wrote a haunted poetry. Yet his is not any conventional or predictable kind of Byronic self-condemnation. It is more a quality of furious self-scrutiny which brings to mind not a flamboyant figure of late nineteenth-century romanticism but one like the American poet, Hart Crane, who burned himself up and finally committed suicide at the age of thirty-two. Mangan too died relatively young, after a lifetime of almost incessant suffering and deprivation.

As a writer, Mangan is erratic and impatient. His poetry is extremely uneven in quality, ranging from exquisite lyricism to rhetorical bombast. He translated from several languages but, of course, in his own personal, inimitable way. Some translations are beautiful, some absolutely atrocious. Most important, however, Mangan had an uncanny knack of self-revelation through translation. Some poets speak with complete personal directness. Others speak through the mouths of dramatic personae. Still others choose mythological characters as their mouthpieces. Mangan spoke through other poets. This is not to say that he could not be shatteringly direct. He could. For the most part, though, he poured out the woes of his heart and soul in poems that came from other languages until they became unmistakable products of his own tormented sensibility. At his best Mangan is profoundly moving, even overwhelming. At his worst he is as bad as any poet can be. But then, that *is* Mangan: a mixture of inspiration and dullness, ecstasy and eccentricity, marvellous compassion and embarrassing self-pity. He delights and exasperates, is at once tragic and trivial, profound, silly, infuriating and lovable. He is the greatest Irish poet before Yeats.

The quantity of poetry produced in the nineteenth century is immense; the quality is frequently poor but with always encouraging exceptions. Patriotism and religion inspired a great number of poems, many of which are hysterically nationalistic or gushingly pious. A few are unsentimental and strong. As always, there were the people's poems: ballads that told of love lost and found; death for, in, and out of Ireland; the struggle for the land; the hope of delivery from the oppressor; the vision of a new, exultant Ireland, freed from her chains, rejoicing in the recovery of an ancient, lost identity. I have included quite a number of nineteenth-century ballads, not only because they are an accurate guide to the feelings and aspirations of the people, or because they turn history into song, but because they also anticipate the ballad rhythms of Yeats, Padraic Colum and F. R. Higgins.

There are always poets who seem to defy any attempt to classify themes and trends. I am thinking of Oscar Wilde and George Darley, two Dubliners whose verse has a vitality which I always find astonishing and admirable. I include a long extract from Wilde's vigorous *The Ballad of Reading Gaol* rather than any of his short pieces where he tends to simper stylishly like many another *fin-de-siècle* poet. And I give extracts from George Darley's *Nepenthe*, a lyrical outburst of almost epic proportions, a poem that is largely ignored nowadays, though it had a strong influence on the early poetry of Austin Clarke.

It is clear then that in nineteenth-century Ireland there was tremendous poetic energy. Yet there was something lacking: a centralizing force, a unifying spirit. W. B. Yeats, himself an important part of nineteenth-century poetry, was such a spirit. He had more solid stamina than Ferguson, more fierce intensity than Mangan. He had a vision for Ireland unequalled in her tradition, as well as the intelligence and energy to turn that vision into reality. Carrying his experience of the nineteenth century and its mythology in his heart and head, he stepped into twentieth-century Ireland, a great poet with a great poet's ideals. Never did a country so badly need a poet. Never did a poet work so tirelessly for his country.

5

The Irish literary revival was largely the work of W. B. Yeats. It may seem odd therefore that he is represented here by only three poems. The main reason for my limited selection is that Yeats is already widely available in paperback; and since I am trying to introduce good Irish poets who are comparatively little known, many who are scarcely available at all, I decided to represent Yeats by three poems which illustrate his development. It is not simply that Yeats went from the tinsel brilliance of conventional Pre-Raphaelite verse to a bare, sensual, symbolic poetry; but his development is parallel, almost identical with, his changing views of a changing Ireland. The three poems given here illustrate this. 'To Ireland in the Coming Times' is youthful and idealistic, and shows the young poet consciously trying to identify himself with the unsung makers of the Irish tradition. 'September 1913' is bitter and disillusioned: Yeats here is middle-aged and openly disgusted by the self-righteous materialism of Irish society. The Easter Rebellion and the Civil War followed; a new

Ireland stumbled into existence and Yeats played his part in the uncertain, exciting creation of the young state. In 'The Statues' he applauds the heroism that made this birth possible and asserts Ireland's dignity in the face of the overwhelming 'filthy modern tide'. Yeats is Ireland's greatest poet, not least because he learned to confront the challenging complexities of Irish life. He recognized that Ireland is always capable of treachery and squalor, but he was also aware of its capacity for heroism and nobility. He witnessed and experienced 'the weasel's twist, the weasel's tooth'. Yet he exhorted later generations to be, and to continue to be, the 'indomitable Irishry'.

Around the massive figure of Yeats cluster a number of interesting minor poets: James Stephens, Oliver Gogarty, Padraic Colum, F. R. Higgins, George Russell (AE) and others. They all made vital contributions to the revival.

Though consciously separating himself from Yeats, James Joyce's verse has an unmistakable vitality. Joyce is Ireland's jester, her high-priest of irreverence, her devoted Rabelais. I find Joyce nearer to Synge than to Yeats both in his art and his life. Just as Synge's drama has drawn attention from his poetry, so Joyce's novels have overshadowed his verse. Though Joyce draws on the city and Synge on the countryside, they are both witty and defiant, tender and vicious.

When Yeats wrote that 'a terrible beauty is born', he had in mind, among others, the poets Pearse, Plunkett and MacDonagh. All three have an intensity lacking in most of the poets who have criticized them adversely. I wish I had the space to include more of their work. I am happy too to give a generous selection of Francis Ledwidge, whose pure lyricism has survived different modes and schools.

After Yeats, Irish poets found themselves in a peculiar position. Yeats, it seemed, had exhausted an entire mythology. His heroic-romantic vision overshadowed the visions of all others. He was disturbingly near in time, a colossus breathing down the necks of the younger generation. The problem facing these writers was to revere and understand his achievement and, at the same time, to absorb and transform his influence. Different poets have tried to solve the problem in different ways. Patrick Kavanagh, for instance, tried to achieve a truly comic vision: 'there is only one Muse,' he said, 'the Comic Muse. In tragedy there is always something of a lie. Great poetry is always comic in the profound sense. Comedy is abundance of life.' In Kavanagh's best work there is certainly this vital abundance. In many ways, his development recalls Yeats's. Like Yeats, he insists on an ultimate gaiety, placing his faith in the joyously irrational. Poetry for him is essentially mystical, a vocation, a way of life. Kavanagh is a rich, rewarding poet who believes, ultimately, in praise and celebration.

Austin Clarke, on the other hand, is essentially a satirist though he has written some fine lyrics. If you wish to get a critical, compassionate view of contemporary Ireland, turn the pages of Clarke's many books. He is prolific, brilliant, incisive. At times, his work suffers because his themes are topical. But his voice is unmistakable, his individuality unquestionable.

Among the younger poets, there is a strong concentration on the long poem. The best have been written by Thomas Kinsella (*Phoenix Park*, *Downstream*, *Nightwalker*). Richard Murphy has produced several impressive narratives (*The Last Galway Hooker*, *The Cleggan Disaster*, *The Battle of Aughrim*). In *The Winning of Etain*, Eavan Boland shows a rare ability in sustaining technical skill and thematic interest; and John Montague is at present engaged in a long work. Yet all these poets are most at home in the compressed lyric form. The point of this apparent paradox is that just as Yeats needed a theatre and a mythology to achieve his purest lyrics, these poets are constantly experimenting, feeling their way towards an appropriate form, a technique which will permit the greatest degree of self-revelation with the least amount of clumsiness or embarrassment.

A great deal of the best contemporary Irish poetry comes out of the North of Ireland. Louis MacNeice and W. R. Rodgers, both now dead, together form a witty, sophisticated foundation. MacNeice is hard and clear, Rodgers religious, comic and profound. John Hewitt's verse, at its best, is as concentrated and strong as granite. Among the younger poets, Heaney, Longley and Mahon are writing with a confidence and expertise which proves that the voice of the North is resonant and distinct and will be heard more and more in time to come.

At the moment, therefore, the Irish scene is encouraging. The English critic, A. Alvárez, says in his introduction to *The New Poetry* (Penguin) that the major threat to English poetry now is its 'gentility'. Not so with contemporary Irish poetry. The danger here is that unless each poet discovers and explores a personal mythology, his work will degenerate into fragmented utterance and transient comment. Patrick Kavanagh was keenly aware of this threat. In his poem 'A Personal Problem' he yearns for a myth and failing to find it says:

> ... I grew
> Uncultivated and now the soil turns sour,
> Needs to be revived by a power not my own,
> Heroes enormous who do astounding deeds –
> Out of this world.

Kavanagh's poem is not only a statement of an artistic dilemma but a warning to all contemporary Irish poets. A poet without a myth is a man confronting famine. Like the body, the imagination gets tired and hungry: myth is a food, a sustaining structure outside the poet that nourishes his inner life and helps him to express it. Most of our young poets realize this, consciously or unconsciously. So, in their different ways, they are shaping their individual myths, frequently in fertile opposition with one another. With every good poem, they enlarge one of the finest poetic traditions in the world.

BRENDAN KENNELLY

A NOTE TO THE SECOND EDITION

SINCE this anthology was first published in 1970, Irish poetry has found a new energy. The sources of that energy are as complex as its manifestations are encouraging. It would take a new, separate anthology to do justice to it. All I can hope to do in this enlarged edition of *The Penguin Book of Irish Verse* is to suggest some of its range and intensity.

A few factors which have helped to promote poetry in Ireland should be mentioned. *The Irish Press*, one of our national newspapers, devotes, each Saturday, a page to new Irish writing, poetry and prose. This page, regular and usually exciting, has done a lot to encourage younger writers. Its editor, Mr David Marcus, has brought an exemplary editorial discipline and reliability into contemporary Irish literature. Quite often in Ireland there's too much talk and too little action; frequently too, when the action *does* happen, it tends to be either murderous or stupid, or both. Mr Marcus, a talented talker himself, is a most effective man of action, always to the benefit of Irish writers and writing.

There's a new interest in creative writing in several of the universities – particularly in Galway, under the guidance of the distinguished novelist and playwright, Thomas Kilroy. Events such as Writers' Week in Listowel, County Kerry, and the Yeats International Summer School in Sligo, with their encouragement of the actual *writing* of verse as well as the promotion of intense discussion in the ordered, enthusiastic atmosphere of workshops, are helpful. And in the publishing area, Gallery Press, the Dolmen Press and Profile Press do excellent work. The Arts Council's *Writers in Schools* programme, sending poets out to schools all over Ireland, is helping to present poetry to students as it really is – a living presence to be joyfully experienced, not a sterile difficulty to be laboriously studied for the sake of examinations. A new society, *Poetry Ireland*, founded by the energetic, efficient John F. Deane, publishes work, organizes poetry readings, and makes valuable information available on a regular basis.

Among the poetry-publishing magazines, the most vigorous and critically discriminating is *The Honest Ulsterman*, edited by the poet, Frank Ormsby.

It would be tempting at this point to talk about the Ulster Movement or the Ulster Poets, but that would be misleading, because the new energy of Irish poetry, and its organization into channels that help to make the poetry available, is not confined to any province or group; though, of course, the inevitable cliques exist in cosy isolation. This energy appears in the work of poets living in different parts of Ireland, whether it be Richard Murphy in the West, John Montague or Paul Durcan in Cork, Seamus Heaney in Dublin, John Ennis in Waterford or Paul Muldoon in Belfast. Geography has little or nothing to do with this energy. It is an inner thing. Places are important only insofar as they excite the imagination into a deeper life, a more intense expression.

Ireland is changing and the poetry of Ireland reflects and embodies the complexity of that change. An increasing awareness of European and other cultures is accompanied by a deepening critical consciousness of the Irish tradition itself. The sense of insularity and isolation is diminishing and young Irish poets turn as readily to Rilke and Mayakovsky, or to Neruda and Amichai, as they do to Yeats and Kavanagh. The claustrophobia and congestion that marked Irish life and literature in the forties, fifties and early sixties are gradually being dispelled and are being replaced by a much more *open* attitude to experience and expression; though the country, North and South, can still be horrifying for its attitudes of barbarism and stupidity, for intolerance both savage and subtle. Poetry is a vital part of our struggle to be free from, and critical of, all such attitudes, and of futile gloom, bumptious self-conscious modernism, the diligent pursuit of ugliness (Dublin is fast becoming an offensively *ugly* city), the dominance of philistinism in public life, pomposity, religiosity, iron respectability, sad suspicion, the cherished profession of cynicism, humourless self-importance and the grotesque, manic materialism of Holy Ireland. More than any other poet of recent times, Patrick Kavanagh is responsible for this liberation. Small wonder that his poetry is being increasingly read and appreciated for, among other things, its imaginative gaiety, its inspired simplicity, its moral grandeur. Many of these qualities are dramatically evident in his long poem *Lough Derg*, included in this edition. The far-reaching consequences of Kavanagh's confrontation of the full spiritual range of Irish life, from grovelling squalor to unconscious magnanimity, have yet to be realized. *Lough Derg* is a monumental example of the energy and courage that mark that confrontation. Like all Kavanagh's best work, *Lough Derg* goes beyond satire and savage criticism to reach his truest tone, his unique music, that of instinctive, celebratory revelation. His poem should be compared with another fascinating poem bearing the same title, by Denis Devlin, also included in this edition. A study of these two poems will show why Kavanagh and Devlin are worthy of sustained critical attention; the poems are two very important moments in modern Irish poetry and point to developments which are even now taking place.

I cannot pretend to be able to indicate the likely future developments of Irish poetry. But I *can* say that good poems are being written in Ireland today and that the signs are that the poets now added to this anthology will go on to produce enjoyable and memorable verse. Some of them may produce much more than that. They are all, as far as I can judge, honest writers, deliberate craftsmen. I wish them well.

I wish to thank Will Sulkin, Donald McFarlan and Robin Robertson for their helpful advice and criticism in compiling this second edition.

BRENDAN KENNELLY

PART ONE

Gaelic translated

ANONYMOUS

8th century

The Deer's Cry

This hymn is also known as 'Patrick's Breastplate'.

I arise today
Through a mighty strength, the invocation of the Trinity,
Through belief in the threeness,
Through confession of the oneness
Of the Creator of Creation.

I arise today
Through the strength of Christ's birth with His baptism,
Through the strength of His crucifixion with His burial,
Through the strength of His resurrection with His ascension,
Through the strength of His descent for the judgement of
    Doom.

I arise today
Through the strength of the love of Cherubim,
In obedience of angels,
In the service of archangels,
In hope of resurrection to meet with reward,
In prayers of patriarchs,
In predictions of prophets,
In preaching of apostles,
In faiths of confessors,
In innocence of holy virgins,
In deeds of righteous men.

I arise today
Through the strength of heaven:
Light of sun,
Radiance of moon,
Splendour of fire,

Speed of lightning,
Swiftness of wind,
Depth of sea,
Stability of earth,
Firmness of rock.

I arise today
Through God's strength to pilot me:
God's might to uphold me,
God's wisdom to guide me,
God's eye to look before me,
God's ear to hear me,
God's word to speak for me,
God's hand to guard me,
God's way to lie before me,
God's shield to protect me,
God's host to save me
From snares of devils,
From temptations of vices,
From every one who shall wish me ill,
Afar and anear,
Alone and in a multitude.

I summon today all these powers between me and those evils,
Against every cruel merciless power that may oppose my body
    and soul,
Against incantations of false prophets,
Against black laws of pagandom,
Against false laws of heretics,
Against craft of idolatry,
Against spells of women and smiths and wizards,
Against every knowledge that corrupts man's body and soul.

Christ to shield me today
Against poison, against burning,
Against drowning, against wounding,
So that there may come to me abundance of reward.
Christ with me, Christ before me, Christ behind me,

Christ in me, Christ beneath me, Christ above me,
Christ on my right, Christ on my left,
Christ when I lie down, Christ when I sit down, Christ when
    I arise,
Christ in the heart of every man who thinks of me,
Christ in the mouth of every one who speaks of me,
Christ in every eye that sees me,
Christ in every ear that hears me.

I arise today
Through a mighty strength, the invocation of the Trinity,
Through belief in the threeness,
Through confession of the oneness
Of the Creator of Creation.

(translated by Kuno Meyer)

ANONYMOUS
7th–13th century

My Story

Here's my story; the stag cries,
Winter snarls as summer dies.

The wind bullies the low sun
In poor light; the seas moan.

Shapeless bracken is turning red,
The wildgoose raises its desperate head.

Birds' wings freeze where fields are hoary.
The world is ice. That's my story.

(translated by Brendan Kennelly)

The Hermit's Song

These verses are from a poetic discussion on the religious life between King Guaire and his hermit brother, Marbhan, both of the seventh century. It is extraordinary how clear and bright the landscape of early Irish poetry is, as though some medieval painter had illustrated it, with its little oratories hung with linen, its woodlands and birds, its fierce winters and gay springs.

A hiding tuft, a green-barked yew-tree
    Is my roof,
While nearby a great oak keeps me
    Tempest-proof.

I can pick my fruit from an apple
    Like an inn,
Or can fill my fist where hazels
    Shut me in.

A clear well beside me offers
   Best of drink,
And there grows a bed of cresses
   Near its brink.

Pigs and goats, the friendliest neighbours,
   Nestle near,
Wild swine come, or broods of badgers,
   Grazing deer.

All the gentry of the county
   Come to call!
And the foxes come behind them,
   Best of all.

To what meals the woods invite me
   All about!
There are water, herbs and cresses,
   Salmon, trout.

A clutch of eggs, sweet mast and honey
   Are my meat,
Heathberries and whortleberries
   For a sweet.

All that one could ask for comfort
   Round me grows,
There are hips and haws and strawberries,
   Nuts and sloes.

And when summer spreads its mantle
   What a sight!
Marjoram and leeks and pignuts,
   Juicy, bright.

Dainty redbreasts briskly forage
   Every bush,
Round and round my hut there flutter
   Swallow, thrush.

Bees and beetles, music-makers,
  Croon and strum;
Geese pass over, duck in autumn,
  Dark streams hum.

Angry wren, officious linnet
  And black-cap,
All industrious, and the woodpecker's
  Sturdy tap.

From the sea the gulls and herons
  Flutter in,
While in upland heather rises
  The grey hen.

In the year's most brilliant weather
  Heifers low
Through green fields, not driven nor beaten,
  Tranquil, slow.

In wreathed boughs the wind is whispering,
  Skies are blue,
Swans call, river water falling
  Is calling too.

(translated by Frank O'Connor)

The Viking Terror

There's a wicked wind tonight,
Wild upheaval in the sea;
No fear now that the Viking hordes
Will terrify me.

(translated by Brendan Kennelly)

A Prayer for Recollection

How my thoughts betray me!
  How they flit and stray!
Well they may appal me
  On great judgement day.

Through the psalms they wander
  Roads that are not right;
Mitching, shouting, squabbling
  In God's very sight.

Through august assemblies
  Groups of gamesome girls,
Then through woods, through cities,
  Like the wind in whirls.

Now down lordly highways
  Boisterously they stride,
Then through desert pathways
  Secretly they glide.

In their whims unferried
  Overseas they fly,
Or in one swift motion
  Spin from earth to sky.

Lost to recollection
  Near and far they roam;
From some monstrous errand
  Slyly they slink home.

Where are ropes to bind them?
  Who has fetters fit?
They who lack all patience
  Cannot stand or sit.

No sharp sword affrights them,
    Nor any threatening whip;
Like an eel's tail, greasy,
    From my grasp they slip.

Lock nor frowning dungeon,
    Nor sentinelled frontier,
Townwall, sea nor fortress
    Halts their mad career.

Christ the chaste, the cherished,
    Searcher of the soul,
Grant the seven-fold spirit
    Keep them in control.

Rule my thoughts and feelings,
    You who brook no ill;
Make me yours forever,
    Bend me to your will.

Grant me, Christ, to reach you,
    With you let me be
Who are not frail nor fickle
    Nor feeble-willed like me.

(translated by Frank O'Connor)

The Priest Rediscovers His Psalm-Book

This exquisite poem gave rise to a two-volume work by George Moore called *A Storyteller's Holiday*, which celebrates the *virgines subintroductae* of the early Irish church. The *virgines subintroductae* were the women who accompanied early saints, but if there were any in Ireland, Crinog, the heroine of this poem, was not one of them. Her name, which means 'Old-Young', is merely a typical donnish joke as a modern scholar, Professor Carney, has shown.

How good to hear your voice again,
    Old love, no longer young, but true,
As when in Ulster I grew up
    And we were bedmates, I and you.

When first they put us twain to bed,
  My love who speaks the tongue of Heaven,
I was a boy with no bad thoughts,
  A modest youth, and barely seven.

We wandered Ireland over then,
  Our souls and bodies free of blame,
My foolish face aglow with love,
  An idiot without fear of blame.

Yours was the counsel that I sought
  Wherever we went wandering;
Better I found your subtle thought
  Than idle converse with some king.

You slept with four men after that,
  Yet never sinned in leaving me,
And now a virgin you return –
  I say but what all men can see.

For safe within my arms again,
  Weary of wandering many ways,
The face I love is shadowed now
  Though lust attends not its last days.

Faultless my old love seeks me out;
  I welcome her with joyous heart –
My dear, you would not have me lost,
  With you I'll learn that holy art.

Since all the world your praises sings,
  And all acclaim your wanderings past
I have but to heed your counsel sweet
  To find myself with God at last.

You are a token and a sign
  To men of what all men must heed;
Each day your lovers learn anew
  God's praise is all the skill they need.

So may He grant me by your grace
    A quiet end, an easy mind,
And light my pathway with His face
    When the dead flesh is left behind.

                    (translated by Frank O'Connor)

The Son of the King of Moy

The son of the King of Moy
Found a girl in a green dell,
Of the rich abounding fruit
She gave him his fill.

                    (translated by Brendan Kennelly)

The Sweetness of Nature

This is one of the songs of the mad king, Suibhne (Sweeney), from a
twelfth-century romance, the material of which goes back to the eighth
century. In this poem Suibhne is flying from the battlefield, driven mad
by the sight of the broken bodies.

Endlessly over the water
    Birds of the Bann are singing;
Sweeter to me their voices
    Than any churchbell's ringing.

Over the plain of Moyra
    Under the heels of foemen
I saw my people broken
    As flax is scutched by women.

But the cries I hear by Derry
    Are not of men triumphant;
I hear their calls in the evening,
    Swans calm and exultant.

ANONYMOUS

I hear the stag's belling
   Over the valley's steepness;
No music on the earth
   Can move me like its sweetness.

Christ, Christ hear me!
   Christ, Christ of Thy meekness!
Christ, Christ love me!
   Sever me not from Thy sweetness!

(translated by Frank O'Connor)

A Love-Song

Such a heart!
Should he leave, how I'd miss him.
Jewel, acorn, youth.
Kiss him!

(translated by Brendan Kennelly)

Storm at Sea

The ascription of this comparatively late poem to an eighth-century poet,
Rumann son of Colman, suggests that it may be part of a romance that
dealt with him.

Tempest on the plain of Lir
Bursts its barriers far and near,
   And upon the rising tide
   Wind and noisy winter ride –
Winter throws a shining spear.

When the wind blows from the east
All the billows seem possessed,
   To the west they storm away
   To the farthest, wildest bay
Where the light turns to its rest.

ANONYMOUS

When the wind is from the north
The fierce and shadowy waves go forth,
   Leaping, snarling at the sky,
   To the southern world they fly
And the confines of the earth.

When the wind is from the west
All the waves that cannot rest
   To the east must thunder on
   Where the bright tree of the sun
Is rooted in the ocean's breast.

When the wind is from the south
The waves turn to a devil's broth,
   Crash in foam on Skiddy's beach,
   For Caladnet's summit reach,
Batter Limerick's grey-green mouth.

Ocean's full! The sea's in flood,
Beautiful is the ships' abode;
   In the Bay of the Two Beasts
   The sandy wind in eddies twists,
The rudder holds a shifting road.

Every bay in Ireland booms
When the flood against it comes –
   Winter throws a spear of fire!
   Round Scotland's shores and by Cantyre
A mountainous surging chaos glooms.

God's Son of hosts that none can tell
The fury of the storm repel!
   Dread Lord of the sacrament,
   Save me from the wind's intent,
Spare me from the blast of Hell.

(translated by Frank O'Connor)

God's Praises

Only a fool would fail
To praise God in His might
When the tiny mindless birds
Praise Him in their flight.

(translated by Brendan Kennelly)

Winter

Winter is a dreary season,
Heavy waters in confusion
　Beat the wide world's strand.
Birds of every place are mournful
But the hot and savage ravens,
　At rough winter's shriek.
Crude and black and dank and smoky;
Dogs about their bones are snarling,
On the fire the cauldron bubbles
　All the long dark day.

(translated by Frank O'Connor)

The Blackbird by Belfast Lough

What little throat
Has framed that note?
What gold beak shot
　It far away?
A blackbird on
His leafy throne
Tossed it alone
　Across the bay.

(translated by Frank O'Connor)

Reconciliation

Do not torment me, woman,
   Let our two minds be as one,
Be my mate in my own land
   Where we may love till life is done.

Put your mouth against my mouth
   You whose skin is fresh as foam,
Take me in your white embrace
   And let us love till kingdom come.

Slender graceful girl, admit
   Me soon into your bed,
Discord, pain will disappear
   When we stretch there side by side.

For your sweet sake, I will ignore
   Every girl who takes my eye,
If it's possible, I implore
   You do the same for me.

As I have given from my heart
   Passion for which alone I live,
Let me now receive from you
   The love you have to give.

(translated by Brendan Kennelly)

ANONYMOUS

The Praise of Fionn

Usheen ('Oisin' or 'Ossian'), son of Fionn, is the great revenant of Irish literature. Translated to the Land of Youth by his love of a fairy queen, he returned to Ireland to find Fionn and his warriors long dead and St Patrick and his monks in power. Although the poem is late so far as language goes – probably sixteenth-century – it has the feeling of the eighth or ninth century.

Patrick you chatter too loud
  And lift your crozier too high,
Your stick would be kindling soon
  If my son Osgar stood by.

If my son Osgar and God
  Wrestled it out on the hill
And I saw Osgar go down
  I'd say that your God fought well.

But how could the God you praise
  And his mild priests singing a tune
Be better than Fionn the swordsman,
  Generous, faultless Fionn?

Just by the strength of their hands
  The Fenians' battles were fought,
With never a spoken lie,
  Never a lie in thought.

There never sat priest in church
  A tuneful psalm to raise
Better spoken than these
  Scarred in a thousand frays.

Whatever your monks have called
  The law of the King of Grace,
That was the Fenians' law;
  His home is their dwelling-place.

If happier house than Heaven
　　There be, above or below,
'Tis there my master Fionn
　　And his fighting men will go.

Ah, priest, if you saw the Fenians
　　Filling the strand beneath
Or gathered in streamy Naas
　　You would praise them with every breath.

Patrick, ask of your God
　　Does he remember their might,
Or has he seen east or west
　　Better men in a fight?

Or known in his own land
　　Above the stars and the moon
For wisdom, courage and strength
　　A man the like of Fionn?

(translated by Frank O'Connor)

Oisin

The teeth you see up here,
　　Up in the ancient skull,
Once cracked yellow nuts
　　And tore the haunch of a bull.

Savage and sharp and huge,
　　Crunching the naked bone,
Every tittle and joint
　　Was mince when they were done.

The eyes you see up here,
　　Up in the aged skull,
Dull they may seem tonight
　　But once they were never dull.

Never in darkest night
   Did they take trip or fall;
Now, though you stand so close,
   I cannot see you at all.

The legs you see below,
   Nothing could weary them then;
Now they totter and ache,
   A bundle of bones and skin.

Though now they run no more,
   All their glory gone,
Once they were quick to follow
   The shadow of golden Fionn.

(translated by Frank O'Connor)

Caoilte

Caoilte is another of the revenant figures who return to an Ireland where, because of St Patrick, everything seems to have become cheapened and diminished. 'Osgar', who is celebrated in 'The Praise of Fionn', is the son of Oisin and grandson of Fionn, and 'Diarmuid', the Tristan of Irish legend, is the hero of another poem, 'Grania'.

Winter time is bleak, the wind
   Drives the stag from height to height;
Belling at the mountain's cold
   Untameable he strays tonight.

The old stag of Carran scarce
   Dare sleep within his den,
While the stag of Aughty hears
   Wolves call in every glen.

Long ago Osgar and I
   And Diarmuid heard that cry;
And we listened to the wolves
   As the frosty night went by.

Now the stag that's filled with sleep
  Lays his lordly side to rest
As if earth had drawn him down
  To the winter's icy breast.

Though I drowse above the fire
  Many a winter morning drear
My hand was tight about a sword
  A battleaxe or spear.

And though I sleep cold tonight,
  God, I offer thanks to you
And to Christ, the Virgin's Son,
  For the mighty men I slew.

(translated by Frank O'Connor)

The Old Woman of Beare

The sea crawls from the shore
Leaving there
The despicable weed,
A corpse's hair.
In me,
The desolate withdrawing sea.

The Old Woman of Beare am I
Who once was beautiful.
Now all I know is how to die.
I'll do it well.

Look at my skin
Stretched tight on the bone.
Where kings have pressed their lips,
The pain, the pain.

I don't hate the men
Who swore the truth was in their lies.

One thing alone I hate –
Women's eyes.

The young sun
Gives its youth to everyone,
Touching everything with gold.
In me, the cold.

The cold. Yet still a seed
Burns there.
Women love only money now.
But when
I loved, I loved
Young men.

Young men whose horses galloped
On many an open plain
Beating lightning from the ground.
I loved such men.

And still the sea
Rears and plunges into me,
Shoving, rolling through my head
Images of the drifting dead.

A soldier cries
Pitifully about his plight;
A king fades
Into the shivering night.

Does not every season prove
That the acorn hits the ground?
Have I not known enough of love
To know it's lost as soon as found?

I drank my fill of wine with kings,
Their eyes fixed on my hair.
Now among the stinking hags
I chew the cud of prayer.

Time was the sea
Brought kings as slaves to me.
Now I near the face of God
And the crab crawls through my blood.

I loved the wine
That thrilled me to my fingertips;
Now the mean wind
Stitches salt into my lips.

The coward sea
Slouches away from me.
Fear brings back the tide
That made me stretch at the side
Of him who'd take me briefly for his bride.

The sea grows smaller, smaller now.
Farther, farther it goes
Leaving me here where the foam dries
On the deserted land,
Dry as my shrunken thighs,
As the tongue that presses my lips,
As the veins that break through my hands.

(translated by Brendan Kennelly)

The King of Connacht

'Have you seen Hugh,
The Connacht king in the field?'
'All that we saw
Was his shadow under his shield.'

(translated by Frank O'Connor)

Liadain

Liadain ('the grey lady') was a Munster poetess who, according to the romance, was courted by another poet, Curithir ('Otter's Son'), with the remarkable plea – 'a child of ours should be famous'. Because, as the romance makes clear, she did not wish to spoil her round of visits, she asked him to join her at home in Munster, but when he arrived, she had already become a nun. In the same romance she is given an equally wonderful but untranslatable poem in which she describes him as 'the ex-poet'. Only those who have known an ex-poet will realize what the word means.

Gain without gladness
    Is in the bargain I have struck;
One that I loved I wrought to madness.

Mad beyond measure
    But for God's fear that numbed her heart
She that would not do his pleasure.

Was it so great
    My treason? Was I not always kind?
Why should it turn his love to hate?

Liadain,
    That is my name, and Curithir
The man I loved; you know my sin.

Alas too fleet!
    Too brief my pleasure at his side;
With him the passionate hours were sweet.

Woods woke
    About us for a lullaby,
And the blue waves in music spoke.

And now too late
    More than for all my sins I grieve
That I turned his love to hate.

Why should I hide
   That he is still my heart's desire
More than all the world beside?

A furnace blast
   Of love has melted down my heart,
Without his love it cannot last.

(translated by Frank O'Connor)

I Shall Not Die

I shall not die because of you
   O woman though you shame the swan,
They were foolish men you killed,
   Do not think me a foolish man.

Why should I leave the world behind
   For the soft hand, the dreaming eye,
The crimson lips, the breasts of snow –
   Is it for these you'd have me die?

Why should I heed the fancy free,
   The joyous air, the eye of blue,
The side like foam, the virgin neck?
   I shall not die because of you.

The devil take the golden hair!
   That maiden look, that voice so gay,
That delicate heel and pillared thigh
   Only some foolish man would slay.

O woman though you shame the swan
   A wise man taught me all he knew,
I know the crooked ways of love,
   I shall not die because of you.

(translated by Frank O'Connor)

Jealousy

Love like heat and cold
   Pierces and then is gone;
Jealousy when it strikes
   Sticks in the marrowbone.

(translated by Frank O'Connor)

The Body's Speech

My grief, my grief, maid without sin,
   Mother of God's Son,
Because of one I cannot win
   My peace is gone.

Mortal love, a raging flood,
   O Mother Maid,
Runs like a fever through my blood,
   Ruins heart and head.

How can I tell her of my fear,
   My wild desire,
When words I speak for my own ear
   Turn me to fire?

I dream of breasts so lilylike,
   Without a fleck,
And hair that, bundled up from her back,
   Burdens her neck.

And praise the cheeks where flames arise
   That shame the rose,
And the soft hands at whose touch flees
   All my repose.

Since I have seen her I am lost,
    A man possessed,
Better to feel the world gone past,
    Earth on my breast;

And from my tomb to hear the choir,
    The hum of prayer;
Without her while her place is here,
    My peace is there.

(translated by Frank O'Connor)

ANONYMOUS

17th–19th century

Kilcash

Kilcash was the home of one branch of the Butler family. Although I
don't think Yeats, who had Butler blood in him, knew this, it was one of
his favourite poems, and there is a good deal of his work in it.

What shall we do for timber?
    The last of the woods is down.
Kilcash and the house of its glory
    And the bell of the house are gone,
The spot where that lady waited
    Who shamed all women for grace
When earls came sailing to greet her
    And Mass was said in the place.

My grief and my affliction
    Your gates are taken away,
Your avenue needs attention,
    Goats in the garden stray.
The courtyard's filled with water
    And the great earls where are they?
The earls, the lady, the people
    Beaten into the clay.

No sound of duck or geese there,
    Hawk's cry or eagle's call,
No humming of the bees there
    That brought honey and wax for all,
Nor even the song of the birds there
    When the sun goes down in the west,
No cuckoo on top of the boughs there,
    Singing the world to rest.

There's mist there tumbling from branches,
    Unstirred by night and by day,
And darkness falling from heaven,
    For our fortune has ebbed away,
There's no holly nor hazel nor ash there,
    The pasture's rock and stone,
The crown of the forest has withered,
    And the last of its game is gone.

I beseech of Mary and Jesus
    That the great come home again
With long dances danced in the garden,
    Fiddle music and mirth among men,
That Kilcash the home of our fathers
    Be lifted on high again,
And from that to the deluge of waters
    In bounty and peace remain.

(translated by Frank O'Connor)

EGAN O'RAHILLY

1670–1726

A Grey Eye Weeping

With the breaking of the Treaty of Limerick by the English in 1691 the Irish Catholics descended into a slavery worse than anything experienced by Negroes in the Southern States. (When the Irish came to America, the Negroes called them 'White Niggers'.) This period is best represented in the few authentic poems of Egan O'Rahilly, a Kerry poet. In this fine poem he approaches, not one of the masters he would have approached fifty years before – the MacCarthys – but Lord Kenmare, one of the new Anglo-Irish gentry. Hence the bitter repetition of the fellow's name. O'Rahilly himself would have considered 'Valentine' a ridiculous name for anyone calling himself a gentleman, and as for 'Brown', he would as soon have addressed a 'Jones' or a 'Robinson'. O'Rahilly *is* a snob, but one of the great snobs of literature.

> That my old bitter heart was pierced in this black doom,
> That foreign devils have made our land a tomb,
> That the sun that was Munster's glory has gone down
> Has made me a beggar before you, Valentine Brown.
>
> That royal Cashel is bare of house and guest,
> That Brian's turreted home is the otter's nest,
> That the kings of the land have neither land nor crown
> Has made me a beggar before you, Valentine Brown.
>
> Garnish away in the west with its master banned,
> Hamburg the refuge of him who has lost his land,
> An old grey eye, weeping for lost renown,
> Have made me a beggar before you, Valentine Brown.

(translated by Frank O'Connor)

Brightness of Brightness

In Irish the poem is pure music, each line beginning with assonantal rhymes on the short vowel 'i' (like 'mistress' and 'bitter'), which gives it the secretive, whispering quality of dresses rustling or of light feet scurrying in the distance.

Brightness of brightness lonely met me where I wandered,
    Crystal of crystal only by her eyes were splendid,
Sweetness of sweetness lightly in her speech she squandered,
    Rose-red and lily-glow brightly in her cheeks contended.

Ringlet on ringlet flowed tress on tress of yellow flaming
        Hair, and swept the dew that glowed on the grass in
            showers behind her,
Vesture her breasts bore, mirror-bright, oh, mirror-shaming
        That her fairy northern land yielded her from birth to
            bind them.

There she told me, told me as one that might in loving
    languish,
        Told me of his coming, he for whom the crown was
            wreathed,
Told me of their ruin who banished him to utter anguish,
        More too she told me I dare not in my song have
            breathed.

Frenzy of frenzy 'twas that her beauty did not numb me,
        That I neared the royal serf, the vassal queen that held
            me vassal,
Then I called on Mary's Son to shield me, she started from me,
        And she fled, the lady, a lightning flash to Luachra
            Castle.

Fleetly too I fled in wild flight with body trembling
        Over reefs of rock and sand, bog and shining plain and
            strand, sure

That my feet would find a path to that place of sad assembling,
    House of houses reared of old in cold dark druid
        grandeur.

There a throng of wild creatures mocked me with elfin
        laughter,
    And a group of mild maidens, tall with twining silken
        tresses,
Bound in bitter bonds they laid me there, and a moment after
    See my lady laughing share a pot-bellied clown's caresses.

Truth of truth I told her in grief that it shamed her
    To see her with a sleek foreign mercenary lover
When the highest peak of Scotland's race already thrice had
        named her,
    And waited in longing for his exile to be over.

When she heard me speak, she wept, but she wept for pride,
    And tears flowed down in streams from cheeks so bright
        and comely,
She sent a watchman with me to lead me to the mountainside –
    Brightness of brightness who met me walking lonely.

(translated by Frank O'Connor)

A Sleepless Night

I have thought long this wild wet night that brought no rest
    Though I have no gold to watch, or horned kine, or
        sheep –
A storm that made the wave cry out has stirred my breast;
    Neither dogfish nor periwinkle was once my neat.

Ah, if the men who knew me were but here tonight
    With their proud company that held me up secure,
Captains of Munster before their great defeat,
    Not long would Corkaguiney see my children poor.

MacCarthy stern and fearless that most upright man,
    MacCarthy of the Lee whose hearth is dark and cold,
MacCarthy of Kanturk and all his kindred gone –
    The heart within me breaks to think their tale is told.

The heart within my breast tonight is wild with grief
    Because, of all the haughty men who ruled this place,
North Munster and South Munster to the wave beneath,
    None lives, and where they lived lives now an alien race.

Ah, famous wave you sang the livelong night below;
    Small wonder if the noise set my wits wandering –
I swear if help could ever come to Ireland now
    I'd strangle in your raucous throat that song you sing.

(translated by Frank O'Connor)

Last Lines

Because, like himself, O'Rahilly seemed the last voice of feudalism,
Yeats used the final line of this poem for one of his own.

I shall not call for help until they coffin me –
    What good for me to call when hope of help is gone?
Princes of Munster who would have heard my cry
    Will not rise from the dead because I am alone.

Mind shudders like a wave in this tempestuous mood,
    My bowels and my heart are pierced and filled with pain
To see our lands, our hills, our gentle neighbourhood,
    A plot where any English upstart stakes his claim.

The Shannon and the Liffey and the tuneful Lee,
    The Boyne and the Blackwater a sad music sing,
The waters of the west run red into the sea –
    No matter what be trumps, their knave will beat our king.

And I can never cease weeping these useless tears;
    I am a man oppressed, afflicted and undone
Who where he wanders mourning no companion hears
    Only some waterfall that has no cause to mourn.

Now I shall cease, death comes, and I must not delay
    By Laune and Laine and Lee, diminished of their pride,
I shall go after the heroes, ay, into the clay –
    My fathers followed theirs before Christ was crucified.

(translated by Frank O'Connor)

ANONYMOUS

Hope

Time has triumphed, the wind has scattered all,
Alexander, Caesar, empires, cities are lost,
Tara and Troy flourished a while and fell
And even England itself, maybe, will bite the dust.

(translated by Brendan Kennelly)

ANONYMOUS

The Questions of Ethne Alba

Who is God
and where is God,
of whom is God,
and where His dwelling?

Has He sons and daughters,
gold and silver, this God of yours?

Is He ever-living?
is He beautiful,
was His son
fostered by many?

Are His daughters
dear and beautiful
to the men of the world?

Is He in heaven
or on the earth?
In the sea,
in the rivers,
in the mountains,
in the valleys?

Speak to us
tidings of Him:
How will He be seen,
how is He loved,
how is He found?

Is it in youth
or is it in old age
He is found?

(translated by James Carney)

EILEEN O'LEARY

18th century

The Lament for Art O'Leary

Arthur or Art O'Leary, a colonel in the Austrian army, outlawed and
killed in Carriganimma, County Cork in 1773 for refusing to sell his
famous mare to a Protestant named Morris for £5.0.0 (Catholics were not
permitted by law to possess a horse of greater value than this), is buried in
the ruined abbey of Kilcrea under an epitaph probably composed by his
wife, the author of this lament, and aunt of Daniel O'Connell.

> Lo Arthur Leary, generous, handsome, brave,
> Slain in his bloom lies in this humble grave.

She is said to have followed up his murderers as she threatened and to
have had the soldiers who shot him transported. Morris himself is sup-
posed to have been shot in Cork by O'Leary's brother. The curious
intervention of O'Leary's sister in the lament strongly suggests that she
had originally composed a lament for her brother in which Eileen
O'Connell was taunted, and that the widow seized on this as a theme and
developed it into the fine poem we know. There is a defensive note about
even the opening lines.

The members of her family – the O'Connells of Derrynane – whom she
mentions are her father, Donal, her brother Connell, who was drowned
in 1765, and her sister Abby, married to another Austrian officer named
O'Sullivan. Abby is the girl who is supposed to have been the companion
of Maria Theresa. Her twin sister, Maire, also named, was married to a
man named Baldwin in Macroom, who appears to have surrendered the
mare to Morris in order to avoid legal complications. The market-house
of the first verse is in Macroom, and the Mill of the penultimate verse is
Millstreet, County Cork.

> My love and my delight,
> The day I saw you first
> Beside the market-house
> I had eyes for nothing else
> And love for none but you.
>
> I left my father's house
> And ran away with you,
> And that was no bad choice;
> You gave me everything.

There were parlours whitened for me,
Bedrooms painted for me,
Ovens reddened for me,
Loaves baked for me,
Joints spitted for me,
Beds made for me
To take my ease on flock
Until the milking time
And later if I pleased.

My mind remembers
That bright spring day,
How your hat with its band
Of gold became you,
Your silver-hilted sword,
Your manly right hand,
Your horse on her mettle
And foes around you
Cowed by your air;
For when you rode by
On your white-nosed mare
The English lowered their head before you
Not out of love for you
But hate and fear,
For, sweetheart of my soul,
The English killed you.

My love and my calf
Of the race of the Earls of Antrim
And the Barrys of Eemokilly,
How well a sword became you,
A hat with a band,
A slender foreign shoe
And a suit of yarn
Woven over the water!

My love and my darling
When I go home

The little lad, Conor,
And Fiach the baby
Will surely ask me
Where I left their father,
I'll say with anguish
'Twas in Kilnamartyr;
They will call the father
Who will never answer.

My love and my mate
That I never thought dead
Till your horse came to me
With bridle trailing,
All blood from forehead
To polished saddle
Where you should be,
Either sitting or standing;
I gave one leap to the threshold,
A second to the gate,
A third upon its back.

I clapped my hands,
And off at a gallop;
I never lingered
Till I found you lying
By a little furze-bush
Without pope or bishop
Or priest or cleric
One prayer to whisper
But an old, old woman,
And her cloak about you,
And your blood in torrents –
Art O'Leary –
I did not wipe it off,
I drank it from my palms.

My love and my delight
Stand up now beside me,

And let me lead you home
Until I make a feast,
And I will roast the meat
And send for company
And call the harpers in,
And I shall make your bed
Of soft and snowy sheets
And blankets dark and rough
To warm the beloved limbs
An autumn blast has chilled.

(*His sister speaks*)

My little love, my calf,
This is the image
That last night brought me
In Cork all lonely
On my bed sleeping,
That the white courtyard
And the tall mansion
That we two played in
As children had fallen,
Ballingeary withered
And your hounds were silent,
Your birds were songless
While people found you
On the open mountain
Without priest or cleric
But an old, old woman
And her coat about you
When the earth caught you –
Art O'Leary –
And your life-blood stiffened
The white shirt on you.

My love and treasure,
Where is the woman
From Cork of the white sails
To the bridge of Tomey

With her dowry gathered
And cows at pasture
Would sleep alone
The night they waked you?

(*His wife replies*)

My darling, do not believe
One word she is saying,
It is a falsehood
That I slept while others
Sat up to wake you –
'Twas no sleep that took me
But the children crying;
They would not rest
Without me beside them.

O people, do not believe
Any lying story!
There is no woman in Ireland
Who had slept beside him
And borne him three children
But would cry out
After Art O'Leary
Who lies dead before me
Since yesterday morning.

Grief on you, Morris!
Heart's blood and bowels' blood!
May your eyes go blind
And your knees be broken!
You killed my darling
And no man in Ireland
Will fire the shot at you.

Destruction pursue you,
Morris the traitor
Who brought death to my husband!
Father of three children –

Two on the hearth
And one in the womb
That I shall not bring forth.

It is my sorrow
That I was not by
When they fired the shots
To catch them in my dress
Or in my heart, who cares?
If you but reached the hills
Rider of the ready hands.

My love and my fortune
'Tis an evil portion
To lay for a giant –
A shroud and a coffin –
For a big-hearted hero
Who fished in the hill-streams
And drank in bright halls
With white-breasted women.

My comfort and my friend,
Master of the bright sword,
'Tis time you left your sleep;
Yonder hangs your whip,
Your horse is at the door,
Follow the lane to the east
Where every bush will bend
And every stream dry up,
And man and woman bow
If things have manners yet
That have them not I fear.

My love and my sweetness,
'Tis not the death of my people,
Donal Mor O'Connell,
Connell who died by drowning,
Or the girl of six and twenty

Who went across the water
To be a queen's companion –
'Tis not all these I speak of
And call in accents broken
But noble Art O'Leary,
Art of hair so golden,
Art of wit and courage,
Art the brown mare's master,
Swept last night to nothing
Here in Carriganimma –
Perish it, name and people!

My love and my treasure,
Though I bring with me
No throng of mourners,
'Tis no shame for me,
For my kinsmen are wrapped in
A sleep beyond waking,
In narrow coffins
Walled up in stone.

Though but for the smallpox,
And the black death,
And the spotted fever,
That hosts of riders
With bridles shaking
Would wake the echoes,
Coming to your waking,
Art of the white breast.

Could my calls but wake my kindred
In Derrynane beyond the mountains,
Or Capling of the yellow apples,
Many a proud and stately rider,
Many a girl with spotless kerchief,
Would be here before tomorrow,
Shedding tears about your body,
Art O'Leary, once so merry.

My love and my secret,
Your corn is stacked,
Your cows are milking;
On me is the grief
There's no cure for in Munster.
Till Art O'Leary rise
This grief will never yield
That's bruising all my heart
Yet shut up fast in it,
As 'twere in a locked trunk
With the key gone astray,
And rust grown on the wards.

My love and my calf,
Noble Art O'Leary,
Son of Conor, son of Cady,
Son of Lewis O'Leary,
West of the Valley
And east of Greenane
Where berries grow thickly
And nuts crowd on branches
And apples in heaps fall
In their own season;
What wonder to any
If Iveleary lighted
And Ballingeary
And Gougane of the saints
For the smooth-palmed rider,
The unwearying huntsman
That I would see spurring
From Grenagh without halting
When quick hounds had faltered?
My rider of the bright eyes,
What happened you yesterday?
I thought you in my heart,
When I bought you your fine clothes,
A man the world could not slay.

'Tis known to Jesus Christ
Nor cap upon my head,
Nor shift upon my back
Nor shoe upon my foot,
Nor gear in all my house,
Nor bridle for the mare
But I will spend at law;
And I'll go oversea
To plead before the King,
And if the King be deaf
I'll settle things alone
With the black-blooded rogue
That killed my man on me.

Rider of the white palms,
Go in to Baldwin,
And face the schemer,
The bandy-legged monster –
God rot him and his children!
(Wishing no harm to Maire,
Yet of no love for her,
But that my mother's body
Was a bed to her for three seasons
And to me beside her.)

Take my heart's love,
Dark women of the Mill,
For the sharp rhymes ye shed
On the rider of the brown mare.

But cease your weeping now,
Women of the soft, wet eyes
Till Art O'Leary drink
Ere he go to the dark school –
Not to learn music or song
But to prop the earth and the stone.

(*translated by Frank O'Connor*)

ANONYMOUS

The Lament for Yellow-haired Donough

An uneducated Connacht girl, or someone speaking in her name, writes the classic lament, the poem that would have been understood in the ninth century as it was in the nineteenth by Yeats.

Ye have seen a marvel in this town,
Yellow-haired Donough and he put down;
In place of his hat a little white cap,
In place of his neck-cloth a hempen rope.

I have come all night without my sleep
Like a little lamb in a drove of sheep,
With naked breast and hair awry
Over Yellow-haired Donough to raise my cry.

I wept the first time by the lake shore,
At the foot of your gallows I wept once more;
I wept again with an aching head
Among the English and you stretched dead.

If only I had you among your kin,
The Ballinrobe or the Sligo men,
They would break the gallows and cut you down
And send you safely among your own.

It was not the gallows that was your due
But to go to the barn and thresh the straw,
And guide your plough-team up and down
Till you had painted the green hill brown.

Yellow-haired Donough, I know your case;
I know what brought you to this bad place:
'Twas the drink going round and the pipes alight
And the dew on the fields at the end of night.

Mullane that brought misfortune on,
My little brother was no stroller's son
But a handsome boy who was bold and quick
And could draw sweet sounds from a hurling stick.

Mullane, may a son not share your floor
Nor a daughter ever leave your door;
The table is empty at foot and head
And Yellow-haired Donough is lying dead.

His marriage portion is in the house,
And it is not horses nor sheep nor cows,
But tobacco and pipes and candles lit –
Not grudging any his share of it.

(translated by Frank O'Connor)

ANTHONY RAFTERY

1784–1835

Mary Hynes

This song has the same sort of wailful charm: a blind man praising a
village beauty whom he cannot see.

Going to Mass by the heavenly mercy,
    The day was rainy, the wind was wild;
I met a lady beside Kiltartan
    And fell in love with the lovely child;
My conversation was smooth and easy,
    And graciously she answered me
'Raftery dear, 'tis yourself that's welcome,
    So step beside me to Ballylee.'

This invitation there was no denying,
    I laughed with joy and my poor heart beat;
We had but to walk across a meadow,
    And in her dwelling I took my seat.
There was laid a table with a jug and glasses,
    And that sweet maiden sat down by me –
'Raftery drink and don't spare the liquor;
    There's a lengthy cellar in Ballylee.'

If I should travel France and England,
    And Spain and Greece and return once more
To study Ireland to the northern ocean,
    I would find no morsel the like of her.
If I was married to that youthful beauty
    I'd follow her through the open sea,
And wander coasts and winding roads
    With the shining pearl of Ballylee.

'Tis fine and bright on the mountainside,
    Looking down on Ballylee,
You can walk the woods, picking nuts and berries,
    And hear the birds sing merrily;

But where's the good if you got no tidings
  Of the flowering branch that resides below –
O summer sky, there's no denying
  It is for you that I ramble so.

My star of beauty, my sun of autumn,
  My golden hair, O my share of life!
Will you come with me this coming Sunday
  And tell the priest you will be my wife?
I'd not grudge you music, nor a feast at evening,
  Nor punch nor wine, if you'd have it be,
And King of Glory, dry up the roadway
  Till I find my posy at Ballylee!

(translated by Frank O'Connor)

BRYAN MERRYMAN

1747–1805

The Midnight Court

I

I liked to walk in the river meadows
In the thick of the dew and the morning shadows,
At the edge of the woods in a deep defile
At peace with myself in the first sunshine.
When I looked at Lough Graney my heart grew bright,
Ploughed lands and green in the morning light,
Mountains in rows with crimson borders
Peering above their neighbours' shoulders.
The heart that never had known relief
In a lonesome old man distraught with grief,
Without money or home or friends or ease,
Would quicken to glimpse beyond the trees
The ducks sail by on a mistless bay
And a swan before them lead the way;
A speckled trout that in their track
Splashed in the air with arching back;
The grey of the lake and the waves around
That foamed at its edge with a hollow sound.
Birds in the trees sang merry and loud;
A fawn flashed out of the shadowy wood;
The horns rang out with the huntsman's cry
And the belling of hounds while the fox slipped by.

Yesterday morning the sky was clear,
The sun fell hot on river and mere,
Its horses fresh and with gamesome eye
Harnessed again to assail the sky;
The leaves were thick upon every bough
And ferns and grass were thick below,
Sheltering bowers of herbs and flowers
That would comfort a man in his dreariest hours.

Longing for sleep bore down my head,
And in the grass I scooped a bed
With a hollow behind to house my back,
A prop for my head and my limbs stretched slack.
What more could one ask? I covered my face
To avert the flies as I dozed a space,
But my mind in dreams was filled with grief
And I tossed and groaned as I sought relief.

I had only begun when I felt a shock,
And all the landscape seemed to rock;
A north wind made my senses tingle
And thunder crackled along the shingle.
As I looked up – as I thought, awake –
I seemed to see at the edge of the lake
As ugly a brute as man could see
In the shape of woman approaching me;
For, if I calculated right,
She must have been twenty feet in height,
With yards and yards of hairy cloak
Trailing behind her in the muck.
There never was seen such a freak of nature;
Without a single presentable feature;
Her grinning jaws with the fangs stuck out
Would be cause sufficient to start a rout,
And in a hand like a weaver's beam
She raised a staff that it might be seen
She was coming on a legal errand,
For nailed to the staff was a bailiff's warrant.

She cried in a voice with a brassy ring:
'Get up out of that, you lazy thing!
That a man like you could think 'tis fitting
To lie in a ditch while the court is sitting!
A decenter court than e'er you knew,
And far too good for the likes of you.
Justice and Mercy hand in hand
Sit in the courts of Fairyland.

Let Ireland think when her trouble's ended
Of those by whom she was befriended.
In Moy Graney palace twelve days and nights
They've sat discussing your wrongs and rights.
All mourned that follow in his train,
Like the king himself, that in his reign
Such unimaginable disaster
Should follow your people, man and master.
Old stock uprooted on every hand
Without claim to rent or law or land;
Nothing to see in a land defiled
Where the flowers were plucked but the weeds and wild;
The best of your breed in foreign places,
And upstart rogues with impudent faces,
Planning with all their guile and spleen
To pick the bones of the Irish clean.
But worst of all those bad reports
Was that truth was darkened in their courts,
And nothing to back a poor man's case
But whispers, intrigue and the lust for place;
The lawyer's craft and the rich man's might,
Cozening, favour, greed and spite;
Maddened with jobs and bribes and malice,
Anarchy loose on cot and palace.

''Twas all discussed, and along with the rest
There were women in scores who came to attest –
A plea that concerns yourself as well –
That the youth of the country's gone to hell,
And men's increase is a sort of crime,
Which only happened within our time;
Nothing but weeds for want of tillage
Since famine and war assailed the village,
And a flighty king and emigration –
And what have you done to restore the nation?
Shame on you without chick nor child
With women in thousands running wild!
The blossoming tree and the young green shoot,

The strap that would sleep with any old root,
The little white saint at the altar rail,
And the proud, cold girl like a ship in sail –
What matter to you if their beauty founder,
If belly and breast will never be rounder,
If, ready and glad to be mother and wife,
They drop unplucked from the boughs of life?

'And having considered all reports,
They agreed that in place of the English courts,
They should select a judge by lot
Who'd hold enquiry on the spot.
Then Eevul, Queen of the Grey Rock,
Who rules all Munster herd and flock,
Arose, and offered to do her share
By putting an end to injustice there.
She took an oath to the council then
To judge the women and the men,
Stand by the poor though all ignore them
And humble the pride of the rich before them;
Make might without right conceal its face
And use her might to give right its place.
Her favour money will not buy,
No lawyer will pull the truth awry,
The smoothest perjurer will not dare
To make a show of falsehood there.
The court is sitting today in Feakle,
So off with you now as quick as you're able!
Come on, I say, and give no back chat,
Or I'll take my stick and knock you flat.'
With the crook of her staff she hooked my cape,
And we went at a speed to make Christians gape
Away through the glens in one wild rush
Till we stood in Moinmoy by the ruined church.

Then I saw with an awesome feeling
A building aglow from floor to ceiling,
Lighted within by guttering torches

Among massive walls and echoing arches.
The Queen of the Fairies sat alone
At the end of the hall on a gilded throne,
While keeping back the thronged beholders
Was a great array of guns and soldiers.
I stared at it all, the lighted hall,
Crammed with faces from wall to wall,
And a young woman with downcast eye,
Attractive, good-looking and shy,
With long and sweeping golden locks
Who was standing alone in the witness box.
The cut of her spoke of some disgrace;
I saw misfortune in her face;
Her tearful eyes were red and hot,
And her passions bubbled as in a pot;
But whatever on earth it was provoked her
She was silent, all but the sobs that choked her.
You could see from the way the speaking failed her
She'd sooner death than the thing that ailed her,
But, unable to express her meaning,
She wrung her hands and pursued her grieving
While all we could do was stand and gaze
Till sobs gave place to a broken phrase,
And bit by bit she mastered her sorrows,
And dried her eyes, and spoke as follows –
'Yourself is the woman we're glad to see,
Eevul, Queen of Carriglee,
Our moon at night, our morning light,
Our comfort in the teeth of spite;
Mistress of the host of delight,
Munster and Ireland stand in your sight.
My chief complaint and principal grief,
The thing that gives me no relief,
Sweeps me from harbour in my mind
And blows me like smoke on every wind
Is all the girls whose charms miscarry
Throughout the land and who'll never marry;
Bitter old maids without house or home,

Put on one side through no fault of their own.
I know myself from the things I've seen
Enough and to spare of the sort I mean,
And to give an example, here am I
While the tide is flowing, left high and dry.
Wouldn't you think I must be a fright,
To be shelved before I get started right;
Heartsick, bitter, dour and wan,
Unable to sleep for the want of a man?
But how can I lie in a lukewarm bed
With all the thoughts that come into my head?
Indeed, 'tis time that somebody stated
The way that the women are situated,
For if men go on their path to destruction
There will nothing be left to us but abduction.
Their appetite wakes with age and blindness
When you'd let them cover you only from kindness,
And offer it up for the wrongs you'd done
In hopes of reward in the life to come:
And if one of them weds in the heat of youth
When the first down is on his mouth
It isn't some woman of his own sort,
Well-shaped, well-mannered or well-taught;
Some mettlesome girl who studied behaviour,
To sit and stand and amuse a neighbour,
But some pious old prude or dour defamer
Who sweated the couple of pounds that shame her.
There you have it! It has me melted,
And makes me feel that the world's demented:
A county's choice for brains and muscle,
Fond of a lark and not scared of a tussle,
Decent and merry and sober and steady,
Good-looking, gamesome, rakish and ready;
A boy in the blush of his youthful vigour
With a gracious flush and a passable figure
Finds a fortune the best attraction
And sires himself off on some bitter extraction;
Some fretful old maid with her heels in the dung,

Pious airs and venomous tongue,
Vicious and envious, nagging and whining,
Snoozing and snivelling, plotting, contriving –
Hell to her soul, an unmannerly sow
With a pair of bow legs and hair like tow
Went off this morning to the altar
And here am I still without hope of the halter!
Couldn't some man love me as well?
Amn't I plump and sound as a bell?
Lips for kissing and teeth for smiling,
Blossomy skin and forehead shining?
My eyes are blue and my hair is thick
And coils in streams about my neck –
A man who's looking for a wife,
Here's a face that will keep for life!
Hand and arm and neck and breast,
Each is better than the rest.
Look at that waist! My legs are long,
Limber as willows and light and strong.
There's bottom and belly that claim attention,
And the best concealed that I needn't mention.
I'm the sort a natural man desires,
Not a freak or a death-on-wires,
A sloven that comes to life in flashes,
A creature of moods with her heels in the ashes,
Or a sluggard stewing in her own grease,
But a good-looking girl that's bound to please.
If I was as slow as some I know
To stand up for my rights and my dress a show,
Some brainless, illbred, country mope
You could understand if I lost hope;
But ask the first you meet by chance:
Hurling match or race or dance,
Pattern or party, market or fair,
Whatever it was, was I not there?
And didn't I make a good impression
Turning up in the height of fashion?
My hair was washed and combed and powdered,

My coif like snow and stiffly laundered;
I'd a little white hood with ribbons and ruff
On a spotted dress of the finest stuff,
And facings to show off the line
Of a cardinal cloak the colour of wine;
A cambric apron filled with showers
Of fruit and birds and trees and flowers;
Neatly-fitting, expensive shoes
With the highest of heels pegged up with screws;
Silken gloves, and myself in spangles
Of brooches, buckles, rings and bangles.
And you mustn't imagine I was shy,
The sort that slinks with a downcast eye,
Solitary, lonesome, cold and wild,
Like a mountainy girl or an only child.
I tossed my cap at the crowds of the races
And kept my head in the toughest places.
Am I not always on the watch
At bonfire, dance or hurling match,
Or outside the chapel after Mass
To coax a smile from fellows that pass?
But I'm wasting my time on a wildgoose-chase,
And my spirit's broken – and that's my case!
After all my shaping, sulks and passions,
All my aping of styles and fashions,
All the times that my cards were spread
And my hands were read and my cup was read;
Every old rhyme, pishrogue and rune,
Crescent, full moon and harvest moon,
Whit and All Souls and the First of May,
I've nothing to show for all they say.
Every night when I went to bed
I'd a stocking of apples beneath my head;
I fasted three canonical hours
To try and come round the heavenly powers;
I washed my shift where the stream was deep
To hear a lover's voice in sleep;
Often I swept the woodstack bare,

Burned bits of my frock, my nails, my hair,
Up the chimney stuck the flail,
Slept with a spade without avail;
Hid my wool in the lime-kiln late
And my distaff behind the churchyard gate;
I had flax on the road to halt coach or carriage
And haystocks stuffed with heads of cabbage,
And night and day on the proper occasions
Invoked Old Nick and all his legions;
But 'twas all no good and I'm broken-hearted
For here I'm back at the place I started;
And this is the cause of all my tears
I am fast in the rope of the rushing years,
With age and need in lessening span,
And death beyond, and no hopes of a man.
But whatever misfortunes God may send
May He spare me at least that lonesome end,
Nor leave me at last to cross alone
Without chick nor child when my looks are gone
As an old maid counting the things I lack
Scowling thresholds that warn me back!
God, by the lightning and the thunder,
The thought of it makes me ripe for murder!
Every idiot in the country
With a man of her own has the right to insult me.
Sal has a slob with a well-stocked farm,
And Molly goes round on a husband's arm,
There's Min and Margery leaping with glee
And never done with their jokes at me.
And the bounce of Sue! and Kitty and Anne
Have children in droves and a proper man,
And all with their kind can mix and mingle
While I go savage and sour and single.

'Now I know in my heart that I've been too quiet
With a remedy there though I scorned to try it
In the matter of draughts and poisonous weeds
And medicine men and darksome deeds

That I know would fetch me a sweetheart plighted
Who'd love me, whether or not invited.
Oh, I see 'tis the thing that most prevails
And I'll give it a trial if all fruit fails –
A powerful aid to the making of splices
Is powdered herbs on apples in slices.
A girl I know had the neighbours yapping
When she caught the best match in the county napping,
And 'twas she that told me under a vow
That from Shrove to All Souls – and she's married now –
She was eating hay like a horse by the pail
With bog-roots burned and stuped in ale –
I've waited too long and was too resigned,
And nothing you say can change my mind;
I'll give you a chance to help me first
And I'm off after that to do my worst.'

II

Then up there jumps from a neighbouring chair
A little old man with a spiteful air,
Staggering legs and panting breath,
And a look in his eye like poison and death;
And this apparition stumps up the hall
And says to the girl in the hearing of all:
'Damnation take you, you bastard's bitch,
Got by a tinkerman under a ditch!
No wonder the seasons are all upset,
Nor every beating Ireland got;
Decline in decency and manners,
And the cows gone dry and the price of bonhams!
Mavrone! what more can we expect
With Doll and Moll and the way they're decked?
You slut of ill-fame, allow your betters
To tell the court how you learned your letters!
Your seed and breed for all your brag
Were tramps to a man with rag and bag;
I knew your da and what passed for his wife,
And he shouldered his traps to the end of his life,

An aimless lout without friend or neighbour,
Knowledge or niceness, wit or favour:
The breeches he wore were riddled with holes
And his boots without a tack of the soles.
Believe me, friends, if you sold at a fair,
Himself and his wife, his kids and gear,
When the costs were met, by the Holy Martyr,
You'd still go short for a glass of porter.
But the devil's child has the devil's cheek –
You that never owned cow nor sheep,
With buckles and brogues and rings to order –
You that were reared in the reek of solder!
However the rest of the world is gypped
I knew you when you went half-stripped;
And I'd venture a guess that in what you lack
A shift would still astonish your back;
And, shy as you seem, an inquisitive gent
Might study the same with your full consent.
Bosom and back are tightly laced,
Or is it the stays that gives you the waist?
Oh, all can see the way you shine,
But your looks are no concern of mine.
Now tell us the truth and don't be shy
How long are you eating your dinner dry?
A meal of spuds without butter or milk,
And dirt in layers beneath the silk.
Bragging and gab are yours by right,
But I know too where you sleep at night,
And blanket or quilt you never saw
But a strip of old mat and a bundle of straw,
In a hovel of mud without a seat,
And slime that settles about your feet,
A carpet of weeds from door to wall
And hens inscribing their tracks on all;
The rafters in with a broken back
And brown rain lashing through every crack –
'Twas there you learned to look so nice,
But now may we ask how you came by the price?

We all admired the way you spoke,
But whisper, treasure, who paid for the cloak?
A sparrow with you would die of hunger –
How did you come by all the grandeur,
All the tassels and all the lace –
Would you have us believe they were got in grace?
The frock made a hole in somebody's pocket,
And it wasn't you that paid for the jacket;
But assuming that and the rest no news,
How the hell did you come by the shoes?

'Your worship, 'tis women's sinful pride
And that alone has the world destroyed.
Every young man that's ripe for marriage
Is hooked like this by some tricky baggage,
And no one is secure, for a friend of my own,
As nice a boy as ever I've known
That lives from me only a perch or two –
God help him! – married misfortune too.
It breaks my heart when she passes by
With her saucy looks and head held high,
Cows to pasture and fields of wheat,
And money to spare – and all deceit!
Well-fitted to rear a tinker's clan,
She waggles her hips at every man,
With her brazen face and bullock's hide,
And such airs and graces, and mad with pride.
And – that God may judge me! – only I hate
A scandalous tongue, I could relate
Things of that woman's previous state
As one with whom every man could mate
In any convenient field or gate
As the chance might come to him early or late!
But now, of course, we must all forget
Her galloping days and the pace she set;
The race she ran in Ibrackane,
In Manishmore and Teermaclane,
With young and old of the meanest rabble

Of Ennis, Clareabbey and Quin astraddle!
Toughs from Tradree out on a fling,
And Cratlee cut-throats sure to swing;
But still I'd say 'twas the neighbours' spite,
And the girl did nothing but what was right,
But the devil take her and all she showed!
I found her myself on the public road,
On the naked earth with a bare backside
And a Garus turf-cutter astride!
Is it any wonder my heart is failing,
That I feel that the end of the world is nearing,
When, ploughed and sown to all men's knowledge,
She can manage the child to arrive with marriage,
And even then, put to the pinch,
Begrudges Charity an inch;
For, counting from the final prayer
With the candles quenched and the altar bare
To the day when her offspring takes the air
Is a full nine months with a week to spare?

'But you see the troubles a man takes on!
From the minute he marries his peace is gone;
Forever in fear of a neighbour's sneer –
And my own experience cost me dear.
I lived alone as happy as Larry
Till I took it into my head to marry,
Tilling my fields with an easy mind,
Going wherever I felt inclined,
Welcomed by all as a man of price,
Always ready with good advice.
The neighbours listened – they couldn't refuse
For I'd money and stock to uphold my views –
Everything came at my beck and call
Till a woman appeared and destroyed it all:
A beautiful girl with ripening bosom,
Cheeks as bright as apple-blossom,
Hair that glimmered and foamed in the wind,
And a face that blazed with the light behind;

A tinkling laugh and a modest carriage
And a twinkling eye that was ripe for marriage.
I goggled and gaped like one born mindless
Till I took her face for a form of kindness,
Though that wasn't quite what the Lord intended
For He marked me down like a man offended
For a vengeance that wouldn't be easy mended
With my folly exposed and my comfort ended.

'Not to detain you here all day
I married the girl without more delay,
And took my share in the fun that followed.
There was plenty for all and nothing borrowed.
Be fair to me now! There was no one slighted;
The beggarmen took the road delighted;
The clerk and mummers were elated;
The priest went home with his pocket weighted.
The lamps were lit, the guests arrived;
The supper was ready, the drink was plied;
The fiddles were flayed, and, the night advancing,
The neighbours joined in the sport and dancing.

'A pity to God I didn't smother
When first I took the milk from my mother,
Or any day I ever broke bread
Before I brought that woman to bed!
For though everyone talked of her carouses
As a scratching post of the public houses
That as sure as ever the glasses would jingle
Flattened herself to married and single,
Admitting no modesty to mention,
I never believed but 'twas all invention.
They added, in view of the life she led,
I might take to the roads and beg my bread,
But I took it for talk and hardly minded –
Sure, a man like me could never be blinded! –
And I smiled and nodded and off I tripped
Till my wedding night when I saw her stripped,

And knew too late that this was no libel
Spread in the pub by some jealous rival –
By God, 'twas a fact, and well-supported:
I was a father before I started!

'So there I was in the cold daylight,
A family man after one short night!
The women around me, scolding, preaching,
The wife in bed and the baby screeching.
I stirred the milk as the kettle boiled
Making a bottle to give the child;
All the old hags at the hob were cooing
As if they believed it was all my doing –
Flattery worse than ever you heard:
"Glory and praise to our blessed Lord,
Though he came in a hurry, the poor little creature,
He's the spit of his da in every feature.
Sal, will you look at the cut of that lip!
There's fingers for you! Feel his grip!
Would you measure the legs and the rolls of fat!
Was there ever a seven-month child like that!"
And they traced away with great preciseness
My matchless face in the baby's likeness;
The same snub nose and frolicsome air,
And the way I laugh and the way I stare;
And they swore that never from head to toe
Was a child that resembled his father so.
But they wouldn't let me go near the wonder –
"Sure, a draught would blow the poor child asunder!"
All of them out to blind me further –
"The least little breath would be noonday murder!"
Malice and lies! So I took the floor,
Mad with rage and I cursed and swore,
And bade them all to leave my sight.
They shrank away with faces white,
And moaned as they handed me the baby:
"Don't crush him now! Can't you handle him easy?
The least thing hurts them. Treat him kindly!

Some fall she got brought it on untimely.
Don't lift his head but leave him lying!
Poor innocent scrap, and to think he's dying!
If he lives at all till the end of day
Till the priest can come 'tis the most we'll pray!"

'I off with the rags and set him free,
And studied him well as he lay on my knee.
That too, by God, was nothing but lies
For he staggered myself with his kicks and cries.
A pair of shoulders like my own,
Legs like sausages, hair fullgrown;
His ears stuck out and his nails were long,
His hands and wrists and elbows strong;
His eyes were bright, his nostrils wide,
And the knee-caps showing beneath his hide –
A champion, begod, a powerful whelp,
As healthy and hearty as myself!

'Young woman, I've made my case entire.
Justice is all that I require.
Once consider the terrible life
We lead from the minute we take a wife,
And you'll find and see that marriage must stop
And the men unmarried must be let off.
And, child of grace, don't think of the race;
Plenty will follow to take our place;
There are ways and means to make lovers agree
Without making a show of men like me.
There's no excuse for all the exploiters;
Cornerboys, clerks and priests and pipers –
Idle fellows that leave you broke
With the jars of malt and the beer they soak,
When the Mother of God herself could breed
Without asking the views of clerk or creed.
Healthy and happy, wholesome and sound,
The come-by-twilight sort abound;
No one assumes but their lungs are ample,
And their hearts as sound as the best example.

When did Nature display unkindness
To the bastard child in disease or blindness?
Are they not handsomer, better-bred
Than many that come of a lawful bed?

'I needn't go far to look for proof
For I've one of the sort beneath my roof –
Let him come here for all to view!
Look at him now! You see 'tis true.
Agreed, we don't know his father's name,
But his mother admires him just the same,
And if in all things else he shines
Who cares for his baptismal lines?
He isn't a dwarf or an old man's error,
A paralytic or walking terror,
He isn't a hunchback or a cripple
But a lightsome, laughing gay young divil.
'Tis easy to see he's no flash in the pan;
No sleepy, good-natured, respectable man,
Without sinew or bone or belly or bust,
Or venom or vice or love or lust,
Buckled and braced in every limb
Spouted the seed that flowered in him:
For back and leg and chest and height
Prove him to all in the teeth of spite
A child begotten in fear and wonder
In the blood's millrace and the body's thunder.

'Down with marriage! It's out of date;
It exhausts the stock and cripples the state.
The priest has failed with whip and blinker,
Now give a chance to Tom the Tinker,
And mix and mash in Nature's can
The tinker and the gentleman!
Let lovers in every lane extended
Struggle and strain as God intended
And locked in frenzy bring to birth
The morning glory of the earth;
The starry litter, girl and boy

Who'll see the world once more with joy.
Clouds will break and skies will brighten,
Mountains bloom and spirits lighten,
And men and women praise your might,
You who restore the old delight.'

III

The girl had listened without dissembling,
Then up she started, hot and trembling,
And answered him with eyes alight
And a voice that shook with squalls of spite:
'By the Crown of the Rock, I thought in time
Of your age and folly and known decline,
And the manners I owe to people and place
Or I'd dye my nails in your ugly face;
Scatter your guts and tan your hide
And ferry your soul to the other side.
I'd honour you much if I gave the lie
To an impudent speech that needs no reply;
'Tis enough if I tell the sort of life
You led your unfortunate, decent wife.

'This girl was poor, she hadn't a home,
Or a single thing she could call her own,
Drifting about in the saddest of lives,
Doing odd jobs for other men's wives,
As if for drudgery created,
Begging a crust from women she hated.
He pretended her troubles were over;
Married to him she'd live in clover;
The cows she milked would be her own,
The feather bed and the decent home,
The stack of turf, the lamp to light,
The good earth wall of a winter's night,
Flax and wool to weave and wind,
The womanly things for which she pined.
Even his friends could not have said

That his looks were such that she lost her head.
How else would he come by such a wife
But that ease was the alms she asked of life?
What possible use could she have at night
For dourness, dropsy, bother and blight,
A basket of bones with thighs of lead,
Knees absconded from the dead,
Fire-speckled shanks and temples whitening,
Looking like one that was struck by lightning?
Is there living a girl who could grow fat
Tied to a travelling corpse like that
Who twice a year wouldn't find a wish
To see what was she, flesh or fish
But dragged the clothes about his head
Like a wintry wind to a woman in bed?

'Now was it too much to expect as right
A little attention once a night?
From all I know she was never accounted
A woman too modest to be mounted.
Gentle, good-humoured and Godfearing
Why should we think she'd deny her rearing?
Whatever the lengths his fancy ran
She wouldn't take fright from a mettlesome man,
And would sooner a boy would be aged a score
Than himself on the job for a week or more;
And an allnight dance or Mass at morning,
Fiddle or flute or choir or organ,
She'd sooner the tune that boy would play
As midnight struck or at break of day.
Damn it, you know we're all the same,
A woman nine months in terror and pain,
The minute that Death has lost the game –
Good morrow my love, and she's off again!
And how could one who longed to please
Feel with a fellow who'd sooner freeze
Than warm himself in a natural way
From All Souls Night to St Brigid's day?

You'd all agree 'twas a terrible fate –
Sixty winters on his pate,
A starved old gelding, blind and lamed
And a twenty year old with her parts untamed.
It wasn't her fault if things went wrong,
She closed her eyes and held her tongue;
She was no ignorant girl from school
To whine for her mother and play the fool
But a competent bedmate smooth and warm
Who cushioned him like a sheaf of corn.
Line by line she bade him linger
With gummy lips and groping finger,
Gripping his thighs in a wild embrace
Rubbing her brush from knee to waist
Stripping him bare to the cold night air,
Everything done with love and care.
But she'd nothing to show for all her labour;
There wasn't a jump in the old deceiver,
And all I could say would give no notion
Of that poor distracted girl's emotion,
Her knees cocked up and the bedposts shaking,
Chattering teeth and sinews aching,
While she sobbed and tossed through a joyless night
And gave it up with the morning light.

'I think you'll agree from the little I've said
A man like this must be off his head
To live like a monk to the end of his life,
Muddle his marriage and blame his wife.
The talk about women comes well from him,
Without hope in body or help in limb;
If the creature that found him such a sell
Has a lover today she deserves him well:
A benefit Nature never denies
To anything born that swims or flies;
Tell me of one that ever went empty
And died of want in the midst of plenty.
In all the wonders west and east

Where will you hear of a breed of beast
That will turn away from fern and hay
To feed on briars and roots and clay?
You silly old fool, you can't reply
And give us at least one reason why
If your supper is there when you come back late
You've such talk of someone that used the plate.
Will it lessen your store, will you sigh for more
If twenty millions cleaned it before?
You must think that women are all like you
To believe they'll go dry for a man or two;
You might as well drink the ocean up
Or empty the Shannon with a cup.
Ah, you must see that you're half insane;
Try cold compresses, avoid all strain,
And stop complaining about the neighbours,
If every one of them owed her favours,
Men by the hundred beneath her shawl
Would take nothing from you in the heel of all.

'If your jealousy even was based on fact
In some hardy young whelp that could keep her packed;
Covetous, quarrelsome, keen on scoring,
Or some hairy old villain hardened with whoring;
A vigorous pusher, a rank outsider,
A jockey of note or a gentleman rider –
But a man disposed in the wrong direction
With a poor mouth shown on a sham erection!

'But oye, my heart will grow grey hairs
Brooding forever on idle cares,
Has the Catholic Church a glimmer of sense
That the priests won't come to the girls' defence?
Is it any wonder the way I moan,
Out of my mind for a man of my own
While there's men around can afford one well
But shun a girl as they shun Hell.
The full of a fair of primest beef,

Warranted to afford relief;
Cherry-red cheeks and bull-like voices
And bellies dripping with fat in slices;
Backs erect and huge hind-quarters,
Hot-blooded men, the best of partners,
Freshness and charm, youth and good looks
And nothing to ease their mind but books!
The best-fed men that travel the country,
With beef and mutton, game and poultry,
Whiskey and wine forever in stock,
Sides of bacon and beds of flock.
Mostly they're hardy under the hood,
And we know like ourselves they're flesh and blood.
I wouldn't ask much of the old campaigners,
Good-for-nothings and born complainers
But petticoat-tossers aloof and idle
And fillies gone wild for bit and bridle!

'Of course I admit that some, more sprightly,
Would like to repent, and I'd treat them lightly.
A pardon and a job for life
To every priest that takes a wife!
For many a good man's chance miscarries
If you scuttle the ship for the crooks it carries;
And though some as we know were always savage,
Gnashing their teeth at the thought of marriage,
And, modest beyond the needs of merit,
Invoked hell-fire on girls of spirit,
Yet some who took to their pastoral labours
Made very good priests and the best of neighbours.
Many a girl filled byre and stall
And furnished her house through a clerical call.
Everyone's heard some priest extolled
For the lonesome women that he consoled;
People I've known throughout the county
Have nothing but praise for the curate's bounty,
Or uphold the canon to lasting fame
For the children he reared in another man's name;

But I hate to think of their lonely lives,
The passions they waste on middle-aged wives
While the girls they'd choose if the choice was theirs
Go by the wall and comb grey hairs.

'I leave it to you, O Nut of Knowledge,
The girls at home and the boys in college,
You cannot persuade me it's a crime
If they make love while they still have time,
But you who for learning have no rival,
Tell us the teachings of the Bible;
Where are we taught to pervert our senses
And make our natural needs offences?
To fly from lust as in Saint Paul
Doesn't mean flight from life and all,
But to leave home and friends behind
And stick to one who pleased one's mind.
But I'm at it again! I'll keep my place;
It isn't for me to judge the case,
When you, a spirit born and queen,
Remember the texts and what they mean,
With apt quotations well-supplied
From the prophets who took the woman's side,
And the words of Christ that were never belied
Who chose for His Mother an earthly bride.

'But oye, what use are pishrogue and spell
To one like myself in the fires of Hell?
What chance can there be for girls like me
With husbands for only one in three?
When there's famine abroad the need advises
To look after yourself as chance arises,
And since crops are thin and weeds are plenty,
And the young without heart and Ireland empty,
And to fill it again is a hopeless job,
Get me some old fellow to sit by the hob;
Tie him down there as best you can –
And leave it to me to make him a man.'

IV

The day crept in and the lights grew pale,
The girl sat down as she ended her tale;
The princess rose with face aglow
And her voice when she spoke was grave and slow.
'Oyez!' said the clerk to quell the riot,
And wielded his mace till all were quiet,
Then from her lips as we sat hushed
Speech like a rainbow glory gushed.
'My child,' she said, 'I will not deny
That you've reason enough to scold and cry,
And, as a woman, I can't but grieve
To see girls like you, and Moll and Maeve,
With your dues diminished and favours gone,
And none to enjoy a likely man
But misers sucking a lonely bone
Or hairy old harpies living alone.
I do enact according then
That all the present unmarried men
Shall be arrested by the guard,
Detained inside the chapel yard
And stripped and tied beside the gate
Until you decide upon their fate.
Those that you find whom the years have thwarted
With masculine parts that were never exerted
To the palpable loss of some woman's employment,
The thrill of the milk and their own enjoyment;
Who, having the chance of wife and home
Went wild and took to the hills to roam,
Are only a burden on the earth
So give it to them for all you're worth.
Roast or pickle them, some reflection
Will frame a suitable correction,
But this you can choose at your own tribunal,
And whatever you do will have my approval.
Fully grown men too old to function
As I say you can punish without compunction;

Nothing you do can have consequences
For middle-aged men with failing senses,
And, whatever is lost or whatever survives,
We need never suppose will affect their wives –
Young men, of course, are another affair;
They still are of use, so strike with care!

'There are poor men working in rain and sleet,
Out of their minds with the troubles they meet,
But, men in name and in deed according,
They quarry their women at night and morning –
A fine traditional consolation! –
And these I would keep in circulation.
In the matter of priests a change is due,
And I think I may say it's coming, too.
Any day now it may be revealed
That the cardinals have it signed and sealed,
And we'll hear no more of the ban on marriage
Before the priests go entirely savage.
Then the cry of the blood in the body's fire
You can quicken or quell to your heart's desire,
But anyone else of woman born,
Flay him alive if he won't reform!
Abolish wherever my judgement reaches
The nancy boy and the flapper in breeches,
And when their rule is utterly ended
We can see the world that the Lord intended.

'The rest of the work must only wait.
I'm due elsewhere and already late;
I've business afoot that I must attend
Though you and I are far from the end,
For I'll sit next month and God help the men
If they haven't improved their ways by then!
But mostly those who sin from pride
With women whose names they do not hide,
Who keep their tally of ruined lives
In whispers, nudges, winks and gibes.

Was ever vanity more misplaced
Than in married women and girls disgraced?
It isn't desire that gives the thrust,
The smoking blood and the ache of lust,
Weakness of love and the body's blindness
But to punish the fools who show them kindness.
Thousands are born without a name
That braggarts may boast of their mothers' shame –
Men lost to Nature through conceit,
And their manhood killed by their own deceit,
For 'tis sure that however their wives may weep
It's never because they go short of sleep.'

I'd listened to every word she uttered,
And then as she stopped my midriff fluttered;
I was took with a sort of sudden reeling
Till my feet seemed resting on the ceiling;
People and place went round and round,
And her words came back as a blur of sound.
Then the bailiff strode along the aisle
And reached for me with an ugly smile;
She nipped my ear as if in sport
And dragged me up before the court.
Then the girl who'd complained of how she was slighted,
Spotted my face and sprang up, excited.
'Is it you?' says she. 'Of all the old crocks!
I'm waiting for years to comb your locks.
You had your chance and you missed your shot,
And devil's cure to you now you're caught!
Will anyone here speak in your favour
Or even think you worth the labour?
What little affair would you care to mention
Or what girl did you honour with your attention?
We'll all agree that the man's no beauty,
But, damn it, he's clearly fit for duty.
I know, he's ill-made and ugly as hell,
But he'd match some poor misfortunate well.
I'd sooner him pale and not quite so fat,

But the hump's no harm; I'd make nothing of that
For it isn't a thing you'd notice much
Or one that goes with the puritan touch.
You'll find bandy legs on men of vigour
And arms like pegs on a frolicsome figure.
Of course there must be some shameful reason
That kept him single out of season.
He's welcome at the country houses,
And at the villagers' carouses,
Called in wherever the fun is going,
And fiddles being tuned and whiskey flowing –
I'll never believe there's truth in a name:
A wonder the Merrymans stand the shame!
The doggedest devil that tramps the hill
With grey in his hair and a virgin still!
Leave me alone to settle the savage!
You can spare your breath to cool your porridge!
The truth of it's plain upon your forehead;
You're thirty at least and still unmarried!
Listen to me, O Fount of Luck,
This fellow's the worst that ever I struck.
All the spite I have locked inside
Won't let me at peace till I've tanned his hide.
Can't ye all help me? Catch him! Mind him!
Winnie, girl, run and get ropes to bind him!
Where are you, Annie, or are you blind?
Sally, tie up his hands behind!
Molly and Maeve, you fools what ails you?
Isn't it soon the courage fails you?
Hand me the rope till I give him a crack;
I'll earth it up in the small of his back.
That, young man, is the place to hurt you;
I'll teach you to respect your virtue!
Steady now, till we give him a sample!
Women alive, he's a grand example!
Set to it now and we'll nourish him well!
One good clout and ye'll hear him yell!
Tan him the more the more he'll yell

Till we teach his friends good manners as well.
And as this is the law to restore the nation
We'll write the date as a great occasion –
"The First of January, Seventeen Eighty – " '

And while I stood there, stripped and crazy,
Knowing that nothing could save my skin,
She opened her book, immersed her pen,
And wrote it down with careful art,
As the girls all sighed for the fun to start.
And then I shivered and gave a shake,
Opened my eyes, and was wide awake.

(translated by Frank O'Connor)

PART TWO

Anglo-Irish

JONATHAN SWIFT

1667-1745

Stella's Birthday

All travellers at first incline
Where'er they see the fairest sign,
And if they find the chambers neat,
And like the liquor and the meat,
Will call again, and recommend
The Angel Inn to every friend.
And though the painting grows decay'd,
The house will never lose its trade:
Nay, though the treach'rous tapster, Thomas,
Hangs a new Angel two doors from us,
As fine as daubers' hands can make it,
In hopes that strangers may mistake it,
We think it both a shame and sin
To quit the true old Angel Inn.
    Now this is Stella's case in fact,
An angel's face a little crack'd.
(Could poets or could painters fix
How angels look at thirty-six:)
This drew us in at first to find
In such a form an angel's mind;
And every virtue now supplies
The fainting rays of Stella's eyes.
See, at her levee crowding swains,
Whom Stella freely entertains
With breeding, humour, wit, and sense,
And puts them to so small expense;
Their minds so plentifully fills,
And makes such reasonable bills,
So little gets for what she gives,
We really wonder how she lives!
And had her stock been less, no doubt
She must have long ago run out.

Then, who can think we'll quit the place,
When Doll hangs out a newer face?
Nail'd to her window full in sight
All Christian people to invite,
Or stop and light at Chloe's head,
With scraps and leavings to be fed?
Then, Chloe, still go on to prate
Of thirty-six and thirty-eight;
Pursue your trade of scandal-picking,
Your hints that Stella is no chicken;
Your innuendoes, when you tell us,
That Stella loves to talk with fellows:
But let me warn you to believe
A truth, for which your soul should grieve;
That should you live to see the day,
When Stella's locks must all be gray,
When age must print a furrow'd trace
On every feature of her face;
Though you, and all your senseless tribe,
Could Art, or Time, or Nature bribe,
To make you look like Beauty's Queen,
And hold for ever at fifteen;
No bloom of youth can ever blind
The cracks and wrinkles of your mind:
All men of sense will pass your door,
And crowd to Stella's at four-score.

OLIVER GOLDSMITH

1728–74

Stanzas: On Woman

When lovely Woman stoops to folly,
And finds too late that men betray,
What charm can soothe her melancholy,
What art can wash her guilt away?

The only art her guilt to cover,
To hide her shame from every eye,
To give repentance to her lover,
And wring his bosom, is – to die.

The Village

Sweet was the sound, when oft at evening's close
Up yonder hill the village murmur rose;
There, as I passed with careless steps and slow,
The mingling notes came soften'd from below:
The swain responsive as the milkmaid sung,
The sober herd that low'd to meet their young;
The noisy geese that gabbled o'er the pool,
The playful children just let loose from school;
The watchdog's voice that bay'd the whisp'ring wind,
And the loud laugh that spoke the vacant mind;
These all in sweet confusion sought the shade,
And fill'd each pause the nightingale had made.
But now the sounds of population fail,
No cheerful murmurs fluctuate in the gale,
No busy steps the grass-grown footway tread,
For all the bloomy flush of life is fled.
All but yon widow'd, solitary thing,
That feebly bends beside the plashy spring:

She, wretched matron, forc'd in age, for bread,
To strip the brook with mantling cresses spread,
To strip her wintry faggot from the thorn,
To seek her nightly shed, and weep till morn;
She only left of all the harmless train,
The sad historian of the pensive plain.

JOHN PHILPOT CURRAN

1750–1817

The Deserter's Meditation

If sadly thinking, with spirits sinking,
    Could more than drinking my cares compose,
A cure for sorrow from sighs I'd borrow,
    And hope to-morrow would end my woes.
But as in wailing there's nought availing,
    And Death unfailing will strike the blow,
Then for that reason, and for a season,
    Let us be merry before we go.

To joy a stranger, a way-worn ranger,
    In every danger my course I've run;
Now hope all ending, and death befriending
    His last aid lending, my cares are done.
No more a rover, or hapless lover,
    My griefs are over – my glass runs low;
Then for that reason, and for a season,
    Let us be merry before we go.

WILLIAM DRENNAN

1754–1820

The Wake of William Orr

There our murdered brother lies;
Wake him not with woman's cries;
Mourn the way that manhood ought –
Sit in silent trance of thought.

Write his merits on your mind;
Morals pure and manners kind;
In his head, as on a hill,
Virtue placed her citadel.

Why cut off in palmy youth?
Truth he spoke, and acted truth.
'Countrymen, UNITE,' he cried,
And died for what our Saviour died.

God of peace and God of love!
Let it not Thy vengeance move –
Let it not Thy lightnings draw –
A nation guillotined by law.

Hapless Nation, rent and torn,
Thou wert early taught to mourn;
Warfare of six hundred years!
Epochs marked with blood and tears!

Hunted thro' thy native grounds,
Or flung *reward* to human hounds,
Each one pulled and tore his share,
Heedless of thy deep despair.

Hapless Nation! hapless Land!
Heap of uncementing sand!

Crumbled by a foreign weight:
And by worse, domestic hate.

God of mercy! God of peace!
Make this mad confusion cease;
O'er the mental chaos move,
Through it SPEAK the light of love.

Monstrous and unhappy sight!
Brothers' blood will not unite;
Holy oil and holy water
Mix, and fill the world with slaughter.

Who is she with aspect wild?
The widow'd mother with her child –
Child new stirring in the womb!
Husband waiting for the tomb!

Angel of this sacred place,
Calm her soul and whisper peace –
Cord, or axe, or guillotine,
Make the sentence – not the sin.

Here we watch our brother's sleep:
Watch with us, but do not weep:
Watch with us thro' dead of night –
But expect the morning light.

RICHARD ALFRED MILLIKEN
1767–1815

The Groves of Blarney

The groves of Blarney
They look so charming,
Down by the purling
   Of sweet, silent brooks,
Being banked with posies
That spontaneous grow there,
Planted in order
   By the sweet 'Rock Close'.
'Tis there the daisy
And the sweet carnation,
The blooming pink
   And the rose so fair,
The daffodowndilly,
Likewise the lily,
All flowers that scent
   The sweet, fragrant air.

'Tis Lady Jeffers
That owns this station;
Like Alexander,
   Or Queen Helen fair,
There's no commander
In all the nation,
For emulation,
   Can with her compare.
Such walls surround her,
That no nine-pounder
Could dare to plunder
   Her place of strength;
But Oliver Cromwell
Her he did pommell,
And made a breach
   In her battlement.

There's gravel walks there
For speculation
And conversation
  In sweet solitude.
'Tis there the lover
May hear the dove, or
The gentle plover
  In the afternoon;
And if a lady
Would be so engaging
As to walk alone in
  Those shady bowers,
'Tis there the courtier
He may transport her
Into some fort, or
  All underground.

For 'tis there's a cave where
No daylight enters,
But cats and badgers
  Are for ever bred;
Being mossed by nature,
That makes it sweeter
Than a coach-and-six or
  A feather bed.
'Tis there the lake is,
Well stored with perches,
And comely eels in
  The verdant mud;
Besides the leeches,
And groves of beeches,
Standing in order
  For to guard the flood.

There's statues gracing
This noble place in –
All heathen gods
  And nymphs so fair;

Bold Neptune, Plutarch,
And Nicodemus,
All standing naked
    In the open air!
So now to finish
This brave narration,
Which my poor genii
    Could not entwine;
But were I Homer,
Or Nebuchadnezzar,
'Tis in every feature
    I would make it shine.

THOMAS MOORE
1779–1852

I Saw From the Beach

I saw from the beach, when the morning was shining,
    A bark o'er the waters move gloriously on;
I came when the sun from that beach was declining,
    The bark was still there, but the waters were gone.

And such is the fate of our life's early promise,
    So passing the spring-tide of joy we have known;
Each wave, that we danc'd on at morning, ebbs from us,
    And leaves us, at eve, on the bleak shore alone.

Ne'er tell me of glories, serenely adorning
    The close of our day, the calm eve of our night; –
Give me back, give me back the wild freshness of Morning,
    Her clouds and her tears are worth Evening's best light.

At the Mid Hour of Night

At the mid hour of night, when stars are weeping, I fly
To the lone vale we lov'd, when life shone warm in thine eye;
    And I think oft, if spirits can steal from the regions of air,
    To revisit past scenes of delight, thou wilt come to me there,
And tell me our love is remember'd, even in the sky.

Then I sing the wild song 'twas once such pleasure to hear!
When our voices commingling breath'd, like one, on the ear;
    And, as Echo far off through the vale my sad orison rolls,
    I think, O my love! 'tis thy voice from the Kingdom of
        Souls,
Faintly answering still the notes that once were so dear.

SIR AUBREY DE VERE
1788–1846

The Rock of Cashel

Royal and saintly Cashel! I would gaze
   Upon the wreck of thy departed powers,
   Not in the dewy light of matin hours,
Nor the meridian pomp of summer's blaze,
But at the close of dim autumnal days,
   When the sun's parting glance, through slanting showers,
   Sheds o'er thy rock-throned battlements and towers
Such awful gleams as brighten o'er Decay's
Prophetic cheek. At such a time, methinks,
   There breathes from thy lone courts and voiceless aisles
A melancholy moral, such as sinks
   On the lone traveller's heart, amid the piles
Of vast Persepolis on her mountain stand,
Or Thebes half buried in the desert sand.

CHARLES WOLFE

1791–1823

The Burial of Sir John Moore

I

Not a drum was heard, not a funeral note,
　　As his corse to the rampart we hurried;
Not a soldier discharged his farewell shot
　　O'er the grave where our hero we buried.

II

We buried him darkly at dead of night,
　　The sods with our bayonets turning;
By the struggling moonbeam's misty light,
　　And the lantern dimly burning.

III

No useless coffin enclosed his breast,
　　Not in sheet or in shroud we wound him
But he lay like a warrior taking his rest,
　　With his martial cloak around him.

IV

Few and short were the prayers we said,
　　And we spoke not a word of sorrow;
But we steadfastly gazed on the face that was dead,
　　And we bitterly thought of the morrow.

V

We thought, as we hollow'd his narrow bed,
　　And smooth'd down his lonely pillow,
That the foe and the stranger would tread o'er his head,
　　And we far away on the billow!

VI

Lightly they'll talk of the spirit that's gone,
   And o'er his cold ashes upbraid him;
But little he'll reck, if they let him sleep on
   In the grave where a Briton has laid him.

VII

But half of our heavy task was done
   When the clock struck the hour for retiring,
And we heard the distant and random gun
   That the foe was sullenly firing.

VIII

Slowly and sadly we laid him down
   From the field of his fame fresh and gory;
We carved not a line, and we raised not a stone –
   But we left him alone with his glory!

JEREMIAH JOSEPH CALLANAN

1795-1829

The Convict of Clonmel

How hard is my fortune
　　And vain my repining;
The strong rope of fate
　　For this young neck is twining!
My strength is departed,
　　My cheeks sunk and sallow,
While I languish in chains
　　In the gaol of Clonmala.

No boy of the village
　　Was ever yet milder;
I'd play with a child
　　And my sport would be wilder;
I'd dance without tiring
　　From morning 'till even,
And the goal-ball I'd strike
　　To the light'ning of Heaven.

At my bed foot decaying
　　My hurl-bat is lying;
Through the boys of the village
　　My goal-ball is flying;
My horse 'mong the neighbours
　　Neglected may fallow,
While I pine in my chains
　　In the gaol of Clonmala.

Next Sunday the patron
　　At home will be keeping,
And the young active hurlers
　　The field will be sweeping;

With the dance of fair maidens
   The evening they'll hallow,
While this heart once so gay
   Shall be cold in Clonmala.

The Outlaw of Loch Lene

O many a day have I made good ale in the glen,
That came not of stream, or malt, like the brewing of men.
My bed was the ground, my roof, the greenwood above,
And the wealth that I sought – one far kind glance from my
    love.

Alas! on that night when the horses I drove from the field,
That I was not near from terror my angel to shield.
She stretched forth her arms, – her mantle she flung to the
    wind,
And swam o'er Loch Lene, her outlawed lover to find.

O would that a freezing sleet-winged tempest did sweep,
And I and my love were alone far off on the deep!
I'd ask not a ship, or a bark, or pinnace to save, –
With her hand round my waist, I'd fear not the wind or the
    wave.

'Tis down by the lake where the wild tree fringes its sides,
The maid of my heart, the fair one of Heaven resides –
I think as at eve she wanders its mazes along,
The birds go to sleep by the sweet wild twist of her song.

GEORGE DARLEY

1795–1846

From *Nepenthe*

Over a bloomy land untrod
    By heavier foot than bird or bee
Lays on the grassy-bosomed sod,
    I passed one day in reverie.
High on his unpavilioned throne
The heaven's hot tyrant sat alone,
And like the fabled king of old
Was turning all he touched to gold.
The glittering fountains seemed to pour
Steep downward rills of molten ore,
Glassily tinkling smooth between
Broom-shaded banks of golden green,
And o'er the yellow pasture straying
Dallying still yet undelaying,
In hasty trips from side to side
Footing adown their steepy slide
Headlong, impetuously playing
With the flowery border pied,
That edged the rocky mountain stair,
They pattered down incessant there,
To lowlands sweet and calm and wide.
With golden lip and glistening bell
Burned every bee-cup on the fell,
Whate'er its native unsunned hue,
Snow-white or crimson or cold blue;
Even the black lustres of the sloe
Glanced as they sided to the glow;
And furze in russet frock arrayed
With saffron knots, like shepherd maid,
Broadly tricked out her rough brocade.
The singed mosses curling here,
A golden fleece too short to shear!

Crumbled to sparkling dust beneath
My light step on that sunny heath.
Light, for the ardour of the clime
Made rare my spirit, that sublime
Bore me as buoyant as young Time
Over the green Earth's grassy prime,
Ere his slouch'd wing caught up her slime;
And sprang I not from clay and crime,
Had from those humming beds of thyme
Lifted me near the starry chime
To learn an empyrean rhyme.

O blest unfabled Incense Tree,
That burns in glorious Araby,
With red scent chalicing the air,
Till earth-life grow Elysian there!

Half buried to her flaming breast
In this bright tree, she makes her nest,
Hundred-sunned Phoenix! when she must
Crumble at length to hoary dust!

Her gorgeous death-bed! her rich pyre
Burnt up with aromatic fire!
Her urn, sight high from spoiler men!
Her birthplace when self-born again!

The mountainless green wilds among,
Here ends she her unechoing song!
With amber tears and odorous sighs
Mourned by the desert where she dies!

Laid like the young fawn mossily
In sun-green vales of Araby,
I woke, hard by the Phoenix tree
That with shadeless boughs flamed over me,
And upward called by a dumb cry
With moonbroad orbs of wonder, I

Beheld the immortal Bird on high
Glassing the great sun in her eye.
Steadfast she gazed upon his fire,
Still her destroyer and her sire!
As if to his her soul of flame
Had flown already, whence it came;
Like those that sit and glare so still,
Intense with their death struggle, till
We touch, and curdle at their chill! –
But breathing yet while she doth burn
  The deathless Daughter of the sun!
Slowly to crimson embers turn
  The beauties of the brightsome one.
O'er the broad nest her silver wings
Shook down their wasteful glitterings;
Her brinded neck high-arched in air
Like a small rainbow faded there;
But brighter glowed her plumy crown
Mouldering to golden ashes down;
With fume of sweet woods, to the skies,
Pure as a Saint's adoring sighs,
Warm as a prayer in Paradise,
Her life-breath rose in sacrifice!
The while with shrill triumphant tone
Sounding aloud, aloft, alone,
Ceaseless her joyful deathwail she
Sang to departing Araby!
  Deep melancholy wonder drew
Tears from my heartspring at that view.
Like cresset shedding its last flare
Upon some wistful mariner,
The Bird, fast blending with the sky,
Turned on me her dead-gazing eye
Once – and as surge to shallow spray
Sank down to vapoury dust away!

O, fast her amber blood doth flow
  From the heart-wounded Incense Tree,

Fast as earth's deep-embosomed woe
   In silent rivulets to the sea!

Beauty may weep her fair first-born,
   Perchance in as resplendent tears,
Such golden dewdrops bow the corn
   When the stern sickleman appears.

But oh! such perfume to a bower
   Never allured sweet-seeking bee,
As to sip fast that nectarous shower
   A thirstier minstrel drew in me!

   My burning soul one drop did quaff –
Heaven reeled and gave a thunder-laugh!
Earth reeled, as if with pendulous swing
She rose each side through half her ring,
That I, head downward, twice uphurled,
Saw twice the deep blue underworld,
Twice, at one glance, beneath me lie
The bottomless, boundless, void sky!
Tho' inland far, me seemed around
Ocean came on with swallowing sound
Like moving mountains serried high!
Methought a thousand daystars burned
By their mere fury as they turned,
Bewildering heaven with too much bright,
Till day looked like a daylight night.
Brief chaos, only of the brain!
Heaven settled on its poles again,
And all stood still, but dizzily . . .

   Winds of the West, arise!
Hesperian balmiest airs, O waft back those sweet sighs
   To her that breathes them from her own pure skies,
   Dew-dropping, mixt with dawn's engoldened dyes,
     O'er my unhappy eyes!
From primrose bed and willow bank, where your moss
   cradle lies,

O from your rushy bowers, to waft back her sweet sighs,
    Winds of the West, arise!

     Over the ocean blown,
Far-winnowing, let my soul be mingled with her own,
  By sighs responsive to each other known!
  Bird unto bird's loved breast has often flown
     From distant zone to zone;
Why must the Darling of the Morn lament him here alone?
Shall not his fleeting spirit be mingled with her own,
    Over the ocean blown?

     From your aerial bourne
Look down, O Mother, and hear your hapless Memnon
    mourn!
  Spectre of my gone self, by sorrow worn,
  Leave me not, Mother beloved! from your embraces torn,
     For ever here forlorn!
For ever, ever lonely here! of all life's glory shorn!
Look down, O Mother! behold your hapless Memnon
    mourn,
     From your aerial bourne!

  The sweet Voice swooned, deep-thrilling;
     then
  Raised its wild monody once more
  As the far murmuring of the main
  Heard in a sea-shell's fairy shore,
  Scarce sensible, made one with pain,
  Wind-lost and fitfuller than before;
  Yet still methought the mystic strain
  Burden like this bewildered bore.

    O could my Spirit wing
Hills over, where salt Ocean hath his fresh headspring
  And snowy curls bedeck the Blue-haired King,
  Up where sweet oral birds articulate sing
     Within the desert ring –

Their mighty shadows o'er broad Earth the Lunar Mountains
    fling,
  Where the Sun's chariot bathes in Ocean's fresh
    headspring –
      O could my Spirit wing!

        O could this Spirit, prisoned here
        Like thine, Immortal Murmurer!
        In hatefullest bounds and bonds of clay,
        O could this Spirit of mine away
        To those strange lands – 'Away! away!'
        Methought the breeze with soft command
        Raised itself in a sigh to say
        After me, whispering still 'Away!'
        Still by my side re-echoing bland
        In fervorous secrecy – 'Away!'
        The desert breeze with pinion gray
        Rustled along the leafless sand,
        Warning me still – 'Away! away!'

        Not less than magic breath had blown
        Ashy ambition now to flame,
        Within me; but like veins in stone
        Red grew the blood in my cold frame:
        Tho' drained this life-spring to the lees
        On lancing rocks – this body worn,
        Weed-wrung, and saturate with seas
        Gulped thro' – by their wild mercy borne
        Half jellied hither, and well nigh
        Piecemeal by those white coursers torn
        That shook their manes of me, foam high,
        Cast on their saviour backs forlorn –
        Tho' thus my flesh, my spirit still
        Is unsubdued! aspiring will
        Buoys up my sinking power. 'Tis thine,
        This quenchless spark! To thee this glow,
        This rise from my sea-grave I owe,
        Nepenthe! vital fire divine!

Yet ah! what boots, if cup of bliss
Have such a bitter dreg as this?
Fragile and faint must I still on
The arduous path that I have gone,
Or burn in my own sighs! Like thee,
A winged cap, O Mercury!
I wear, that lifts me still to heaven,
Tho' down to herd with mortals driven.

   By that visionary shore
Steep channel of continual roar,
Billowy duct of flowing thunder,
That wallows the rooted woodland under,
Wandering I, in dizzy wonder,
Tread the hollow crust that caves
The rueful Erebus of waves
Beneath me surging. Blind I roam
The wilderness. O gentle Eve!
Pale daughter of the Day, receive
My greeting glad! – All hail, thou dome
Of God's great Temple, lit so bright
With lamps of ever-living light,
Kept trim within those censers rare
By Virgins quiring to their care,
Voice-joined, tho' separate in far air.
Awful Night! thy sombre plumes,
Shadowed athwart the moonlight pale,
Make this rock-bestudded vale
Gleam like an antique place of tombs,
With lustre cold that chills the gale.
Grateful now to fallen me
This deep tranquillity!
Here in folded silence fast
Shall I fix myself at last,
Till I grow by age as grey
As the rocks, and stiff as they,
Making ever here my own
Statue and monumental stone!

Lo! in the mute mid wilderness,
What wondrous creature, of no kind,
His burning lair doth largely press,
Gaze fixt, and feeding on the wind?
His fell is of the desert dye,
And tissue adust, dun-yellow and dry,
Compact of living sands; his eye
Black luminary, soft and mild,
With its dark lustre cools the wild.
From his stately forehead springs,
Piercing to heaven, a radiant horn!
Lo, the compeer of lion-kings,
The steed self-armed, the Unicorn!
Ever heard of, never seen,
With a main of sands between
Him and approach; his lonely pride
To course his arid arena wide,
Free as the hurricane, or lie here,
Lord of his couch as his career!
Wherefore should this foot profane
His sanctuary, still domain?
Let me turn, ere eye so bland
Perchance be fire-shot, like heaven's brand,
To wither my boldness! Northward now,
Behind the white star on his brow
Glittering straight against the Sun,
Far athwart his lair I run.

What marvellous things I saw besides,
Wandering heaven's wide furnace thro',
With floor of burning sands, and sides
And glowing cope of glassy blue,
Ne'er could mortal tongue nor ear
Intelligibly tell or hear!
Enow to have seen and sung of those
Beauteous chimeras, called in scorn,
Single of species both, and born
Mid among mankind, that but knows

The Phœnix and the Unicorn
Ev'n now, as dim-seen thro' a horn!
Both symbols of proud solitude,
One of melancholy gladness,
One of most majestic sadness,
And therefore to such neighbourhood
I won, by sympathetic madness,
Where let no other steps intrude!

    Across the desert's shrivelled scroll
I past, myself almost to sands
Crumbling, to make another knoll
Amidst the numberless of those lands.
Welcome! Before my bloodshot eyes,
Steed of the East, a camel stands,
Mourning his fallen lord that dies.
Now, as forth his spirit flies,
Ship of the Desert! bear me on,
O'er this wavy-bosomed lea,
That solid seemed and staid anon,
But now looks surging like a sea. —
On she bore me, as the blast
Whirling a leaf, to where in calm
A little fount poured dropping-fast
On dying Nature's heart its balm.
Deep we sucked the spongy moss,
And cropt for dates the sheltering palm,
Then with fleetest amble cross
Like desert, fed upon like alm.
That most vital beverage still,
Tho' near exhaust, preserved me till
Now the broad Barbaric shore
Spread its havens to my view,
And mine ear rung with ocean's roar,
And mine eye glistened with its blue!
Till I found me once again
By the ever-murmuring main,
Listening across the distant foam

My native church bells ring me home.
Alas! why leave I not this toil
Thro' stranger lands, for mine own soil?
Far from ambition's worthless coil,
From all this wide world's wearying moil, –
Why leave I not this busy broil,
For mine own clime, for mine own soil,
My calm, dear, humble, native soil!
There to lay me down at peace
In my own first nothingness?

EUGENE O'CURRY

1796–1862

Do You Remember That Night?

Do you remember that night
When you were at the window
With neither hat nor gloves
Nor coat to shelter you?
I reached out my hand to you
And you ardently grasped it,
I remained to converse with you
Until the lark began to sing.

Do you remember that night
That you and I were
At the foot of the rowan-tree
And the night drifting snow?
Your head on my breast,
And your pipe sweetly playing?
Little thought I that night
That our love ties would loosen!

Beloved of my inmost heart,
Come some night, and soon,
When my people are at rest,
That we may talk together.
My arms shall encircle you
While I relate my sad tale,
That your soft, pleasant converse
Hath deprived me of heaven.

The fire is unraked,
The light unextinguished,
The key under the door,
Do you softly draw it.

EUGENE O'CURRY

My mother is asleep,
But I am wide awake;
My fortune in my hand,
I am ready to go with you.

(from the Irish, 17th century)

JAMES CLARENCE MANGAN

1803–49

Dark Rosaleen

O my Dark Rosaleen,
  Do not sigh, do not weep!
The priests are on the ocean green,
  They march along the Deep.
There's wine . . . from the royal Pope
  Upon the ocean green;
And Spanish ale shall give you hope,
  My Dark Rosaleen!
  My own Rosaleen!
Shall glad your heart, shall give you hope,
Shall give you health, and help, and hope,
  My Dark Rosaleen.

Over hills and through dales
  Have I roamed for your sake;
All yesterday I sailed with sails
  On river and on lake.
The Erne . . . at its highest flood
  I dashed across unseen,
For there was lightning in my blood,
  My Dark Rosaleen!
  My own Rosaleen!
Oh! there was lightning in my blood,
Red lightning lightened through my blood,
  My Dark Rosaleen!

All day long in unrest
  To and fro do I move,
The very soul within my breast
  Is wasted for you, love!
The heart . . . in my bosom faints
  To think of you, my Queen,

My life of life, my saint of saints,
  My Dark Rosaleen!
  My own Rosaleen!
To hear your sweet and sad complaints,
My life, my love, my saint of saints,
  My Dark Rosaleen!

Woe and pain, pain and woe,
  Are my lot night and noon,
To see your bright face clouded so,
  Like to the mournful moon.
But yet . . . will I rear your throne
  Again in golden sheen;
'Tis you shall reign, shall reign alone,
  My Dark Rosaleen!
  My own Rosaleen!
'Tis you shall have the golden throne,
'Tis you shall reign, and reign alone,
  My Dark Rosaleen!

Over dews, over sands
  Will I fly for your weal:
Your holy delicate white hands
  Shall girdle me with steel.
At home . . . in your emerald bowers,
  From morning's dawn till e'en,
You'll pray for me, my flower of flowers,
  My Dark Rosaleen!
  My fond Rosaleen!
You'll think of me through Daylight's hours,
My virgin flower, my flower of flowers,
  My Dark Rosaleen!

I could scale the blue air,
  I could plough the high hills,
Oh, I could kneel all night in prayer,
  To heal your many ills!

And one . . . beamy smile from you
   Would float like light between
My toils and me, my own, my true,
   My Dark Rosaleen!
   My fond Rosaleen!
Would give me life and soul anew,
A second life, a soul anew,
   My Dark Rosaleen!

O! the Erne shall run red
   With redundance of blood,
The earth shall rock beneath our tread,
   And flames wrap hill and wood,
And gun-peal, and slogan cry,
   Wake many a glen serene,
Ere you shall fade, ere you shall die,
   My Dark Rosaleen!
   My own Rosaleen!
The Judgement Hour must first be nigh,
Ere you can fade, ere you can die,
   My Dark Rosaleen!

O'Hussey's Ode to the Maguire

Where is my Chief, my Master, this bleak night, *mavrone!*
O, cold, cold, miserably cold is this bleak night for Hugh,
It's showery, arrowy, speary sleet pierceth one through and
    through,
Pierceth one to the very bone!

Rolls real thunder? Or was that red, livid light
Only a meteor? I scarce know; but through the midnight dim
The pitiless ice-wind streams. Except the hate that persecutes
    him
Nothing hath crueller venomy might.

An awful, a tremendous night is this, meseems!
The flood-gates of the rivers of heaven, I think, have been
    burst wide –
Down from the overcharged clouds, like unto headlong
    ocean's tide,
Descends grey rain in roaring streams.

Though he were even a wolf ranging the round green woods,
Though he were even a pleasant salmon in the unchainable
    sea,
Though he were a wild mountain eagle, he could scarce bear,
    he,
This sharp, sore sleet, these howling floods.

O, mournful is my soul this night for Hugh Maguire!
Darkly, as in a dream, he strays! Before him and behind
Triumphs the tyrannous anger of the wounding wind,
The wounding wind, that burns as fire!

It is my bitter grief – it cuts me to the heart –
That in the country of Clan Darry this should be his fate!
O, woe is me, where is he? Wandering, houseless, desolate,
Alone, without or guide or chart!

Medreams I see just now his face, the strawberry bright,
Uplifted to the blackened heavens, while the tempestuous
    winds
Blow fiercely over and round him, and the smiting sleet-
    shower blinds
The hero of Galang to-night!

Large, large affliction unto me and mine it is,
That one of his majestic bearing, his fair, stately form,
Should thus be tortured and o'erborne – that this unsparing
    storm
Should wreak its wrath on head like his!

That his great hand, so oft the avenger of the oppressed,
Should this chill, churlish night, perchance, be paralysed by
    frost –
While through some icicle-hung thicket – as one lorn and
    lost –
He walks and wanders without rest.

The tempest-driven torrent deluges the mead,
It overflows the low banks of the rivulets and ponds –
The lawns and pasture-grounds lie locked in icy bonds
So that the cattle cannot feed.

The pale bright margins of the streams are seen by none.
Rushes and sweeps along the untamable flood on every side –
It penetrates and fills the cottagers' dwellings far and wide –
Water and land are blent in one.

Through some dark woods, 'mid bones of monsters, Hugh
    now strays,
As he confronts the storm with anguished heart, but manly
    brow –
O! what a sword-wound to that tender heart of his were now
A backward glance at peaceful days.

But other thoughts are his – thoughts that can still inspire
With joy and an onward-bounding hope the bosom of
    Mac-Nee –
Thoughts of his warriors charging like bright billows of the
    sea,
Borne on the wind's wings, flashing fire!

And though frost glaze to-night the clear dew of his eyes,
And white ice-gauntlets glove his noble fine fair fingers o'er,
A warm dress is to him that lightning-garb he ever wore,
The lightning of the soul, not skies.

AVRAN*

Hugh marched forth to the fight – I grieved to see him so
   depart;
And lo! to-night he wanders frozen, rain-drenched, sad,
   betrayed –
But the memory of the limewhite mansions his right hand hath
   laid
In ashes, warms the hero's heart!

(from the Irish of O'Hussey)

*A concluding stanza, generally intended as a recapitulation of the
entire poem.

The Woman of Three Cows

O woman of Three Cows, *agra!* don't let your tongue thus
   rattle!
O, don't be saucy, don't be stiff, because you may have cattle.
I have seen – and, here's my hand to you, I only say what's
   true –
A many a one with twice your stock not half so proud as you.

Good luck to you, don't scorn the poor, and don't be their
   despiser,
For worldly wealth soon melts away, and cheats the very
   miser,
And Death soon strips the proudest wreath from haughty
   human brows;
Then don't be stiff, and don't be proud, good Woman of
   Three Cows!

See where Momonia's heroes lie, proud Owen More's
   descendants,
'Tis they that won the glorious name, and had the grand
   attendants!
If *they* were forced to bow to Fate, as every mortal bows,
Can *you* be proud, can *you* be stiff, my Woman of Three Cows!

The brave sons of the Lord of Clare, they left the land to
    mourning;
Mavrone! for they were banished, with no hope of their
    returning –
Who knows in what abodes of want those youths were driven
    to house?
Yet *you* can give yourself these airs, O Woman of Three Cows!

O, think of Donnell of the Ships, the Chief whom nothing
    daunted –
See how he fell in distant Spain, unchronicled, unchanted!
He sleeps, the great O'Sullivan, where thunder cannot rouse –
Then ask yourself, should *you* be proud, good Woman of
    Three Cows!

O'Ruark, Maguire, those souls of fire, whose names are
    shrined in story –
Think how their high achievements once made Erin's highest
    glory –
Yet now their bones lie mouldering under weeds and cypress
    boughs,
And so, for all your pride, will yours, O Woman of Three
    Cows!

The O'Carrolls, also, famed when Fame was only for the
    boldest,
Rest in forgotten sepulchres with Erin's best and oldest;
Yet who so great as they of yore in battle or carouse?
Just think of that, and hide your head, good Woman of
    Three Cows!

Your neighbour's poor, and you, it seems, are big with vain
    ideas,
Because, *inagh!* you've got three cows – one more, I see, than
    she has.
That tongue of yours wags more at times than Charity allows,
But if you're strong, be merciful, great Woman of Three
    Cows!

Now, there you go! You still, of course, keep up your
    scornful bearing,
And I'm too poor to hinder you; but, by the cloak I'm
    wearing,
If I had but *four* cows myself, even though you were my
    spouse,
I'd thwack you well to cure your pride, my Woman of Three
    Cows!

(from the Irish)

Gone in the Wind

Solomon! where is thy throne? It is gone in the wind.
Babylon! where is thy might? It is gone in the wind.
Like the swift shadows of Noon, like the dreams of the Blind,
Vanish the glories and pomps of the earth in the wind.

Man! canst thou build upon aught in the pride of thy mind?
Wisdom will teach thee that nothing can tarry behind;
Though there be thousand bright actions embalmed and
    enshrined,
Myriads and millions of brighter are snow in the wind.

Solomon! where is thy throne? It is gone in the wind.
Babylon! where is thy might? It is gone in the wind.
All that the genius of Man hath achieved or designed
Waits but its hour to be dealt with as dust by the wind.

Say, what is Pleasure? A phantom, a mask undefined;
Science? An almond, whereof we can pierce but the rind;
Honour and Affluence? Firmans that Fortune hath signed
Only to glitter and pass on the wings of the wind.

Solomon! where is thy throne? It is gone in the wind.
Babylon! where is thy might? It is gone in the wind.
Who is the Fortunate? He who in anguish hath pined!
He shall rejoice when his relics are dust in the wind!

Mortal! be careful with what thy best hopes are entwined;
Woe to the miners for Truth – where the Lampless have
    mined!
Woe to the seekers on earth for – what none ever find!
They and their trust shall be scattered like leaves on the wind.

Solomon! where is thy throne? It is gone in the wind.
Babylon! where is thy might? It is gone in the wind.
Happy in death are they only whose hearts have consigned
All Earth's affections and longings and cares to the wind.

Pity, thou, reader! the madness of poor Humankind,
Raving of Knowledge, – and Satan so busy to blind!
Raving of Glory, – like me, – for the garlands I bind
(Garlands of song) are but gathered, and – strewn in the wind!

Solomon! where is thy throne? It is gone in the wind.
Babylon! where is thy might? It is gone in the wind.
I, Abul-Namez, must rest; for my fire hath declined,
And I hear voices from Hades like bells on the wind.

And Then No More

I saw her once, one little while, and then no more:
'Twas Eden's light on Earth awhile, and then no more.
Amid the throng she passed along the meadow-floor:
Spring seemed to smile on Earth awhile, and then no more:
But whence she came, which way she went, what garb she
    wore
I noted not; I gazed awhile, and then no more!

I saw her once, one little while, and then no more:
'Twas Paradise on Earth awhile, and then no more.
Ah! what avail my vigils pale, my magic lore?
She shone before mine eyes awhile, and then no more.
The shallop of my peace is wrecked on Beauty's shore.
Near Hope's fair isle it rode awhile, and then no more!

I saw her once, one little while, and then no more:
Earth looked like Heaven a little while, and then no more.
Her presence thrilled and lighted to its inner core
My desert breast a little while, and then no more.
So may, perchance, a meteor glance at midnight o'er
Some ruined pile a little while, and then no more!

I saw her once, one little while, and then no more:
The earth was Peri-land awhile, and then no more.
Oh, might I see but once again, as once before,
Through chance or wile, that shape awhile, and then no more!
Death soon would heal my griefs! This heart, now sad and
    sore,
Would beat anew a little while, and then no more.

The Lover's Farewell

Slowly through the tomb-still streets I go –
    Morn is dark, save one swart streak of gold –
Sullen rolls the far-off river's flow,
    And the moon is very thin and cold.

Long and long before the house I stand
    Where sleeps she, the dear, dear one I love –
All undreaming that I leave my land,
    Mute and mourning, like the moon above!

Wishfully I stretch abroad mine arms
    Towards the well-remembered casement-cell –
Fare thee well! Farewell thy virgin charms!
    And thou stilly, stilly house, farewell!

And farewell the dear dusk little room,
    Redolent of roses as a dell,
And the lattice that relieved its gloom –
    And its pictured lilac walls, farewell!

Forth upon my path! I must not wait –
    Bitter blows the fretful morning wind:
Warden, wilt thou softly close the gate
    When thou knowest I leave my heart behind?

A Vision of Connaught in the Thirteenth Century

        I walked entranced
           Through a land of Morn;
    The sun, with wondrous excess of light,
        Shone down and glanced
           Over seas of corn
    And lustrous gardens aleft and right
        Even in the clime
        Of resplendent Spain,
    Beams no such sun upon such a land;
        But it was the time,
        'Twas in the reign,
    Of Cáhal Mór of the Wine-red Hand.

        Anon stood nigh
           By my side a man
    Of princely aspect and port sublime.
        Him queried I –
        'O, my Lord and Khan,[1]
    What clime is this, and what golden time?'
        When he – 'The clime
        Is a clime to praise,
    The clime is Erin's, the green and bland;
        And it is the time,
        These be the days,
    Of Cáhal Mór of the Wine-red Hand!'

        Then saw I thrones,
           And circling fires,
    And a Dome rose near me, as by a spell,

Whence flowed the tones
　　Of silver lyres,
And many voices in wreathed swell;
　　And their thrilling chime
　　　Fell on mine ears
As the heavenly hymn of an angel-band –
　　'It is now the time,
　　　These be the years,
Of Cáhal Mór of the Wine-red Hand!'

　　I sought the hall,
　　　And, behold! – a change
From light to darkness, from joy to woe!
　　King, nobles, all,
　　　Looked aghast and strange;
The minstrel-group sate in dumbest show!
　　Had some great crime
　　　Wrought this dread amaze,
This terror? None seemed to understand
　　'Twas then the time
　　　We were in the days,
Of Cáhal Mór of the Wine-red Hand.

　　I again walked forth,
　　　But lo! the sky
Showed fleckt with blood, and an alien sun
　　Glared from the north,
　　　And there stood on high,
Amid his shorn beams, a skeleton!
　　It was by the stream
　　　Of the castled Maine,
One Autumn eve, in the Teuton's land,
　　That I dreamed this dream
　　　Of the time and reign
Of Cáhal Mór of the Wine-red Hand!

1. *Ceann*, the Gaelic title for a chief.

The Nameless One

Roll forth, my song, like the rushing river,
   That sweeps along to the mighty sea;
God will inspire me while I deliver
    My soul of thee!

Tell thou the world, when my bones lie whitening
   Amid the last homes of youth and eld,
That there was once one whose veins ran lightning
    No eye beheld.

Tell how his boyhood was one drear night-hour,
   How shone for *him*, through his griefs and gloom,
No star of all heaven sends to light our
    Path to the tomb.

Roll on, my song, and to after ages
   Tell how, disdaining all earth can give,
He would have taught men, from wisdom's pages,
    The way to live.

And tell how trampled, derided, hated,
   And worn by weakness, disease, and wrong,
He fled for shelter to God, who mated
    His soul with song –

With song which alway, sublime or vapid,
   Flowed like a rill in the morning beam,
Perchance not deep, but intense and rapid –
    A mountain stream.

Tell how this Nameless, condemned for years long
   To herd with demons from hell beneath,
Saw things that made him, with groans and tears, long
    For even death.

Go on to tell how, with genius wasted,
   Betrayed in friendship, befooled in love,
With spirit shipwrecked, and young hopes blasted,
    He still, still strove.

Till, spent with toil, dreeing death for others,
   And some whose hands should have wrought for *him*
(If children live not for sires and mothers),
    His mind grew dim.

And he fell far through that pit abysmal
   The gulf and grave of Maginn and Burns,
And pawned his soul for the devil's dismal
    Stock of returns.

But yet redeemed it in days of darkness
   And shapes and signs of the final wrath,
When death, in hideous and ghastly starkness,
    Stood on his path.

And tell how now, amid wreck and sorrow,
   And want, and sickness, and houseless nights,
He bides in calmness the silent morrow,
    That no ray lights.

And lives he still, then? Yes! Old and hoary
   At thirty-nine, from despair and woe,
He lives enduring what future story
    Will never know.

Him grant a grave to, ye pitying noble,
   Deep in your bosoms! There let him dwell!
He, too, had tears for all souls in trouble,
    Here and in hell.

Siberia

In Siberia's wastes
   The Ice-wind's breath
Woundeth like the toothed steel;
Lost Siberia doth reveal
   Only blight and death.

Blight and death alone.
   No Summer shines.
Night is interblent with Day.
In Siberia's wastes alway
   The blood blackens, the heart pines.

In Siberia's wastes
   No tears are shed,
For they freeze within the brain.
Nought is felt but dullest pain,
   Pain acute, yet dead;

Pain as in a dream,
   When years go by
Funeral-paced, yet fugitive,
When man lives, and doth not live,
   Doth not live – nor die.

In Siberia's wastes
   Are sands and rocks
Nothing blooms of green or soft,
But the snow-peaks rise aloft
   And the gaunt ice-blocks.

And the exile there
   Is one with those;
They are part, and he is part,
For the sands are in his heart,
   And the killing snows.

Therefore, in those wastes
   None curse the Czar.
Each man's tongue is cloven by
The North Blast, that heweth nigh
   With sharp scimitar.

And such doom each drees,
   Till, hunger-gnawn,
And cold-slain, he at length sinks there,
Yet scarce more a corpse than ere
   His last breath was drawn.

Lament for the Princes of Tir-Owen and Tirconnell

O Woman of the Piercing Wail,
   Who mournest o'er yon mound of clay
      With sigh and groan
Would God thou wert among the Gael!
   Thou wouldst not then from day to day
      Weep thus alone.
'Twere long before, around a grave
   In green Tirconnell, one could find
      This loneliness;
Near where Beann-Boirche's banners wave,
   Such grief as thine could ne'er have pined
      Companionless.

Beside the wave, in Donegal,
   In Antrim's glen, or fair Dromore,
      Or Killillee,
Or where the sunny waters fall
   At Assaroe, near Erna's shore,
      This could not be.
On Derry's plains – in rich Drumcliff –
   Throughout Armagh the Great, renowned
      In olden years,

No day could pass but woman's grief
  Would rain upon the burial-ground
    Fresh floods of tears!

Oh no! – from Shannon, Boyne, and Suir,
  From high Dunluce's castle-walls,
    From Lissadill,
Would flock alike both rich and poor.
  One wail would rise from Cruachan's halls
    To Tara's hill;
And some would come from Barrow-side,
  And many a maid would leave her home
    On Leitrim's plains,
And by melodious Banna's tide,
  And by the Mourne and Erne, to come
    And swell thy strains!

Oh! horse's hoofs would trample down
  The mount whereon the martyr-saint
    Was crucified.
From glen and hill, from plain and town,
  One loud lament, one thrilling plaint,
    Would echo wide.
There would not soon be found, I ween,
  One foot of ground among those bands
    For museful thought,
So many shriekers of the *keen*
  Would cry aloud, and clap their hands,
    All woe-distraught!

Two princes of the line of Conn
  Sleep in their cells of clay beside
    O'Donnell Roe.
Three royal youths, alas! are gone,
  Who lived for Erin's weal, but died
    For Erin's woe!
Ah! could the men of Ireland read
  The names these noteless burial stones
    Display to view,

Their wounded hearts afresh would bleed,
  Their tears gush forth again, their groans
    Resound anew!

The youths whose relics moulder here
  Were sprung from Hugh, high Prince and Lord
    Of Aileach's lands;
Thy noble brothers, justly dear,
  Thy nephew, long to be deplored
    By Ulster's bands.
Theirs were not souls wherein dull Time
  Could domicile Decay or house
    Decrepitude!
They passed from Earth ere Manhood's prime,
  Ere years had power to dim their brows
    Or chill their blood.

And who can marvel o'er thy grief,
  Or who can blame thy flowing tears,
    That knows their source?
O'Donnell, Dunnasana's chief,
  Cut off amid his vernal years,
    Lies here a corse
Beside his brother Cathbar, whom
  Tirconnell of the Helmets mourns
    In deep despair –
For valour, truth, and comely bloom,
  For all that greatens and adorns,
    A peerless pair.

Oh! had these twain, and he, the third,
  The Lord of Mourne, O'Niall's son,
    Their mate in death –
A prince in look, in deed and word –
  Had these three heroes yielded on
    The field their breath;
Oh! had they fallen on Criffan's plain,
  There would not be a town or clan
    From shore to sea

But would with shrieks bewail the slain,
  Or chant aloud the exulting *rann*
    Of jubilee.

When high the shout of battle rose
  On fields where Freedom's torch still burned
    Through Erin's gloom,
If one, if barely one of those
  Were slain, all Ulster would have mourned
    The hero's doom!
If at Athboy, where hosts of brave
  Ulidian horsemen sank beneath
    The shock of spears,
Young Hugh O'Neill had found a grave,
  Long must the north have wept his death
    With heart-wrung tears!

If on the day of Ballachmyre,
  The Lord of Mourne had met, thus young,
    A warrior's fate,
In vain would such as those desire
  To mourn, alone, the champion sprung
    From Niall the Great!
No marvel this – for all the dead,
  Heaped on the field, pile over pile,
    At Mullach-brack,
Were scarce an *eric* for his head,
  If Death had stayed his footsteps while
    On victory's track!

If on the Day of Hostages
  The fruit had from the parent bough
    Been rudely torn
In sight of Munster's bands – Mac-Nee's
  Such blow the blood of Conn, I trow,
    Could ill have borne.
If on the day of Balloch-boy,
  Some arm had laid, by foul surprise,
    The chieftain low,

Even our victorious shout of joy
    Would soon give place to rueful cries
      And groans of woe!

If on the day the Saxon host
    Were forced to fly – a day so great
      For Ashanee –
The Chief had been untimely lost,
    Our conquering troops should moderate
      Their mirthful glee.
There would not lack on Lifford's day,
    From Galway, from the glens of Boyle,
      From Limerick's towers,
A marshalled file, a long array,
    Of mourners to bedew the soil
      With tears in showers!

If on the day a sterner fate
    Compelled his flight from Athenree,
      His blood had flowed,
What numbers all disconsolate
    Would come unasked, and share with thee
      Affliction's load!
If Derry's crimson field had seen
    His life-blood offered up, though 'twere
      On Victory's shrine,
A thousand cries would swell the *keen*,
    A thousand voices of despair
      Would echo thine!

Oh! had the fierce Dalcassian swarm,
    That bloody night on Fergus' banks,
      But slain our Chief;
When rose his camp in wild alarm,
    How would the triumph of his ranks
      Be dashed with grief!
How would the troops of Murbach mourn,
    If on the Curlew Mountains' day –
      Which England rued –

Some Saxon hand had left them lorn:
　　By shedding there, amid the fray,
　　　Their prince's blood!

Red would have been our warriors' eyes,
　　Had Roderick found on Sligo's field
　　　A gory grave.
No Northern Chief would soon arise,
　　So sage to guide, so strong to shield,
　　　So swift to save.
Long would Leith-Cuinn have wept if Hugh
　　Had met the death he oft had dealt
　　　Among the foe;
But, had our Roderick fallen too,
　　All Erin must, alas! have felt
　　　The deadly blow.

What do I say? Ah, woe is me –
　　Already we bewail in vain
　　　Their fatal fall!
And Erin, once the Great and Free,
　　Now vainly mourns her breakless chain,
　　　And iron thrall!
Then daughter of O'Donnell, dry
　　Thine overflowing eyes, and turn
　　　Thy heart aside;
For Adam's race is born to die,
　　And sternly the sepulchral urn
　　　Mocks human pride.

Look not, nor sigh, for earthly throne,
　　Nor place thy trust in arm of clay:
　　　But on thy knees
Uplift thy soul to God alone,
　　For all things go their destined way,
　　　As He decrees.

(from the Irish)

Shapes and Signs

I see black dragons mount the sky,
  I see earth yawn beneath my feet –
  I feel within the asp, the worm
That will not sleep and cannot die,
  Fair though may show the winding-sheet!
  I hear all night as through a storm
  Hoarse voices calling, calling
    My name upon the wind –
  All omens monstrous and appalling
    Affright my guilty mind.

I exult alone in one wild hour –
  That hour in which the red cup drowns
  The memories it anon renews
In ghastlier guise, in fiercer power –
  Then Fancy brings me golden crowns,
  And visions of all brilliant hues
  Lap my lost soul in gladness,
    Until I wake again,
  And the dark lava-fires of madness
    Once more sweep through my brain.

Kinkora

O, where, Kinkora! is Brian the Great?
  And where is the beauty that once was thine?
O, where are the princes and nobles that sate
  At the feast in thy halls, and drank the red wine!
                    Where, O Kinkora?

O, where, Kinkora! are thy valorous lords?
  O, whither, thou Hospitable! are they gone

O, where are the Dalcassians of the golden swords![1]
   And where are the warriors Brian led on?
                       Where, O Kinkora?

And where is Morrogh, the descendant of kings;
   The defeater of a hundred – the daringly brave –
Who set but slight store by jewels and rings –
   Who swam down the torrent and laughed at its wave?
                       Where, O Kinkora?

And where is Donogh, King Brian's worthy son?
   And where is Conaing, the beautiful chief?
And Kian and Corc? Alas! they are gone –
   They have left me this night alone with my grief
                       Left me, Kinkora!

And where are the chiefs with whom Brian went forth,
   The never-vanquished sons of Erin the brave,
The great King of Onaght, renowned for his worth,
   And the hosts of Baskinn from the western wave?
                       Where, O Kinkora?

O, where is Duvlann of the Swift-footed Steeds?
   And where is Kian, who was son of Molloy?
And where is King Lonergan, the fame of whose deeds
   In the red battle-field no time can destroy?
                       Where, O Kinkora?

And where is that youth of majestic height,
   The faith-keeping Prince of the Scots? Even he,
As wide as his fame was, as great as was his might,
   Was tributary, O Kinkora, to thee!
                       Thee, O Kinkora!

They are gone, those heroes of royal birth,
   Who plundered no churches, and broke no trust;
'Tis weary for me to be living on earth
   When they, O Kinkora, lie low in the dust!
                       Low, O Kinkora!

O, never again will Princes appear,
   To rival the Dalcassians[2] of the Cleaving Swords;
I can never dream of meeting afar or anear,
   In the east or the west, such heroes and lords!
                          Never, Kinkora!

O, dear are the images my memory calls up
   Of Brian Boru! – how he never would miss
To give me at the banquet, the first bright cup!
   Ah! why did he heap on me honour like this?
                          Why, O Kinkora?

I am Mac-Liag, and my home is on the Lake:
   Thither often, to that palace whose beauty is fled,
Came Brian, to ask me, and I went for his sake,
   O, my grief! that I should live, and Brian be dead!
                          Dead, O Kinkora!

    1. *Colg n-or*, or the swords *of Gold*, *i.e.* of the *Gold-hilted* Swords
      2. The Dalcassians were Brian's body-guard

To Joseph Brenan

Friend and brother, and yet more than brother,
   Thou endowed with all of Shelley's soul!
Thou whose heart so burneth for thy mother,
That, like *his*, it may defy all other
    Flames, while time shall roll!

Thou of language bland, and manner meekest,
   Gentle bearing, yet unswerving will –
Gladly, gladly, list I when thou speakest,
Honoured highly is the man thou seekest
    To redeem from ill!

Truly showest thou me the one thing needful!
   Thou art not, nor is the world yet blind.

Truly have I been long years unheedful
Of the thorns and tares, that choked the weedful
  Garden of my mind!

Thorns and tares, which rose in rank profusion
  Round my scanty fruitage and my flowers,
Till I almost deemed it self-delusion,
Any attempt or glance at their extrusion
  From their midnight bowers.

Dream and waking life have now been blended
  Longtime in the caverns of my soul –
Oft in daylight have my steps descended
Down to that dusk realm where all is ended,
  Save remeadless dole!

Oft, with tears, I have groaned to God for pity –
  Oft gone wandering till my way grew dim –
Oft sung unto Him a prayerful ditty –
Oft, all lonely in this throngful city
  Raised my soul to Him!

And from path to path His mercy tracked me –
  From many a peril snatched He me,
When false friends pursued, betrayed, attacked me,
When gloom overdarked, and sickness racked me
  He was by to save and free!

Friend! thou warnest me in truly noble
  Thoughts and phrases! I will heed thee well –
Well will I obey thy mystic double
Counsel, through all scenes of woe and trouble,
  As a magic spell!

Yes! to live a bard, in thought and feeling!
  Yes! to act my rhyme, by self-restraint,
This is truth's, is reason's deep revealing,
Unto me from thee, as God's to a kneeling
  And entranced saint!

Fare thee well! we now know each the other,
  Each has struck the other's inmost chords –
Fare thee well, my friend and more than brother
And may scorn pursue me if I smother
  In my soul thy words!

The One Mystery

'Tis idle! we exhaust and squander
  The glittering mine of thought in vain;
All-baffled reason cannot wander
  Beyond her chain.
The flood of life runs dark – dark clouds
  Make lampless night around its shore:
The dead, where are they? In their shrouds –
  Man knows no more.

Evoke the ancient and the past,
  Will one illumining star arise?
Or must the film, from first to last,
  O'erspread thine eyes?
When life, love, glory, beauty, wither,
  Will wisdom's page, or science' chart,
Map out for thee the region whither
  Their shades depart?

Supposest thou the wondrous powers,
  To high imagination given,
Pale types of what shall yet be ours,
  When earth is heaven?
When this decaying shell is cold,
  Oh! sayest thou the soul shall climb
That magic mount she trod of old,
  Ere childhood's time?

And shall the sacred pulse that thrilled,
　　Thrill once again to glory's name?
And shall the conquering love that filled
　　All earth with flame,
Reborn, revived, renewed, immortal,
　　Resume his reign in prouder might,
A sun beyond the ebon portal
　　Of death and night?

No more, no more – with aching brow
　　And restless heart, and burning brain,
We ask the When, the Where, the How,
　　And ask in vain.
And all philosophy, all faith,
　　All earthly – all celestial lore,
Have but one voice, which only saith –
　　Endure – adore!

To *the Ingleezee Khafir, calling himself Djaun Bool Djenkinzun*

Thus writeth Meer Djafrit –
　　I hate thee, Djaun Bool,
Worse than Márid or Afrit,
　　Or corpse-eating Ghool.
I hate thee like Sin,
　　For thy mop-head of hair,
Thy snub nose and bald chin,
　　And thy turkeycock air.
Thou vile Ferindjee!
　　That thou thus shouldst disturb an
Old Moslim like me,
　　With my Khizzilbash turban,
Old fogy like me,
　　With my Khizzilbash turban.

I spit on thy clothing,
  That garb for baboons
I eye with deep loathing
  Thy tight pantaloons!
I curse the cravat
  That encircles thy throat,
And thy cooking-pot hat,
  And thy swallow-tailed coat!
Go, hide thy thick sconce
  In some hovel suburban;
Or else don at once
  The red Moosleman turban.
Thou dog, don at once
  The grand Khizzilbash turban!

(from the Persian)

The Time of the Barmecides

My eyes are filmed, my beard is grey,
  I am bowed with the weight of years;
I would I were stretched in my bed of clay,
  With my long-lost youth's compeers.
For back to the Past, though the thought brings woe,
  My memory ever glides –
To the old, old time, long, long ago,
  The time of the Barmecides.

Then Youth was mine, and a fierce wild will,
  And an iron arm in war,
And a fleet foot high up on Ishkar's hill,
  When the watch-lights glimmered afar,
And a barb as fiery as any I know,
  That Khoord or Beddaween rides,
Ere my friends lay low – long, long ago,
  In the time of the Barmecides,
Ere my friends lay low – long, long ago,
  In the time of the Barmecides.

One golden goblet illumed my board,
    One silver dish was there;
At hand my tried Karamanian sword,
    Lay always bright and bare;
For those were the days when the angry blow
    Supplanted the word that chides –
When hearts could glow – long, long ago,
    In the time of the Barmecides:
When hearts could glow – long, long ago,
    In the time of the Barmecides.

Through city and desert my mates and I
    Were free to rove and roam,
Our diapered canopy the deep of the sky,
    Or the roof of the palace dome –
O! ours was that vivid life to and fro
    Which only sloth derides –
Men spent Life so, long, long ago,
    In the time of the Barmecides,
Men spent Life so, long, long ago,
    In the time of the Barmecides.

I see rich Bagdad once again,
    With its turrets of Moorish mould,
And the Khalif's twice five hundred men,
    Whose binishes flamed with gold;
I call up many a gorgeous show
    Which the Pall of Oblivion hides –
All passed like snow, long, long ago,
    With the time of the Barmecides;
All passed like snow, long, long ago,
    With the time of the Barmecides!

But mine eye is dim, and my beard is grey,
    And I bend with the weight of years –
May I soon go down to the House of Clay
    Where slumber my Youth's compeers!

For with them and the Past, though the thought wakes woe,
   My memory ever abides;
And I mourn for the Times gone long ago,
   For the Times of the Barmecides!
I mourn for the Times gone long ago,
   For the Times of the Barmecides!

Twenty Golden Years Ago

O, the rain, the weary, dreary rain,
   How it plashes on the window-sill!
Night, I guess, too, must be on the wane,
   Strass and Gass around are grown so still.
Here I sit, with coffee in my cup –
   Ah! 'twas rarely I beheld it flow
In the tavern where I loved to sup
   Twenty golden years ago!

Twenty years ago, alas! – but stay –
   On my life, 'tis half-past twelve o'clock!
After all, the hours *do* slip away –
   Come, here goes to burn another block!
For the night, or morn, is wet and cold;
   And my fire is dwindling rather low –
I had fire enough, when young and bold
   Twenty golden years ago.

Dear! I don't feel well at all, somehow:
   Few in Weimar dream how bad I am;
Floods of tears grow common with me now,
   High-Dutch floods, that Reason cannot dam.
Doctors think I'll neither live nor thrive
   If I mope at home so – I don't know –
Am I living *now*? I *was* alive
   Twenty golden years ago.

Wifeless, friendless, flagonless, alone,
  Not quite bookless, though, unless I chuse,
Left with nought to do, except to groan,
  Not a soul to woo – except the muse –
O! this is hard for *me* to bear,
  Me, who whilome lived so much *en haut*,
Me, who broke all hearts like china-ware,
  Twenty golden years ago!

Perhaps 'tis better; – time's defacing waves
  Long have quenched the radiance of my brow –
They who curse me nightly from their graves,
  Scarce could love me were they living now;
But my loneliness hath darker ills –
  Such dun duns as Conscience, Thought and Co.,
Awful Gorgons! worse than tailors' bills
  Twenty golden years ago!

Did I paint a fifth of what I feel,
  O, how plaintive you would ween I was!
But I won't, albeit I have a deal
  More to wail about than Kerner has!
Kerner's tears are wept for withered flowers,
  Mine for withered hopes, my scroll of woe
Dates, alas! from youth's deserted bowers,
  Twenty golden years ago!

Yet, may Deutschland's bardlings flourish long.
  Me, I tweak no beak among them: – hawks
Must not pounce on hawks: besides, in song
  I could once beat all of them by chalks.
Though you find me as I near my goal,
  Sentimentalizing like Rousseau,
O! I had a grand Byronian soul
  Twenty golden years ago!

Tick-tick, tick-tick – not a sound save Time's,
  And the windgust as it drives the rain –

Tortured torturer of reluctant rhymes,
    Go to bed, and rest thine aching brain!
Sleep! no more the dupe of hopes or schemes;
    Soon thou sleepest where the thistles blow –
Curious anticlimax to thy dreams
    Twenty golden years ago!

ANONYMOUS

The Night Before Larry Was Stretched

The night before Larry was stretched,
   The boys they all paid him a visit;
A bait in their sacks, too, they fetched;
   They sweated their duds till they riz it:
For Larry was ever the lad,
   When a boy was condemned to the squeezer,
Would fence all the duds that he had
   To help a poor friend to a sneezer,
     And warm his gob 'fore he died.

The boys they came crowding in fast,
   They drew all their stools round about him,
Six glims round his trap-case were placed,
   He couldn't be well waked without 'em.
When one of us asked could he die
   Without having duly repented,
Says Larry, 'That's all in my eye;
   And first by the clargy invented,
     To get a fat bit for themselves.'

'I'm sorry, dear Larry,' says I,
   'To see you in this situation;
And, blister my limbs if I lie,
   I'd as lieve it had been my own station.'
'Ochone! it's all over,' says he,
   'For the neckcloth I'll be forced to put on
And by this time to-morrow you'll see
   Your poor Larry as dead as a mutton,
     Because, why, his courage was good.

'And I'll be cut up like a pie,
   And my nob from my body be parted.'
'You're in the wrong box, then,' says I,
   'For blast me if they're so hard-hearted:

A chalk on the back of your neck
   Is all that Jack Ketch dares to give you;
Then mind not such trifles a feck,
    For why should the likes of them grieve you?
     And now, boys, come tip us the deck.'

The cards being called for, they played,
   Till Larry found one of them cheated;
A dart at his napper he made
    (The boy being easily heated):
'Oh, by the hokey, you thief,
   I'll scuttle your nob with my daddle!
You cheat me because I'm in grief,
    But soon I'll demolish your noddle,
     And leave you your claret to drink.'

Then the clergy came in with his book,
   He spoke him so smooth and so civil;
Larry tipped him a Kilmainham look,
   And pitched his big wig to the devil:
Then sighing, he threw back his head
   To get a sweet drop of the bottle,
And pitiful sighing, he said:
    'Oh, the hemp will be soon round my throttle
     And choke my poor windpipe to death.

'Though sure it's the best way to die,
   Oh, the devil a better- a-livin'!
For, sure, when the gallows is high
   Your journey is shorter to Heaven:
But what harasses Larry the most,
   And makes his poor soul melancholy,
Is to think of the time when his ghost
    Will come in a sheet to sweet Molly –
     Oh, sure it will kill her alive!'

So moving these last words he spoke,
   We all vented our tears in a shower;

For my part, I thought my heart broke,
  To see him cut down like a flower.
On his travels we watched him next day;
  Oh, the throttler! I thought I could kill him;
But Larry not one word did say,
  Nor changed till he come to 'King William' –
    Then, *musha!* his colour grew white.

When he came to the nubbling chit,
  He was tucked up so neat and so pretty,
The rumbler jogged off from his feet,
  And he died with his face to the city;
He kicked, too – but that was all pride,
  For soon you might see 'twas all over;
Soon after the noose was untied,
  And at darky we waked him in clover,
    And sent him to take a ground sweat.

GERALD GRIFFIN

1803-40

Aileen Aroon

When, like the early rose,
       Aileen aroon!
Beauty in childhood blows,
       Aileen aroon!
When, like a diadem,
Buds blush around the stem,
Which is the fairest gem?
       Aileen aroon!

Is it the laughing eye?
       Aileen aroon!
Is it the timid sigh?
       Aileen aroon!
Is it the tender tone,
Soft as the stringed harp's moan?
Oh, it is truth alone,
       Aileen aroon!

When, like the rising day,
       Aileen aroon!
Love sends his early ray,
       Aileen aroon!
What makes his dawning glow
Changeless through joy or woe?
Only the constant know,
       Aileen aroon!

I know a valley fair,
       Aileen aroon!
I knew a cottage there,
       Aileen aroon!

Far in that valley's shade
I knew a gentle maid,
Flower of the hazel glade,
   Aileen aroon!

Who in the song so sweet,
   Aileen aroon!
Who in the dance so sweet,
   Aileen aroon!
Dear were her charms to me,
Dearer her laughter free,
Dearest her constancy,
   Aileen aroon!

Were she no longer true,
   Aileen aroon!
What should her lover do?
   Aileen aroon!
Fly with his broken chain
Far o'er the sounding main,
Never to love again,
   Aileen aroon!

Youth must with time decay,
   Aileen aroon!
Beauty must fade away,
   Aileen aroon!
Castles are sacked in war,
Chieftains are scattered far,
Truth is a fixed star,
   Aileen aroon!

(from the Irish, 14th century)

FRANCIS SYLVESTER MAHONY
(FATHER PROUT)
1804–66

The Bells of Shandon

With deep affection and recollection
   I often think of the Shandon bells,
Whose sounds so wild would, in days of childhood,
   Fling round my cradle their magic spells.
On this I ponder, where'er I wander,
    And thus grow fonder, sweet Cork, of thee;
        With thy bells of Shandon,
        That sound so grand on
The pleasant waters of the river Lee.

I have heard bells chiming full many a clime in,
   Tolling sublime in cathedral shrine;
While at a glib rate brass tongues would vibrate,
   But all their music spoke nought to thine;
For memory dwelling on each proud swelling
    Of thy belfry knelling its bold notes free,
        Made the bells of Shandon
        Sound far more grand on
The pleasant waters of the river Lee.

I have heard bells tolling 'old Adrian's mole' in,
   Their thunder rolling from the Vatican,
With cymbals glorious, swinging uproarious
   In the gorgeous turrets of Notre Dame;
But thy sounds were sweeter than the dome of Peter
    Flings o'er the Tiber, pealing solemnly.
        Oh! the bells of Shandon
        Sound far more grand on
The pleasant waters of the river Lee.

There's a bell in Moscow, while on tower and Kiosko
  In St Sophia the Turkman gets,
And loud in air calls men to prayer
  From the tapering summit of tall minarets.
Such empty phantom I freely grant 'em,
   But there's an anthem more dear to me:
     'Tis the bells of Shandon,
     That sound so grand on
The pleasant waters of the river Lee.

EDWARD WALSH

1805–51

The Dawning of the Day

At early dawn I once had been
　Where Lene's blue waters flow,
When summer bid the groves be green,
　The lamp of light to glow.
As on by bower, and town, and tower,
　And widespread fields I stray,
I meet a maid in the greenwood shade
　At the dawning of the day.

Her feet and beauteous head were bare,
　No mantle fair she wore;
But down her waist fell golden hair,
　That swept the tall grass o'er.
With milking-pail she sought the vale,
　And bright her charms' display;
Outshining far the morning star
　At the dawning of the day.

Beside me sat that maid divine
　Where grassy banks outspread.
'Oh, let me call thee ever mine,
　Dear maid,' I sportive said.
'False man, for shame, why bring me blame?'
　She cried, and burst away –
The sun's first light pursued her flight
　At the dawning of the day.

GEORGE FOX

The County of Mayo

On the deck of Patrick Lynch's boat I sat in woeful plight,
Through my sighing all the weary day and weeping all the
    night.
Were it not that full of sorrow from my people forth I go,
By the blessed sun, 'tis royally I'd sing thy praise, Mayo.

When I dwelt at home in plenty, and my gold did much
    abound,
In the company of fair young maids the Spanish ale went
    round.
Tis a bitter change from those gay days that now I'm forced
    to go,
And must leave my bones in Santa Cruz, far from my own
    Mayo.

They are altered girls in Irrul now; 'tis proud they're grown
    and high,
With their hair-bags and their top-knots – for I pass their
    buckles by.
But it's little now I heed their airs, for God will have it so,
That I must depart for foreign lands, and leave my sweet
    Mayo.

'Tis my grief that Patrick Loughlin is not Earl in Irrul still,
And that Brian Duff no longer rules as Lord upon the Hill;
And that Colonel Hugh McGrady should be lying dead and
    low,
And I sailing, sailing swiftly from the county of Mayo.

SAMUEL FERGUSON

1810–86

The Burial of King Cormac

'Crom Cruach and his sub-gods twelve,'
　　Said Cormac, 'are but carven treene;
The axe that made them, haft or helve,
　　Had worthier of our worship been.

'But He who made the tree to grow,
　　And hid in earth the iron-stone,
And made the man with mind to know
　　The axe's use, is God alone.'

Anon to priests of Crom was brought –
　　Where, girded in their service dread,
They minister'd on red Moy Slaught –
　　Word of the words King Cormac said.

They loosed their curse against the king;
　　They cursed him in his flesh and bones;
And daily in their mystic ring
　　They turn'd the maledictive stones,

Till, where at meat the monarch sate,
　　Amid the revel and the wine,
He choked upon the food he ate,
　　At Sletty, southward of the Boyne.

High vaunted then the priestly throng,
　　And far and wide they noised abroad
With trump and loud liturgic song
　　The praise of their avenging God.

But ere the voice was wholly spent
　　That priest and prince should still obey,
To awed attendants o'er him bent
　　Great Cormac gather'd breath to say, –

'Spread not the beds of Brugh for me
   When restless death-bed's use is done:
But bury me at Rossnaree
   And face me to the rising sun.

'For all the kings who lie in Brugh
   Put trust in gods of wood and stone;
And 'twas at Ross that first I knew
   One, Unseen, who is God alone.

'His glory lightens from the east;
   His message soon shall reach our shore;
And idol-god, and cursing priest
   Shall plague us from Moy Slaught no more.'

Dead Cormac on his bier they laid: –
   'He reign'd a king for forty years,
And shame it were,' his captains said,
   'He lay not with his royal peers.

'His grandsire, Hundred-Battle, sleeps
   Serene in Brugh: and, all around,
Dead kings in stone sepulchral keeps
   Protect the sacred burial ground.

'What though a dying man should rave
   Of changes o'er the eastern sea?
In Brugh of Boyne shall be his grave,
   And not in noteless Rossnaree.'

Then northward forth they bore the bier,
   And down from Sletty side they drew,
With horsemen and with charioteer,
   To cross the fords of Boyne to Brugh.

There came a breath of finer air
   That touch'd the Boyne with ruffling wings,
It stirr'd him in his sedgy lair
   And in his mossy moorland springs.

And as the burial train came down
  With dirge and savage dolorous shows,
Across their pathway, broad and brown
  The deep, full-hearted river rose;

From bank to bank through all his fords,
  'Neath blackening squalls he swell'd and boil'd;
And thrice the wondering gentile lords
  Essay'd to cross, and thrice recoil'd.

Then forth stepp'd grey-hair'd warriors four:
  They said, 'Through angrier floods than these,
On link'd shields once our king we bore
  From Dread-Spear and the hosts of Deece.

'And long as loyal will holds good,
  And limbs respond with helpful thews,
Nor flood, nor fiend within the flood,
  Shall bar him of his burial dues.'

With slanted necks they stoop'd to lift;
  They heaved him up to neck and chin;
And, pair and pair, with footsteps swift,
  Lock'd arm and shoulder, bore him in.

'Twas brave to see them leave the shore;
  To mark the deep'ning surges rise,
And fall subdued in foam before
  The tension of their striding thighs.

'Twas brave, when now a spear-cast out,
  Breast-high the battling surges ran;
For weight was great, and limbs were stout,
  And loyal man put trust in man.

But ere they reach'd the middle deep,
  Nor steadying weight of clay they bore,
Nor strain of sinewy limbs could keep
  Their feet beneath the swerving four.

And now they slide, and now they swim,
   And now, amid the blackening squall,
Grey locks afloat, with clutching grim,
   They plunge around the floating pall.

While, as a youth with practised spear
   Through justling crowds bears off the ring,
Boyne from their shoulders caught the bier
   And proudly bore away the king.

At morning, on the grassy marge
   Of Rossnaree, the corpse was found,
And shepherds at their early charge
   Entomb'd it in the peaceful ground.

A tranquil spot: a hopeful sound
   Comes from the ever youthful stream,
And still on daisied mead and mound
   The dawn delays with tenderer beam.

Round Cormac Spring renews her buds:
   In march perpetual by his side,
Down come the earth-fresh April floods,
   And up the sea-fresh salmon glide;

And life and time rejoicing run
   From age to age their wonted way;
But still he waits the risen Sun,
   For still 'tis only dawning Day.

Cashel of Munster

I'd wed you without herds, without money, or rich array,
And I'd wed you on a dewy morning at day-dawn grey;
My bitter woe it is, love, that we are not far away
In Cashel town, though the bare deal board were our
   marriage-bed this day!

Oh, fair maid, remember the green hill side,
Remember how I hunted about the valleys wide;
Time now has worn me; my locks are turn'd to grey,
The year is scarce and I am poor, but send me not, love, away!

Oh, deem not my blood is of base strain, my girl,
Oh, deem not my birth was as the birth of the churl;
Marry me, and prove me, and say soon you will,
That noble blood is written on my right side still!

My purse holds no red gold, no coin of the silver white,
No herds are mine to drive through the long twilight!
But the pretty girl that would take me, all bare though I be
   and lone,
Oh, I'd take her with me kindly to the county Tyrone.

Oh, my girl, I can see 'tis in trouble you are,
And, oh, my girl, I see 'tis your people's reproach you bear:
'I am a girl in trouble for his sake with whom I fly,
And, oh, may no other maiden know such reproach as I!'

Cean Dubh Deelish[1]

Put your head, darling, darling, darling,
   Your darling black head my heart above;
Oh, mouth of honey, with the thyme for fragrance,
   Who, with heart in breast, could deny you love?
Oh, many and many a young girl for me is pining,
   Letting her locks of gold to the cold wind free,
For me, the foremost of our gay young fellows;
   But I'd leave a hundred, pure love, for thee!
Then put your head, darling, darling, darling,
   Your darling black head my heart above;
Oh, mouth of honey, with the thyme for fragrance,
   Who, with heart in breast, could deny you love?

(*Irish song*)

1. Pronounced *cawn dhu deelish*, i.e. dear, black head.

The Lapful of Nuts

Whene'er I see soft hazel eyes
    And nut-brown curls,
I think of those bright days I spent
    Among the Limerick girls;
When up through Cratla woods I went,
    Nutting with thee;
And we pluck'd the glossy clustering fruit
    From many a bending tree.

Beneath the hazel boughs we sat,
    Thou, love, and I,
And the gather'd nuts lay in thy lap,
    Beneath thy downcast eye:
But little we thought of the store we'd won,
    I, love, or thou;
For our hearts were full, and we dare not own
    The love that's spoken now.

Oh, there's wars for willing hearts in Spain,
    And high Germanie!
And I'll come back, ere long, again,
    With knightly fame and fee:
And I'll come back, if I ever come back,
    Faithful to thee,
That sat with thy white lap full of nuts
    Beneath the hazel tree.

(from the Irish)

The Fair Hills of Ireland

A plenteous place is Ireland for hospitable cheer,
     Uileacan dubh O!
Where the wholesome fruit is bursting from the yellow barley
    ear;
     Uileacan dubh O!
There is honey in the trees where her misty vales expand,
And her forest paths, in summer, are by falling waters fann'd,
There is dew at high noontide there, and springs i'the yellow
    sand,
  On the fair hills of holy Ireland.

Curl'd he is and ringletted, and plaited to the knee,
     Uileacan dubh O!
Each captain who comes sailing across the Irish sea;
     Uileacan dubh O!
And I will make my journey, if life and health but stand,
Unto that pleasant country, that fresh and fragrant strand,
And leave your boasted braveries, your wealth and high
    command,
  For the fair hills of holy Ireland.

Large and profitable are the stacks upon the ground,
     Uileacan dubh O!
The butter and the cream do wondrously abound,
     Uileacan dubh O!
The cresses on the water and the sorrels are at hand,
And the cuckoo's calling daily his note of mimic bland,
And the bold thrush sings so bravely his song i'the forests
    grand,
  On the fair hills of holy Ireland.

(Old Irish song)

The Fairy Thorn

'Get up, our Anna dear, from the weary spinning-wheel;
   For your father's on the hill, and your mother is asleep:
Come up above the crags, and we'll dance a highland reel
   Around the fairy thorn on the steep.'

At Anna Grace's door 'twas thus the maidens cried,
   Three merry maidens fair in kirtles of the green;
And Anna laid the rock and the weary wheel aside,
   The fairest of the four, I ween.

They're glancing through the glimmer of the quiet eve,
   Away in milky wavings of neck and ankle bare;
The heavy-sliding stream in its sleepy song they leave,
   And the crags in the ghostly air:

And linking hand and hand, and singing as they go,
   The maids along the hill-side have ta'en their fearless way,
Till they come to where the rowan trees in lonely beauty grow
   Beside the Fairy Hawthorn grey.

The Hawthorn stands between the ashes tall and slim,
   Like matron with her twin grand-daughters at her knee;
The rowan berries cluster o'er her low head grey and dim
   In ruddy kisses sweet to see.

The merry maidens four have ranged them in a row,
   Between each lovely couple a stately rowan stem,
And away in mazes wavy, like skimming birds they go,
   Oh, never caroll'd bird like them!

But solemn is the silence of the silvery haze
   That drinks away their voices in echoless repose,
And dreamily the evening has still'd the haunted braes,
   And dreamier the gloaming grows.

And sinking one by one, like lark-notes from the sky
   When the falcon's shadow saileth across the open shaw,
Are hush'd the maidens' voices, as cowering down they lie
   In the flutter of their sudden awe.

For, from the air above, and the grassy ground beneath,
   And from the mountain-ashes and the old whitethorn
      between,
A Power of faint enchantment doth through their beings
      breathe,
   And they sink down together on the green.

They sink together silent, and stealing side to side,
   They fling their lovely arms o'er their drooping necks so
      fair,
Then vainly strive again their naked arms to hide,
   For their shrinking necks again are bare.

Thus clasp'd and prostrate all, with their heads together
      bow'd,
   Soft o'er their bosoms' beating – the only human sound –
They hear the silky footsteps of the silent fairy crowd,
   Like a river in the air, gliding round.

No scream can any raise, nor prayer can any say,
   But wild, wild, the terror of the speechless three –
For they feel fair Anna Grace drawn silently away,
   By whom they dare not look to see.

They feel their tresses twine with her parting locks of gold,
   And the curls elastic falling, as her head withdraws;
They feel her sliding arms from their tranced arms unfold,
   But they may not look to see the cause:

For heavy on their senses the faint enchantment lies
   Through all that night of anguish and perilous amaze;
And neither fear nor wonder can ope their quivering eyes
   Or their limbs from the cold ground raise,

Till out of night the earth has roll'd her dewy side,
  With every haunted mountain and streamy vale below;
When, as the mist dissolves in the yellow morning tide,
  The maidens' trance dissolveth so.

Then fly the ghastly three as swiftly as they may,
  And tell their tale of sorrow to anxious friends in vain –
They pined away and died within the year and day,
  And ne'er was Anna Grace seen again.

(an Ulster ballad)

Deirdre's Lament for the Sons of Usnach

The lions of the hill are gone,
And I am left alone – alone –
Dig the grave both wide and deep,
For I am sick, and fain would sleep!

The falcons of the wood are flown,
And I am left alone – alone –
Dig the grave both deep and wide,
And let us slumber side by side.

The dragons of the rock are sleeping,
Sleep that wakes not for our weeping:
Dig the grave and make it ready;
Lay me on my true Love's body.

Lay their spears and bucklers bright
By the warriors' sides aright;
Many a day the Three before me
On their linkèd bucklers bore me.

Lay upon the low grave floor,
'Neath each head, the blue claymore;
Many a time the noble Three
Redden'd those blue blades for me.

Lay the collars, as is meet,
Of their greyhounds at their feet;
Many a time for me have they
Brought the tall red deer to bay.

Oh! to hear my true Love singing,
Sweet as sound of trumpets ringing:
Like the sway of ocean swelling
Roll'd his deep voice round our dwelling.

Oh! to hear the echoes pealing
Round our green and fairy sheeling,
When the Three, with soaring chorus,
Pass'd the silent skylark o'er us.

Echo now, sleep, morn and even –
Lark alone enchant the heaven! –
Ardan's lips are scant of breath, –
Neesa's tongue is cold in death.

Stag, exult on glen and mountain –
Salmon, leap from loch to fountain –
Heron, in the free air warm ye –
Usnach's Sons no more will harm ye!

Erin's stay no more you are,
Rulers of the ridge of war;
Never more 'twill be your fate
To keep the beam of battle straight.

Woe is me! by fraud and wrong –
Traitors false and tyrants strong –
Fell Clan Usnach, bought and sold,
For Barach's feast and Conor's gold!

Woe to Eman, roof and wall! –
Woe to Red Branch, hearth and hall! –
Tenfold woe and black dishonour
To the false and foul Clan Conor!

Dig the grave both wide and deep,
Sick I am, and fain would sleep!
Dig the grave and make it ready,
Lay me on my true Love's body.

(from the Irish)

The Lark in the Clear Air

Dear thoughts are in my mind
And my soul soars enchanted,
As I hear the sweet lark sing
In the clear air of the day.
For a tender beaming smile
To my hope has been granted,
And tomorrow she shall hear
All my fond heart would say.

I shall tell her all my love,
All my soul's adoration;
And I think she will hear me
And will not say me nay.
It is this that fills my soul
With its joyous elation,
As I hear the sweet lark sing
In the clear air of the day.

Lament for the Death of Thomas Davis

I walked through Ballinderry in the springtime,
    When the bud was on the tree,
And I said, in every fresh-ploughed field beholding
    The sowers striding free,
Scattering broadcast for the corn in golden plenty,
    On the quick, seed-clasping soil,
Even such this day among the fresh-stirred hearts of Erin
    Thomas Davis, is thy toil!

I sat by Ballyshannon in the summer,
    And saw the salmon leap,
And I said, as I beheld the gallant creatures
    Spring glittering from the deep,
Through the spray and through the prone heaps striving
      onward
    To the calm, clear streams above,
So seekest thou thy native founts of freedom, Thomas Davis,
    In thy brightness of strength and love!

I stood on Derrybawn in the autumn,
    I heard the eagle call,
With a clangorous cry of wrath and lamentation
    That filled the wide mountain hall,
O'er the bare, deserted place of his plundered eyrie,
    And I said, as he screamed and soared,
So callest thou, thou wrathful-soaring Thomas Davis,
    For a nation's rights restored.

Young husbandman of Erin's fruitful seed-time,
    In the fresh track of danger's plough!
Who will walk the heavy, toilsome, perilous furrow,
    Girt with freedom's seed-sheets now?
Who will banish with the wholesome crop of knowledge
    The flaunting weed and the bitter thorn,
Now that thou thyself art but a seed for hopeful planting
    Against the resurrection morn?

Young salmon of the flood-time of freedom
    That swells round Erin's shore,
Thou wilt leap against their loud, oppressive torrents
    Of bigotry and hate no more!
Drawn downward by their prone material instinct,
    Let them thunder on their rocks, and foam;
Thou hast leaped, aspiring soul, to founts beyond their raging,
    Where troubled waters never come.

But I grieve not, eagle of the empty eyrie,
    That thy wrathful cry is still,

And that the songs alone of peaceful mourners
    Are heard to-day on Erin's hill.
Better far if brothers' wars are destined for us –
    God avert that horrid day, I pray! –
That ere our hands be stained with slaughter fratricidal,
    Thy warm heart should be cold in clay.

But my trust is strong in God who made us brothers,
    That He will not suffer these right hands,
Which thou hast joined in holier rites than wedlock,
    To draw opposing brands.
O many a tuneful tongue that thou madest vocal,
    Would lie cold and silent then,
And songless long once more should often-widowed Erin
    Mourn the loss of her brave young men.

O brave young men, my love, my pride, my promise,
    'Tis on you my hopes are set,
In manliness, in kindliness, in justice,
    To make Erin a nation yet;
Self-respecting, self-relying, self-advancing,
    In union or in severance, free and strong,
And if God grant this, then, under God, to Thomas Davis
    Let the greater praise belong!

The Forging of the Anchor

Come, see the Dolphin's anchor forged – 'tis at a white heat
    now:
The bellows ceased, the flames decreased though on the forge's
    brow
The little flames still fitfully play through the sable mound,
And fitfully you still may see the grim smiths ranking round,
All clad in leathern panoply, their broad hands only bare:
Some rest upon their sledges here, some work the windlass
    there.

The windlass strains the tackle chains, the black mound
    heaves below,
And red and deep a hundred veins burst out at every throe:
It rises, roars, rends all outright – O, Vulcan, what a glow!
'Tis blinding white, 'tis blasting bright – the high sun shines
    not so!
The high sun sees not, on the earth, such fiery fearful show,
The roof-ribs swarth, the candent hearth, the ruddy lurid row
Of smiths that stand, an ardent band, like men before the foe,
As, quivering through his fleece of flame, the sailing monster,
    slow
Sinks on the anvil: – all about the faces fiery grow;
'Hurrah!' they shout, 'leap out – leap out;' bang, bang the
    sledges go:
Hurrah! the jetted lightnings are hissing high and low –
A hailing fount of fire is struck at every squashing blow;
The leathern mail rebounds the hail, the rattling cinders strow
The ground around; at every bound the sweltering fountains
    flow,
And thick and loud the swinking crowd at every stroke pant
    'ho!'
Leap out, leap out, my masters; leap out and lay on load!
Let's forge a goodly anchor – a bower thick and broad;
For a heart of oak is hanging on every blow, I bode;
I see the good ship riding all in a perilous road –
The low reef roaring on her lee – the roll of ocean pour'd
From stem to stern, sea after sea, the mainmast by the board,
The bulwarks down, the rudder gone, the boats stove at the
    chains!
But courage still, brave mariners – the bower yet remains,
And not an inch to flinch he deigns, save when ye pitch sky
    high;
Then moves his head, as though he said, 'Fear nothing – here
    am I.'
Swing in your strokes in order, let foot and hand keep time;
Your blows make music sweeter far than any steeple's chime:
But, while you sling your sledges, sing – and let the burthen
    be,

The anchor is the anvil-king, and royal craftsmen we!
Strike in, strike in – the sparks begin to dull their rustling red;
Our hammers ring with sharper din, our work will soon be
      sped.
Our anchor soon must change his bed of fiery rich array,
For a hammock at the roaring bows, or an oozy couch of
      clay;
Our anchor soon must change the lay of merry craftsmen
      here,
For the yeo-heave-o', and the heave-away, and the sighing
      seaman's cheer;
When, weighing slow, at eve they go – far, far from love and
      home;
And sobbing sweethearts, in a row, wail o'er the ocean foam.

In livid and obdurate gloom he darkens down at last:
A shapely one he is, and strong, as e'er from cat was cast:
O trusted and trustworthy guard, if thou hadst life like me,
What pleasures would thy toils reward beneath the deep
      green sea!
O deep-Sea-diver, who might then behold such sights as thou?
The hoary monster's palaces! methinks what joy 'twere now
To go plumb plunging down amid the assembly of the whales,
And feel the churn'd sea round me boil beneath their
      scourging tails!
Then deep in tangle-woods to fight the fierce sea unicorn,
And send him foil'd and bellowing back, for all his ivory horn;
To leave the subtle sworder-fish of bony blade forlorn;
And for the ghastly-grinning shark, to laugh his jaws to scorn:
To leap down on the kraken's back, where 'mid Norwegian
      isles
He lies, a lubber anchorage for sudden shallow'd miles;
Till snorting, like an under-sea volcano, off he rolls;
Meanwhile to swing, a-buffeting the far astonished shoals
Of his back-browsing ocean-calves; or, haply, in a cove,
Shell-strown, and consecrate of old to some Undiné's love,
To find the long-hair'd mermaidens; or, hard by icy lands,
To wrestle with the Sea-serpent, upon cerulean sands.

O broad-arm'd Fisher of the deep, whose sports can equal
    thine?
The Dolphin weighs a thousand tons, that tugs thy cable line;
And night by night, 'tis thy delight, thy glory day by day,
Through sable sea and breaker white the giant game to play –
But shamer of our little sports! forgive the name I gave –
A fisher's job is to destroy – thine office is to save.
O lodger in the sea-kings' halls, couldst thou but understand
Whose be the white bones by thy side, or whose that dripping
    band,
Slow swaying in the heaving waves, that round about thee
    bend,
With sounds like breakers in a dream blessing their ancient
    friend –
Oh, couldst thou know what heroes glide with larger steps
    round thee,
Thine iron side would swell with pride; thou'dst leap within
    the sea!
Give honour to their memories who left the pleasant strand,
To shed their blood so freely for the love of Fatherland –
Who left their chance of quiet age and grassy churchyard
    grave,
So freely, for a restless bed amid the tossing wave –
Oh, though our anchor may not be all I have fondly sung,
Honour him for their memory, whose bones he goes among!

SAMUEL FERGUSON

The Vengeance of the Welshmen of Tirawley

Several Welsh families, associates in the invasion of Strongbow, settled in the west of Ireland. Of these, the principal whose names have been preserved by the Irish antiquarians were the Walshes, Joyces, Heils (*a quibus* MacHale), Lawlesses, Tomlyns, Lynotts, and Barretts, which last drew their pedigree from Walynes, son of Guyndally, the Ard Maor, or High Steward of the Lordship of Camelot, and had their chief seats in the territory of the two Bacs, in the barony of Tirawley, and county of Mayo. Clochan-na-n'all, i.e. 'the Blind Men's Stepping-stones', are still pointed out on the Duvowen river, about four miles north of Crossmolina, in the townland of Garranard; and Tubber-na-Scorney, or 'Scragg's Well', in the opposite townland of Carns, in the same barony. The earldom was in the hands of de Burgo, who, living as an Irish chieftain named himself MacWilliam; the de Burgo name became Burke.

Scorna Boy, the Barretts' bailiff, lewd and lame,
To lift the Lynotts' taxes when he came,
Rudely drew a young maid to him;
Then the Lynotts rose and slew him,
And in Tubber-na-Scorney threw him –
  Small your blame,
  Sons of Lynott!
Sing the vengeance of the Welshmen of Tirawley.

Then the Barretts to the Lynotts proposed a choice,
Saying, 'Hear, ye murderous brood, men and boys,
For this deed today ye lose
Sight or manhood: say and choose
Which ye keep and which refuse;
  And rejoice
  That our mercy
Leaves you living for a warning to Tirawley.'

Then the little boys of the Lynotts, weeping, said,
'Only leave us our eyesight in our head.'
But the bearded Lynotts then
Made answer back again,
'Take our eyes, but leave us men,

Alive or dead,
Sons of Wattin!'
Sing the vengeance of the Welshmen of Tirawley.

So the Barretts, with sewing needles sharp and smooth,
Let the light out of the eyes of every youth,
And of every bearded man
Of the broken Lynott clan;
Then their darken'd faces wan
Turning south
To the river –
Sing the vengeance of the Welshmen of Tirawley!

O'er the slippery stepping-stones of Clochan-na-n'all
They drove them, laughing loud at every fall,
As their wandering footsteps dark
Fail'd to reach the slippery mark
And the swift stream swallow'd stark,
One and all,
As they stumbled –
From the vengeance of the Welshmen of Tirawley.

Of all the blinded Lynotts one alone
Walk'd erect from stepping-stone to stone:
So back again they brought you,
And the second time they wrought you
With their needles; but never got you
Once to groan,
Emon Lynott,
For the vengeance of the Welshmen of Tirawley.

But with prompt-projected footstep sure as ever,
Emon Lynott again cross'd the river,
Though Duvowen was rising fast,
And the shaking stones o'ercast
By cold floods boiling past;
Yet you never,
Emon Lynott,
Faltered once before your foemen of Tirawley!

But, turning on Ballintubber bank you stood,
And the Barretts thus bespoke o'er the flood –
'Oh, ye foolish sons of Wattin,
Small amends are these you've gotten,
For, while Scorna Boy lies rotten,
      I am good
      For vengeance!'
Sing the vengeance of the Welshmen of Tirawley.

'For 'tis neither in eye nor eyesight that a man
Bears the fortunes of himself and his clan,
But in the manly mind,
And loins with vengeance lined,
That your needles could never find
      Though they ran
      Through my heart-strings!'
Sing the vengeance of the Welshmen of Tirawley.

'But little your women's needles do I reck:
For the night from heaven never fell so black,
But Tirawley, and abroad
From the Moy to Cuan-an-fod,
I could walk it, every sod,
      Path and track,
      Ford and togher,
Seeking vengeance on you, Barretts of Tirawley!

'The night when Dathy O'Dowda broke your camp,
What Barrett among you was it held the lamp –
Show'd the way to those two feet,
When through wintry wind and sleet,
I guided your blind retreat
      In the swamp
      Of Beal-an-asa?
O ye vengeance-destined ingrates of Tirawley!'

So leaving loud-shriek-echoing Garranard,
The Lynott like a red dog hunted hard,

With his wife and children seven,
'Mong the beasts and fowls of heaven
In the hollows of Glen Nephin,
      Light-debarr'd,
      Made his dwelling,
Planning vengeance on the Barretts of Tirawley.

And e'er the bright-orb'd year its course had run,
On his brown round-knotted knee he nurs'd a son,
A child of light, with eyes
As clear as are the skies
In summer, when sunrise
      Has begun;
      So the Lynott
Nursed his vengeance on the Barretts of Tirawley.

And, as ever the bright boy grew in strength and size,
Made him perfect in each manly exercise,
The salmon in the flood,
The dun deer in the wood,
The eagle in the cloud
      To surprise
      On Ben Nephin,
Far above the foggy fields of Tirawley.

With the yellow-knotted spear-shaft, with the bow,
With the steel, prompt to deal shot and blow,
He taught him from year to year
And train'd him, without a peer,
For a perfect cavalier,
      Hoping so –
      Far his forethought –
For vengeance on the Barretts of Tirawley.

And, when mounted on his proud-bounding steed,
Emon Oge sat a cavalier indeed;
Like the ear upon the wheat
When winds in Autumn beat
On the bending stems, his seat;

And the speed
Of his courser
Was the wind from Barna-na-gee o'er Tirawley!

Now when fifteen sunny summers thus were spent,
(He perfected in all accomplishment) –
The Lynott said, 'My child,
We are over long exiled
From mankind in this wild –
– Time we went
Through the mountain
To the countries lying over-against Tirawley.'

So, out over mountain-moors, and mosses brown,
And green stream-gathering vales, they journey'd down;
Till, shining like a star,
Through the dusky gleams afar,
The bailey of Castlebar,
And the town
Of Mac William
Rose bright before the wanderers of Tirawley.

'Look southward, my boy, and tell me as we go,
What seest thou by the loch-head below.'
'Oh, a stone-house strong and great,
And a horse-host at the gate,
And their captain in armour of plate –
Grand the show!
Great the glancing!
High the heroes of this land below Tirawley!

'And a beautiful Woman-chief by his side,
Yellow gold on all her gown-sleeves wide;
And in her hand a pearl
Of a young, little, fair-hair'd girl.' –
Said the Lynott, 'It is the Earl!
Let us ride
To his presence!'
And before him came the exiles of Tirawley.

'God save thee, Mac William,' the Lynott thus began;
'God save all here besides of this clan;
For gossips dear to me
Are all in company –
For in these four bones you see
   A kindly man
   Of the Britons –
Emon Lynott of Garranard of Tirawley.

'And hither, as kindly gossip-law allows,
I come to claim a scion of thy house
To foster; for thy race
Since William Conquer's days,
Have ever been wont to place
   With some spouse
   Of a Briton,
A Mac William Oge, to foster in Tirawley.

'And to show thee in what sort our youth are taught,
I have hither to thy home of valour brought
This one son of my age,
For a sample and a pledge
For the equal tutelage,
   In right thought,
   Word, and action,
Of whatever son ye give into Tirawley.'

When Mac William beheld the brave boy ride and run,
Saw the spear-shaft from his white shoulder spun –
With a sigh, and with a smile,
He said, – 'I would give the spoil
Of a county, that Tibbot Moyle,
   My own son,
   Were accomplish'd
Like this branch of the kindly Britons of Tirawley.'

When the Lady Mac William she heard him speak,
And saw the ruddy roses on his cheek,

She said, 'I would give a purse
Of red gold to the nurse
That would rear my Tibbot no worse;
  But I seek
  Hitherto vainly –
Heaven grant that I now have found her in Tirawley!'

So they said to the Lynott, 'Here, take our bird!
And as pledge for the keeping of thy word
Let this scion here remain
Till thou comest back again:
Meanwhile the fitting train
  Of a lord
  Shall attend thee
With the lordly heir of Connaught into Tirawley.'

So back to strong-throng-gathering Garranard,
Like a lord of the country with his guard,
Came the Lynott, before them all,
Once again over Clochan-na-n'all,
Steady-striding, erect, and tall,
  And his ward
  On his shoulders;
To the wonder of the Welshmen of Tirawley.

Then a diligent foster-father you would deem
The Lynott, teaching Tibbot, by mead and stream,
To cast the spear, to ride,
To stem the rushing tide,
With what feats of body beside,
  Might beseem
  A Mac William,
Foster'd free among the Welshmen of Tirawley.

But the lesson of hell he taught him in heart and mind:
For to what desire soever he inclined,
Of anger, lust or pride,
He had it gratified,
Till he ranged the circle wide

Of a blind
Self-indulgence,
Ere he came to youthful manhood in Tirawley.

Then, even as when a hunter slips a hound,
Lynott loosed him – God's leashes all unbound –
In the pride of power and station,
And the strength of youthful passion,
On the daughters of thy nation,
All around,
Wattin Barrett!
Oh! the vengeance of the Welshmen of Tirawley!

Bitter grief and burning anger, rage and shame,
Fill'd the houses of the Barretts where'er he came;
Till the young men of the Bac
Drew by night upon his track,
And slew him at Cornassack –
Small your blame,
Sons of Wattin!
Sing the vengeance of the Welshmen of Tirawley.

Said the Lynott, 'The day of my vengeance is drawing
near,
The day for which, through many a long dark year,
I have toil'd through grief and sin –
Call ye now the Brehons in,
And let the plea begin
Over the bier
Of Mac William,
For an eric upon the Barretts of Tirawley.'

Then the Brehons to Mac William Burke decreed
An eric upon Clan Barrett for the deed;
And the Lynotts' share of the fine,
As foster-father, was nine
Ploughlands and nine score kine;

But no need
Had the Lynott,
Neither care, for land or cattle in Tirawley.

But rising, while all sat silent on the spot,
He said, 'The law says – doth it not? –
If the foster-sire elect
His portion to reject,
He may then the right exact
To applot
The short eric.'
''Tis the law,' replied the Brehons of Tirawley.

Said the Lynott, 'I once before had a choice
Proposed me, wherein law had little voice;
But now I choose, and say,
As lawfully I may,
I applot the mulct today;
So rejoice
In your ploughlands
And your cattle which I renounce throughout Tirawley.

'And thus I applot the mulct: I divide
The land throughout Clan Barrett on every side
Equally, that no place
May be without the face
Of a foe of Wattin's race –
That the pride
Of the Barretts
May be humbled hence for ever throughout Tirawley.

'I adjudge a seat in every Barrett's hall
To Mac William: in every stable I give a stall
To Mac William: and, beside,
Whenever a Burke shall ride
Through Tirawley, I provide
At his call
Needful grooming,
Without charge from any hosteler of Tirawley.

'Thus lawfully I avenge me for the throes
Ye lawlessly caused me and caused those
Unhappy shamefaced ones,
Who, their mothers expected once,
Would have been the sires of sons –
        O'er whose woes
        Often weeping
I have groan'd in my exile from Tirawley.

'I demand not of you your manhood; but I take –
For the Burkes will take it – your Freedom! for the sake
Of which all manhood's given,
And all good under heaven,
And, without which, better even
        Ye should make
        Yourselves barren,
Than see your children slaves throughout Tirawley!

'Neither take I your eyesight from you; as you took
Mine and ours: I would have you daily look
On one another's eyes,
When the strangers tyrannize
By your hearths, and blushes arise,
        That ye brook,
        Without vengeance,
The insults of troops of Tibbots throughout Tirawley!

'The vengeance I design'd, now is done,
And the days of me and mine nearly run –
For, for this, I have broken faith,
Teaching him who lies beneath
This pall, to merit death;
        And my son
        To his father
Stands pledged for other teaching in Tirawley.'

Said Mac William – 'Father and son, hang them high!'
And the Lynott they hang'd speedily;

But across the salt sea water,
To Scotland, with the daughter
Of Mac William – well you got her! –
      Did you fly,
      Edmund Lindsay,
The gentlest of all the Welshmen of Tirawley!

'Tis thus the ancient Ollaves of Erin tell
How, through lewdness and revenge, it befell
That the sons of William Conquer
Came over the sons of Wattin,
Throughout all the bounds and borders
Of the land of Auley MacFiachra;
Till the Saxon Oliver Cromwell,
With his valiant Bible-guided
Free heretics of Clan London
Coming in, in their succession,
Rooted out both Burke and Barrett,
And in their empty places
New stems of freedom planted,
With many a goodly sapling
Of manliness and virtue;
Which while their children cherish
Kindly Irish of the Irish,
Neither Saxon nor Italian,
May the mighty God of Freedom
      Speed them well
      Never taking
Further vengeance on his people of Tirawley.

AUBREY DE VERE

1814–1902

Song

The little Black Rose shall be red at last!
  What made it black but the East wind dry,
And the tear of the widow that fell on it fast?
  It shall redden the hills when June is nigh!

The Silk of the Kine shall rest at last!
  What drave her forth but the dragon-fly?
In the golden vale she shall feed full fast
  With her mild gold horn, and her slow dark eye.

The wounded wood-dove lies dead at last:
  The pine long-bleeding, it shall not die!
– This song is secret. Mine ear it pass'd
  In a wind o'er the stone plain of Athenry.

The Year of Sorrow

Ireland – 1849

SPRING

Once more, through God's high will and grace
  Of hours that each its task fulfils,
Heart-healing Spring resumes its place; –
  The valley throngs and scales the hills,

In vain. From earth's deep heart o'ercharged,
  The exulting life runs o'er in flowers; –
The slave unfed is unenlarged:
  In darkness sleep a Nation's powers.

Who knows not Spring? Who doubts, when blows
 Her breath, that Spring is come indeed?
The swallow doubts not; nor the rose
 That stirs, but wakes not; nor the weed.

I feel her near, but see her not;
 For these with pain uplifted eyes
Fall back repulsed; and vapours blot
 The vision of the earth and skies.

I see her not – I feel her near,
 As, charioted in mildest airs,
She sails through yon empyreal sphere,
 And in her arms and bosom bears

That urn of flowers and lustral dews,
 Whose sacred balm, o'er all things shed,
Revives the weak, the old renews,
 And crowns with votive wreaths the dead.

Once more the cuckoo's call I hear;
 I know in many a glen profound
The earliest violets of the year
 Rise up like water from the ground.

The thorn I know once more is white;
 And far down many a forest dale
The anemones in dubious light
 Are trembling like a bridal veil.

By streams released that singing flow
 From craggy shelf, through sylvan glades,
The pale narcissus, well I know,
 Smiles hour by hour on greener shades.

The honeyed cowslip tufts once more
 The golden slopes; with gradual ray
The primrose stars the rock, and o'er
 The wood-path strews its milky way.

From ruined huts and holes come forth
  Old men, and look on yonder sky!
The Power Divine is on the earth:
  Give thanks to God before ye die!

And ye, O children worn and weak,
  Who care no more with flowers to play,
Lean on the grass your cold, thin cheek,
  And those slight hands, and whispering, say,

'Stern mother of a race unblest,
  In promise kindly, cold in deed! –
Take back, O Earth, into thy breast,
  The children whom thou wilt not feed.'

WINTER

Fall, snow, and cease not! Flake by flake
  The decent winding-sheet compose;
Thy task is just and pious; make
  An end of blasphemies and woes.

Fall flake by flake! by thee alone,
  Last friend, the sleeping draught is given;
Kind nurse, by thee the couch is strown –
  The couch whose covering is from heaven.

Descend and clasp the mountain's crest;
  Inherit plain and valley deep:
This night, in thy maternal breast,
  A vanquished nation dies in sleep.

Lo! from the starry Temple gates
  Death rides, and bears the flag of peace;
The combatants he separates;
  He bids the wrath of ages cease.

Descend, benignant Power! But O,
  Ye torrents, shake no more the vale;

Dark streams, in silence seaward flow;
    Thou rising storm, remit thy wail.

Shake not, to-night, the cliffs of Moher,
    Nor Brandon's base, rough sea! Thou Isle,
The rite proceeds! From shore to shore,
    Hold in thy gathered breath the while.

Fall, snow! in stillness fall, like dew,
    On temple's roof and cedar's fan;
And mould thyself on pine and yew,
    And on the awful face of man.

Without a sound, without a stir,
    In streets and wolds, on rock and mound,
O omnipresent Comforter,
    By thee, this night, the lost are found!

On quaking moor, and mountain moss,
    With eyes upstaring at the sky,
And arms extended like a cross,
    The long-expectant sufferers lie.

Bend o'er them, white-robed Acolyte!
    Put forth thine hand from cloud and mist,
And minister the last sad rite,
    Where altar there is none, nor priest.

Touch thou the gates of soul and sense;
    Touch darkening eyes and dying ears;
Touch stiffening hands and feet, and thence
    Remove the trace of sin and tears:

And ere thou seal those filmed eyes,
    Into God's urn thy fingers dip,
And lay, 'mid eucharistic sighs,
    The sacred wafer on the lip.

The Combat at the Ford

From *The Foray of Queen Meave*

Queen Meave sends her herald to Ferdia the Firbolg, requiring him to engage with Cuchullain in single combat. Ferdia refuses to fight against his ancient friend; yet, later he attends a royal banquet given in his honour; and there, being drawn aside through the witcheries of the Princess Finobar, he consents to the fight. The charioteer of Ferdia sees Cuchullain advancing in his war-car to the Ford, and, rapt by a prophetic spirit, sings his triumph. For two days the ancient friends contend against each other with reluctance and remorse: but on the third day the battle-rage bursts fully forth: and on the fourth, Cuchullain, himself pierced through with wounds innumerable, slays Ferdia by the Gae-Bulg. He lays his friend upon the bank, at its northern side, and, standing beside him, sings his dirge.

> Well they knew,
Both warriors, that the fortunes of that day
Must end the conflict; that for one, or both,
The sun that hour ascending shone his last:
Therefore all strength of onset till that hour
By either loosed or hoarded, craft of fight
Reined in one moment but to spring the next
Forward in might more terrible, compared
With that last battle was a trivial thing;
Whilst every weapon, javelin, spear, or sword,
Lawful alike that day, scattered abroad
Huge flakes of dinted mail; from every wound
Bounded the life-blood of a heart athirst
For victory or for death. The vernal day
Panted with summer ardours, while aloft
Noontide, a fire-tressed Fury, waved her torch,
Kindling the lit grove and its youngling green
From the azure-blazing zenith. As the heat
So waxed the warriors' frenzy. Hours went by:
That day they sought not rest on rock or mound,
Held no discourse. Slowly the sun declined;
And as wayfarers oft when twilight falls

Advance with strength renewed, so they, refreshed,
Surpassed their deeds at morning. With a bound
Cuchullain, from the bank high springing, lit
Full on the broad boss of Ferdia's shield,
His dagger-point down turned. With spasm of arm
Instant the Firbolg from its sable rim
Cast him astonished. Upward from the Ford
Again Cuchullain reached that shield: again
With spasm of knee Ferdia flung him far,
While Leagh in scorn reviled him: 'As the flood
Shoots on the tempest's blast its puny foam;
The oak-tree casts its dead leaf on the wave;
The mill-wheel showers its spray; the shameless woman
Hurls on the mere that babe which was her shame,
So hurls he forth that fairy-child bewitched
Whom men misdeemed for warrior!'
                                    Then from heaven
Came down upon Cuchullain, like the night,
The madness-rage. The Foes confronted met:
Shivered their spears from point to haft: their swords
Flashed lightnings round them. Fate-compelled, their feet
Drew near, then reached that stream which backward fled
Leaving its channel dry. While raged that fight
Cuchullain's stature rose, huge bulk, immense,
Ascending still: as high Ferdia towered
Like Fomor old, or Nemed from the sea,
Those shields, their covering late from foot to helm,
Shrinking, so seemed it, till above them beamed
Shoulders and heads. So close that fight, their crests
That waved defiance, mingled in mid air;
While all along the circles of their shields,
And all adown their swords, viewless for speed
Ran, mad with rage, the demons of dark moors
And war-sprites of the valleys, Bocanachs
And Banacahs, whose scream, so keen its edge,
Might shear the centuried forest as the scythe
Shears meadow grass. To these in dread response
Thundered far off from sea-caves billow-beat

And halls rock-vaulted 'neath the eternal hills,
That race Tuatha, giant once, long since
To pigmy changed, that forge from molten ores
For aye their clanging weapons, shield or spear,
On stony anvils, waiting still their day
Of vengeance on the Gael. That tumult scared
The horses of the host of Meave that brake
From war-car or the tethering rope, and spread
Ruin around. Camp-followers first, then chiefs
Innumerable were dragged along, or lay
'Neath broken axle, dead. The end was nigh:
Cuchullain's shield splintered upon his arm
Served him no more; and through his fenceless side
Ferdia drave the sword. Then first the Gael
Hurled forth this taunt; 'The Firbolg, bribed by Meave,
Has sold his ancient friend!' Ferdia spake,
'No Firbolg he, the man in Scatha's Isle,
That won a maid, then left her!' Backward stepp'd
Cuchullain paces three: he reached the bank;
He uttered low; 'The Gae-Bulg!' Instant, Leagh
Within his hand had lodged it. Bending low,
Low as that stream, the war-game's crowning feat,
He launched it on Ferdia's breast. The shield,
The iron plate beneath, the stone within it,
Like shallow ice-films 'neath a courser's hoof
Burst. All was o'er. To earth the warrior sank:
Dying, he spake: 'Not thine this deed, O friend –
'Twas Meave who winged that bolt into my heart!'

  Then ran Cuchullain to that great one dead,
And raised him in his arms, and laid him down
Beside the Ford, but on its northern bank,
Not in that realm by Ailill swayed and Meave:
Long time he looked the dead man in the face;
Then by him fell in swoon. 'Cuchullain, rise!
The men of Erin be upon thee! Rise!'
Thus Leagh. He answered, waking; 'Let them come!
To me what profit if I live or die?
The man I loved is dead!'

But by the dead
Cuchullain stood; and thus he made lament:
'Ferdia! On their head the curse descend
Who sent thee to thy death! We meet no more;
Never while sun, and moon, and earth endure.
    'Ferdia! Far away in Scatha's Isle
A great troth bound us and a vow eterne
Never to raise war-weapons, each on each: –
'Twas Finobar that snared thee! She shall die.
    'Ferdia! dearer to my heart wert thou
Than all beside if all were joined in one:
Dear was thy clouded face, and darksome eye;
Thy deep, sad voice; thy words so wise and few;
Dear was thy silence: dear thy slow, grave ways,
Not boastful like the Gael's.'

Silent he stood
While Leagh in reverence from the dead man's breast
Loosened his mail. There shone the torque of Meave:
There where the queen had fixed it yet it lay.
Cuchullain clutched it. 'Ha! that torque I spurned!
Dark gem ill-lifted from the seas of Death!
Swart planet bickering from the heavens of Fate!
With what a baleful beam thou look'st on me!
'Twas thou, 'twas thou, not I, that slew'st this man' –
He dashed it on the rock, and with his heel
Smote it to fragments.

Then, as one from trance
Waking, once more he spake: 'Oh me – oh me,
That I should see that face so great and pale!
Today face-whitening death is on that face;
And in my hand my sword: – 'tis crimson yet.
That day when he and I triumphed in fight
By Formait's lake o'er Scatha's pirate foes
The woman fetched a beaker forth of wine,
And made us drink it both; and made us vow
Friendship eterne. O friend, my hand this day
Tendered a bloody beaker to thy lip.'
    Again he sang; 'Queen Meave to Uladh's bound

Came down; and dark the deed that grew thereof;
Came down with all the hosting of her kings;
And dark the deed that grew thereof. We two
Abode with Scatha in her northern isle,
Her pupils twinned. The sea-girt warrioress
That honoured few men honoured us alike:
We ate together of the self-same dish:
We couched together 'neath the self-same shield:
Now living man I stand, and he lies dead!'
  He raised again his head: once more he sang:
'Each battle was a game, a jest, a sport
Till came, fore-doomed, Ferdia to the Ford.
I loved the warrior though I pierced his heart.
Each battle was a game, a jest, a sport
Till stood, self-doomed, Ferdia by the Ford.
Huge lion of the forestry of war;
Fair, central pillar of the House of Fame;
But yesterday he towered above the world:
This day he lies along the earth, a shade.'

THOMAS DAVIS

1814–45

Lament for the Death of Eoghan Ruadh O'Neill

Time – 10 November, 1649. *Scene* – Ormond's Camp, County Waterford.
Speakers – A veteran of Eoghan O'Neill's clan, and one of the horsemen,
just arrived with an account of his death.

'Did they dare – did they dare, to slay Owen Roe O'Neill?'
'Yes, they slew with poison him they feared to meet with
    steel.'
'May God wither up their hearts! May their blood cease to
    flow!
May they walk in living death who poisoned Owen Roe!

'Though it break my heart to hear, say again the bitter words.'
'From Derry, against Cromwell, he marched to measure
    swords;
But the weapon of the Sassanach met him on his way.
And he died at Cloch Uachtar upon St Leonard's Day.

'Wail, wail ye for the Mighty One! Wail, wail, ye for the
    Dead!
Quench the hearth, and hold the breath – with ashes strew the
    head.
How tenderly we loved him! How deeply we deplore!
Holy Saviour! but to think we shall never see him more!

'Sagest in the council was he, kindest in the hall:
Sure, we never won a battle – 'twas Owen won them all.
Had he lived – had he lived, our dear country had been free;
But he's dead – but he's dead, and 'tis slaves we'll ever be.

'O'Farrell and Clanrickarde, Preston and Red Hugh,
Audley and MacMahon, ye are valiant, wise, and true;
But what – what are ye all to our darling who is gone?
The Rudder of our ship was he – our Castle's corner-stone!

'Wail, wail him through the island! Weep, weep for our pride!
Would that on the battlefield our gallant chief had died!
Weep the victor of Beinn Burb – weep him, young men and
    old!
Weep for him, ye women – your Beautiful lies cold!

'We thought you would not die – we were sure you would
    not go,
And leave us in our utmost need to Cromwell's cruel blow –
Sheep without a shepherd, when the snow shuts out the sky –
Oh! why did you leave us, Owen? Why did you die?

'Soft as woman's was your voice, O'Neill! Bright was your
    eye.
Oh! why did you leave us, Owen? Why did you die?
Your troubles are all over; you're at rest with God on high:
But we're slaves, and we're orphans, Owen! Why did you
    die?'

WILLIAM McBURNEY

The Croppy Boy

A BALLAD OF '98

'Good men and true! in this house who dwell,
To a stranger *bouchal*, I pray you tell
Is the Priest at home? or may he be seen?
I would speak a word with Father Green.'

'The Priest's at home, boy, and may be seen;
'Tis easy speaking with Father Green;
But you must wait, till I go and see
If the holy Father alone may be.'

The youth has entered an empty hall –
What a lonely sound has his light foot-fall!
And the gloomy chamber's chill and bare,
With a vested Priest in a lonely chair.

The youth has knelt to tell his sins.
'*Nomine Dei*,' the youth begins:
At '*mea culpa*' he beats his breast,
And in broken murmurs he speaks the rest.

'At the siege of Ross did my father fall,
And at Gorey my loving brothers all.
I alone am left of my name and race;
I will go to Wexford and take their place.

'I cursed three times since last Easter Day –
At Mass-time once I went to play;
I passed the churchyard one day in haste,
And forgot to pray for my mother's rest.

'I bear no hate against living thing;
But I love my country above my King.

Now, Father! bless me, and let me go
To die, if God has ordained it so.'

The Priest said nought, but a rustling noise
Made the youth look above in wild surprise;
The robes were off, and in scarlet there
Sat a yeoman captain with fiery glare.

With fiery glare and with fury hoarse,
Instead of blessing, he breathed a curse:
' 'Twas a good thought, boy, to come here and shrive;
For one short hour is your time to live.

'Upon yon river three tenders float;
The Priest's in one, if he isn't shot;
We hold his house for our Lord the King,
And – "Amen," say I – may all traitors swing!'

At Geneva barrack that young man died,
And at Passage they have his body laid.
Good people who live in peace and joy,
Breathe a prayer and a tear for the Croppy boy.

ARTHUR G. GEOGHEGAN

1810–89

After Aughrim

Do you remember, long ago,
    Kathaleen?
When your lover whispered low,
'Shall I stay or shall I go,
    Kathaleen?'
And you answered proudly, 'Go!
And join King James and strike a blow
    For the Green!'

Mavrone, your hair is white as snow,
    Kathaleen;
Your heart is sad and full of woe.
Do you repent you made him go,
    Kathaleen?
And quick you answer proudly, 'No!
For better die with Sarsfield so
Than live a slave without a blow
    For the Green!'

LADY WILDE

1820–96

The Famine Year

Weary men, what reap ye? – 'Golden corn for the stranger.'
What sow ye? – 'Human corses that await for the Avenger.
Fainting forms, all hunger-stricken, what see you in the offing?
'Stately ships to bear our food away amid the stranger's
    scoffing.
There's a proud array of soldiers – what do they round your
    door?
They guard our master's granaries from the thin hands of the
    poor.'
Pale mothers, wherefore weeping? – 'Would to God that we
    were dead –
Our children swoon before us, and we cannot give them
    bread!'

Little children, tears are strange upon your infant faces,
God meant you but to smile within your mother's soft
    embraces.
'Oh! we know not what is smiling, and we know not what is
    dying;
But we're hungry, very hungry, and we cannot stop our
    crying;
And some of us grow cold and white – we know not what it
    means.
But as they lie beside us we tremble in our dreams.'
There's a gaunt crowd on the highway – are ye come to pray
    to man,
With hollow eyes that cannot weep, and for words your faces
    wan?

'No; the blood is dead within our veins; we care not now for
    life;
Let us die hid in the ditches, far from children and from wife;

1– 232 –

We cannot stay to listen to their raving, famished cries –
Bread! Bread! Bread! – and none to still their agonies.
We left an infant playing with her dead mother's hand:
We left a maiden maddened by the fever's scorching brand:'
Better, maiden, thou wert strangled in thy own dark-twisted
      tresses!
Better, infant, thou wert smothered in thy mother's first
      caresses.

'We are fainting in our misery, but God will hear our groan;
Yea, if fellow-men desert us, He will hearken from His
      throne!
Accursed are we in our own land, yet toil we still and toil;
But the stranger reaps our harvest – the alien owns our soil.
O Christ, how have we sinned, that on our native plains
We perish houseless, naked, starved, with branded brow, like
      Cain's?
Dying, dying wearily, with a torture sure and slow –
Dying as a dog would die, by the wayside as we go.

'One by one they're falling round us, their pale faces to the
      sky;
We've no strength left to dig them graves – there let them lie.
The wild bird, when he's stricken, is mournèd by the others,
But we, we die in Christian land – we die amid our brothers –
In the land which God has given – like a wild beast in his cave,
Without a tear, a prayer, a shroud, a coffin, or a grave.
Ha! but think ye the contortions on each dead face ye see,
Shall not be read on judgement-day by the eyes of Deity?

'We are wretches, famished, scorned, human tools to build
      your pride,
But God will yet take vengeance for the souls for whom
      Christ died.
Now is your hour of pleasure, bask ye in the world's caress;
But our whitening bones against ye will arise as witnesses,
From the cabins and the ditches, in their charred, uncoffined
      masses,

For the ANGEL OF THE TRUMPET will know them as he
    passes.
A ghastly, spectral army before great God we'll stand
And arraign ye as our murderers, O spoilers of our land!'

JOHN KELLS INGRAM

1823–1907

The Memory of the Dead

Who fears to speak of Ninety-Eight?
  Who blushes at the name?
When cowards mock the patriot's fate,
  Who hangs his head for shame?
He's all a knave or half a slave
  Who slights his country thus:
But a true man, like you, man,
  Will fill your glass with us.

We drink the memory of the brave,
  The faithful and the few –
Some lie far off beyond the wave,
  Some sleep in Ireland, too;
All, all are gone – but still lives on
  The fame of those who died;
And true men, like you, men,
  Remember them with pride.

Some on the shores of distant lands
  Their weary hearts have laid,
And by the stranger's heedless hands
  Their lonely graves were made;
But though their clay be far away
  Beyond the Atlantic foam,
In true men, like you, men,
  Their spirit's still at home.

The dust of some is Irish earth;
  Among their own they rest;
And the same land that gave them birth
  Has caught them to her breast;

And we will pray that from their clay
   Full many a race may start
Of true men, like you, men,
   To act as brave a part.

They rose in dark and evil days
   To right their native land;
They kindled here a living blaze
   That nothing shall withstand.
Alas! that Might can vanquish Right –
   They fell, and passed away;
But true men, like you, men,
   Are plenty here today.

Then here's their memory – may it be
   For us a guiding light,
To cheer our strife for liberty,
   And teach us to unite!
Through good and ill, be Ireland's still,
   Though sad as theirs, your fate;
And true men, be you, men,
   Like those of Ninety-Eight.

MICHAEL JOSEPH McCANN

1824–83

O'Donnell Aboo

Proudly the note of the trumpet is sounding,
Loudly the war-cries arise on the gale;
Fleetly the steed by Lough Swilly is bounding,
To join the thick squadrons in Saimear's green vale.
    On, ev'ry mountaineer,
    Strangers to flight and fear!
Rush to the standard of dauntless Red Hugh!
    Bonnaught and gallowglass,
    Throng from each mountain pass;
On for old Erin, 'O'Donnell Aboo!'

Princely O'Neill to our aid is advancing
With many a chieftain and warrior clan,
A thousand proud steeds in his vanguard are prancing
'Neath the borderers brave from the banks of the Bann;
    Many a heart shall quail
    Under its coat of mail;
Deeply the merciless foeman shall rue,
    When on his ear shall ring,
    Borne on the breezes' wing,
Tir Connell's dread war-cry, 'O'Donnell Aboo!'

Wildly o'er Desmond the war-wolf is howling,
Fearless the eagle sweeps over the plain,
The fox in the streets of the city is prowling;
All, all who would scare them are banished or slain.
    Grasp every stalwart hand
    Hackbut and battle brand,
Pay them all back the debt so long due;
    Norris and Clifford well
    Can of Tir Connell tell;
Onward to glory, 'O'Donnell Aboo!'

Sacred the cause of Clan Connaill's defending,
The altars we kneel at, the homes of our sires;
Ruthless the ruin the foe is extending,
Midnight is red with the plunderers' fires.
  On with O'Donnell, then,
  Fight the old fight again,
Sons of Tir Connell, all valiant and true.
  Make the false Saxon feel
  Erin's avenging steel!
Strike for your country, 'O'Donnell Aboo!'

THOMAS CAULFIELD IRWIN

1823–92

'The apples ripen under yellowing leaves'

The apples ripen under yellowing leaves,
And in the farm yards by the little bay
The shadows come and go amid the sheaves,
And on the long dry inland winding way:
Where, in the thinning boughs each air bereaves,
Faint sunlights golden, and the spider weaves.
Grey are the low-laid sleepy hills, and grey
The autumn solitude of the sea day,
Where from the deep 'mid-channel, less and less
You hear along the pale east afternoon
A sound, uncertain as the silence, swoon –
The tide's sad voice ebbing toward loneliness:
And past the sands and seas' blue level line,
Ceaseless, the faint far murmur of the brine.

'A roadside inn this summer Saturday'

A roadside inn this summer Saturday:
The doors are open to the wide warm air,
The parlour, whose old window views the bay,
Garnished with cracked delph full of flowers fair
From the fields round, and whence you see the glare
Fall heavy on the hot slate roofs and o'er
The wall's tree shadows drooping in the sun.
Now rumbles slowly down the dusty street
The lazy drover's clattering cart; and crows
Fainter through afternoon the cock; with hoes
Tan-faced harvest folk trudge in the heat:
The neighbours at their shady doors swept clean,
Gossip, and with cool eve fresh scents of wheat,
Grasses and leaves, come from the meadows green.

'I walk of grey noons by the old canal'

I walk of grey noons by the old canal
   Where rain-drops patter on the autumn leaves,
Now watching from some ivied orchard wall
   In slopes of stubble figures pile the sheaves;
Or under banks in shadow of their grass,
Blue water-flies by starts jettingly pass
'Mid large leaves level on the glassy cool;
   Or noiseless dizzy midges winking round
The yellow sallows of the meadow pool;
   While into cloudy silence ebbs each sound,
And sifts the moulting sunlight warm and mellow
O'er sandy beach remote, or slumberous flood,
Or rooky, red brick mansion by the wood,
   Mossed gate, or farmyard hay-stacks tanned and yellow.

'Now, winter's dolorous days are o'er'

Now, winter's dolorous days are o'er, and through
March morning casements comes the sharp spring air,
And noises from the distant city, where
The steeples stand up keenly in the blue:
No more the clouds by crispy frost defined,
Pile the pale North, but float, dispersed shapes;
Though still around the cool grey twilight capes,
The sullen sea is dark with drifts of wind.
Like a forgotten fleck of snow still left,
The cascade gleams in the far mountain cleft;
Brown rushes by the river's brimming bank
Rustle, and matted sedges sway and sigh,
Where grasses in sleek shallows waver dank,
Or drift in windy ripples greyly by.

WILLIAM ALLINGHAM

1824–89

The Winding Banks of Erne:

OR, THE EMIGRANT'S ADIEU TO BALLYSHANNON

Adieu to Ballyshannon! where I was bred and born;
Go where I may, I'll think of you, as sure as night and morn,
The kindly spot, the friendly town, where everyone is known,
And not a face in all the place but partly seems my own;
There's not a house or window, there's not a field or hill,
But, east or west, in foreign lands, I'll recollect them still.
I leave my warm heart with you, though my back I'm forced
    to turn –
So adieu to Ballyshannon, and the winding banks of Erne!

No more on pleasant evenings we'll saunter down the Mall,
When the trout is rising to the fly, the salmon to the fall.
The boat comes straining on her net, and heavily she creeps,
Cast off, cast off! – she feels the oars, and to her berth she
    sweeps;
Now fore and aft keep hauling, and gathering up the clue,
Till a silver wave of salmon rolls in among the crew.
Then they may sit, with pipes a-lit, and many a joke and
    'yarn'; –
Adieu to Ballyshannon, and the winding banks of Erne!

The music of the waterfall, the mirror of the tide,
When all the green-hill'd harbour is full from side to side –
From Portnasun to Bulliebawns, and round the Abbey Bay,
From rocky Inis Saimer to Coolnargit sandhills grey;
While far upon the southern line, to guard it like a wall,
The Leitrim mountains, clothed in blue, gaze calmly over
    all,
And watch the ship sail up or down, the red flag at her stern; –
Adieu to these, adieu to all the winding banks of Erne!

Farewell to you, Kildoney lads, and them that pull an oar,
A lug-sail set, or haul a net, from the Point to Mullaghmore;
From Killybegs to bold Slieve-League, that ocean-mountain
    steep,
Six hundred yards in air aloft, six hundred in the deep;
From Dooran to the Fairy Bridge, and round by Tullen
    strand,
Level and long, and white with waves, where gull and curlew
    stand; –
Head out to sea when on your lee the breakers you discern! –
Adieu to all the billowy coast, and winding banks of Erne!

Farewell Coolmore, – Bundoran! and your summer crowds
    that run
From inland homes to see with joy th' Atlantic-setting sun;
To breathe the buoyant salted air, and sport among the waves;
To gather shells on sandy beach, and tempt the gloomy
    caves;
To watch the flowing, ebbing tide, the boats, the crabs, the
    fish;
Young men and maids to meet and smile, and form a tender
    wish;
The sick and old in search of health, for all things have their
    turn –
And I must quit my native shore, and the winding banks of
    Erne!

Farewell to every white cascade from the Harbour to Belleek,
And every pool where fins may rest, and ivy-shaded creek;
The sloping fields, the lofty rocks, where ash and holly grow,
The one split yew-tree gazing on the curving flood below;
The Lough, that winds through islands under Turaw
    mountain green;
And Castle Caldwell's stretching woods, with tranquil bays
    between;
And Breesie Hill, and many a pond among the heath and
    fern, –
For I must say adieu – adieu to the winding banks of Erne!

The thrush will call through Camlin groves the live-long
    summer day;
The waters run by mossy cliff, and bank with wild flowers gay;
The girls will bring their work and sing beneath a twisted
    thorn,
Or stray with sweethearts down the path among the growing
    corn;
Along the river side they go, where I have often been, –
O, never shall I see again the days that I have seen!
A thousand chances are to one I never may return, –
Adieu to Ballyshannon, and the winding banks of Erne!

Adieu to evening dances, when merry neighbours meet,
And the fiddle says to boys and girls, 'Get up and shake your
    feet!'
To 'shanachus' and wise old talk of Erin's days gone by –
Who trench'd the rath on such a hill, and where the bones
    may lie
Of saint, or king, or warrior chief; with tales of fairy power,
And tender ditties sweetly sung to pass the twilight hour.
The mournful song of exile is now for me to learn –
Adieu, my dear companions on the winding banks of Erne!

Now measure from the Commons down to each end of the
    Purt,
Round the Abbey, Moy, and Knather, – I wish no one any
    hurt;
The Main Street, Back Street, College Lane, the Mall, and
    Portnasun,
If any foes of mine are there, I pardon every one.
I hope that man and womankind will do the same by me;
For my heart is sore and heavy at voyaging the sea.
My loving friends I'll bear in mind, and often fondly turn
To think of Ballyshannon, and the winding banks of Erne.

If ever I'm a money'd man, I mean, please God, to cast
My golden anchor in the place where youthful years were
    pass'd;

Though heads that now are black and brown must meanwhile
    gather grey,
New faces rise by every hearth, and old ones drop away –
Yet dearer still that Irish hill than all the world beside;
It's home, sweet home, where'er I roam, through lands and
    waters wide.
And if the Lord allows me, I surely will return
To my native Ballyshannon, and the winding banks of Erne.

Tenants at Will

From *Lawrence Bloomfield in Ireland*

The steady world pursued its common way;
Yet some good luck, before that evil day,
Might intercept the hand outstretch'd to tear
Those cottage roofs, and leave their hearthstones bare.
If coming ills be distant half a mile,
Poor Paddy can forget, and gaily smile,
From carelessness, or fatalism, or sense
Profound of overruling Providence.

    But Pigot's ruddy cheek and sharp black eye
Display no softer hint, as months go by;
And now the trembling tenants whisper sad, –
'O Queen of Heaven! and would he be so bad?
And will they send us begging, young and old,
And seize the fields, and make the firesides cold,
Where, God's our witness, poor enough we live,
But still content with what the Lord may give,
Our hearts with love and veneration tied
To where our fathers' fathers lived and died'
Or else more fiercely, – ''Tis our native land!
But cruel tyrants have us at command,
To let us grow, if best it serves their needs,
Or tear and cast us forth like poison-weeds.

The law's their implement: who make the law?
The rich men for the rich, and leave no flaw.
And what's the poor man's part? to drudge and sweat
For food and shelter. Does the poor man get
Bare food and shelter? – praties, cabin, rags.
Now fling him out to famish – or he drags
His weary body to that gaol and grave
The Poorhouse; – he must live and die a slave,
Toil, starve, and suffer, creep, and crouch, and crawl,
Be cursed and trampled, and submit to all
Without one murmur, one rebellious trace
Among the marks of misery on his face!'

Each tongue around old Oona feared to tell
The great misfortune, worse than yet befell
In all her length of journey. When they tried
To move her – 'Would they take her life?' she cried;
At which it rested, hap what happen might.
And scarcely one, in truth, prepared for flight;
Imprudence, anger, fatalism, despair,
And *vis inertiae*, kept them as they were;
'God and the world will see it,' – so they said,
'Let all the wrong be on the doer's head!'

In early morning twilight, raw and chill,
Damp vapours brooding on the barren hill,
Through miles of mire in steady grave array
Threescore well-arm'd police pursue their way;
Each tall and bearded man a rifle swings,
And under each greatcoat a bayonet clings;
The Sheriff on his sturdy cob astride
Talks with the chief, who marches by their side,
And, creeping on behind them, Paudeen Dhu
Pretends his needful duty much to rue.
Six big-boned labourers, clad in common frieze,
Walk in the midst, the Sheriff's staunch allies;
Six crowbar men, from distant county brought, –
Orange, and glorying in their work, 'tis thought,

But wrongly, – churls of Catholics are they,
And merely hired at half a crown a day.

   The Hamlet clustering on its hill is seen,
A score of petty homesteads, dark and mean;
Poor always, not despairing until now;
Long used, as well as poverty knows how,
With life's oppressive trifles to contend.
This day will bring its history to an end.
Moveless and grim against the cottage walls
Lean a few silent men: but some one calls
Far off; and then a child 'without a stitch'
Runs out of doors, flies back with piercing screech,
And soon from house to house is heard the cry
Of female sorrow, swelling loud and high,
Which makes the men blaspheme between their teeth.
Meanwhile, o'er fence and watery field beneath,
The little army moves through drizzling rain;
A 'Crowbar' leads the Sheriff's nag; the lane
Is enter'd, and their plashing tramp draws near;
One instant, outcry holds its breath to hear;
'Halt!' – at the doors they form in double line,
And ranks of polish'd rifles wetly shine.

The Sheriff's painful duty must be done;
He begs for quiet – and the work's begun.
The strong stand ready; now appear the rest,
Girl, matron, grandsire, baby on the breast,
And Rosy's thin face on a pallet borne;
A motley concourse, feeble and forlorn.
One old man, tears upon his wrinkled cheek,
Stands trembling on a threshold, tries to speak,
But, in defect of any word for this,
Mutely upon the doorpost prints a kiss,
Then passes out for ever. Through the crowd
The children run bewilder'd, wailing loud;
Where needed most, the men combine their aid;
And, last of all, is Oona forth convey'd,

Reclined in her accustom'd strawen chair,
Her aged eyelids closed, her thick white hair
Escaping from her cap; she feels the chill,
Looks round and murmurs, then again is still.

Now bring the remnants of each household fire.
On the wet ground the hissing coals expire;
And Paudeen Dhu, with meekly dismal face,
Receives the full possession of the place.

Whereon the Sheriff, 'We have legal hold.
Return to shelter with the sick and old.
Time shall be given; and there are carts below
If any to the workhouse choose to go.'
A young man makes him answer, grave and clear,
'We're thankful to you! but there's no one here
Goin' back into them houses: do your part.
Nor we won't trouble Pigot's horse and cart.'
At which name, rushing into th' open space,
A woman flings her hood from off her face,
Falls on her knees upon the miry ground,
Lifts hands and eyes, and voice of thrilling sound, –
'Vengeance of God Almighty fall on you,
James Pigot! – may the poor man's curse pursue,
The widow's and the orphan's curse, I pray,
Hang heavy round you at your dying day!'
Breathless and fix'd one moment stands the crowd
To hear this malediction fierce and loud.

But now (our neighbour Neal is busy there)
On steady poles be lifted Oona's chair,
Well-heap'd with borrow'd mantles; gently bear
The sick girl in her litter, bed and all;
Whilst others hug the children weak and small
In careful arms, or hoist them pick-a-back;
And, 'midst the unrelenting clink and thwack
Of iron bar on stone, let creep away
The sad procession from that hill-side gray,

Through the slow-falling rain. In three hours more
You find, where Ballytullagh stood before,
Mere shatter'd walls, and doors with useless latch,
And firesides buried under fallen thatch.

   The Doran household, shadow'd with dismay,
Can still perform a pious part today;
Jack Doran's mother, now deceased a year,
Was Oona's cousin; Oona's welcomed here;
Nor will her grandson in his duty fail,
Though far across the sea compell'd to sail.
'Man, woman, child, – they're gone, dear!' Mary said,
'And here we sit and mourn them like the dead.
It falls like death, as cowld upon the heart,
For kin and kindly neighbours thus to part.
There won't be one face left we used to know,
Not one companion out of long-ago.
The good oul' people! – why should this befall?
Och, *murneen* boys and girls, where are ye all?
Through the wide world they're scatter'd, *fareer gair!*
Sarch for them, barrin' Ireland, everywhere.
Sure Ireland once was blest, – and was she curst
Since then? or what has made her last and worst?
The Heretics that robb'd the Church, some say:
But glory be to God, amin, this day!' –
For gentle Maureen seldom said so much;
And this was theme too perilous to touch.
   So was the little Hamlet's crowd at last
Whirl'd off like leaves before misfortune's blast.
Some from a seaport, and their lot the best,
On Neptune's Highway follow'd, east or west,
The myriads of their kindred gone before, –
If Irish still, yet Ireland's nevermore.
Some wander'd through the country; some went down,
Like Rose, to back-lane lodgings in the Town;
And some to those high-built repulsive walls
Where Doctor Larmour paid his daily calls.
Dispensary and workhouse own'd his care,

An Antrim Presbyterian, short and spare,
Quick, busy, cool; with lancet or with pill
Acknowledged first in Æsculapian skill.
Catholicism he openly despised,
But ailing Papists cleverly advised,
And men of every creed his talent prized.
Him Bloomfield knew. For Ballytullagh's fall
The Doctor's pity, Bloomfield found, was small.
'They lived in filth, perpetual sickness bred,
Lazy of hand, and obstinate of head;
Gave rent too much for all they really made,
Being well-nigh savage in the farming trade,
Too small for what they wasted and o'erran.
At risk of bloodshed let another plan
Improvement, lawful owner though he be, –
Mere owner! what the devil right has he?
Poorer, of course, they could not fail to grow;
But humble, willing to be taught? O no!
See vice and crime and folly now array'd
Conspirators, in ragged masquerade;
Erin-go-bragh! – yet scoundrels ten times worse,
And more deserving the true patriot's curse
Than these poor scurvy rogues, are some who claim
With public voice the patriot's lofty name;
That *mimber*, soaring on the rabble's yell;
This journalist, his rotten page to sell;
Or briefless barrister, whose frantic word,
A cry for victual, must and will be heard.

'Ireland, forsooth, "a nation once again!"
If Ireland was a nation, tell me when?
For since the civil modern world began
What's Irish History? Walks the child a man?
Or strays he still perverse and immature,
Weak, slothful, rash, irresolute, unsure;
Right bonds rejecting, hugging rusty chains,
Nor one clear view, nor one bold step attains?
What Ireland might have been, if wisely school'd,

I know not: far too briefly Cromwell ruled.
We see the melting of a barbarous race
(Sad sight, I grant, sir), from their ancient place;
But always, everywhere, it has been so;
Red-Indians, Bushmen, Irish, – they must go!'

The Doctor harshly spoke; yet did his best
To cure the sick, and comfort the distress'd;
And tended Rosy kindly, – to whose aid
A rill of Bloomfield's bounty he convey'd.

Those, too, with less to spare, and those with nought,
To this poor girl their friendly succour brought.
Here in a neighbouring house, but whence no noise
Can reach her, some well-wishing girls and boys
Have clubb'd their moneys, raffling for a shawl;
Of Rose's other shreds the pawn has all.
Three simple pence entitle to a throw;
Down on a slate the names and numbers go;
The wooden cubes mark'd with a red-hot wire
(No better dice or dice-box they require)
In old tin porringer flung rattling fast,
A warmer interest watches every cast;
'Follie' your han'!' 'You're lucky, throw for me!'
'More power!' 'Tim Ryan has it – fifty-three!'
Then silver, copper, mix'd, a bulky pound
Makes haste to Rosy, feebly turning round
With grateful smile; and back the shawl comes too,
The winner swearing 'twas for her he threw.

Meanwhile, no raffle ends without a dance:
My boy, choose out a partner, and advance
To ask the fiddler for her favourite tune,
Slipping into his hand the penny boon.
Polthoge, or *Washerwoman*, let him play,
Heart of my Kitty, or *The Fields in May*;
She makes a pretty quibbling with her toes,

But he his agile power untiring shows
In many a double-shuffle, stamp and fling;
Nor slack in praises are the crowded ring, –
'Success to both! – my boul' you wor'! – ay *that!*
Don't spare him, Peggy dear! – Hurroo for Pat!'
They meet, change sides, the rapid steps renew,
A second wind inspires the fiddler too,
Till *Colleen Dhas*, well-flush'd in cheek, but grave
As courtly dames in minuets behave,
Signals; when hand in hand the two give o'er,
Bow to the music, and resign the floor;
Where other pairs achieve with equal zeal
The busy jig, or winding four-hand reel.

The dance-house, all the better for being bare,
Its broken roof admitting fresher air,
This poor and merry company befits;
With jest and mimicry and clash of wits
Con 'Pastime' keeps them laughing long and loud;
Sweethearts draw close together in the crowd;
Gay groups of damsels, gather'd near the door
Banter to death each awkward bachelor,
And dart some flying jokes at Denis Coyle,
Whose travell'd wit such weapons well can foil,
For, do their utmost, Denis will not dance,
And slips away upon the earliest chance.

But all is not amusement. Near to these
Stands one at watch; and ever when he sees
A man expected, pushing through the line,
By look or touch conveys a rapid sign.
As Denis goes, the grip salutes his hand
Which greets a Brother of the Midnight Band;
And soon the whisper none may safely slight
Commands his presence on tomorrow night
With hour and place; for Neal and Denis both
Have sworn the Ribbonman's unlawful oath.

The dark and lonely streets young Denis treads,
With mind confused, and fill'd with shapeless dreads;
Where Doctor Larmour's lamp shoots forth a ray,
He shuns the light, and slinks across the way.

murneen: darling   *fareer gair:* bitter grief

Colleen Dhas: the pretty girl

THOMAS D'ARCY McGEE

1825–68

The Celts

Long, long ago, beyond the misty space
    Of twice a thousand years,
In Erin old there dwelt a mighty race,
    Taller than Roman spears;
Like oaks and towers they had a giant grace,
    Were fleet as deers,
With wind and waves they made their 'biding place,
    These western shepherd seers.

Their Ocean-God was Manannan MacLir,
    Whose angry lips,
In their white foam, full often would inter
    Whole fleets of ships;
Cromah their Day-God, and their Thunderer
    Made morning and eclipse;
Bride was their Queen of Song, and unto her
    They prayed with fire-touched lips.

Great were their deeds, their passions and their sports;
    With clay and stone
They piled on strath and shore those mystic forts,
    Not yet o'erthrown;
On cairn-crowned hills they held their council-courts;
    While youths alone,
With giant dogs, explored the elk resorts,
    And brought them down.

Of these was Fin, the father of the Bard
    Whose ancient song
Over the clamour of all change is heard,
    Sweet-voiced and strong.

Fin once o'ertook Grania, the golden-haired,
   The fleet and young;
From her the lovely, and from him the feared,
   The primal poet sprung.

Ossian! two thousand years of mist and change
   Surround thy name –
Thy Finian heroes now no longer range
   The hills of fame.
The very names of Fin and Gaul sound strange –
   Yet thine the same –
By miscalled lake and desecrated grange –
   Remains, and shall remain!

The Druid's altar and the Druid's creed
   We scarce can trace,
There is not left an undisputed deed
   Of all your race,
Save your majestic song, which hath their speed,
   And strength and grace;
In that sole song, they live and love, and bleed –
   It bears them on through space.

O, inspired giant! Shall we e'er behold,
   In our own time,
One fit to speak your spirit on the wold,
   Or seize your rhyme?
One pupil of the past, as mighty-souled
   As in the prime,
Were the fond, fair, and beautiful, and bold –
   They, of your song sublime!

JOHN TODHUNTER

1839–1916

Aghadoe

There's a glen in Aghadoe, Aghadoe, Aghadoe,
There's a green and silent glade in Aghadoe,
   Where we met, my Love and I, Love's fair planet in the sky,
O'er that sweet and silent glen in Aghadoe.

There's a glen in Aghadoe, Aghadoe, Aghadoe,
There's a deep and secret glen in Aghadoe,
   Where I hid him from the eyes of the redcoats and their
     spies
That year the trouble came to Aghadoe!

Oh! my curse on one black heart in Aghadoe, Aghadoe,
On Shaun Dhuv,[1] my mother's son in Aghadoe,
   When your throat fries in hell's drouth salt the flame be in
     your mouth,
For the treachery you did in Aghadoe!

For they tracked me to that glen in Aghadoe, Aghadoe,
When the price was on his head in Aghadoe;
   O'er the mountain through the wood, as I stole to him
     with food,
When in hiding low he lay in Aghadoe.

But they never took him living in Aghadoe, Aghadoe;
With the bullets in his heart in Aghadoe,
   There he lay, the head – my breast keeps the warmth where
     once 'twould rest –
Gone, to win the traitor's gold from Aghadoe!

1. *Seán Dubh:* Black-haired John.

A Moment

'Was that the wind?' she said,
And turned her head
To where, on a green bank, the primrose flowers
Seemed with new beauty suddenly endowed,
As though they gazed out of their mortal cloud
On things unseen, communing with strange powers.

Then upon that green place
Fell a new grace,
As when a sun-gleam visits drops of dew,
And every drop shines like a mystic gem,
Set in the front of morning's diadem,
With hues more tender than e'er a diamond knew.

And something seemed to pass –
As through the grass
The presence of the gentlest wind will go –
Delicately through her bosom and her hair,
Till, with delight, she found herself more fair,
And her heart sang, unutterably low.

The Fate of the Sons of Usna

From *The First Duan: The Coming of Deirdré*

So Kings and Chiefs and Bards, in Eman of the Kings,
Feasted with Felimy; and rank and order due
Were kept between them all, each Bard, or Chief, or King
Being marshalled to his place by stewards of the feast.
But Conchobar alone came armed into the hall.

And there the amber mead, crowning the golden cup,
Welcomed each noble guest. There Conall Carnach sat,

Whose eyes, renowned in song, the blue eye and the brown,
Abashed his foes; but now beamed kindly as he pledged,
The man of glorious heart who laughed a realm away –
Fergus MacRoy; who now pledged him again, and laughed,
With frank heart-easing roar, the laugh that all men loved.

So Fergus laughed, and looked a mighty man of men;
Ruddy his face, and red the great beard on his breast,
Fergus whose heart contained the laughter and the tears
Of all the world; who held the freedom of his mood,
Love, and the dreaming harp that made the world a dream,
The comradeship of feasts, the wild joy of the chase,
Dearer than power; Fergus, who sang in after-years
The raid of red Queen Meave, the wasting of the Branch,
Breaches in famous loves, long wars, and deaths renowned
Of many a feaster there; where Conall now in mirth
Pledged his old friend, whose son ere long by him should fall.

And there Fardia felt the broad hand of his death
Laid on his shoulder now in comrade's love; for there,
A friend beside his friend, unarmed Cuchullin sat,
Like a swift hound for strength and graceful slenderness,
In the first flower of his youth; the colours of his face
Fresh as the dawning day, and in his clear blue eyes
The glad undaunted light of life's unsullied morn.

There in his royal state, a grave man among Kings,
Sat Conchobar, still, stern. The dark flame of his face
Tamed, as the sun the stars, all faces else: a face
Of subtle splendour; brows of wisdom, broad and high,
Where strenuous youth had scored the runes of hidden power
Not easily read; a mouth pliant for speech, an eye
Whose ambushed fires at need could terribly outleap
In menace or command, mastering the wills of men.

He wore upon him all the colours of a King
By ancient laws ordained: the three colours, the white,

Crimson, and black; with these blending, by ancient law,
The four colours, the red, yellow, and green, and blue,
Enriched with gleaming gold. But subtly Conchobar
Loved to display the seven fair colours of a King
Inwoven and intertwined in traceries quaint and rare;
And his keen eye would search the play of shimmering hues,
Even as his ear the turns and tricks of tuneful art
Of skilled harpers. For craft of hand as craft of mind
Was ever his delight, and subtle as his mind
Ever his dress. No King in splendour was his peer;
Each looked a gaudy clown, at vie with Conchobar.
Over his chair of state four silver posts upheld
A silken canopy; and by him were his arms:
'The Hawk', his casting-spear, that never left his hand
But death sang in its scream; and, in its jewelled sheath,
His sword, 'Flame of the Sea', won by his sires, of yore,
From some slain Eastern King – the blade, with wizard spells,
Tempered in magic baths under the Syrian moon.
But in the House of Arms bode his long thrusting-spear,
'Spoil-winner'; there, too, bode, far-famed in bardic song,
'The Bellower', his great shield, seven-bossed, whose pealing
        voice,
Loud o'er the battle's roar, would call its vassal waves,
The wave of Toth, the wave of Rury, and the wave
Of Cleena, the three waves, to thunder on their shores,
Ireland's three magic waves, at danger of her King.

On the High-King's right hand sat Cathvah, that white peer
Of hoary Time, like Time wrinkled and hoar; the beard
Upon his breast, the hair upon his druid head
Wintered with eld; Cathvah, whose voice was like a sea's
For mystery and awe, and like the brooding sea
Blue were his druid eyes, and sad with things to come.

And on his left was set old Shancha of the Laws,
His Councillor; none lived wiser in all the lore
Of statecraft, and the laws and customs of old time.
Thin was his shaven face; deep under the black brows

Gleamed his keen eyes that weighed coldly each thing they
    saw;
Long was his head and high, fringed round with silver hair;
Smooth as an egg above, where baldness on the dome
Sat in grave state, yet looked no blemish where it sat.
These two after the King were honoured in the hall.

On wings of song flew by the hastening day, and song
Led in the hooded night, soft stealing on the feast;
And without stint the wife of Felimy the Bard
Crowned the great horn with ale, with mead the golden cup,
To circle the great hall. Praised for her open hand,
She served with nimble cheer, though now her hour drew
    nigh.

But when the hearts of all were merry, and their brains
Hummed with the humming ale, and drowsily the harps
Murmured of deeds long done, till sleep with downy wing
Fanned heavy lids, a cry – a thin, keen, shuddering cry –
Rang eerily through the hall, dumbing all tongues, for lo!
Foreboding birth's dread hour, loud shrieked the babe
    unborn.

Then cheeks grew pale that ne'er in danger's grimmest hour
Failed of their wholesome red; and ghastly looks met looks
As ghastly in the eyes of champions whose proud names
Were songs of valour. First came loosing of the tongue
To Felimy. His words shook on the breath of fear:
'Woman, what woeful voice that rends my heart like steel,
Keenes from thee now?' His wife with trembling hands of
    prayer
Sank pale at Cathvah's feet: 'From what night-shrieking
    wraith,
O Druid, came that voice? A hand of ice is laid
Upon my heart: the *keene* comes to the house of death!'

And Cathvah said: 'A child cries in the gate of birth
For terror of this world; yet shall she be the queen

Of all this world for beauty. Ushered by fear she comes,
And "Dread" shall be her name; Deirdré I name her now,
For dear shall Eri dree her beauty and her birth.'

Then, with her pangs upon her, the mother from the hall
Was hurried by her maids; and ere they rose that night
A wail was in the house, for Death came to that birth,
And Deirdré's mother passed with the coming of her child.

Anon the aged crones that haunt with equal feet
The house of joy or tears, priestesses hoar like-skilled
In rites of death or birth, solemnly up the hall
Paced slow, bearing the babe; and with a weeping word,
'Thy dead wife sends thee this,' laid it in its father's arms.
And Felimy bent down and, dazed with sudden grief,
Kissed it without a tear. Then Cathvah took the child
And o'er its new-born head murmured his druid song:

THE DRUID SONG OF CATHVAH

I

O Deirdré, terrible child,
For thee, red star of our ruin,
Great weeping shall be in Eri –
Woe, woe, and a breach in Ulla!

II

The flame of thy dawn shall kindle
The pride of Kings to possess thee,
The spite of Queens or thy slander:
In seas of blood is thy setting.

III

War, war is thy bridesmaid,
Thou soft, small whelp of terror;
Thy feet shall trample the mighty,
Yet stumble on heads thou lovest.

IV

The little heap of thy grave
Shall dwell in thy desolation;
Sad songs shall wail over Eri
Thy dolorous name, O Deirdré!

To the nurse he gave the child. In silence from the hall
Deirdré was borne. Anon the vast hush of the night
Was filled with dreadful sound: the shield of Conchobar,
Raising its brazen voice within the House of Arms,
Bellowed; and at its call a mighty voice they knew
Thundered from the far shore, the voice of the great Wave
Of Rury. And the voice of the great Wave of Toth,
And the great Wave of Cleena, answered him from afar,
Thundering upon their shores at danger of their King.[1]

1. According to the legend, the magic shield of Conchobar roared like
the sea when the king was in danger, and the seas of Erinn answered it,
thundering upon their beaches.

EDWARD DOWDEN

1843–1913

In the Cathedral Close

In the Dean's porch a nest of clay
  With five small tenants may be seen,
Five solemn faces, each as wise
  As though its owner were a Dean;

Five downy fledglings in a row,
  Packed close, as in the antique pew
The schoolgirls are whose foreheads clear
  At the *Venite* shine on you.

Day after day the swallows sit
  With scarce a stir, with scarce a sound,
But dreaming and digesting much
  They grow thus wise and soft and round.

They watch the Canons come to dine,
  And hear, the mullion-bars across,
Over the fragrant fruit and wine
  Deep talk of rood-screen and reredos.

Her hands with field-flowers drenched, a child
  Leaps past in wind-blown dress and hair,
The swallows turn their heads askew –
  Five judges deem that she is fair.

Prelusive touches sound within,
  Straightway they recognize the sign,
And, blandly nodding, they approve
  The minuet of Rubinstein.

They mark the cousins' schoolboy talk,
  (Male birds flown wide from minster bell)
And blink at each broad term of art,
  Binomial or bicycle.

Ah! downy young ones, soft and warm,
   Doth such a stillness mask from sight
Such swiftness? can such peace conceal
   Passion and ecstasy of flight?

Yet somewhere 'mid your Eastern suns,
   Under a white Greek architrave
At morn, or when the shaft of fire
   Lies large upon the Indian wave,

A sense of something dear gone-by
   Will stir, strange longings thrill the heart
For a small world embowered and close,
   Of which ye some time were a part.

The dew-drench'd flowers, the child's glad eyes,
   Your joy unhuman shall control,
And in your wings a light and wind
   Shall move from the Maestro's soul.

JOHN BOYLE O'REILLY

1844–90

A White Rose

The red rose whispers of passion,
And the white rose breathes of love;
O, the red rose is a falcon,
And the white rose is a dove.

But I send you a cream-white rosebud,
With a flush on its petal tips;
For the love that is purest and sweetest
Has a kiss of desire on the lips.

ARTHUR O'SHAUGHNESSY

1844–81

Ode

We are the music-makers
  And we are the dreamers of dreams,
Wandering by lone sea-breakers,
  And sitting by desolate streams; –
World-losers and world-forsakers,
  On whom the pale moon gleams:
Yet we are the movers and shakers
  Of the world for ever, it seems.

With wonderful deathless ditties
We build up the world's great cities,
  And out of a fabulous story
  We fashion an empire's glory:
One man with a dream, at pleasure,
  Shall go forth and conquer a crown;
And three with a new song's measure
  Can trample an empire down.

We, in the ages lying
  In the buried past of the earth,
Built Nineveh with our sighing,
  And Babel itself with our mirth;
And o'erthrew them with prophesying,
  To the old of the new world's worth;
For each age is a dream that is dying,
  Or one that is coming to birth.

EMILY LAWLESS

1845-1913

After Aughrim

She said, 'They gave me of their best,
They lived, they gave their lives for me;
I tossed them to the howling waste,
And flung them to the foaming sea.'

She said, 'I never gave them aught,
Not mine the power, if mine the will;
I let them starve, I let them bleed, –
They bled and starved, and loved me still.'

She said, 'Ten times they fought for me,
Ten times they strove with might and main,
Ten times I saw them beaten down,
Ten times they rose, and fought again.'

She said, 'I stayed alone at home,
A dreary woman, grey and cold;
I never asked them how they fared,
Yet still they loved me as of old.'

She said, 'I never called them sons,
I almost ceased to breathe their name,
Then caught it echoing down the wind,
Blown backwards from the lips of Fame.'

She said, 'Not mine, not mine that fame;
Far over sea, far over land,
Cast forth like rubbish from my shores,
They won it yonder, sword in hand.'

She said, 'God knows they owe me nought,
I tossed them to the foaming sea,
I tossed them to the howling waste,
Yet still their love comes home to me.'

ALFRED PERCEVAL GRAVES

1846–1931

Father O'Flynn

'Of priests we can offer a charmin' variety,
Far renowned for larnin' and piety;
Still, I'd advance ye widout impropriety,
   Father O'Flynn as the flower of them all.

CHORUS
Here's a health to you, Father O'Flynn,
Sláinte, and *sláinte*, and *sláinte* agin;
   Powerfulest preacher, and
   Tinderest teacher, and
Kindliest creature in ould Donegal.

Don't talk of your Provost and Fellows of Trinity
Famous for ever at Greek and Latinity,
Faix! and the divels and all at Divinity –
   Father O'Flynn 'd make hares of them all!
   Come, I vinture to give ye my word,
   Niver the likes of his logic was heard,
     Down from mythology
     Into thayology,
Troth! and conchology if he'd the call.

CHORUS
Here's a health to you, Father O'Flynn,
Sláinte and *sláinte*, and *sláinte* agin;
   Powerfulest preacher, and
   Tinderest teacher, and
Kindliest creature in ould Donegal.

Och! Father O'Flynn, you've the wonderful way wid you,
All the ould sinners are wishful to pray wid you,
All the young childer are wild for to play wid you,
   You've such a way wid you, Father avick!

Still, for all you've so gentle a soul,
Gad, you've your flock in the grandest control,
Checking the crazy ones,
Coaxin' onaisy ones,
Liftin' the lazy ones on wid the stick.

CHORUS

Here's a health to you, Father O'Flynn,
Sláinte, and *sláinte*, and *sláinte* agin;
Powerfulest preacher, and
Tinderest teacher, and
Kindliest creature in ould Donegal.

And though quite avoidin' all foolish frivolity
Still, at all seasons of innocent jollity,
Where was the play-boy could claim an equality
At comicality, Father, wid you?
Once the Bishop looked grave at your jest,
Till this remark set him off wid the rest:
'Is it lave gaiety
All to the laity?
Cannot the clargy be Irishmen too?'

CHORUS

Here's a health to you, Father O'Flynn,
Sláinte, and *sláinte*, and *sláinte* agin;
Powerfulest preacher, and
Tinderest teacher, and
Kindliest creature in ould Donegal.

WILLIAM LARMINIE

1850–1899

The Nameless Doon

Who were the builders? Question not the silence
That settles on the lake for evermore,
Save when the sea-bird screams and to the islands
The echo answers from the steep-cliffed shore.
O half-remaining ruin, in the lore
Of human life a gap shall all deplore
Beholding thee; since thou art like the dead
Found slain, no token to reveal the why,
The name, the story. Some one murdered
We know, we guess; and gazing upon thee,
And, filled by thy long silence of reply,
We guess some garnered sheaf of tragedy; –
Of tribe or nation slain so utterly
That even their ghosts are dead, and on their grave
Springeth no bloom of legend in its wildness;
And age by age weak washing round the islands
No faintest sigh of story lisps the wave.

The Speech of Emer

From Fand

Cuhoolin has been lured from his home by the goddess Fand; his wife
Emer discovers him, and pleads with him:

Heed her not, O Cuhoolin, husband mine;
Delusive is the bliss she offers thee –
Bliss that will to torment turn,
Like one bright colour for ever before thine eyes,
Since of mortal race thou art.
Man is the shadow of a changing world;
As the image of a tree
By the breeze swayed to and fro

On the grass, so changeth he;
Night and day are in his breast;
Winter and summer, all the change
Of light and darkness and the seasons marching;
Flowers that bud and fade,
Tides that rise and fall.
Even with the waxing and the waning moon
His being beats in tune;
The air that is his life
Inhales he with alternate heaving breath;
Joyous to him is effort, sweet is rest;
Life he hath and death.

Then seek not thou too soon that permanence
Of changeless joy that suits unchanging gods,
In whom no tides of being ebb and flow.
Out of the flux and reflux of the world
Slowly man's soul doth gather to itself,
Atom by atom, the hard elements –
Firm, incorruptible, indestructible –
Whereof, when all his being is compact,
No more it wastes nor hungers, but endures,
Needing not any food of changing things,
But fit among like-natured gods to live,
Amongst whom, entering too soon, he perishes,
Unable to endure their fervid gaze.
Though now thy young, heroic soul
Be mate for her immortal might,
Yet think: thy being is still but as a lake
That, by the help of friendly streams unfed,
Full soon the sun drinks up.
Wait till thou hast sea-depths –
Till all the tides of life and deed,
Of action and of meditation,
Of service unto others and their love,
Shall pour into the caverns of thy being
The might of their unconquerable floods.
Then canst thou bear the glow of eyes divine,

And like the sea beneath the sun at noon
Shalt shine in splendour inexhaustible.
Therefore be no more tempted by her lures –
Not that way lies thine immortality:
But thou shalt find it in the ways of men,
Where many a task remains for thee to do,
And shall remain for many after thee,
Till all the storm-winds of the world be bound.

Epilogue to *Fand*

Is there one desires to hear
If within the shores of Eirè
Eyes may still behold the scene
Fair from Fand's enticements?

Let him seek the southern hills
And those lakes of loveliest water
Where the richest blooms of spring
Burn to reddest autumn:
And the clearest echo sings
Notes a goddess taught her.

Ah! 'twas very long ago,
And the words are now denied her:
But the purple hillsides know
Still the tones delightsome,
And their breasts, impassioned, glow
As were Fand beside them.

And though many an isle be fair,
Fairer still is Inisfallen,
Since the hour Cuhoolin lay
In the bower enchanted.
See! the ash that waves today,
Fand its grandsire planted.

When from wave to mountain-top
All delight thy sense bewilders,
Thou shalt own the wonder wrought
Once by her skilled fingers,
Still, though many an age be gone,
Round Killarney lingers.

Consolation

From *Fand*

Yes, let us speak, with lips confirming
  The inner pledge that eyes reveal –
Bright eyes that death shall dim for ever,
  And lips that silence soon shall seal.

Yes, let us make our claim recorded
  Against the powers of earth and sky,
And that cold boon their laws award us –
  Just once to live and once to die.

Thou sayest that fate is frosty nothing,
  But love the flame of souls that are:
'Two spirits approach, and at their touching,
  Behold! an everlasting star.'

High thoughts, O love: well, let us speak them!
  Yet bravely face at least this fate:
To know the dreams of us that dream them
  On blind, unknowing things await.

If years from winter's chill recover,
  If fields are green and rivers run,
If thou and I behold each other,
  Hangs it not all on yonder sun?

So while that mighty lord is gracious
  With prodigal beams to flood the skies,

Let us be glad that he can spare us
  The light to kindle lovers' eyes.

And die assured, should life's new wonder
  In any world our slumbers break,
These the first words that each will utter:
  'Beloved, art thou too awake?'

The Sword of Tethra

From *Moytura*

The sword of Tethra is captured by the sun-god Lu. This sword is
Death.

The Sword: I am the breath of Tethra, voice of Tethra
The tongue of an utterance harsh:
I am the beat of the heart
Of the inmost darkness, that sends
Night to the world's far ends.
I am the raven of Tethra, mate of Tethra, slave of Tethra:
My joy is the storm
That strews the ground with the fruit –
Half-living, bleeding, and bruised –
From life's tree shaken.
I desire the flame of battle;
I desire gore-spouting wounds;
Flanks that are gashed, trunks that are headless
Heads that are trunkless in piles and in mounds;

*

Do you seek to bind me, ye gods,
And the deeds of me only beginning?
Shall I gloat over triumphs achieved
When the greatest remains for the winning?
Ye boast of this world ye have made,
This corpse-built world?
Show me an atom thereof
That hath not suffered and struggled,

And yielded its life to Tethra?
The rocks they are built of the mould,
And the mould of the herb that was green,
And the beast from the herb,
And man from the beast,
And downward in hurried confusion,
Through shapes that are loathsome,
Beast, man, worm, pellmell,
What does it matter to me?
All that have lived go back to the mould,
To stiffen through ages of pain
In the rock-rigid realms of death.

Ah, ah!
Loose me, ye gods!
I stifle, I faint in your hands:
Your presence benumbs me:
An effluence from you exhales,
Life deadly to death,
The poison whereof overcomes me,
And it is not my doom to perish;
Gods ye have slain that were brave and mighty,
But Tethra ye never shall slay.
    Lu: We will not loose thee till thou be subdued –
Thy venom quenched a little; till thy song
In milder music sheathe its jagged edge,
And choose a smoother speech that shall not rend.
    The Sword: Ah, ah! I gash! Alas, alas!
That even of me should soft things be averred;
I am the song unheard,
Shall ofttimes lure men's falt'ring souls away;
Soft as from summer's eve the tender light
Stolen by northern night,
My gentle call they gladly shall obey:
From them regretful tears shall flow not,
But eyes shine bright with hope to see the land they
    know not.
Loose me! loose me!

JOHN KEEGAN CASEY

1846–70

The Rising of the Moon A.D. 1798

'Oh! then tell me, Shawn O'Ferrall,
    Tell me why you hurry so?'
'Hush, ma bouchal, hush and listen,'
    And his cheeks were all a-glow.
'I bear ordhers from the captain,
    Get you ready quick and soon,
For the pikes must be together
    At the risin' of the moon.'

'Oh! then tell me, Shawn O'Ferrall
    Where the gatherin' is to be?'
'In the ould spot by the river,
    Right well known to you and me.
One word more – for signal token
    Whistle up the marching tune,
With your pike upon your shoulder
    By the risin' of the moon.'

Out from many a mud-wall cabin
    Eyes were watching thro' that night,
Many a manly chest was throbbing
    For the blessed warning light.
Murmurs passed along the valleys
    Like the banshee's lonely croon,
And a thousand blades were flashing
    At the risin' of the moon.

There beside the singing river
    That dark mass of men was seen,
Far above the shining weapons
    Hung their own beloved green.

'Death to every foe and traitor!
    Forward! strike the marchin' tune,
And hurrah, my boys, for freedom!
    'Tis the risin' of the moon.'

Well they fought for poor old Ireland
    And full bitter was their fate
(Oh! what glorious pride and sorrow
    Fill the name of Ninety-Eight.)
Yet, thank God, e'en still are beating
    Hearts in manhood's burning noon,
Who would follow in their footsteps
    At the risin' of the moon!

FANNY PARNELL

1854–82

After Death

Shall mine eyes behold thy glory, oh, my country?
  Shall mine eyes behold thy glory?
Or shall the darkness close around them ere the sun-blaze
  Break at last upon thy story?

When the nations ope for thee their queenly circle,
  As sweet new sister hail thee,
Shall these lips be sealed in callous death and silence,
  That have known but to bewail thee?

Shall the ear be deaf that only loved thy praises,
  When all men their tribute bring thee?
Shall the mouth be clay that sang thee in thy squalor,
  When all poets' mouths shall sing thee?

Ah! the harpings and the salvos and the shoutings
  Of thy exiled sons returning,
I should hear, tho' dead and mouldered, and the grave-damps
  Should not chill my bosom's burning.

Ah! the tramp of feet victorious! I should hear them
  'Mid the shamrocks and the mosses,
And my heart should toss within the shroud and quiver
  As a captive dreamer tosses.

I should turn and rend the cere-cloths round me –
  Giant sinews I should borrow –
Crying 'Oh, my brothers, I have also loved her
  In her loneliness and sorrow!

'Let me join with you the jubilant procession,
  Let me chant with you her story;
Then, contented, I shall go back to the shamrocks,
  Now mine eyes have seen her glory.'

OSCAR WILDE

1854–1900

From *The Ballad of Reading Gaol*

He did not wear his scarlet coat,
  For blood and wine are red,
And blood and wine were on his hands
  When they found him with the dead,
The poor dead woman whom he loved,
  And murdered in her bed.

He walked amongst the Trial Men
  In a suit of shabby grey;
A cricket cap was on his head,
  And his step seemed light and gay;
But I never saw a man who looked
  So wistfully at the day.

I never saw a man who looked
  With such a wistful eye
Upon that little tent of blue
  Which prisoners call the sky,
And at every drifting cloud that went
  With sails of silver by.

I walked, with other souls in pain,
  Within another ring,
And was wondering if the man had done
  A great or little thing,
When a voice behind me whispered low,
  '*That fellow's got to swing.*'

*

Six weeks the guardsman walked the yard,
  In the suit of shabby grey:
His cricket cap was on his head,
  And his step seemed light and gay,

But I never saw a man who looked
   So wistfully at the day.

I never saw a man who looked
   With such a wistful eye
Upon that little tent of blue
   Which prisoners call the sky,
And at every wandering cloud that trailed
   Its ravelled fleeces by.

He did not wring his hands, as do
   Those witless men who dare
To try to rear the changeling Hope
   In the cave of black Despair:
He only looked upon the sun,
   And drank the morning air.

He did not wring his hands nor weep,
   Nor did he peek or pine,
But he drank the air as though it held
   Some healthful anodyne;
With open mouth he drank the sun
   As though it had been wine!

And I and all the souls in pain,
   Who tramped the other ring,
Forgot if we ourselves had done
   A great or little thing,
And watched with gaze of dull amaze
   The man who had to swing.

For strange it was to see him pass
   With a step so light and gay,
And strange it was to see him look
   So wistfully at the day,
And strange it was to think that he
   Had such a debt to pay.

*

For oak and elm have pleasant leaves
   That in the spring-time shoot;
But grim to see is the gallows-tree,
   With its adder-bitten root,
And, green or dry, a man must die
   Before it bears its fruit!

The loftiest place is that seat of grace
   For which all worldlings try:
But who would stand in hempen band
   Upon a scaffold high,
And through a murderer's collar take
   His last look at the sky?

It is sweet to dance to violins
   When Love and Life are fair:
To dance to flutes, to dance to lutes,
   Is delicate and rare:
But it is not sweet with nimble feet
   To dance upon the air!

So with curious eyes and sick surmise
   We watched him day by day,
And wondered if each one of us
   Would end the self-same way,
For none can tell to what red Hell
   His sightless soul may stray.

At last the dead man walked no more
   Amongst the Trial Men,
And I knew that he was standing up
   In the black dock's dreadful pen,
And that never would I see his face
   For weal or woe again.

Like two doomed ships that pass in storm
   We had crossed each other's way:
But we made no sign, we said no word,
   We had no word to say;

For we did not meet in the holy night,
　　But in the shameful day.

A prison wall was round us both,
　　Two outcast men we were:
The world had thrust us from its heart,
　　And God from out His care:
And the iron gin that waits for Sin
　　Had caught us in its snare.

*

In Debtors' Yard the stones are hard,
　　And the dripping wall is high,
So it was there he took the air
　　Beneath the leaden sky,
And by each side a Warder walked,
　　For fear the man might die.

Or else he sat with those who watched
　　His anguish night and day;
Who watched him when he rose to weep,
　　And when he crouched to pray;
Who watched him lest himself should rob
　　Their scaffold of its prey.

*

And twice a day he smoked his pipe,
　　And drank his quart of beer:
His soul was resolute, and held
　　No hiding-place for fear;
He often said that he was glad
　　The hangman's day was near.

But why he said so strange a thing
　　No warder dared to ask:
For he to whom a watcher's doom
　　Is given as his task,
Must set a lock upon his lips
　　And make his face a mask.

Or else he might be moved, and try
    To comfort or console:
And what should Human Pity do
    Pent up in Murderer's Hole?
What word of grace in such a place
    Could help a brother's soul?

*

We tore the tarry rope to shreds
    With blunt and bleeding nails;
We rubbed the doors, and scrubbed the floors,
    And cleaned the shining rails:
And, rank by rank, we soaped the plank,
    And clattered with the pails.

We sewed the sacks, we broke the stones,
    We turned the dusty drill:
We banged the tins, and bawled the hymns,
    And sweated on the mill:
But in the heart of every man
    Terror was lying still.

So still it lay that every day
    Crawled like a weed-clogged wave:
And we forgot the bitter lot
    That waits for fool and knave,
Till once, as we tramped in from work,
    We passed an open grave.

With yawning mouth the yellow hole
    Gaped for a living thing;
The very mud cried out for blood
    To the thirsty asphalt ring:
And we knew that ere one dawn grew fair
    Some prisoner had to swing.

Right in we went, with soul intent
    On Death and Dread and Doom:

The hangman, with his little bag,
    Went shuffling through the gloom:
And I trembled as I groped my way
    Into my numbered tomb.

*

That night the empty corridors
    Were full of forms of Fear,
And up and down the iron town
    Stole feet we could not hear,
And through the bars that hide the stars
    White faces seemed to peer.

He lay as one who lies and dreams
    In a pleasant meadow-land,
The watchers watched him as he slept,
    And could not understand
How one could sleep so sweet a sleep
    With a hangman close at hand.

But there is no sleep when men must weep
    Who never yet have wept:
So we – the fool, the fraud, the knave –
    That endless vigil kept,
And through each brain on hands of pain
    Another's terror crept.

*

There is no chapel on the day
    On which they hang a man:
The Chaplain's heart is far too sick,
    Or his face is far too wan,
Or there is that written in his eyes
    Which none should look upon.

So they kept us close till nigh on noon,
    And then they rang the bell,
And the warders with their jingling keys
    Opened each listening cell,

And down the iron stair we tramped,
    Each from his separate Hell.

Out into God's sweet air we went,
    But not in wonted way,
For this man's face was white with fear,
    And that man's face was grey,
And I never saw sad men who looked
    So wistfully at the day.

I never saw sad men who looked
    With such a wistful eye
Upon that little tent of blue
    We prisoners called the sky,
And at every happy cloud that passed
    In such strange freedom by.

*

The warders strutted up and down,
    And watched their herd of brutes,
Their uniforms were spick and span,
    And they wore their Sunday suits,
But we knew the work they had been at,
    By the quicklime on their boots.

For where a grave had opened wide,
    There was no grave at all:
Only a stretch of mud and sand
    By the hideous prison-wall,
And a little heap of burning lime,
    That the man should have his pall.

*

For three long years they will not sow
    Or root or seedling there:
For three long years the unblessed spot
    Will sterile be and bare,
And look upon the wondering sky
    With unreproachful stare.

They think a murderer's heart would taint
    Each simple seed they sow.
It is not true! God's kindly earth
    Is kindlier than men know,
And the red rose would but blow more red,
    The white rose whiter blow.

T. W. ROLLESTON

1857–1920

Clonmacnoise

In a quiet water'd land, a land of roses,
  Stands Saint Kieran's city fair;
And the warriors of Erin in their famous generations
  Slumber there.

There beneath the dewy hillside sleep the noblest
  Of the clan of Conn,
Each below his stone with name in branching Ogham
  And the sacred knot thereon.

There they laid to rest the seven Kings of Tara,
  There the sons of Cairbrè sleep –
Battle-banners of the Gael that in Kieran's plain of crosses
  Now their final hosting keep.

And in Clonmacnoise they laid the men of Teffia,
  And right many a lord of Breagh;
Deep the sod above Clan Creidè and Clan Conaill,
  Kind in hall and fierce in fray.

Many and many a son of Conn the Hundred-fighter
  In the red earth lies at rest;
Many a blue eye of Clan Colman the turf covers,
  Many a swan-white breast.

(from the Irish of Angus O'Gillan)

JOHN SYNGE

1871–1909

Prelude

Still south I went and west and south again,
Through Wicklow from the morning till the night,
And far from cities, and the sites of men,
Lived with the sunshine and the moon's delight.

I knew the stars, the flowers, and the birds,
The grey and wintry sides of many glens,
And did but half remember human words,
In converse with the mountains, moors, and fens.

On an Anniversary

After reading the dates in a book of Lyrics

With Fifteen-ninety or Sixteen-sixteen
We end Cervantes, Marot, Nashe or Green:
Then Sixteen-thirteen till two score and nine,
Is Crashaw's niche, that honey-lipped divine.
And so when all my little work is done
They'll say I came in Eighteen-seventy-one,
And died in Dublin. . . . What year will they write
For my poor passage to the stall of Night?

Queens

Seven dog-days we let pass
Naming Queens in Glenmacnass,
All the rare and royal names
Wormy sheepskin yet retains,

Etain, Helen, Maeve, and Fand,
Golden Deirdre's tender hand,
Bert, the big-foot, sung by Villon,
Cassandra, Ronsard found in Lyon.
Queens of Sheba, Meath and Connaught,
Coifed with crown, or gaudy bonnet,
Queens whose finger once did stir men,
Queens were eaten of fleas and vermin,
Queens men drew like Monna Lisa,
Or slew with drugs in Rome and Pisa,
We named Lucrezia Crivelli,
And Titian's lady with amber belly,
Queens acquainted in learned sin,
Jane of Jewry's slender shin:
Queens who cut the bogs of Glanna,
Judith of Scripture, and Gloriana,
Queens who wasted the East by proxy,
Or drove the ass-cart, a tinker's doxy,
Yet these are rotten – I ask their pardon –
And we've the sun on rock and garden,
These are rotten, so you're the Queen
Of all are living, or have been.

Beg-Innish

Bring Kateen-beug and Maurya Jude
To dance in Beg-Innish,
And when the lads (they're in Dunquin)
Have sold their crabs and fish,
Wave fawny shawls and call them in,
And call the little girls who spin,
And seven weavers from Dunquin,
To dance in Beg-Innish.

I'll play you jigs, and Maurice Kean,
Where nets are laid to dry,

I've silken strings would draw a dance
From girls are lame or shy;
Four strings I've brought from Spain and France
To make your long men skip and prance,
Till stars look out to see the dance
Where nets are laid to dry.

We'll have no priest or peeler in
To dance in Beg-Innish;
But we'll have drink from M'riarty Jim
Rowed round while gannets fish,
A keg with porter to the brim,
That every lad may have his whim,
Till we up sails with M'riarty Jim
And sail from Beg-Innish.

To the Oaks of Glencree

My arms are round you, and I lean
Against you, while the lark
Sings over us, and golden lights, and green
Shadows are on your bark.

There'll come a season when you'll stretch
Black boards to cover me:
Then in Mount Jerome I will lie, poor wretch,
With worms eternally.

The Curse

*To a sister of an enemy of the author's who
disapproved of 'The Playboy'*

Lord, confound this surly sister,
Blight her brow with blotch and blister,
Cramp her larynx, lung, and liver,
In her guts a galling give her.
Let her live to earn her dinners
In Mountjoy with seedy sinners:
Lord, this judgment quickly bring,
And I'm your servant, J. M. Synge.

In Kerry

We heard the thrushes by the shore and sea,
And saw the golden stars' nativity,
Then round we went the lane by Thomas Flynn,
Across the church where bones lie out and in;
And there I asked beneath a lonely cloud
Of strange delight, with one bird singing loud,
What change you'd wrought in graveyard, rock and sea,
This new wild paradise to wake for me . . .
Yet knew no more than knew these merry sins
Had built this stack of thigh-bones, jaws and shins.

On a Birthday

Friend of Ronsard, Nashe, and Beaumont,
Lark of Ulster, Meath and Thomond,
Heard from Smyrna and Sahara
To the surf of Connemara,
Lark of April, June, and May,
Sing loudly this my Lady-day.

A Question

I asked if I got sick and died, would you
With my black funeral go walking too,
If you'd stand close to hear them talk or pray
While I'm let down in that steep bank of clay.

And, No, you said, for if you saw a crew
Of living idiots, pressing round that new
Oak coffin – they alive, I dead beneath
That board, – you'd rave and rend them with your teeth.

THOMAS MACDONAGH

1878–1916

John-John

I dreamt last night of you, John-John,
   And thought you called to me;
And when I woke this morning, John,
   Yourself I hoped to see;
But I was all alone, John-John,
   Though still I heard your call:
I put my boots and bonnet on,
   And took my Sunday shawl,
And went, full sure to find you, John,
         To Nenagh fair.

The fair was just the same as then,
   Five years ago today,
When first you left the thimble men
   And came with me away;
For there again were thimble men
   And shooting galleries,
And card-trick men and Maggie men
   Of all sorts and degrees –
But not a sight of you, John-John,
         Was anywhere.

I turned my face to home again,
   And called myself a fool
To think you'd leave the thimble men
   And live again by rule,
And go to mass and keep the fast
   And till the little patch:
My wish to have you home was past
   Before I raised the latch
And pushed the door and saw you, John,
         Sitting down there.

How cool you came in here, begad,
  As if you owned the place!
But rest yourself there now, my lad,
  'Tis good to see your face;
My dream is out, and now by it
  I think I know my mind:
At six o'clock this house you'll quit,
  And leave no grief behind; –
But until six o'clock, John-John,
        My bit you'll share.

My neighbours' shame of me began
  When first I brought you in;
To wed and keep a tinker man
  They thought a kind of sin;
But now this three year since you're gone
  'Tis pity me they do,
And that I'd rather have John-John,
  Than that they'd pity you.
Pity for me and you, John-John,
        I could not bear.

Oh, you're my husband right enough,
  But what's the good of that?
You know you never were the stuff
  To be the cottage cat,
To watch the fire and hear me lock
  The door and put out Shep –
But there now, it is six o'clock
  And time for you to step.
God bless and keep you far, John-John!
        And that's my prayer.

THOMAS MACDONAGH

The Yellow Bittern

The yellow bittern that never broke out
   In a drinking bout, might as well have drunk;
His bones are thrown on a naked stone
   Where he lived alone like a hermit monk.
O yellow bittern! I pity your lot,
   Though they say that a sot like myself is curst –
I was sober a while, but I'll drink and be wise
   For I fear I should die in the end of thirst.

It's not for the common birds that I'd mourn,
   The black-bird, the corn-crake, or the crane,
But for the bittern that's shy and apart
   And drinks in the marsh from the lone bog-drain.
Oh! if I had known you were near your death,
   While my breath held out I'd have run to you,
Till a splash from the Lake of the Son of the Bird
   Your soul would have stirred and waked anew.

My darling told me to drink no more
   Or my life would be o'er in a little short while;
But I told her 'tis drink gives me health and strength
   And will lengthen my road by many a mile.
You see how the bird of the long smooth neck
   Could get his death from the thirst at last –
Come, son of my soul, and drain your cup,
   You'll get no sup when your life is past.

In a wintering island by Constantine's halls
   A bittern calls from a wineless place,
And tells me that hither he cannot come
   Till the summer is here and the sunny days.
When he crosses the stream there and wings o'er the sea
   Then a fear comes to me he may fail in his flight –
Well, the milk and the ale are drunk every drop,
   And a dram won't stop our thirst this night.

(from the Irish of Cathal Buidhe Mac Giolla Ghunna)

PATRICK PEARSE

1879–1916

I am Ireland

I am Ireland:
I am older than the Old Woman of Beare.

Great my glory:
I that bore Cuchulainn the valiant.

Great my shame:
My own children that sold their mother.

I am Ireland:
I am lonelier than the Old Woman of Beare.

Renunciation

Naked I saw thee,
O beauty of beauty,
And I blinded my eyes
For fear I should fail.

I heard thy music,
O melody of melody,
And I closed my ears
For fear I should falter.

I tasted thy mouth,
O sweetness of sweetness,
And I hardened my heart
For fear of my slaying.

I blinded my eyes,
And I closed my ears,

I hardened my heart
And I smothered my desire.

I turned my back
On the vision I had shaped,
And to this road before me
I turned my face.

I have turned my face
To this road before me,
To the deed that I see
And the death I shall die.

The Mother

I do not grudge them: Lord, I do not grudge
My two strong sons that I have seen go out
To break their strength and die, they and a few,
In bloody protest for a glorious thing,
They shall be spoken of among their people,
The generations shall remember them,
And call them blessed;
But I will speak their names to my own heart
In the long nights;
The little names that were familiar once
Round my dead hearth.
Lord, thou art hard on mothers:
We suffer in their coming and their going;
And tho' I grudge them not, I weary, weary
Of the long sorrow – And yet I have my joy:
My sons were faithful, and they fought.

The Fool

Since the wise men have not spoken, I speak that am only a
fool;
A fool that hath loved his folly,
Yea, more than the wise men their books or their counting
houses, or their quiet homes,
Or their fame in men's mouths;
A fool that in all his days hath done never a prudent thing,
Never hath counted the cost, nor recked if another reaped
The fruit of his mighty sowing, content to scatter the seed;
A fool that is unrepentant, and that soon at the end of all
Shall laugh in his lonely heart as the ripe ears fall to the
reaping-hooks
And the poor are filled that were empty,
Tho' he go hungry.

I have squandered the splendid years that the Lord God gave
to my youth
In attempting impossible things, deeming them alone worth
the toil.
Was it folly or grace? Not men shall judge me, but God.

I have squandered the splendid years:
Lord, if I had the years I would squander them over again,
Aye, fling them from me!
For this I have heard in my heart, that a man shall scatter, not
hoard,
Shall do the deed of today, nor take thought of tomorrow's
teen,
Shall not bargain or huxter with God; or was it a jest of
Christ's
And is this my sin before men, to have taken Him at His word?

The lawyers have sat in council, the men with the keen, long
faces,

And said, 'This man is a fool,' and others have said, 'He
　　blasphemeth';
And the wise have pitied the fool that hath striven to give a
　　life
In the world of time and space among the bulks of actual
　　things,
To a dream that was dreamed in the heart, and that only the
　　heart could hold.

O wise men, riddle me this: what if the dream come true?
What if the dream come true? and if millions unborn shall
　　dwell
In the house that I shaped in my heart, the noble house of my
　　thought?
Lord, I have staked my soul, I have staked the lives of my kin
On the truth of Thy dreadful word. Do not remember my
　　failures,
But remember this my faith.

And so I speak.
Yea, ere my hot youth pass, I speak to my people and say:
Ye shall be foolish as I; ye shall scatter, not save;
Ye shall venture your all, lest ye lose what is more than all;
Ye shall call for a miracle, taking Christ at His word.
And for this I will answer, O people, answer here and
　　hereafter,
O people that I have loved shall we not answer together?

The Rebel

I am come of the seed of the people, the people that sorrow,
That have no treasure but hope,
No riches laid up but a memory
Of an Ancient glory.
My mother bore me in bondage, in bondage my mother was
　　born,

I am of the blood of serfs;
The children with whom I have played, the men and women
  with whom I have eaten,
Have had masters over them, have been under the lash of
  masters,
And, though gentle, have served churls;
The hands that have touched mine, the dear hands whose
  touch is familiar to me,
Have worn shameful manacles, have been bitten at the wrist
  by manacles,
Have grown hard with the manacles and the task-work of
  strangers,
I am flesh of the flesh of these lowly, I am bone of their bone,
I that have never submitted;
I that have a soul greater than the souls of my people's
  masters,
I that have vision and prophecy and the gift of fiery speech,
I that have spoken with God on the top of His holy hill.

And because I am of the people, I understand the people,
I am sorrowful with their sorrow, I am hungry with their
  desire:
My heart has been heavy with the grief of mothers,
My eyes have been wet with the tears of children,
I have yearned with old wistful men,
And laughed or cursed with young men;
Their shame is my shame, and I have reddened for it,
Reddened for that they have served, they who should be free,
Reddened for that they have gone in want, while others have
  been full,
Reddened for that they have walked in fear of lawyers and of
  their jailors
With their writs of summons and their handcuffs,
Men mean and cruel!
I could have borne stripes on my body rather than this shame
  of my people.

And now I speak, being full of vision;

I speak to my people, and I speak in my people's name to the
    masters of my people.
I say to my people that they are holy, that they are august,
    despite their chains,
That they are greater than those that hold them, and stronger
    and purer,
That they have but need of courage, and to call on the name of
    their God,
God the unforgetting, the dear God that loves the peoples
For whom He died naked, suffering shame.
And I say to my people's masters: Beware,
Beware of the thing that is coming, beware of the risen people,
Who shall take what ye would not give. Did ye think to
    conquer the people,
Or that Law is stronger than life and than men's desire to be
    free?
We will try it out with you, ye that have harried and held,
Ye that have bullied and bribed, tyrants, hypocrites, liars!

Christmas 1915

O King that was born
To set bondsmen free,
In the coming battle,
Help the Gael!

JOSEPH PLUNKETT

1887–1916

I See His Blood upon the Rose

I see his blood upon the rose
And in the stars the glory of his eyes,
His body gleams amid eternal snows,
His tears fall from the skies.

I see his face in every flower;
The thunder and the singing of the birds
Are but his voice – and carven by his power
Rocks are his written words.

All pathways by his feet are worn,
His strong heart stirs the ever-beating sea,
His crown of thorns is twined with every thorn,
His cross is every tree.

My Lady Has the Grace of Death

My lady has the grace of Death
Whose charity is quick to save,
Her heart is broad as heaven's breath,
Deep as the grave.

She found me fainting by the way
And fed me from her babeless breast
Then played with me as children play,
Rocked me to rest.

When soon I rose and cried to heaven
Moaning for sins I could not weep
She told me of her sorrows seven
Kissed me to sleep.

And when the morn rose bright and ruddy
And sweet birds sang on the branch above
She took my sword from her side all bloody
And died for love.

FRANCIS LEDWIDGE

1891–1917

The Wife of Llew

And Gwydion said to Math, when it was Spring:
'Come now and let us make a wife for Llew.'
And so they broke broad boughs yet moist with dew,
And in a shadow made a magic ring:
They took the violet and the meadowsweet
To form her pretty face, and for her feet
They built a mound of daisies on a wing,
And for her voice they made a linnet sing
In the wide poppy blowing for her mouth.
And over all they chanted twenty hours.
And Llew came singing from the azure south
And bore away his wife of birds and flowers.

June

Broom out the floor now, lay the fender by,
And plant this bee-sucked bough of woodbine there,
And let the window down. The butterfly
Floats in upon the sunbeam, and the fair
Tanned face of June, the nomad gipsy, laughs
Above her widespread wares, the while she tells
The farmers' fortunes in the fields, and quaffs
The water from the spider-peopled wells.

The hedges are all drowned in green grass seas,
And bobbing poppies flare like Elmo's light,
While siren-like the pollen-stainéd bees
Drone in the clover depths. And up the height
The cuckoo's voice is hoarse and broke with joy.
And on the lowland crops the crows make raid,
Nor fear the clappers of the farmer's boy,
Who sleeps, like drunken Noah, in the shade.

And loop this red rose in that hazel ring
That snares your little ear, for June is short
And we must joy in it and dance and sing,
And from her bounty draw her rosy worth.
Ay! soon the swallows will be flying south,
The wind wheel north to gather in the snow,
Even the roses spilt on youth's red mouth
Will soon blow down the road all roses go.

The Coming Poet

'Is it far to the town?' said the poet,
As he stood 'neath the groaning vane,
And the warm lights shimmered silver
On the skirts of the windy rain.
'There are those who call me,' he pleaded,
'And I'm wet and travel-sore.'
But nobody spoke from the shelter,
And he turned from the bolted door.

And they wait in the town for the poet
With stones at the gates, and jeers,
But away on the wolds of distance
In the blue of a thousand years
He sleeps with the age that knows him,
In the clay of the unborn, dead,
Rest at his weary insteps,
Fame at his crumbled head.

Thomas McDonagh

He shall not hear the bittern cry
In the wild sky, where he is lain,
Nor voices of the sweeter birds
Above the wailing of the rain.

Nor shall he know when loud March blows
Thro' slanting snows her fanfare shrill,
Blowing to flame the golden cup
Of many an upset daffodil.

But when the Dark Cow leaves the moor,
And pastures poor with greedy weeds,
Perhaps he'll hear her low at morn
Lifting her horn in pleasant meads.

The Blackbirds

I heard the Poor Old Woman say:
'At break of day the fowler came,
And took my blackbirds from their songs
Who loved me well thro' shame and blame.

No more from lovely distances
Their songs shall bless me mile by mile,
Nor to white Ashbourne call me down
To wear my crown another while.

With bended flowers the angels mark
For the skylark the place they lie,
From there its little family
Shall dip their wings first in the sky.

And when the first surprise of flight
Sweet songs excite, from the far dawn
Shall there come blackbirds loud with love,
Sweet echoes of the singers gone.

But in the lonely hush of eve
Weeping I grieve the silent bills.'
I heard the Poor Old Woman say
In Derry of the little hills.

Ireland

I called you by sweet names by wood and linn,
You answered not because my voice was new,
And you were listening for the hounds of Finn
    And the long hosts of Lugh.

And so, I came unto a windy height
And cried my sorrow, but you heard no wind,
For you were listening to small ships in flight,
    And the wail on hills behind.

And then I left you, wandering the war
Armed with will, from distant goal to goal,
To find you at the last free as of yore,
    Or die to save your soul.

And then you called to us from far and near
To bring your crown from out the deeps of time,
It is my grief your voice I couldn't hear
    In such a distant clime.

PART THREE

Yeats and After

W. B. YEATS

1865-1939

To Ireland in the Coming Times

Know, that I would accounted be
True brother of a company
That sang, to sweeten Ireland's wrong,
Ballad and story, rann and song;
Nor be I any less of them,
Because the red-rose-bordered hem
Of her, whose history began
Before God made the angelic clan,
Trails all about the written page.
When Time began to rant and rage
The measure of her flying feet
Made Ireland's heart begin to beat;
And Time bade all his candles flare
To light a measure here and there;
And may the thoughts of Ireland brood
Upon a measured quietude.

Nor may I less be counted one
With Davis, Mangan, Ferguson,
Because, to him who ponders well,
My rhymes more than their rhyming tell
Of things discovered in the deep,
Where only body's laid asleep.
For the elemental creatures go
About my table to and fro,
That hurry from unmeasured mind
To rant and rage in flood and wind;
Yet he who treads in measured ways
May surely barter gaze for gaze.
Man ever journeys on with them
After the red-rose-bordered hem.
Ah, faeries, dancing under the moon,
A Druid land, a Druid tune!

While still I may, I write for you
The love I lived, the dream I knew.
From our birthday, until we die,
Is but the winking of an eye;
And we, our singing and our love,
What measurer Time has lit above,
And all benighted things that go
About my table to and fro,
Are passing on to where may be,
In truth's consuming ecstasy,
No place for love and dream at all;
For God goes by with white footfall.
I cast my heart into my rhymes,
That you, in the dim coming times,
May know how my heart went with them
After the red-rose-bordered hem.

September 1913

What need you, being come to sense,
But fumble in a greasy till
And add the halfpence to the pence
And prayer to shivering prayer, until
You have dried the marrow from the bone?
For men were born to pray and save:
Romantic Ireland's dead and gone,
It's with O'Leary in the grave.

Yet they were of a different kind,
The names that stilled your childish play,
They have gone about the world like wind,
But little time had they to pray
For whom the hangman's rope was spun,
And what, God help us, could they save?
Romantic Ireland's dead and gone,
It's with O'Leary in the grave.

Was it for this the wild geese spread
The grey wing upon every tide;
For this that all that blood was shed,
For this Edward Fitzgerald died,
And Robert Emmet and Wolfe Tone,
All that delirium of the brave?
Romantic Ireland's dead and gone,
It's with O'Leary in the grave.

Yet could we turn the years again,
And call those exiles as they were
In all their loneliness and pain,
You'd cry, 'Some woman's yellow hair
Has maddened every mother's son':
They weighed so lightly what they gave.
But let them be, they're dead and gone,
They're with O'Leary in the grave.

The Statues

Pythagoras planned it. Why did the people stare?
His numbers, though they moved or seemed to move
In marble or in bronze, lacked character.
But boys and girls, pale from the imagined love
Of solitary beds, knew what they were,
That passion could bring character enough,
And pressed at midnight in some public place
Live lips upon a plummet-measured face.

No! Greater than Pythagoras, for the men
That with a mallet or a chisel modelled these
Calculations that look but casual flesh, put down
All Asiatic vague immensities,
And not the banks of oars that swam upon
The many-headed foam at Salamis.
Europe put off that foam when Phidias
Gave women dreams and dreams their looking-glass.

One image crossed the many-headed, sat
Under the tropic shade, grew round and slow,
No Hamlet thin from eating flies, a fat
Dreamer of the Middle Ages. Empty eyeballs knew
That knowledge increases unreality, that
Mirror on mirror mirrored is all the show.
When gong and conch declare the hour to bless
Grimalkin crawls to Buddha's emptiness.

When Pearse summoned Cuchulain to his side,
What stalked through the Post Office? What intellect,
What calculation, number, measurement, replied?
We Irish, born into that ancient sect
But thrown upon this filthy modern tide
And by its formless spawning fury wrecked,
Climb to our proper dark, that we may trace
The lineaments of a plummet-measured face.

GEORGE RUSSELL (AE)

1867–1935

On Behalf of Some Irishmen Not Followers of Tradition

They call us aliens, we are told,
Because our wayward visions stray
From that dim banner they unfold,
The dreams of worn-out yesterday.
The sum of all the past is theirs,
The creeds, the deeds, the fame, the name,
Whose death-created glory flares
And dims the spark of living flame.
They weave the necromancer's spell,
And burst the graves where martyrs slept,
Their ancient story to retell,
Renewing tears the dead have wept.
And they would have us join their dirge,
This worship of an extinct fire
In which they drift beyond the verge
Where races all outworn expire.
The worship of the dead is not
A worship that our hearts allow,
Though every famous shade were wrought
With woven thorns above the brow.
We fling our answer back in scorn:
'We are less children of this clime
Than of some nation yet unborn
Or empire in the womb of time.
We hold the Ireland in the heart
More than the land our eyes have seen,
And love the goal for which we start
More than the tale of what has been.'
The generations as they rise
May live the life men lived before,
Still hold the thought once held as wise,
Go in and out by the same door.

We leave the easy peace it brings:
The few we are shall still unite
In fealty to unseen kings
Or unimaginable light.
We would no Irish sign efface,
But yet our lips would gladlier hail
The firstborn of the Coming Race
Than the last splendour of the Gael.
No blazoned banner we unfold –
One charge alone we give to youth,
Against the sceptred myth to hold
The golden heresy of truth.

OLIVER ST JOHN GOGARTY

1878–1957

Ringsend
(*After reading Tolstoi*)

I will live in Ringsend
With a red-headed whore,
And the fan-light gone in
Where it lights the hall-door;
And listen each night
For her querulous shout,
As at last she streels in
And the pubs empty out.
To soothe that wild breast
With my old-fangled songs,
Till she feels it redressed
From inordinate wrongs,
Imagined, outrageous,
Preposterous wrongs,
Till peace at last comes,
Shall be all I will do,
Where the little lamp blooms
Like a rose in the stew;
And up the back-garden
The sound comes to me
Of the lapsing, unsoilable,
Whispering sea.

JOSEPH CAMPBELL

1879–1944

Days

The days of my life
Come and go.

One is a black valley,
Rising to blue goat-parks
On the crowns of distant hills.
I hear the falling of water
And the whisper of ferns' tongues,
And, still more, I hear
The silence.

One is a moon,
Distorted, cold –
A window without light.
The rain pits the rock-face.
The beeches cast their deadness
Into the sea.

One is a cloud of gulls
Over a plough.
The sun-married air
Is filled with their wings and their crying.
Slowly, slowly,
The lea breaks
In deep furrows of red.

The days of my life
Come and go.

SEAMAS O'SULLIVAN

1879–1958

Nelson Street

There is hardly a mouthful of air
In the room where the breakfast is set,
For the blind is still down though it's late,
And the curtains are redolent yet
Of tobacco smoke, stale from last night.
There's the little bronze teapot, and there
The eggs on the blue willow-plate,
And the sleepy canary, a hen,
Starts faintly her chirruping tweet
And I know, could she speak, she would say,
'Hullo there – what's wrong with the light?
Draw the blind up, let's look at the day.'
I see that it's Monday again,
For the man with the organ is there;
Every Monday he comes to the street
(Lest I, or the bird there, should miss
Our count of monotonous days)
With his reed-organ, wheezy and sweet,
And stands by the window and plays
'There's a Land that is Fairer than This.'

PADRAIC COLUM

1881–

Plougher

Sunset and silence! A man; around him earth savage, earth
  broken;
Beside him two horses, a plough!

Earth savage, earth broken, the brutes, the dawn-man there
  in the sunset,
And the plough that is twin to the sword, that is founder of
  cities!

'Brute-tamer, plough-maker, earth-breaker! Canst hear?
  There are ages between us –
Is it praying you are as you stand there alone in the sunset?

Surely our sky-born gods can be naught to you, earth-child
  and earth-master –
Surely your thoughts are of Pan, or of Wotan, or Dana?

Yet why give thought to the gods? Has Pan led your brutes
  where they stumble?
Has Dana numbed pain of the child-bed, or Wotan put hands
  to your plough?

What matter your foolish reply? O man standing lone and
  bowed earthward,
Your task is a day near its close. Give thanks to the night-
  giving god.'

Slowly the darkness falls, the broken lands blend with the
  savage;
The brute-tamer stands by the brutes, a head's breadth only
  above them.

A head's breadth? Aye, but therein is hell's depth and the
    height up to heaven,
And the thrones of the gods and their halls, their chariots,
    purples, and splendours.

JAMES JOYCE

1882–1941

Gas from a Burner

In September 1909, Joyce, then on a visit to Dublin, signed a contract with the Dublin firm of Maunsel and Co. to publish *Dubliners*. But George Roberts, the manager of the firm, began to find reasons first for delaying and then for censoring the manuscript. Negotiations dragged along for three years, until finally Joyce returned to Dublin in July 1912, and brought the matter to a head. Both Joyce and Roberts consulted solicitors; Roberts was advised that the use of actual names for public houses and the like was libellous, and began to demand so many changes that there was no possibility of agreement. At length he decided to accept Joyce's offer to purchase the sheets for the book, which John Falconer, a Dublin printer, had finished. But Falconer, hearing of the dispute, decided he wanted nothing to do with so unpleasant a book, and guillotined the sheets. Joyce left Dublin full of bitterness, which he vented by writing this broadside on the back of his contract with Maunsel and Co. for the publication of *Dubliners*, while he was on the train between Flushing and Salzburg.

> Ladies and gents, you are here assembled
> To hear why earth and heaven trembled
> Because of the black and sinister arts
> Of an Irish writer in foreign parts.
> He sent me a book ten years ago.[1]
> I read it a hundred times or so,
> Backwards and forwards, down and up,
> Through both ends of a telescope.
> I printed it all to the very last word
> But by the mercy of the Lord
> The darkness of my mind was rent
> And I saw the writer's foul intent.
> But I owe a duty to Ireland:
> I hold her honour in my hand,
> This lovely land that always sent
> Her writers and artists to banishment
> And in a spirit of Irish fun
> Betrayed her own leaders, one by one.

'Twas Irish humour, wet and dry,
Flung quicklime into Parnell's eye;[2]
'Tis Irish brains that save from doom
The leaky barge of the Bishop of Rome
For everyone knows the Pope can't belch
Without the consent of Billy Walsh.[3]
O Ireland my first and only love
Where Christ and Caesar are hand and glove!
O lovely land where the shamrock grows!
(Allow me, ladies, to blow my nose)
To show you for strictures I don't care a button
I printed the poems of Mountainy Mutton[4]
And a play he wrote (you've read it I'm sure)
Where they talk of 'bastard', 'bugger' and 'whore'[5]
And a play on the Word and Holy Paul
And some woman's legs that I can't recall
Written by Moore, a genuine gent
That lives on his property's ten per cent:[6]
I printed mystical books in dozens:
I printed the table-book of Cousins[7]
Though (asking your pardon) as for the verse
'Twould give you a heartburn on your arse:[8]
I printed folklore from North and South
By Gregory of the Golden Mouth:[9]
I printed poets, sad, silly and solemn:
I printed Patrick What-do-you-Colm:[10]
I printed the great John Milicent Synge
Who soars above on an angel's wing
In the playboy shift[11] that he pinched as swag
From Maunsel's manager's travelling-bag.[12]
But I draw the line at that bloody fellow,
That was over here dressed in Austrian yellow,
Spouting Italian by the hour
To O'Leary Curtis[13] and John Wyse Power[14]
And writing of Dublin, dirty and dear,
In a manner no blackamoor printer could bear.
Shite and onions![15] Do you think I'll print
The name of the Wellington Monument,

Sydney Parade and Sandymount tram,
Downes's cakeshop and Williams's jam?
I'm damned if I do – I'm damned to blazes!
Talk about *Irish Names of Places*![16]
It's a wonder to me, upon my soul,
He forgot to mention Curly's Hole.[17]
No, ladies, my press shall have no share in
So gross a libel on Stepmother Erin.[18]
I pity the poor – that's why I took
A red-headed Scotchman[19] to keep my book.
Poor sister Scotland! Her doom is fell;
She cannot find any more Stuarts to sell.
My conscience is fine as Chinese silk:
My heart is as soft as buttermilk.
Colm can tell you I made a rebate
Of one hundred pounds on the estimate
I gave him for his Irish Review.[20]
I love my country - by herrings I do!
I wish you could see what tears I weep
When I think of the emigrant train and ship.
That's why I publish far and wide
My quite illegible railway guide.
In the porch of my printing institute
The poor and deserving prostitute
Plays every night at catch-as-catch-can
With her tight-breeched British artilleryman
And the foreigner learns the gift of the gab
From the drunken draggletail Dublin drab.
Who was it said: Resist not evil?[21]
I'll burn that book, so help me devil.
I'll sing a psalm as I watch it burn
And the ashes I'll keep in a one-handled urn.
I'll penance do with farts and groans
Kneeling upon my marrowbones.
This very next lent I will unbare
My penitent buttocks to the air
And sobbing beside my printing press
My awful sin I will confess.

My Irish foreman from Bannockburn[22]
Shall dip his right hand in the urn
And sign crisscross with reverent thumb
Memento homo[23] upon my bum.

1. George Roberts is the speaker.

2. This incident, which Joyce also mentions in 'The Shade of Parnell', occurred at Castlecomer in the summer of 1891, according to Parnell's biographer and friend, R. Barry O'Brien.

3. His Grace the Most Reverend William J. Walsh, D.D., Archbishop of Dublin.

4. Joseph Campbell, author of *The Mountainy Singer*, published by Maunsel in 1909.

5. Campbell's *Judgment: a Play in Two Acts*, published by Maunsel in 1912, contains on p. 25 the words 'bastard' and 'whore'.

6. *The Apostle*, published by Maunsel in 1911. Moore's play, in which Christ (the Word) and Paul meet after Christ's death, includes a dialogue between Christ and Mary in which Mary laments her lost beauty. In a long preface Moore surveys the Bible for evidence of sensuality and remarks (p. 9) 'In Samuel we read how David was captured by the sweetness of Bathsheba's legs while bathing . . .', and (p. 26) 'It may be doubted whether Paul always succeeded in subduing these infirmities of the flesh, but we would not love him less, even if we knew that he had loved St Eunice not wisely but too well.'

7. James Cousins, a Dublin Theosophist and poet. The 'table-book' is probably his *Etain the Beloved and Other Poems*, published by Maunsel in 1912.

8. An expression of Joyce's father; see *Ulysses*, Penguin Books, p. 125 (115).

9. Maunsel published Lady Gregory's *Kiltartan History Book* in 1909 and *The Kiltartan Wonder Book* in 1910.

10. Padraic Colum.

11. The word 'shift', spoken by a character in Synge's *Playboy of the Western World*, caused a riot at the Abbey Theatre in 1907; Maunsel published the play in the same year.

12. Roberts was a traveller in ladies' underwear.

13. A Dublin journalist.

14. An official in the Royal Irish Constabulary in Dublin Castle, and a man of considerable cultivation. He figures largely in *Ulysses* in the characters of Jack Power and John Wyse Nolan.

15. An expression of Joyce's father; see *Ulysses*, p. 127 (117).

16. *The Origin and History of Irish Names of Places*, by Patrick Weston Joyce, no relation to James.

17. A bathing pool at Dollymount, Clontarf.

18. As Dr Oliver Gogarty remarks, in *Mourning Becomes Mrs Spendlove* (N.Y., 1948) p. 61, Roberts was an Ulster Scot, so Erin is only his step-mother.

19. Roberts himself.

20. The *Irish Review* was edited by Colum from March 1912 to July 1913.

21. Christ, in the Sermon on the Mount.

22. In Scotland.

23. 'Memento, homo, quia pulvis es', the words of the priest on Ash Wednesday as he marks the cross of ashes on the communicant's forehead.

JAMES STEPHENS

1882–1950

A Glass of Beer

The lanky hank of a she in the inn over there
Nearly killed me for asking the loan of a glass of beer;
May the devil grip the whey-faced slut by the hair,
And beat bad manners out of her skin for a year.

That parboiled ape, with the toughest jaw you will see
On virtue's path, and a voice that would rasp the dead,
Came roaring and raging the minute she looked at me,
And threw me out of the house on the back of my head!

If I asked her master he'd give me a cask a day;
But she, with the beer at hand, not a gill would arrange!
May she marry a ghost and bear him a kitten, and may
The High King of Glory permit her to get the mange.

AUSTIN CLARKE

1896–1974

Martha Blake

Before the day is everywhere
And the timid warmth of sleep
Is delicate on limb, she dares
The silence of the street
Until the double bells are thrown back
For Mass and echoes bound
In the chapel yard, O then her soul
Makes bold in the arms of sound.

But in the shadow of the nave
Her well-taught knees are humble,
She does not see through any saint
That stands in the sun
With veins of lead, with painful crown:
She waits that dreaded coming,
When all the congregation bows
And none may look up.

The word is said, the Word sent down,
The miracle is done
Beneath those hands that have been rounded
Over the embodied cup,
And with a few, she leaves her place
Kept by an east-filled window
And kneels at the communion rail
Starching beneath her chin.

She trembles for the Son of Man,
While the priest is murmuring
What she can scarcely tell, her heart
Is making such a stir;
But when he picks a particle
And she puts out her tongue,

That joy is the glittering of candles
And benediction sung.

Her soul is lying in the Presence
Until her senses, one
By one, desiring to attend her,
Come as for feast and run
So fast to share the sacrament,
Her mouth must mother them:
'Sweet tooth grow wise, lip, gum be gentle,
I touch a purple hem.'

Afflicted by that love she turns
To multiply her praise,
Goes over all the foolish words
And finds they are the same;
But now she feels within her breast
Such calm that she is silent,
For soul can never be immodest
Where body may not listen.

On a holy day of obligation
I saw her first in prayer,
But mortal eye had been too late
For all that thought could dare.
The flame in heart is never grieved
That pride and intellect
Were cast below, when God revealed
A heaven for this earth.

So to begin the common day
She needs a miracle,
Knowing the safety of angels
That see her home again,
Yet ignorant of all the rest,
The hidden grace that people
Hurrying to business
Look after in the street.

The Straying Student

On a holy day when sails were blowing southward,
A bishop sang the Mass at Inishmore,
Men took one side, their wives were on the other
But I heard the woman coming from the shore:
And wild in despair my parents cried aloud
For they saw the vision draw me to the doorway.

Long had she lived in Rome when Popes were bad,
The wealth of every age she makes her own,
Yet smiled on me in eager admiration,
And for a summer taught me all I know,
Banishing shame with her great laugh that rang
As if a pillar caught it back alone.

I learned the prouder counsel of her throat,
My mind was growing bold as light in Greece;
And when in sleep her stirring limbs were shown,
I blessed the noonday rock that knew no tree:
And for an hour the mountain was her throne,
Although her eyes were bright with mockery.

They say I was sent back from Salamanca
And failed in logic, but I wrote her praise
Nine times upon a college wall in France.
She laid her hand at darkfall on my page
That I might read the heavens in a glance
And I knew every star the Moors have named.

Awake or in my sleep, I have no peace now,
Before the ball is struck, my breath has gone,
And yet I tremble lest she may deceive me
And leave me in this land, where every woman's son
Must carry his own coffin and believe,
In dread, all that the clergy teach the young.

MONK GIBBON
1896–

Salt

Often,
Stepping so delicately through the shrubbery of learning,
The spring mist lighter than a wisp of cloud,
Pearling the leaves and spider-webs with jewels,
Tiptoe, excited, full of hope,
The greedy thumb and index tightly pressed,
But ready in an instant to release
Some grains of less-than-Attic apprehension,
I thought, 'With but a little further zeal she's mine!'
The tracery of her three-toed imprint patterned
Even the mud with tiny hieroglyphics;
And Plato's diligence had brandished once
Handfuls of gem-bright feathers. All was well.
It was delight merely to sniff the morning
And know the wood was haunted by her. Others had said
She hung, in safety caged, above a hundred doorways,
Twittering her daily reassurance.
O mystery of existence, shy as air,
Sometimes a thought, a single phrase, a sentence,
Some intimation not in words at all
But in some earth-borne and earth-bitter fragrance
Seemed to presage for me the ecstatic moment
When, lip to finger, poised for the final step,
I'd launch myself, and with wild joy would feel
Under my hand at last her pulsing heart.
Time was when such hopes were. I did not know
Truth tumbles in the vast and limitless heaven,
Hops, out of reach, a yard or so away,
Or perches in the branch her soul has chosen.

F. R. HIGGINS

1896–1941

Father and Son

Only last week, walking the hushed fields
Of our most lovely Meath, now thinned by November,
I came to where the road from Laracor leads
To the Boyne river – that seemed more lake than river,
Stretched in uneasy light and stript of reeds.

And walking longside an old weir
Of my people's, where nothing stirs – only the shadowed
Leaden flight of a heron up the lean air –
I went unmanly with grief, knowing how my father,
Happy though captive in years, walked last with me there.

Yes, happy in Meath with me for a day
He walked, taking stock of herds hid in their own breathing;
And naming colts, gusty as wind, once steered by his hand,
Lightnings winked in the eyes that were half shy in greeting
Old friends – the wild blades, when he gallivanted the land.

For that proud, wayward man now my heart breaks –
Breaks for that man whose mind was a secret eyrie,
Whose kind hand was sole signet of his race,
Who curbed me, scorned my green ways, yet increasingly
    loved me
Till Death drew its grey blind down his face.

And yet I am pleased that even my reckless ways
Are living shades of his rich calms and passions –
Witnesses for him and for those faint namesakes
With whom now he is one, under yew branches,
Yes, one in a graven silence no bird breaks.

R. N. D. WILSON

1899–1953

Enemies

... And you, O most of all
I hate, whose wisdom is
But to be cynical, –
The knave's analysis.
You who have never known
The heart set wild with a word,
Or seen the swallows blown
Northward when spring has stirred
The wing's rebellion.
I wonder if you found,
Beaten with wind and sun,
A swallow on the ground,
Would even a moment's thought
Trouble you with a fleet
Pain, that such daring brought
Such passionate defeat.

PATRICK MACDONOGH

1902–61

The Widow of Drynam

I stand in my door and look over the low fields of Drynam.
No man but the one man has known me, no child but the one
Grew big at my breast, and what are my sorrows beside
That pride and that glory? I come from devotions on Sunday
And leave them to pity or spite, and though I who had music
    have none
But crying of seagulls at morning and calling of curlews at
    night,
I wake and remember my beauty and think of my son
Who would stare the loud fools into silence
And rip the dull parish asunder.

Small wonder indeed he was wild with breeding and beauty
And why would my proud lad not straighten his back from
    the plough?
My son was not got and I bound in a cold bed of duty
Nor led to the side of the road by some clay-clabbered lout!
No, but rapt by a passionate poet away from the dancers
To curtains and silver and firelight.
O wisely and gently he drew down the pale shell of satin
And all the bright evening's adornment and clad me
Again in the garment of glory, the joy of his eyes.

I stand in my door and look over the low fields of Drynam
When skies move westward, the way he will come from the
    war;
Maybe on a morning of March when a thin sun is shining
And starlings have blackened the thorn,
He will come, my bright limb of glory, my mettlesome wild
    one,
With coin in his pocket and tales on the tip of his tongue;

And the proud ones that slight me will bring back forgotten
  politeness
To see me abroad on the roads with my son,
The two of us laughing together or stepping in silence.

EWART MILNE

1903–

Ballad for an Orphan

My mother was of Ireland,
My father came to dance.
He laid her down in Ireland
As time and fate and chance
Did work. A fiddle played in France.
The stars shook off their trance.

My father was of England,
He wore the English red,
But he laid his head in Ireland
Deep in my mother's bed –
His foolish head –
Deep in her emerald bed.

A shout arose in Ireland
And to drive the English out,
My father shook his handsome head,
His pipe smoked in and out.
A business man need never heed
Such foolish shout.

My mother died, my father wept,
Oh on my bed his head he dropped –
His handsome head –
And there he wept and I lay still.
Mavrone, I said, there is a mill
Grinds sure for all who wed.

My father lies in Ireland
Forgotten and unmourned.
He lies upon her grass-green grave
That by her hearth he scorned;

The fiddle played in France is gone,
And about the world has roamed.

Now, Father dear, this is your son
That wears both green and red,
And battles for the commonweal –
The iron road to tread –
His mother's breastbone sings upon
Your lion head.

C. DAY LEWIS

1904–72

Remembering Con Markievicz

Child running wild in woods of Lissadell:
Young lady from the Big House, seen
In a flowered dress gathering wild flowers: Ascendancy queen
Of hunts, house-parties, practical jokes – who could foretell
(Oh fiery shade, impetuous bone)
Where all was regular, self-sufficient, gay,
Their lovely hoyden lost in a nation's heroine?
Laughterless now the sweet demesne,
And the gaunt house looks blank on Sligo Bay
A nest decayed, an eagle flown.

The Paris studio, your playboy Count
Were not enough, nor Castle splendour
And fame of horsemanship. You were the tinder
Waiting a match, a runner tuned for the pistol's sound,
Impatient shade, long-suffering bone.
In a Balally cottage you found a store
Of Sinn Fein papers. You read (maybe the old sheets can
      while
The time.) The flash lights up a whole
Ireland which you have never known before,
A nest betrayed, its eagles gone.

The road to Connolly and Stephen's Green
Showed clear. The great heart which defied
Irish prejudice, English snipers, died
A little not to have shared a grave with the fourteen.
Oh fiery shade, intransigent bone!
And when the Treaty emptied the British jails,
A haggard woman returned and Dublin went wild to greet her.
But still it was not enough: an iota
Of compromise, she cried, and the Cause fails
Nest disarrayed, eagles undone.

Fanatic, bad actress, figure of fun –
She was called each. Ever she dreamed,
Fought, suffered for a losing side, it seems,
(The side which always at last is seen to have won).
Oh fiery shade and unvexed bone!
Remember a heart impulsive, gay and tender,
Still to an ideal Ireland and its real poor alive.
When she died in a pauper bed, in love
All the poor of Dublin rose to lament her.
A nest is made, an eagle flown.

PADRAIC FALLON

1905–

Field Observation

There died last night
In a poor thatch that whiskered heavy man
Who used to go my road
Peaceful as Saturn and as countryfied;

In a flit of moonlight,
With the town dwarf complaining in his sleep,
He left corpse and corner,
A broken pot and one bright glass of water.

No more will all things cast
His measure, horoscope or the great size of his breath,
Who was each year reborn
In the annual excursion of the corn;

Who moved in the gravity
Of some big sign, and slowly on the plough
Came out anew in orbit
With birds and seasons circling him by habit;

Morning fell upon
His horses, and the weather moved behind;
From cold Christmas he
Moved up the hill in every leafing tree.

Now the windy fallow
For harmony must invent him in its turn,
Whiskers, seeds and eyes,
His bags about him and his flapping skies;

One day the low-fired sun
In hedges bare and barbed as rolls of wire,

An old stiff half-rayed figure, the sole reason
For each divulging season;

In hayloads lost in June, in
Autumn the wheaten man, while
At their harps together
His strawpale daughters tinkling in the weather;

No other kin, not one
Beam from the blues in the cold cowyards round
The mountain where the crows knew him but never
The women clinging to the winter flaws;

And leaves no name
A season won't erase, old Walrus-face
Who lined the surging team
On a long furrow straight as the morning beam.

BRYAN GUINNESS

1905–

By Loch Etive

The flowers of the flags
Are like yellow birds, hanging
Over the secret pool.

The fronds of the ferns
Are like green serpents, curling
Beside the silent path.

The lashes of your lids
Are like a bird's wing, sweeping
Across your regard.

The softness of your speech
Is like rain, falling
Among parched thoughts.

The lenience of your lips
Is like a cloud, dissolving
At the kiss of the wind.

From your deep consideration
Runs the dark stream, nourishing
The lake of my delight.

PATRICK KAVANAGH

1905–67

Shancoduff

My black hills have never seen the sun rising,
Eternally they look north towards Armagh.
Lot's wife would not be salt if she had been
Incurious as my black hills that are happy
When dawn whitens Glassdrummond chapel.

My hills hoard the bright shillings of March
While the sun searches in every pocket.
They are my Alps and I have climbed the Matterhorn
With a sheaf of hay for three perishing calves
In the field under the Big Forth of Rocksavage.

The sleety winds fondle the rushy beards of Shancoduff
While the cattle-drovers sheltering in the Featherna Bush
Look up and say: 'Who owns them hungry hills
That the water-hen and snipe must have forsaken?
A poet? Then by heavens he must be poor.'
I hear and is my heart not badly shaken?

Prelude

Give us another poem, he said
Or they will think your muse is dead;
Another middle-age departure
Of Apollo from the trade of archer.
Bring out a book as soon as you can
To let them see you're a living man,
Whose comic spirit is untamed
Though sadness for a little claimed

The precedence; and tentative
You pulled your punch and wondered if
Old cunning Silence might not be
A better bet than poetry.

You have not got the countenance
To hold the angle of pretence,
That angry bitter look for one
Who knows that art's a kind of fun;
That all true poems laugh inwardly
Out of grief-born intensity.
Dullness alone can get you beat
And so can humour's counterfeit.
You have not got a chance with fraud
And might as well be true to God.

Then link your laughter out of doors
In sunlight past the sick-faced whores
Who chant the praise of love that isn't
And bring their bastards to be Christened
At phoney founts by bogus priests
With rites mugged up by journalists.
Walk past professors looking serious
Fondling an unpublished thesis –
'A child! my child! my darling son'
Some Poets of Nineteen Hundred and One.
Note well the face profoundly grave.
An empty mind can house a knave.
Be careful to show no defiance.
They've made pretence into a science:
Card-sharpers of the art committees
Working all the provincial cities,
They cry 'Eccentric' if they hear
A voice that seems at all sincere.
Fold up their table and their gear
And with the money disappear.
But satire is unfruitful prayer,

Only wild shoots of pity there,
And you must go inland and be
Lost in compassion's ecstasy,
Where suffering soars in summer air –
The millstone has become a star.

Count then your blessings, hold in mind
All that has loved you or been kind:
Those women on their mercy missions,
Rescue work with kiss or kitchens,
Perceiving through the comic veil
The poet's spirit in travail.

Gather the bits of road that were
Not gravel to the traveller
But eternal lanes of joy
On which no man who walks can die.
Bring in the particular trees
That caught you in their mysteries.
And love again the weeds that grew
Somewhere specially for you.
Collect the river and the stream
That flashed upon a pensive theme,
And a positive world make,
A world man's world cannot shake,
And do not lose love's resolution
Though face to face with destitution.

If Platitude should claim a place
Do not denounce his humble face;
His sentiments are well-intentioned
He has a part in the larger legend.

So now my gentle tiger burning
In the forest of no-yearning
Walk on serenely, do not mind
That Promised Land you thought to find

Where the worldly-wise and rich take over
The mundane problems of the lover.
Ignore Power's schismatic sect
Lovers alone lovers protect.

Lough Derg

From Cavan and from Leitrim and from Mayo,
From all the thin-faced parishes where hills
Are perished noses running peaty water,
They come to Lough Derg to fast and pray and beg
With all the bitterness of nonentities, and the envy
Of the inarticulate when dealing with the artist.
Their hands push closed the doors that God holds open;
Love-sunlit is an enchanter in June's hours
And flowers and light. These to shopkeepers and small lawyers
Are heresies up beauty's sleeve.
The naïve and simple go on pilgrimage too,
Lovers trying to take God's truth for granted . . .
Listen to the chanted
Evening devotions in the limestone church,
For this is Lough Derg, St Patrick's Purgatory.
He came to this island-acre of limestone once
To be shut of the smug too-faithful. The story
Is different now.
Solicitors praying for cushy jobs
To be County Registrar or Coroner,
Shopkeepers threatened with sharper rivals
Than any hook-nosed foreigner.
Mothers whose daughters are Final Medicals,
Too heavy-hipped for thinking,
Wives whose husbands have angina pectoris,
Wives whose husbands have taken to drinking.

But there were the sincere as well
The innocent who feared the hell

Of sin. The girl who had won
A lover and the girl who had none
Were both in trouble
Trying to encave in the rubble
Of these rocks the Real,
The part that can feel.
And the half-pilgrims too,
They who are the true
Spirit of Ireland, who joke
Through the Death-mask and take
Virgins of heaven or flesh,
Were on Lough Derg Island
Wanting some half-wish.

Over the black waves of the lake trip the last echoes
Of the bell that has shooed through the chapel door
The last pilgrims, like hens to roost.
The sun through Fermanagh's furze fingers
Looks now on the deserted penance rings of stone
Where only John Flood on St Kevin's Bed lingers
With the sexton's heaven-sure stance, the man who knows
The ins and outs of religion . . .
'Hail glorious St Patrick' a girl sings above
The old-man drone of the harmonium.
The rosary is said and Benediction.
The sacramental sun turns round and 'Holy, Holy, Holy'
The pilgrims cry, striking their breasts in Purgatory.
The same routine and ritual now
As serves for street processions or congresses
That take all shapes of souls as a living theme
In a novel refuses nothing. No truth oppresses.

Women and men in bare feet turn again
To the iron crosses and the rutted Beds,
Their feet are swollen and their bellies empty –
But something that is Ireland's secret leads
These petty mean people
For here's the day of a poor soul freed

To a marvellous beauty above its head.
The Castleblaney grocer trapped in the moment's need
Puts out a hand and writes what he cannot read,
A wisdom astonished at every turn
By some angel that writes in the oddest words.
When he will walk again in Muckno Street
He'll hear from the kitchens of fair-day eating houses
In the after-bargain carouses
News from a country beyond the range of birds.
The lake waves caught the concrete stilts of the Basilica
That spread like a bulldog's hind paws. A Leitrim man
With a face as sad as a flooded hay-field,
Leaned in an angle of the walls with his rosary beads in his
    hands.
Beside St Brigid's Cross – an ancient relic
A fragment of the Middle Ages set
Into the modern masonry of the conventional Basilica
Where everything is ordered and correct –
A queue of pilgrims waiting to renounce
The World, the Flesh, the Devil and all his house.

    Like young police recruits being measured
Each pilgrim flattened backwards to the wall
And stretched his arms wide
As he cried:
'I renounce the World, the Flesh and the Devil';
Three times they cried out. A country curate
Stared with a curate leer – he was proud.
The booted
Prior passes by ignoring all the crowd.

    'I renounce the World', a young woman cried
Her breasts stood high in the pagan sun.
'I renounce . . .' an old monk followed. Then a fat lawyer.
They rejected one by one
The music of Time's choir.
A half-pilgrim looked up at the Carrara marbles,
St Patrick wearing an alb with no stitch dropped.

Once he held a shamrock in his hand
But the stem was flawed and it got lost.
St Brigid and the Blessed Virgin flanked
Ireland's national apostle
On the south-west of the island on the gravel-path
Opposite the men's hostel.
Around the island like soldiers quartered round a barrack-
    yard
There were houses and a stall where *Agnus Dei*s
And Catholic Truth pamphlets were sold.
And at the pier end, the grey chapel of St Mary's.

The middle of the island looked like the memory
Of some village evicted by the Famine,
Some corner of a field beside a well
Old stumps of walls where a stunted boortree is growing.
These were the holy cells of saintly men –
O that was the place where Mickey Fehan lived
And the Reillys before they went to America in the Fifties.
No, this is Lough Derg in County Donegal –
So much alike is our historical
And spiritual pattern, a heap
Of stones anywhere is consecrated
By love's terrible need.

On Lough Derg, too, the silver strands
Of the individual sometimes show
Through the fabric of prison anonymity.
One man's private trouble transcending the divinity
Of the prayer-locked multitude.
A vein of humanity that can bleed
Through the thickest hide.
And such a plot unfolds a moment, so –

In a crevice between the houses and the lake
A tall red-headed man of thirty slouches,
A half-pilgrim who hated prayer,
All truth for which St Patrick's Purgatory vouches.

He was a small farmer who was fond of literature
In a country-schoolmaster way.
He skimmed the sentiment of every pool of experience
And talked heresy lightly from distances
Where nothing was terrifying Today
Where he felt he could be safe and say or sin –
But Christ sometimes bleeds in the museum.
It was the first day of his pilgrimage.
He came to Lough Derg to please the superstition
Which says: 'At least the thing can do no harm'
Yet he alone went out with Jesus fishing.

An ex-monk from Dublin, a broad-faced man
With his Franciscan habit, staggering in a megrim
Between doubt and vanity's courtesan.
He had fallen once and secretly, no shame
Tainted the young girl's name,
A convent schoolgirl knowing
Nothing of earth sowing.
He took her three times
As in his day-dreams
These things happened.
Three times finds all
The notes of body's madrigal.
'Twas a failing otherwise
Lost him his priestly faculties.

Barefoot in the kitchen
Of John Flood's cottage
Where the girls of Donegal sat, laughing round on stools,
And iron cranes and crooks
Were loaded with black pots,
And holy-looking women kept going in and out of the rooms
As though some man was a-waking . . .
The red-haired man came in
And saw among the loud cold women one who
Was not a Holy Biddy
With a rat-trap on her diddy,

But something from the unconverted kingdom
The beauty that has turned
Convention into forests
Where Adam wanders deranged with half a memory;
And red-haired Robert Fitzsimons
Saw Aggie Meegan, and quietly
An angel was turning over the pages of Mankind's history.
He must have her, she was waiting
By the unprotected gable
Of asceticism's granite castle. The masonry's down
And the sun coming in its blood
The green of trees is lust
He saw from the unpeopled country into a town.

   Let beauty bag or burst
The sharp points of truth may not be versed
Too smoothly, but the truth must go in as it occurred
A bulb of light in the shadows of Lough Derg.

   The first evening they prayed till nine o'clock
Around the gravel rings, a hundred decades
Of rosaries until they hardly knew what words meant –
Their own names when they spoke them sounded mysterious.
They knelt and prayed and rose and prayed
And circled the crosses and kissed the stones
Never looking away from the brimstone bitterness
To the little islands of Pan held in the crooked elbow of the
     lake,
They closed their eyes to Donegal and the white houses
On the slope of the northern hills
And these pilgrims of a western reason
Were not pursuing French-hot miracles.
There were hundreds of them tripping one another
Upon the pilgrim way (O God of Truth
Keep him who tells this story straight,
Let no cheap insincerity shape his mouth).
These men and boys were not led there
By priests of Maynooth or stories of Italy or Spain

For this is the penance of the poor
Who knows what beauty hides in misery
As beggars, fools and eastern fakirs know.

Black tea, dry bread.
Yesterday's pilgrims went upstairs to bed
And as they slept
The vigil in St Patrick's prison was kept
By the others. The Evening Star
Looked into Purgatory whimsically. Night dreams are
Simple and catching as music-hall tunes
Of the Nineties. We'll ramble through the brambles of starry-
      strange Junes.

On a seat beside the women's hostel four men
Sat and talked spare minutes away;
It was like Sunday evening on a country road
Light and gay.
The talk was 'There's a man
Who must be twenty stone weight – a horrid size . . .'
'Larry O'Duff . . . yes, like a balloon
Or a new tick of chaff . . . Lord, did anyone ever see clearer
      skies?'
'No rain a while yet, Joe
And the turnips could be doing with a sup, you know'.
And in the women's talk too, was woven
Such earth to cool the burning brain of Heaven.
On the steps of the church the monks talked
To Robert of art, music, literature.
'Genius is not measured', he said,
'In prudent feet and inches
Old Justice burns the work of Raphael –
Justice was God until he saw His Son
Falling in love with earth's fantastic one,
The woman in whose dunghill of emotion
Grows flowers of poetry, music, and the old
Kink in the mind, the fascination
Of sin troubled the mind of God

Until He thought of Charity . . .
Have you known Charity? Have I?'
Aggie Meegan passed by
To vigil. Robert was puzzled, where
Grew the germ of this crooked prayer?
The girl was thrilling as joy's despair.

  A schoolmaster from Roscommon led
The vigil prayer that night
'Hail Queen of Heaven' they sang at twelve.
Someone snored near the porch. A bright
Moon sailed in from the County Tyrone
By the water route that he might make
Queer faces in the stained-glassed windows. Why should sun
Have all the fun?
'Our vows of Baptism we again take . . .'
Every Rosary brought the morning nearer.
The schoolmaster looked at his watch and said:
'Out now for a mouthful of fresh air –
A ten-minute break to clear the head'.
It was cold in the rocky draughts between the houses
Old women tried
To pull bare feet close to their bellies.
Three o'clock rang from the Prior's house clock.
In the hostel pilgrims slept away a three day fast.

  On the cell wall beside the sycamore tree
The tree that never knew a bird
Aggie sat fiddling with her Rosary
And doubting the power of Lough Derg
To save the season's rose of life
With the ponderous fingers of prayer's philosophy.
Robert was a philosopher, a false one
Who ever takes a sledge to swat a fly.
He talked to the girls as a pedant professor
Talking in a university.

  The delicate precise immediacy

That sees a flower half a foot away
He could not learn. He spoke to Aggie
Of powers, passions, with the *naïveté*
Of a ploughman. She did not understand –
She only knew that she could hold his hand
If he stood closer. 'Virtue is sublime'
He said, 'and it is virtue is the frame
Of all love and learning . . .'
'I want to tell you something', she whispered,
'Because you are different and will know . . .'
'You don't need to tell me anything, you could not,
For your innocence is pure glass that I see through'.
'You'd be surprised', she smiled. O God, he gasped
To his soul, what could she mean by that?
They watched the lake waves clapping cold hands together
And saw the morning breaking as it breaks
Over a field where a man is watching a calving cow.
New life, new day.
A half-pilgrim saw it as a rabbiter
Poaching in wood sees
Primeval magic among the trees.

The rusty cross of St Patrick had a dozen
Devotees clustered around it at four o'clock.
Bare knees were going round Saint Brendan's Bed.
A boy was standing like a ballet dancer poised on the rock
Under the belfry; he stared over at Donegal
Where the white houses on the side of the hills
Popped up like mushrooms in September.
The sun was smiling on a thousand hayfields
That hour, and he must have thought Lough Derg
More unreasonable than ordinary stone.
Perhaps it was an iceberg
That he had glanced at on his journey from Japan,
But the iceberg filled a glass of water
And poured it to the honour of the sun.

Lough Derg in the dawn poured rarer cups. Prayer

And fast that makes the sourest drink rare,
Was that St Paul
Riding his ass down a lane in Donegal?
Christ was lately dead,
Men were afraid
With a new fear, the fear
Of love. There was a laugh freed
For ever and for ever. The Apostles' Creed
Was a fireside poem, the talk of the town ...
They remember a man who has seen Christ in his thorny
    crown.

John Flood came out and climbed the rock to ring
His bell for six o'clock. He spoke to the pilgrims:
'Was the night fine?'
'Wonderful, wonderful', they answered, 'not too cold –
Thank God we have the worst part over us'.

The bell brought the sleepers from their cubicles.
Grey-faced boatmen were getting out a boat.
Mass was said. Another day began.
The penance wheel turned round again.
Pilgrims went out in boats, singing
'O Fare Thee Well, Lough Derg' as they waved
Affection to the persecuting stones.

The Prior went with them – suavely, goodily
Priestly, painfully directing the boats.
They who were left behind
Felt like the wellwishers who keep house when the funeral
Has left for the chapel.

Lough Derg overwhelmed the individual imagination
And the personal tragedy.
Only God thinks of the dying sparrow
In the middle of a war.
The ex-monk, farmer and the girl
Melted in the crowd

– 353 –

Where only God, the poet
Followed with interest till he found
Their secret, and constructed from
The chaos of its fire
A reasonable document.

A man's the centre of the world,
A man is not anonymous
Member of the general public.
The Communion of Saints
Is a Communion of Individuals.
God the Father is the Father
Of each one of us.

Then there was war, the slang, the contemporary
     touch
The ideologies of the daily papers
They must seem realer, Churchill, Stalin, Hitler,
Than ideas in the contemplative cloister.
The battles where ten thousand men die
Are more significant than a peasant's emotional problem.
But wars will be merely dry bones in histories
And these common people real living creatures in it
On the unwritten spaces between the lines.
A man throws himself prostrate
And God lies down beside him like a woman
Consoling the hysteria of her lover
That sighs his passion emptily:
'The next time, love, you shall faint in me'.

'Don't ask for life', the monk said,
'If you meet her
Be easy with your affection
She's a traitor
To those who love too much
As I have done'.
'What have you done?' said Robert
'That you've come

To St Patrick's Purgatory?'
The monk told his story
Of how he thought that he
Could make reality
Of the romance of the books
That told of Popes,
Men of genius who drew
Wild colours on the flat page. He knew
Now that madness is not knowing
That laws for the mown hay
Will not serve that which is growing.
Through Lough Derg's fast and meditation
He learned the wisdom of his generation.
He was satisfied now his heart
Was free from the coquetry of art.
Something was unknown
To Robert, not long,
For Aggie told him all
That hour as they sat on the wall
Of Brendan's cell:
Birth, bastardy and murder –
He only heard rocks crashing distantly
When John Flood rang the mid-day bell.

Now the three of them got out of the story altogether
Almost. Now they were not three egotists
But part of the flood of humanity
Anonymous, never to write or be written.
They vanish among the forests and we see them
Appearing among the trees for seconds.
Lough Derg rolls its caravan before us
And as the pilgrims pass their thoughts are reckoned.
St Patrick was there, that peasant-faced man,
Whose image was embroidered on political banners
In the days of the A.O.H. and John Redmond.
A kindly soft man this Patrick was, like a farmer
To whom no man might be afraid to tell a story
Of bawdy life as it goes on in country places.

Was St Patrick like that?
A shamrock in a politician's hat
Yesterday. Today
The sentimentality of an Urban Councillor
Moving an address of welcome to the Cardinal.
All Ireland's Patricks were present on Lough Derg.
All Ireland that froze for want of Europe.

'And who are you?' said the poet speaking to
The old Leitrim man.
He said, 'I can tell you
What I am.
Servant girls bred my servility:
When I stoop
It is my mother's mother mother's mother
Each one in turn being called in to spread –
"Wider with your legs" the master of the house said.
Domestic servants taken back and front.
That's why I'm servile. It is not the poverty
Of soil in Leitrim that makes me raise my hat
To fools with fifty pounds in a paper bank.
Domestic servants, no one has told
Their generations as it is, as I
Show the cowardice of the man whose mothers were whored
By five generations of capitalist and lord'.

Time passed
Three boatloads of Dublin's unemployed came in
At three o'clock led by a priest from Thomas Street
To glutton over the peat-filtered water
And sit back drunk when jobs are found
In the Eternal factory where the boss
Himself must punch the clock.

And the day crawled lazily
Along the orbit of Purgatory.
A baker from Rathfriarland
A solicitor from Derry

A parish priest from Wicklow
A civil servant from Kerry
Sat on the patch of grass,
Their stations for the day
Completed – all things arranged,
Nothing in doubt, nothing gone astray.

    O the boredom of Purgatory
Said the poet then,
Their piety that hangs like a fool's unthought,
This certainty in men,
This three days too-goodness,
Too-neighbourly cries
Temptation to murder
Mediocrities.

    The confession boxes in St Mary's chapel hum
And it is evening now. Prose prayers become
Odes and sonnets.
There is a shrine with money heaped upon it
Before Our Lady of Immaculate Succour.

    A woman said her Litany:
That my husband may get his health
    We beseech Thee to hear us
That my son Joseph may pass the Intermediate
    We beseech Thee to hear us
That my daughter Eileen may do well at her music
    We beseech Thee to hear us
That her aunt may remember us in her will
    We beseech Thee to hear us
That there may be good weather for the hay
    We beseech Thee to hear us
That my indigestion may be cured
    We beseech Thee to hear us
O Mother of Perpetual Succour! in temptation
    Be you near us.
And some of the prayers were shaped like sonnets –

O good St Anthony your poor client asks
That he may have one moment in his arms
The girl I am thinking of this minute –
I'd love her even if she had no farms
Or a four-footed beast in a stable;
Her father is old, doting down the lanes,
There isn't anyone as able
As I am for cocking hay or cleaning drains
All this that I am is an engine running
Light down the narrow-gauge railway of life.
St Anthony, I ask for Mary Gunning
Of Rathdrumskean to be my wife.
My strength is a skull battering the wall
Where a remand-prisoner is losing his soul.

Saint Anne, I am a young girl from Castleblaney,
One of a farmer's six grown daughters
Our little farm, when the season's rainy,
Is putty spread on stones. The surface waters
Soak all the fields of this north-looking townland.
Last year we lost our acre of potatoes
And my mother with unmarried daughters round her
Is soaked like our soil in savage natures.
She tries to be as kind as any mother
But what can a mother be in such a house
With arguments going on and such a bother
About the half-boiled pots and unmilked cows.
O Patron of the pure woman who lacks a man
Let me be free I beg you, St Anne.

O Sacred Heart of Jesus I ask of you
A job so I can settle down and marry;
I want to live a decent life. And through
The flames of St Patrick's Purgatory
I go offering every stone-bruise, all my hunger;
In the back-room of my penance I am weaving
An inside-shirt for charity. How longer
Must a fifty-shilling-a-week job be day-dreaming?

The dole and empty minds and empty pockets,
Cup Finals seen from the branches of a tree,
Old firms that break the eye-balls in their sockets,
A toss-pit. This is life for such as me.
And I know a girl and I know a room to be let
And a job in a builder's yard to be given yet.

I have sinned old; my lust's a running sore
That drains away my strength. Each morning shout:
'Last night will's a bone that will not knit.
I slip on the loose rubble of remorse
And grasp at tufts of cocksfoot grass that yield
My belly in a bankrupt's purse.
My mind is a thrice-failed cropping field
Where the missed ridges give out their ecstasy
To weeds that seed through gaps of indiscretion.
Nettles where barley or potatoes should be.
I set my will in Communion and Confession
But still the sore is dribbling – blood, and will
In spite of penance, prayer and canticle.'

This was the banal
Beggary that God heard. Was he bored
As men are with the poor? Christ Lord
Hears in the voices of the meanly poor
Homeric utterances, poetry sweeping through.

More pilgrims came that evening
From the pier.
The old ones watched the boats come in
And smothered the ridiculous cheer
That breaks, like a hole in pants,
Whether the heroic armies advance.

Somebody brought a newspaper
With news of war.
When they killed in Time they knew
What men killed each other for –

Was it something different in the spelling
Of a useless law?
A man from the campanile said:
'Kipper is fish – nice'
Somebody else talked of Dempsey:
'Greater than Tunney'. Then a girl's voice
Called: 'You'll get cigarettes inside'.

It was six o'clock in the evening
Robert sat looking over the lake
Seeing the green islands that were his morning hope
And his evening despair.
The sharp knife of Jansen
Cuts all the green branches,
Not sunlight comes in
But the hot-iron sin
Branding the shame
Of a beast in the Name
Of Christ on the breast
Of a child of the West.
It was this he had read.
All day he was smitten
By this foul legend written
In the fields, in the skies,
In the sanctuaries.
But now the green tree
Of humanity
Was leafing again
Forgiveness of sin.
A shading hand over
The brow of the lover.

And as the hours of Lough Derg's time
Stretch long enough to hold a generation
He sat beside her and promised that no word
Of what he knew should ever be heard.
The bell at nine o'clock closed the last station,
The pilgrims kissed good-bye to stone and clay.

The Prior had declared the end of day.

Morning from the hostel windows was like the
    morning
In some village street after a dance carouse,
Debauchees of Venus and Bacchus
Half-alive stumbling wearily out of a bleary house.
So these pilgrims stumbled below in the sun
Out of God's publichouse.

The Mass was said.
Pilgrims smiled at one another
How good God was
How much a loving Father!
How wonderful the punishing stones were!
Another hour and the boats will sail
Into the port of time.
Are you not glad you came?

John Flood stared at the sky
And shook his head knowingly.
No storm nor rain.
The boats are ready to sail.

The monk appears once more
Not trailing his robe as before
But different, his pride gone,
Green hope growing where the feet of Pan
Had hoofed the grass.
Lough Derg, St Patrick's Purgatory in Donegal,
Christendom's purge. Heretical
Around the edges: the centre's hard
As the commonplace of a flamboyant bard.
The twentieth century blows across it now
But deeply it has kept an ancient vow.
It knows the secret of pain –
O moralist, your preaching is in vain
To tell men of the germ in the grain.

All happened on Lough Derg as it is written
In June nineteen-forty-two
When the Germans were fighting outside Rostov.
The poet wrote it down as best he knew
As integral and completed as the emotion
Of men and women cloaking a burning emotion
In the rags of the commonplace, will permit him.
He too was one of them. He too denied
The half of him that was his pride
Yet found it waiting, and the half untrue
Of this story is his pride's rhythm.
The turnips were a-sowing in the fields around Pettigo
As our train passed through.
A horse-cart stopped near the eye of the railway bridge.
By Monaghan, Cavan and Dundalk
By Bundoran and by Omagh the pilgrims went
And three sad people had found the key to the lock
Of God's delight in disillusionment.

SAMUEL BECKETT

1906–

Poem

I would like my love to die
and the rain to be falling on the graveyard
and on me walking the streets
mourning the first and last to love me

(translated from the French by the author)

JOHN HEWITT

1907–

The Glens

Groined by deep glens and walled along the west
by the bare hilltops and the tufted moors,
this rim of arable that ends in foam
has but to drop a leaf or snap a branch
and my hand twitches with the leaping verse
as hazel twig will wrench the straining wrists
for untapped jet that thrusts beneath the sod.

Not these my people, of a vainer faith
and a more violent lineage. My dead
lie in the steepled hillock of Kilmore
in a fat country rich with bloom and fruit.
My days, the busy days I owe the world,
are bound to paved unerring roads and rooms
heavy with talk of politics and art.
I cannot spare more than a common phrase
of crops and weather when I pace these lanes
and pause at hedge gap spying on their skill,
so many fences stretch between our minds.

I fear their creed as we have always feared
the lifted hand between the mind and truth.
I know their savage history of wrong
and would at moments lend an eager voice,
if voice avail, to set that tally straight.

And yet no other corner in this land
offers in shape and colour all I need
for sight to torch the mind with living light.

LOUIS MACNEICE
1907–63

Valediction

Their verdure dare not show . . . their verdure dare not
    show . . .
Cant and randy – the seals' heads bobbing in the tide-flow
Between the islands, sleek and black and irrelevant
They cannot depose logically what they want:
Died by gunshot under borrowed pennons,
Sniped from the wet gorse and taken by the limp fins
And slung like a dead seal in a boghole, beaten up
By peasants with long lips and the whisky-drinker's cough.
Park your car in the city of Dublin, see Sackville Street
Without the sandbags in the old photos, meet
The statues of the patriots, history never dies,
At any rate in Ireland, arson and murder are legacies
Like old rings hollow-eyed without their stones
Dumb talismans.
See Belfast, devout and profane and hard,
Built on reclaimed mud, hammers playing in the shipyard;
Time punched with holes like a steel sheet, time
Hardening the faces, veneering with a grey and speckled rime
The faces under the shawls and caps:
This was my mother-city, these my paps.
Country of callous lava cooled to stone,
Of minute sodden haycocks, of ship-sirens' moan,
Of falling intonations – I would call you to book
I would say to you, Look;
I would say, This is what you have given me
Indifference and sentimentality
A metallic giggle, a fumbling hand
A heart that leaps to a fife band:
Set these against your water-shafted air
Of amethyst and moonstone, the horses' feet like bells of hair
Shambling beneath the orange-cart, the beer-brown spring
Guzzling between the heather, the green gush of Irish spring.

Cursèd be he that curses his mother. I cannot be
Anyone else than what this land engendered me:
In the back of my mind are snips of white, the sails
Of the Lough's fishing-boats, the bellropes lash their tails
When I would peal my thoughts, the bells pull free –
Memory in apostasy.
I would tot up my factors
But who can stand in the way of his soul's steam-tractors?
I can say Ireland is hooey, Ireland is
A gallery of fake tapestries,
But I cannot deny my past to which my self is wed,
The woven figure cannot undo its thread.
On a cardboard lid I saw when I was four
Was the trade-mark of a hound and a round tower,
And that was Irish glamour, and in the cemetery
Sham Celtic crosses claimed our individuality,
And my father talked about the West where years back
He played hurley on the sands with a stick of wrack.
Park your car in Killarney, buy a souvenir
Of green marble or black bog-oak, run up to Clare,
Climb the cliff in the postcard, visit Galway city,
Romanticise on our Spanish blood, leave ten per cent of pity
Under your plate for the emigrant,
Take credit for our sanctity, our heroism and our sterile want
Columba Kevin and briny Brandan the accepted names,
Wolfe Tone and Grattan and Michael Collins the accepted
        names,
Admire the suavity with which the architect
Is rebuilding the burnt mansion, recollect
The palmy days of the Horse Show, swank your fill,
But take the Holyhead boat before you pay the bill;
Before you face the consequence
Of inbred soul and climatic maleficence
And pay for the trick beauty of a prism
In drug-dull fatalism.
I will exorcise my blood
And not to have my baby-clothes my shroud
I will acquire an attitude not yours

And become as one of your holiday visitors,
And however often I may come
Farewell, my country, and in perpetuum;
Whatever desire I catch when your wind scours my face
I will take home and put in a glass case
And merely look on
At each new fantasy of badge and gun.
Frost will not touch the hedge of fuchsias,
The land will remain as it was,
But no abiding content can grow out of these minds
Fuddled with blood, always caught by blinds;
The eels go up the Shannon over the great dam;
You cannot change a response by giving it a new name.
Fountain of green and blue curling in the wind
I must go east and stay, not looking behind,
Not knowing on which day the mist is blanket-thick
Nor when sun quilts the valley and quick
Winging shadows of white clouds pass
Over the long hills like a fiddle's phrase.
If I were a dog of sunlight I would bound
From Phoenix Park to Achill Sound,
Picking up the scent of a hundred fugitives
That have broken the mesh of ordinary lives,
But being ordinary too I must in course discuss
What we mean to Ireland or Ireland to us;
I have to observe milestone and curio
The beaten buried gold of an old king's bravado,
Falsetto antiquities, I have to gesture,
Take part in, or renounce, each imposture;
Therefore I resign, goodbye the chequered and the quiet hills
The gaudily-striped Atlantic, the linen-mills
That swallow the shawled file, the black moor where half
A turf-stack stands like a ruined cenotaph;
Goodbye your hens running in and out of the white house
Your absent-minded goats along the road, your black cows
Your greyhounds and your hunters beautifully bred
Your drums and your dolled-up Virgins and your ignorant
    dead.

DENIS DEVLIN

(1908–59)

The Colours of Love

I

Women that are loved are more than lovable,
    Their beauty absolute blows:
But wastes away the urgent, carnal soul
    More than its leaves so mortal in the rose.

O rose! O more than red mortality!
    What can my love have said
That made her image more than be?
    Her mind more than mind, blood more than red?

II

Those beautiful women shone against the dark
With flowers upon the breast, and birds
Disturbed by foreknowledge, sang some notes.
There were unshed tears, reproach and fret;
I wondered if their women's time was yet.

And the flowers like milk in a dark pantry at night
Offered themselves to the groping hand;
The cliffs fell faster than tears
Reaching that pain where feeling does not matter;
Nor through the house the ghosts' averse patter,

Repeating their old theme of the unknown
Birds or women never did translate:
It was as if eternity were breathing
Through the small breathing of the flowers
Shining upon its breast with speechless light.

III

It cannot well be said of love and death
That love is better and that death is worse,
Unless we buy death off with loving breath
So he may rent his beauty with our purse.

But is that beauty, is that beauty death?
No, it's the mask by which we're drawn to him,
It is with our consent death finds his breath;
Love is death's beauty and annexes him.

IV

At the *Bar du Départ* drink farewell
And say no word you'll be remembered by;
Nor Prince nor President can ever tell
Where love ends or when it does or why.

Down the boulevard the lights come forth
Like my rainflowers trembling all through Spring,
Blue and yellow in the Celtic North . . .
The stone's ripple weakens, ring by ring.

Better no love than love, which, through loving
Leads to no love. The ripples come to rest . . .
Ah me! how all that young year I was moving
To take her dissolution to my breast!

Lough Derg

The poor in spirit on their rosary rounds,
The jobbers with their whiskey-angered eyes,
The pink bank clerks, the tip-hat papal counts,
And drab, kind women their tonsured mockery tries,

Glad invalids on penitential feet
Walk the Lord's majesty like their village street.

With mullioned Europe shattered, this Northwest,
Rude-sainted isle would pray it whole again:
(Peasant Apollo! Troy is worn to rest.)
Europe that humanized the sacred bane
Of God's chance who yet laughed in his mind
And balanced thief and saint: were they this kind?

Low rocks, a few weasels, lake
Like a field of burnt gorse; the rooks caw;
Ours, passive, for man's gradual wisdom take
Firefly instinct dreamed out into law;
The prophets' jeweled kingdom down at heel
Fires no Augustine here. Inert, they kneel;

All is simple and symbol in their world,
The incomprehended rendered fabulous.
Sin teases life whose natural fruits withheld
Sour the deprived nor bloom for timely loss:
Clan Jansen! less what magnanimity leavens
Man's wept-out, fitful, magniloquent heavens

Where prayer was praise, O Lord! the Temple trumpets
Cascaded down Thy sunny pavilions of air,
The scroll-tongued priests, the galvanic strumpets,
All clash and stridency gloomed upon Thy stair;
The pharisees, the exalted boy their power
Sensually psalmed in Thee, their coming hour!

And to the sun, earth turned her flower of sex,
Acanthus in the architects' limpid angles;
Close priests allegorized the Orphic egg's
Brood, and from the Academy, tolerant wranglers
Could hear the contemplatives of the Tragic Choir
Drain off man's sanguine, pastoral death-desire.

It was said stone dreams and animal sleeps and man
Is awake; but sleep with its drama on us bred
Animal articulate, only somnambulist can
Conscience like Cawdor give the blood its head
For the dim moors to reign through druids again.
O first geometer! tangent-feelered brain

Clearing by inches the encircled eyes,
Bolder than the peasant tiger whose autumn beauty
Sags in the expletive kill, or the sacrifice
Of dearth puffed positive in the stance of duty
With which these pilgrims would propitiate
Their fears; no leafy, medieval state

Of paschal cathedrals backed on earthy hooves
Against the craftsmen's primary-coloured skies
Whose gold was Gabriel on the patient roofs,
The parabled windows taught the dead to rise,
And Christ the Centaur in two natures whole,
With fable and proverb joinered body and soul.

Water withers from the oars. The pilgrims blacken
Out of the boats to masticate their sin
Where Dante smelled among the stones and bracken
The door to Hell (O harder Hell where pain
Is earthed, a casuist sanctuary of guilt!).
Spirit bureaucracy on a bet built

Part by this race when monks in convents of coracles
For the Merovingian centuries left their land,
Belled, fragrant; and honest in their oracles
Bespoke the grace to give without demand,
Martyrs Heaven winged nor tempted with reward.
And not ours, doughed in dogma, who never have dared

Will with surrogate palm distribute hope:
No better nor worse than I who, in my books,
Have angered at the stake with Bruno and, by the rope

Wat Tyler swung from, leagued with shifty looks
To fuse the next rebellion with the desperate
Serfs in the sane need to eat and get;

Have praised, on its thunderous canvas, the Florentine smile
As man took to wearing his death, his own
Sapped crisis through cathedral branches (while
Flesh groped loud round dissenting skeleton)
In soul, reborn as body's appetite:
Now languisht back in body's amber light,

Now is consumed. O earthly paradise!
Hell is to know our natural empire used
Wrong, by mind's moulting, brute divinities.
The vanishing tiger's saved, his blood transfused.
Kent is for Jutes again and Glasgow town
Burns high enough to screen the stars and moon.

Well may they cry who have been robbed, their wasting
Shares in justice legally lowered until
Man his own actor, matrix, mould and casting,
Or man, God's image, sees, his idol spill.
Say it was pride that did it, or virtue's brief:
To them that suffer it is no relief.

All indiscriminate, man, stone, animal
Are woken up in nightmare. What John the Blind
From Patmos saw works and we speak it. Not all
The men of God nor the priests of mankind
Can mend or explain the good and broke, not one
Generous with love prove communion.

Behind the eyes the winged ascension flags,
For want of spirit by the market blurbed,
And if hands touch, such fraternity sags
Frightened this side the dikes of death disturbed
Like Aran Islands' bibulous, unclean seas:
Pieta: but the limbs ache; it is not peace.

Then to see less, look little, let hearts' hunger
Feed on water and berries. The pilgrims sing:
Life will fare well from elder to younger,
Though courage fail in a world-end, rosary ring.
Courage kills its practitioners and we live,
Nothing forgotten, nothing to forgive.

We pray to ourself. The metal moon, unspent
Virgin eternity sleeping in the mind,
Excites the form of prayer without content;
Whitethorn lightens, delicate and blind,
The negro mountain, and so, knelt on her sod,
This woman beside me murmuring *My God! My God!*

ROBERT FARREN

1909–

The Mason

Nothing older than stone but the soil and the sea and the sky.
Nothing stronger than stone but water and air and fire.
Nothing worthier than stone but the harpstring, the word and
    the tree.
Nothing humbler or stubborner than stone – whatever it be!

Stone is the bone of the world, under moor, under loam,
under ocean and churchyard-corruption of buried bone;
floor of the mountain, pound of the ocean, the world's cord.
God's creature, stone, that once was the vault of its Lord.
God gave me stone to know for a womb with child,
the time of delivery come but waiting the knife:
I free the stone-born glory into the air,
rounded and grooved and edged and grained and rare.

I have mastered the grain, the make, the temper of stone,
fingering it and considering, touching with hand and with soul,
quarrying it out of the course, piercing and severing it,
with a chirp of meeting metals like a bird's chirp.

Basalt I know – bottle-green still pools of stone
harder than hawk's beak, shark's tooth or tusk of the boar;
basalt – the glass-stone, stone without pore or wart;
causeway-stone stepped across Moyle-fjord in the north.

Granite I know – dust-pearl with silver eyes –
that moulds domed hills, with snow, rain, wind and time.
Marble – the multiple-tinted, – the satin-flesh –
daughter of the King of white Greece in the lands of the west.

Dark flint I know with the feel of a fox's tongue,
the unconsumed cold carrier of fire its young,

stone of hairedges and thornpoints, the dagger stone,
spearstone, swordstone, hatchet-stone, hearth-gilly stone.

O Christ, the stone which the builders rejected
and which is become the head of the corner,
part me from them the stone shall grind when it fall;
leave me not a stone in thine enemies' hand!

W. R. RODGERS

1909–69

The Net

Quick, woman in your net
Catch the silver I fling!
O I am deep in your debt,
Draw tight, skin-tight, the string,
And rake the silver in.
No fisher ever yet
Drew such a cunning ring.

Ah, shifty as the fin
Of any fish this flesh
That, shaken to the shin,
Now shoals into your mesh,
Bursting to be held in;
Purse-proud and pebble-hard,
Its pence like shingle showered.

Open the haul, and shake
The fill of shillings free,
Let all the satchels break
And leap about the knee
In shoals of ecstasy.
Guineas and gills will flake
At each gull-plunge of me.

Though all the Angels, and
Saint Michael at their head,
Nightly contrive to stand
On guard about your bed,
Yet none dare take a hand,
But each can only spread
His eagle-eye instead.

But I, being man, can kiss
And bed-spread-eagle too;
All flesh shall come to this,
Being less than angel is,
Yet higher far in bliss
As it entwines with you.

Come, make no sound, my sweet·
Turn down the candid lamp
And draw the equal quilt
Over our naked guilt.

Home Thoughts from Abroad

Hearing, this June day, the thin thunder
Of far-off invective and old denunciation
Lambasting and lambegging the homeland,
I think of that brave man Paisley, eyeless
In Gaza, with a daisy-chain of millstones
Round his neck; groping, like blind Samson,
For the soapy pillars and greased poles of lightning
To pull them down in rains and borborygmic roars
Of rhetoric. (There but for the grace of God
Goes God.) I like his people and I like his guts
But I dislike his gods who always end
In gun-play. Some day, of course, he'll be one
With the old giants of Ireland – such as
Denis of the Drought, or Iron-Buttocks –
Who had at last to be reduced to size,
Quietly shrunken into 'wee people'
And put out to grass on the hills for good,
Minimized like cars or skirts or mums;
Photostatted to fit a literate age
And filed safely away on the dark shelves
Of memory; preserved in ink, oak-gall,
Alcohol, aspic, piety, wit. A pity,

Perhaps, if it is drama one wants. But,
Look at it this way: in this day and age
We can't really have giants lumbering
All over the place, cluttering it up,
With hair like ropes, flutes like telegraph poles,
And feet like tramcars, intent only on dogging
The fled horse of history and the Boyne.
So today across the Irish Sea I wave
And wish him well from the bottom of my heart
Where truth lies bleeding, its ear-drums burst
By the blather of his hand-me-down talk.
In fond memory of his last stand
I dedicate this contraceptive pill
Of poetry to his unborn followers,
And I place
This bunch of beget-me-nots on his grave.

W. B. STANFORD

1910–

Undertone

When the landfolk of Galway converse with a stranger,
softly the men speak, more softly the women,
light words on their lips, and an accent that sings
in traditional cadences (once plucked by harpists
to cheer melancholic carousals of kings),
when the landfolk of Galway converse with a stranger.

But under the cadences, under the light lips,
under the lilt of the harp-plucking bard,
threaded deep in its socket of anger and loneliness
a passion, with piercing and tightening screw, grips
their minds' inner engine and presses it hard.

When the landfolk of Galway converse with a stranger,
softly the men speak, more softly the women;
yet older than harp-playing, older than welcomes,
an undertone threatens Fomorian danger,
when the landfolk of Galway converse with a stranger.

DONAGH MACDONAGH

1912–68

The Hungry Grass

Crossing the shallow holdings high above sea
Where few birds nest, the luckless foot may pass
From the bright safety of experience
Into the terror of the hungry grass.

Here in a year when poison from the air
First withered in despair the growth of spring
Some skull-faced wretch whom nettle could not save
Crept on four bones to his last scattering,

Crept, and the shrivelled heart which drove his thought
Towards platters brought in hospitality
Burst as the wizened eyes measured the miles
Like dizzy walls forbidding him the city.

Little the earth reclaimed from that poor body,
And yet remembering him the place has grown
Bewitched and the thin grass he nourishes
Racks with his famine, sucks marrow from the bone.

SIGERSON CLIFFORD

1913–

The Ballad of the Tinker's Wife

When cocks curved throats for crowing
And cows in slumber kneeled,
She tiptoed out the half-door
And crossed her father's field.

Down the mountain shoulders
The ragged dawnlight came
And a cold wind from the westland
Blew out the last star's flame.

Her father, the strong farmer,
Had horses, sheep and cows,
One hundred verdant acres
And slates upon his house.

And she stole with the starlight
From where her life began
To roam the roads of Ireland
With a travelling tinker man.

His hair was brown and curling,
His eyes were brown as well,
His tongue would charm the hinges
Off the gates of hell.

At Caher fair she saw him
As she was hurrying by,
And the song that he was singing
Would lure lark from the sky.

Her footsteps slowed to standing,
She stood and stared that day;
He made a noose of music
And pulled her heart away.

And so she left her slate-roof
And her father rich and strong
Because her mind was turning
About a tinker's song.

They walked the roads of Ireland,
Went up the hills and down,
Passed many an empty bogland,
Through many a noisy town.

She rode upon the ass-cart
To rest a tired leg,
She learned the lore of tinkers,
And he taught her how to beg.

'The tree-tied house of planter
Is colder than east wind,
The hall-door of the gombeen
Has no welcome for our kind.

'The farmstead of the grabber
Is hungry as a stone,
But the little homes of Kerry
Will give us half their own.'

She cut the cards for girls
And made their eyes glow bright,
She read the palms of women
And saw their lips go tight.

'A dark man will marry you
On a day of June;
There's money across water
Coming to you soon.

'Oh, he'll be rich and handsome
And I see a bridal feast;
Your daughter will dwell in Dublin,
Your son will be a priest.'

They rode along together,
The woman pale and wan,
The black ass young and giddy,
And the brown-eyed tinker man.

He bought up mules and jennets
And sang songs far and wide;
But she never gave him children
To fill his heart with pride.

She never gave him children
To spoil his sleep with cries,
But she saw his empty arms
And the hunger in his eyes.

She saw the lonely bogland,
She felt the killing wind,
And the fine home of her father
Kept turning in her mind.

She felt the chill rain falling,
She grew tired of it all,
And twisting in the darkness
She died within her shawl.

They dug a cold grave for her
And left her all alone,
And the tinker man went with them,
His heart as grey as stone.

'She was the best of women,
The flower of the ball,
She never gave me children
But that's no blame at all.

'A lass may break her mother's heart,
A son his father's head:
Maybe she is happier now
Sleeping with the dead.'

He drank his fill of porter
And turned his face to life,
And hit the road fór Puck Fair
To get another wife.

planter: one of the landed gentry of English origin.
gombeen: an unscrupulous shopkeeper.
grabber: one who buys a farm from which the hereditary owners have
been evicted. A very unpopular person in Ireland.

VALENTIN IREMONGER

1918–

Icarus

As, even today, the airman, feeling the plane sweat
Suddenly, seeing the horizon tilt up gravely, the wings shiver,
Knows that, for once, Daedalus has slipped up badly,
Drunk on the job, perhaps, more likely dreaming, high-flier
    Icarus,
Head butting down, skidding along the light-shafts
Back, over the tones of the sea-waves and the slip-stream,
    heard
The gravel-voiced, stuttering trumpets of his heart

Sennet among the crumbling court-yards of his brain the
    mistake
Of trusting somebody else on an important affair like this;
And, while the flat sea, approaching, buckled into oh!
    avenues
Of acclamation, he saw the wrong story fan out into history,
Truth, undefined, lost in his own neglect. On the hills,
The summer-shackled hills, the sun spanged all day;
Love and the world were young and there was no ending:

But star-chaser, big-time going, chancer Icarus
Like a dog on the sea lay and the girls forgot him,
And Daedalus, too busy hammering another job,
Remembered him only in pubs. No bugler at all
Sobbed taps for the young fool then, reported missing,
Presumed drowned, wing-bones and feathers on the tides
Drifting in casually, one by one.

KEVIN FALLER

1920–

Landscape

Where painted women
in the neons pass
hid by a smile
I lift my glass

to that grey lady,
the western sky,
embracing Corrib
with a sigh –

trailing her veils
in the mourning gleam
where castle and church
entomb a dream.

ROY McFADDEN

1922–

Saint Francis and the Birds

Hearing him, the birds came in a crowd,
Wing upon wing, from stone and blade and twig,
From tilted leaf and thorn and lumbering cloud,
Falling from hill, soaring from meadowland,
Wing upon widening wing, until the air
Wrinkled with sound and ran like watery sand
Round the sky's gleaming bowl. Then, like a flower
They swung, hill-blue and tremulous, each wing
A petal palpitating in a shower
Of words, till he beneath felt the stale crust
Of self crinkle and crumble and his words
Assume an independence, pure and cold,
Cageless, immaculate, one with the birds
Fattening their throats in song. Identity
Lost, he stood in swollen ecstasy.

PADRAIC FIACC

1924–

Alive Alive O

The altar boy from a Mass for the dead
Romps through the streets of the town,
Lolls on brick studded grass
Jumps up, bolts back down
With wild pup eyes . . .

This morning at twist of winter to spring
Small hands clutched a big brass cross
Followed the stern brow of the priest
Encircle the man in the box . . .

A bell-tossed head sneezed
In a blue daze of incense on
Shrivelled bit lips, then
Just to stay awake, prayed
Too loud for the man to be at rest . . .

O now where has he got to
But climbed an apple tree!

ANTHONY CRONIN

1925–

For a Father

With the exact length and pace of his father's stride
The son walks,
Echoes and intonations of his father's speech
Are heard when he talks.

Once when the table was tall,
And the chair a wood,
He absorbed his father's smile and carefully copied
The way that he stood.

He grew into exile slowly,
With pride and remorse,
In some ways better than his begetters,
In others worse.

And now having chosen, with strangers,
Half glad of his choice,
He smiles with his father's hesitant smile
And speaks with his voice.

JEROME KIELY
1925–

Lizard

O lizard,
chinking up the new made wall
come down: the moderns do not make you inns.
Come down to me,
green lightning of the day,
and lie upon the frond-dress of the ground
like such a pin as white necked Deirdre wore.
Ah! you are down.
Where will you go to now?
Not up the palm,
for there the urchin sun
lies spikey white in his great lair of sky,
and I am here between you and your cave
where you skid round boy-glad on roller skates.
No, lagartijo, I take that image back.
Not skates.
For you have claws like fairy forks
that feed in autumn on the red and berried ground.
Oh, calm your pulsing neck.
That's right. Lie still,
so I can marvel at your mosaiced back
your carpet-threaded tail
your head of fish
your mould of yacht hull curves,
water in sand
your miming wisdom's torch
your anchored grace.
You raise yourself upon a twig to preach;
I read the message in your watching eye
that I am some dead thing lit by the sun
mere moon of your amaze.
And moving ants
are all the passion of your livelier eye.

If I be naught to you, yet you are now
the biggest of God's fingers in my world,
my friend,
my image-maker,
poet-wife.
O little dragon, where is the scoundrel knight
would tilt at you?
Tell me, and I will kill him in my verse.

EUGENE R. WATTERS

1925–

From *The Week-End of Dermot and Grace*

It is late, late,
Gaslight is a green disease in the hall.
Three flights up,
Easy now with the wound not properly healed.
She'll not be expecting me.
Maybe a bit of a fire and a book with her feet up,
I'd laugh but for the pain it brings me in the belly.
Hell of a climb up always.
But I was young myself once,
I was myself once,
And if we could warm the damp sheets again,
Haha, I was myself once,
And if we could but warm the sheets dear heart
– Do not touch me!

Throb of the controlled wheel turning.
Let us alone. The bright blood is free.
He stays inlaid, the voice that broke
Out of the nightshifting long mosaic
Of cut stones and lazuli chipped eyes
Falls back again spent and stylised
Into the plainsong of the antiphonal wheel.
Alone. Alone. All one. Why trouble us?
They died in their own day, the blood is free.
Love, the dark did not devour your little sparrow,
It nips and chirps out of the same furrow
Twinkling a wing between the ellipticals.
He sleeps, nursing the intangible.
It may be our sour galactic galled his lips
Till he cried out of a dream of cracked windows
Buried among streets of old paving
And gangling rails, lit knots, the lamps

Of unfleshed sweethearts gibbering out at us.
Hide us from the ghosts of ourselves.
Where gaslight is a green slime on the cobblestones,
Where the town yet stinks of a damp fecundity.
Hide us from the sea, our mother.
Hell, brother, it was a famous thing,
A leap out of the muttering rhythm of the deep
Into the splinter of the sun on the shingle banks
And the scream of the pterodactyl.
Intractable
Wingdrifting memories,
Awkwardly fingering
Under a skirt's edge for the femoral bone.
And Strasburg lace on the family skeleton.
Atone. Let us atone. And a flowered kimono
That burned its roses on the original skin.
Love, born among the flame of underclothes,
In foam of silk and two nude rimes
Long-legged, long-legged, wingfingered,
And all the time the nailed beak bickering
Between the lines, between the legs, all one,
Hide us from our cheap cupidity
Manhandling always what the hands disclose.
This is the deliberate breaking of a rose.
Leave us alone. The blood is sick with thinking,
Neither bird nor bone is innocent any longer,
And a white rose against a brick wall in Drumcondra
Is simply a shattering thing.

PEARSE HUTCHINSON

1927–

Look, No Hands

for Ernie Hughes

> Lengua sin manos, cuemo osas fablar?
> – *Poema del Cid*

I blame old women for buying paper roses,
yet pluck a dandelion: by the time
it reaches my lapel it's turned to paper.

I hate the winter, and blame drinkers
for hiding in dark pubs when the sun shines outside,
and could be enjoyed at sidewalk tables;
yet every time I visit a crowded beach
I bring a sun-ray lamp along.

I praise trust above all,
yet cannot let a friend post a letter
In case he might stop on the way for a drink.

I admire a stone for its hardness,
resembling it only in barrenness;
admire a butterfly's brightness,
resembling it only in brittleness.

I like speed, summer, the country roads,
but never could master a bike.
Believing in God because of the need to praise –
though fear alone, so far, makes me long to pray –
if granted another hundred years
I might learn
                    how to say prayers.

RICHARD KELL

1927–

Spring Night

(For Muriel)

Out on Killiney Hill that night, you said
'Remember how we promised to come up here
When snow is lying under a full moon?'
And I made no reply – to hide my sadness,
Thinking we might not satisfy that whim,
Ever perhaps, at least for years to come,
Since it was spring, and winter would see us parted.

Sitting on the Druid's Chair recalled
The last time we were there, a night of icy
Wind and moonlight when the sea was churning
Silver and the distant hills were clear;
How we belonged to them and they to us.
Now there was no brightness – only a vast
Obscurity confusing sea and sky,
Dalkey Island and the lights of Bray
Submerged and suffocating in the mist.

And there was no belonging now; no vivid
Elemental statement to compel
Refusal or assent, making decision
Easy; but a dumb neutrality
That challenged us to give it character
And view our own minds large as a landscape.
To you it was tranquil. Sinister to me.

Lying under the pine tree, looking up
At the small stars and breathing the wood's sweetness,
We spoke hardly a word. I could not tell you
I was afraid of something out there
In the future, like that dark and bitter sea;

And how my love for you would have me lonely
Until the fear was broken. I could say
'Be close to me this winter and every winter;
We'll come up here to watch the snow by moonlight' –
And that would be too easy. For I must give
To you whose meaning transcends moods and moments
Nothing half-hearted or ambiguous,
But the perfected diamond of my will.

RICHARD MURPHY

1927–

The Poet on the Island

To Theodore Roethke

On a wet night, laden with books for luggage,
And stumbling under the burden of himself,
He reached the pier, looking for a refuge.

Darkly he crossed to the island six miles off:
The engine pulsed, the sails invented rhythm,
While the sea expanded and the rain drummed softly.

Safety on water, he rocked with a new theme:
And in the warmth of his mind's greenhouse bloomed
A poem nurtured like a chrysanthemum.

His forehead, a Prussian helmet, moody, domed,
Relaxed in the sun: a lyric was his lance.
To be loved by the people, he, a stranger, hummed

In the herring-store on Sunday crammed with drunks
Ballads of bawdry with a speakeasy stress.
Yet lonely they left him, 'one of the Yanks'.

The children understood. This was not madness.
How many orphans had he fathered in words
Robust and cunning, but never heartless.

He watched the harbour scouted by sea-birds:
His fate was like fish under poetry's beaks:
Words began weirdly to take off inwards.

Time that they calendar in seasons not in clocks,
In gardens dug over and houses roofed,
Was to him a see-saw of joys and shocks,

Where his body withered but his style improved.
A storm shot up, his glass cracked in a gale:
An abstract thunder of darkness deafened

The listeners he'd once given roses, now hail.
He'd burst the lyric barrier: logic ended.
Doctors were called, and he agreed to sail.

JOHN B. KEANE

1928–

Certainty

This is the place, I was told.
See the tall grass lie low.
They rested here and made bold
Now for a certainty I know.

Take note of the blue-bell broken,
The fern mangled and dead
And look at this for a token –
Here's a hair from her head.

ULICK O'CONNOR

1928–

Oscar Wilde

Oscar Wilde, Poète et Dramaturge, né a Dublin le 15 Octobre, 1856, est
mort dans cette maison le 30 Novembre, 1900.

After all the wit
In a sudden fit
Of fear, he skipped it.
Stretched in the twilight
That body once lively
Dumb in the darkness.
Quiet, but for candles
Blazing beside him,
His elegant form
And firm gaze exhausted.
In an empty cold room
With a spiteful concierge
Impatient at waiting
For a foreign waster
Who left without paying
The ten per cent service.
Exiled now from Flore
To sanctity's desert
The young prince of Sin
Broken and withered.
Lust left behind him
Gem without lustre
No Pernod for a stiffener
But cold holy water
The young king of Beauty
Narcissus broken.
But the pure star of Mary
As a gleam on the ocean.

ULICK O'CONNOR

ENVOI

Sweet is the way of the sinner
Sad, death without God's praise
My life on you, Oscar boy
Yourself had it both ways.

(translated from the Irish of Brendan Behan)

BASIL PAYNE

1928–

Lines in Memory of my Father

Fishing, one morning early in July
From the canal bank – that was the closest ever
We came to entering each other's world;
That, and one wintry day at the Museum,
Looking at ancient coins and skeletons,
Dead butterflies, old guns and precious stones;
Each of us slightly awed, and slightly bored,
And slightly uneasy at each other's boredom.
I cried, of course, the morning that you died,
Frightened by Mother's tears and your grey spittle,
And frightened at being suddenly bereft
Of someone I had never loved enough,
But vaguely understood had loved me.

Today in Dublin, passing the Museum,
A dead leaf blew across my instep, stabbing
My memory suddenly: little frightened fishes
Flapping bewildered in a cheap white net,
Then gliding in a water-filled jam jar;
Nudging their awkward heads against the glass,
Groping in vain for green and spacious freedom.

THOMAS KINSELLA

1929–

Downstream II[1]

Drifting to meet us on the darkening stage
A pattern shivered; whorling in its place
Another held us in a living cage
Then broke to its reordered phase of grace.

*

Again in the mirrored dusk the paddles sank.
  We thrust forward, swaying both as one.
  The ripples scattered to the ghostly bank

Where willows, with their shadows half undone,
  Hung to the water, mowing like the blind.
  The current seized our skiff. We let it run

Grazing the reeds, and let the land unwind
  In stealth on either hand. Dark woods: a door
  Opened and shut. The clear sky fell behind,

The channel shrank. Thick slopes from shore to shore
  Lowered a matted arch. I thought of roots
  Crawling full of pike on the river-floor

To cage us in, sensed the furred night-brutes
  Halt in their trails, twitching their tiny brushes.
  What plopped in the reeds, stirred between the shoots?

Then I remembered how among those bushes
  A man one night fell sick and left his shell
  Collapsed, half eaten, like a rotten thrush's

To frighten stumbling children. 'You could tell,'
  My co-shadow murmured, 'by the hands
  He died in terror.' And the cold of hell,

– 403 –

A limb-lightness, a terror in the glands,
   Pierced again as when that story first
   Froze my blood: the soil of other lands

Drank lives that summer with a body thirst;
   Nerveless by the European pit
   – Ourselves through seven hundred years accurst –

We saw the barren world obscurely lit
   By tall chimneys flickering in their pall,
   The haunt of swinish man – each day a spit

That, turning, sweated war, each night a fall
   Back to the evil dream where rodents ply,
   Man-rumped, sow-headed, busy with whip and maul

Among nude herds of the damned. It seemed that I,
   Coming to conscience on that lip of dread,
   Still dreamed, impervious to calamity,

Imagining a formal drift of the dead
   Stretched calm as effigies on velvet dust,
   Scattered on starlit slopes with arms outspread

And eyes of silver – when that story thrust
   Pungent horror and an actual mess
   Into my very face, and taste I must.

Then hungry joy and sickening distress
   Fumbled together by the brimming flood,
   And night consumed a hopeless loneliness.

Like mortal jaws, the alleys of the wood
   Fell-to behind us. In its heart, a ghost
   Glimmered briefly with my gift of blood

– Spreadeagled on a rack of leaves, almost
   Remembering. It looked full at the sky,
   Calmly encountering the starry host,

Meeting their silver eyes with silver eye.
  An X of wavering flesh, a skull of light,
  Extinguished in our wake without a sigh.

Then the current shuddered in its flight
  And swerved on pliant muscle; we were sped
  Through sudden peace into a pit of night:

The Mill-Hole, whose rocky fathoms fed
  On moss and pure depth and the cold fin
  Turning in its heart. The river bed

Called to our flesh. Across the watery skin,
  Breathless, our shell trembled. The abyss ...
  We shipped our oars in dread. Now, deeper in,

Something shifted in sleep, a quiet hiss
  As we slipped by. Adrift ... A milk-white breast ...
  A shuffle of wings betrayed with a feathery kiss

A soul of white with darkness for a nest.
  The creature bore the night so tranquilly
  I lifted up my eyes. There without rest

The phantoms of the overhanging sky
  Occupied their stations and descended;
  Another moment, to the starlit eye,

The slow, downstreaming dead, it seemed, were blended
  One with those silver hordes, and briefly shared
  Their order, glittering. And then impended

A barrier of rock that turned and bared
  A varied barrenness as toward its base
  We glided – blotting heaven as it towered –

Searching the darkness for a landing place.

  1. A revision of the poem 'Downstream' published in the book *Down-stream* in 1962. It was printed in roughly this form in the *Massachusetts Review*, Winter 1964.

JOHN MONTAGUE

1929–

The Trout

Flat on the bank I parted
Rushes to ease my hands
In the water without a ripple
And tilt them slowly downstream
To where he lay, light as a leaf,
In his fluid sensual dream.

Bodiless lord of creation
I hung briefly above him
Savouring my own absence
Senses expanding in the slow
Motion, the photographic calm
That grows before action.

As the curve of my hands
Swung under his body
He surged, with visible pleasure.
I was so preternaturally close
I could count every stipple
But still cast no shadow, until

The two palms crossed in a cage
Under the lightly pulsing gills.
Then (entering my own enlarged
Shape, which rode on the water)
I gripped. To this day I can
Taste his terror on my hands.

PATRICK GALVIN

1930–

The Madwoman of Cork

To-day
Is the feast day of Saint Anne
Pray for me
I am the madwoman of Cork.

Yesterday
In Castle Street
I saw two goblins at my feet
I saw a horse without a head
Carrying the dead
To the graveyard
Near Turner's Cross.

I am the madwoman of Cork
No one talks to me

When I walk in the rain
The children throw stones at me
Old men persecute me
And women close their doors.
When I die
Believe me
They'll set me on fire.

I am the madwoman of Cork
I have no sense.

Sometimes
With an eagle in my brain
I can see a train
Crashing at the station
If I told people that
They'd choke me.
Then where would I be?

I am the madwoman of Cork
The people hate me.

When Canon Murphy died
I wept on his grave
That was twenty-five years ago.
When I saw him just now
In Dunbar Street
He had clay in his teeth
He blest me.

I am the madwoman of Cork
The clergy pity me.

I see death
In the branches of a tree
Birth in the feathers of a bird.
To see a child with one eye
Or a woman buried in ice
Is the worst thing
And cannot be imagined.

I am the madwoman of Cork
My mind fills me.

I should like to be young
To dress up in silk
And have nine children.
I'd like to have red lips
But I'm eighty years old
I have nothing
But a small house with no windows.

I am the madwoman of Cork
Go away from me.

And if I die now
Don't touch me.

I want to sail in a long boat
From here to Roche's Point
And there I will anoint
The sea
With oil of alabaster.

I am the madwoman of Cork
And to-day
Is the feast day of Saint Anne.
Feed me.

SEAN LUCY

1931–

Senior Members

Tadhg sat up on his hills
Sniping at passing Tommies from the barracks,
Growling in Gaelic,
Plowtilth on his boots.

Vincent was just a boy
Kept in at curfew by a careful Da
In a soft suburb
Of the cautious city.

Tadhg was two-and-three with Fionn the Hero
(Meaning his cousin)
And helped to shoot him
After the treaty split them.

Vincent is solid stock:
His uncle was Home Rule M.P.:
His face is sleek with merchant generation;
'Liberal plumbing makes a cultured nation.'

Tadhg is a bully on the commitées,
As full of malice as intelligence;
His language is as hairy as his ears;
He has a drover's voice.

Vincent works mainly for the money men.
Deep in his heart he fears the tinker's shout,
The eyes of mountain goats,
The gunman's shot.

Save us Saint Patrick! Is it gin and plush,
Or the grey ash-plant that shall master us?

The bourgeois coma or the bully's push?
This is a dilemma, not a choice.

Footnote
The new politico answers my sad voice:

Vincent and Tadhg, though sadly out of date,
Each taught me in his way to rule the state,
Ruthless as mountain rocks, slick as the city street
I am the inheritor. Kneel at my feet.

RICHARD WEBER

1932–

Lady & Gentleman

Of himself to think this: she does not
Know my meaning, nor ever will,
Though the leaves like late butterflies
Twist and turn, falter and fall
In the outside racing, interlacing winds.

And she, seeing this, that and that
Other yet sees nothing of these,
Is contemplative in her conducted contempt
Of this contact of the customary, this always
And always to be expected, the look of love.

And all else but herself: herself she sees
And is pleased and displeased by turns
Of her thought, of her head also.
One can see it in the constant
Constrained movements of her denying head.

So fine a thing this is, balanced like held
Breath between beauty and plainness.
When the eyes hold one they hold so fast
It is only by one's arrival at their awaiting
Uninterest that one releases, is released, dropped.

To fall as one can in one's napkin,
Like a soupdrop, desiring not to be noticed.
Nevertheless, nerveless, one looks up to see
If she can see. Then what joy that she sees.
What, you? No, she watches not you, not

Even now the appearance of you. What, then?
He has seen already that in that steady

Amazing gaze of her eyes there is merely
Awareness of self, her self, and maybe not
Only that but of whole hordes of women

Who have come together in this one woman.
It is not enough, he knows, but it is more
Than one man, representing only himself,
Can bear, which is why shortly he must dab
At his dismayed mouth with his already raised napkin.

SEAN O'MEARA

1933–

The Lady of the Restaurant

Of all the womenfolk I knew
The lush, the gamey-eyed, the gaunt
Not one could hold a candle to
The Lady of the Restaurant.

In Limerick city I sat down
A-weary of the stranger's face
For 'tis a pain to be alone
In such a populated place.

I asked a man who chanced to pass
If he could recommend to me
A place where I could break my fast
And drink a mug or two of tea.

He pointed and I wandered in
Where there were lights and people sat
By china-covered table cloths
Passing the hours in idle chat.

There as I tilted up the cup
And gorged my belly out of want
Who should I see there looking up:
The Lady of the Restaurant!

I whispered low, now child of grace
What a predicament you're in
With muddy lanes writ on your face
And hairy acres on your chin,

For could you but have seen her, boys
With health or wealth you'd gladly part

Or with your wisdom if you're wise
To set her image on your heart.

Within her love and beauty lurk
Her hair is pressed into a bun
No daubing brushes handiwork
Would dare to tarnish such a one.

O boys, my wonder was threefold
To see a mouth so ripe and sweet
A limb that had so fine a mould
The fluted leather on her feet.

All things shall come to one who waits
By god I waited far too long
Around me were the nodding pates
But she had vanished in the throng.

For me the Fates select such tricks
I drank no more when she was gone
She was a siren of twenty six
And I a year of twenty one.

JAMES SIMMONS

1933–

Art and Reality

for James Boyce

From twenty yards I saw my old love
Locking up her car.
She smiled and waved, as lovely still
As girls of twenty are.

That cloud of auburn hair that bursts
Like sunrise round her head,
The smile that made me smile
At ordinary things she said.

But twenty years have gone and flesh
Is perishable stuff;
Can art and exercise and diet
Ever be enough

To save the tiny facial muscles
And keep taut the skin,
And have the waist, in middle-age,
Still curving firmly in?

Beauty invites me to approach,
And lies make truth seem hard
As my old love assumes her age,
A year for every yard.

JAMES LIDDY

1934–

To the Memory of Bernard Berenson

He was beautifully arrayed,
features superb as any Correggio,
grey Slavonic eyes with purring lids
and priest's hands brittle as the
ivory paper-weight on his desk –
a frail elderly Prospero in his Italian
castle wanding off progress with
the conversation of dead friends, Wilde,
Montesquiou, d' Annunzio, Proust,
preferring society women; an age bowed
itself out in the long silence before dinner.

At rose light-fall discovering he
was unable to love, more of
an exotic caressing creature
than a human being with a heart;
dignified he did not weep for himself or
send down for police protection;
he passed the morning in the library
looking at catalogues and at lunch
talked like the survivor of the Argonauts,
the guest or the mere traveller took
home pieces of the golden legend.

His difficulty was every old saint's
how to keep the soul in its cage,
walking on the Bergamo hills the red earth
tore him apart with its lovely claws:
if only he had been Adam who named
the animals roaring, creeping, flying,
swimming over the ground, in the water
or in the air, or Solomon
who could name all the flowers in the field.

Such men dance no more who were outrageous
like angels and had a whim to transfix
the knowledge of the serpent and the spider;
civilisation threw him its last jewels
before it put on its plain dress.
Earth of Bergamo, lavish sweetness on these
bones and whisper gently to them: such a head
shall not bite again the four corners
of our European dust and glory.

RIVERS CAREW

1935–

Catching Trout

Each autumn, brown trout in the middle pond
Stocked by my grandfather, moved into the stream
And steered through shallow water over stones
Until they reached the spawning-beds upstream.

For an adventure we went fishing there,
Equipped with buckets. Water slithering past
Our ankles, we dipped and dipped again, and soon
We'd landed several on the bank. Aghast

To be precipitated into air
They beat in mortal anguish on the grass
And we, confronting terror, found that it
Was mimicked in our flesh as in a glass.

Dumb agony defeated us in the end.
We gave them back their atmosphere and scheme
Half glad to see them break the glossy water,
Harness it and zigzag up the stream.

Balked, with buckets empty, we trudged home.
But now it's different. Landing trout, I pounce,
Grip them and crack them sharply on the head.
They quiver and they die almost at once.

JAMES McAULEY

1935–

Stella

Cassiopeia stirs
With fond escort.
He rolls in his head the drums of love
Under her influence;
A still figure in the garden,
Scarcely observed where he stands
In darkness among dissolving
Summer flowers.

The swan pierced by an arrow lies
Immortal on sharp stars
Above the bowed head ringing with the tones,
Vibrations, plangent chords of love.
About him, night sounds:
A leaf touching his shoulder
Whispered, descended, dying
At his feet.

Orion's hectic music
Plays perpetua mobile
For the dancing trees,
Sensuous black branches posing
In sibilant mime the thunder in his blood.
Breath crept from his lips
And fled into the sky
Carrying love's despatches.

Taurus, urgent,
Potent in that sky's sculpture,
Commands his gaze to rise
And meet the rowdy challenge of his beam.
Allowed a leniency, denied a right, he bends

Again his head and turns eyes down,
Reflecting inclinations of the spheres
That hold his secret.

At a far window, Stella rests
Fine brow against the pane
And mingles under Hesperus
Her breath with his.

DESMOND O'GRADY

1935-

Homecoming

The familiar pull of the slow train
trundling after a sinking sun on shadowed fields.
White light splicing the broad span of the sky.
Evening deepens grass, the breeze,
like purple smoke, ruffles its surface.
Straight into herring-dark skies the great cathedral spire
is sheer Gothic; slender and singular,
grey as the slate at school when a child looking up –
a bottle of raspberry in one hand, a brown bag of biscuits in
    t'other –
Feathereye Mykie my uncle told me a man
shot down a hawk dead from the cross
with a telescope fixed to his rifle.

Pulling home now into the station. Cunneen waving
a goatskin of wine from the Spain he has never seen
like an acolyte swinging a thurible.
My father, behind him, as ever in clerical grey,
white hair shining, his hand raised,
preaching away to the Poet Ryan.
And after a drink at the White House – out home.

The house in bedlam. He's here says my father.
Sober? my mother. She's looking me over.
Bring out the bottle. Pull round the fire.
Talk of the journey, living abroad:
Paris and London, Rome and New York.
What is it like in an airplane? my sister.
Glad you could make it – my brother.
Everything here the same tuppence ha'penny – the
    neighbours;
just as you left it; the same old roast chestnut.

After the songs, the one for the road,
the last caller gone – up to my room.

As I used find it home for the Christmas from school.
The great brass bed. The box still under it full
of old prayerbooks, assorted mementos,
the untouched bundle of letters mottled with mould.
Now it's a house of doorways and walls
and no laughter. A place for two old people
who speak to each other but rarely. And that only
when children return. Old people mumbling
low in the night of change and of ageing
when they think you asleep and not listening –
and we wide awake in the dark,
as when we were children.

BRENDAN KENNELLY

1936–

My Dark Fathers

My dark fathers lived the intolerable day
Committed always to the night of wrong,
Stiffened at the hearthstone, the woman lay,
Perished feet nailed to her man's breastbone.
Grim houses beckoned in the swelling gloom
Of Munster fields where the Atlantic night
Fettered the child within the pit of doom,
And everywhere a going down of light.

And yet upon the sandy Kerry shore
The woman once had danced at ebbing tide
Because she loved flute music – and still more
Because a lady wondered at the pride
Of one so humble. That was long before
The green plant withered by an evil chance;
When winds of hunger howled at every door
She heard the music dwindle and forgot the dance.

Such mercy as the wolf receives was hers
Whose dance became a rhythm in a grave,
Achieved beneath the thorny savage furze
That yellowed fiercely in a mountain cave.
Immune to pity, she, whose crime was love,
Crouched, shivered, searched the threatening sky,
Discovered ready signs, compelled to move
Her to her innocent appalling cry.

Skeletoned in darkness, my dark fathers lay
Unknown, and could not understand
The giant grief that trampled night and day,
The awful absence moping through the land.

Upon the headland, the encroaching sea
Left sand that hardened after tides of Spring,
No dancing feet disturbed its symmetry
And those who loved good music ceased to sing.

Since every moment of the clock
Accumulates to form a final name,
Since I am come of Kerry clay and rock,
I celebrate the darkness and the shame
That could compel a man to turn his face
Against the wall, withdrawn from light so strong
And undeceiving, spancelled in a place
Of unapplauding hands and broken song.

RUDI HOLZAPFEL

1938–

The Employee

Is all that fire put out, that passion spent
On buggar all, that I now worry what the boss
May think, and how to pay the bloody rent?
So I'm the rebel digit on his loss
Account . . . well, damn him and his cookie shop!
Can't I dream, and love, or try and treat all
Passers-by as human beings and drop
A bob from off some battered article?
I tell you, Mate, to please one poor old face,
To make it laugh again, or even smile,
I'd T.N.T. their bastard commonplace
And have them running up and down the aisle.
It is not time, but give my ghost re-birth –
I'll burn away such sickness from the Earth!

SEAMUS HEANEY

1939–

At a Potato Digging

I

A mechanical digger wrecks the drill,
Spins up a dark shower of roots and mould.
Labourers swarm in behind, stoop to fill
Wicker creels. Fingers go dead in the cold.

Like crows attacking crow-black fields, they stretch
A higgledy line from hedge to headland;
Some pairs keep breaking ragged ranks to fetch
A full creel to the pit and straighten, stand

Tall for a moment but soon stumble back
To fish a new load from the crumbled surf.
Heads bow, trunks bend, hands fumble towards the black
Mother. Processional stooping through the turf

Recurs mindlessly as autumn. Centuries
Of fear and homage to the famine god
Toughen the muscles behind their humbled knees,
Make a seasonal altar of the sod.

II

Flint-white, purple. They lie scattered
like inflated pebbles. Native
to the black hutch of clay
where the halved seed shot and clotted
these knobbed and slit-eyed tubers seem
the petrified hearts of drills. Split
by the spade, they show white as cream.

Good smells exude from crumbled earth.
The rough bark of humus erupts
knots of potatoes (a clean birth)

whose solid feel, whose wet inside
promises taste of ground and root.
To be piled in pits; live skulls, blind-eyed.

III

Live skulls, blind-eyed, balanced on
wild higgledy skeletons
scoured the land in 'forty-five,
wolfed the blighted root and died.

The new potato, sound as stone,
putrefied when it had lain
three days in the long clay pit.
Millions rotted along with it.

Mouths tightened in, eyes died hard,
faces chilled to a plucked bird.
In a million wicker huts
beaks of famine snipped at guts.

A people hungering from birth,
grubbing, like plants, in the bitch earth,
were grafted with a great sorrow.
Hope rotted like a marrow.

Stinking potatoes fouled the land,
pits turned pus into filthy mounds:
and where potato diggers are
you still smell the running sore.

IV

Under a gay flotilla of gulls
The rhythm deadens, the workers stop.
Brown bread and tea in bright canfuls
Are served for lunch. Dead-beat, they flop

Down in the ditch and take their fill,
Thankfully breaking timeless fasts;
Then, stretched on the faithless ground, spill
Libations of cold tea, scatter crusts.

MICHAEL LONGLEY

1939–

Leaving Inishmore

Rain and sunlight and the boat between them
Shifted whole hillsides through the afternoon –
Quiet variations on an urgent theme
Reminding me now that we left too soon
The island awash in wave and anthem.

Miles from the brimming enclave of the bay
I hear again the Atlantic's voices,
The gulls above us as we pulled away –
So munificent their final noises
These are the broadcasts from our holiday.

Oh, the crooked walkers on that tilting floor!
And the girls singing on the upper deck
Whose hair took the light like a downpour –
Interim nor change of scene shall shipwreck
Those folk on the move between shore and shore.

Summer and solstice as the seasons turn
Anchor our boat in a perfect standstill,
The harbour wall of Inishmore astern
Where the Atlantic waters overspill –
I shall name this the point of no return

Lest that excursion out of light and heat
Take on a January idiom –
Our ocean icebound when the year is hurt,
Wintertime past cure – the curriculum
Vitae of sailors and the sick at heart.

SEAMUS DEANE

1940-

Derry

I

The unemployment in our bones
Erupting on our hands in stones;

The thought of violence a relief,
The act of violence a grief;

Our bitterness and love
Hand in glove.

II

At the very most
The mind's eye
Perceives the ghost
Of the hands try
To timidly knock
On the walled rock.
But nothing will come
And the hands become
As they insist
Mailed fists.

III

The Scots and English
Settling for the best.
The unfriendly natives
Ready for the worst.
It has been like this for years
Someone says,
It might be so forever, someone fears,
Or for days.

TIMOTHY BROWNLOW

1941–

Portrait

She paces mindlessly her shuttered room,
An old rook straying among winter trees,
Whose blatant intricacies of dead bloom
Recall her careless eye from fantasies.
A dead child's faded clothes and shoes confess
What might have been, are objects which decline
Through every syllable of loneliness,
Her soul, caged by capricious nets of time.
When light enters, as her nonchalant hand
Allows it, with flick of withered curtain,

Tinges with habitual love each strand
Of hair, its gaze reveals her furtive den.
Startled eyes, like a stoat pinned on a stake,

Wedged in her skull, where God's candles confer
No sacrament, tell of her plight. Pray, break
Bread for her darkness, which no love can stir.

MICHAEL HARTNETT

1941–

mo ghrá thú[1]

with me, so you call me man,
stay: winter is harsh to us,
my self is worth no money.
but with your self spread over
me, eggs under woodcock-wings,
the grass will not be meagre:
where we walk will be white flowers.

so rare will my flesh cry out
I will not call at strange times,
we will couple when you wish:
for your womb estranges death.
jail me in this gentle land,
let your hands hold me: I am
not man until less than man.

1. I love you (Gaelic).

DEREK MAHON

1941–

In Carrowdore Churchyard

(at the grave of Louis MacNeice)

Your ashes will not stir, even on this high ground,
However the wind tugs, the headstones shake –
This plot is consecrated, for your sake,
To what lies in the future tense. You lie
Past tension now, and spring is coming round
Igniting flowers on the peninsula.

Your ashes will not fly, however the rough winds burst
Through the wild brambles and the reverend trees.
All we may ask of you we have, the rest
Is not for publication, will not be heard.
Maguire, I believe, suggested a blackbird,
And over your grave a phrase from Euripides.

Which suits you down to the ground, like this churchyard
With its play of shadow, its humane perspective.
Locked in the winter's fist, these hills are hard
As nail, yet soft and feminine in their turn
When fingers open and the hedges burn.
This you implied, is how we ought to live –

The ironical, loving crush of roses against snow,
Each fragile, solving ambiguity. So
From the pneumonia of the ditch, from the ague
Of the blind poet and the bombed-out town you bring
The all-clear to the empty holes of spring,
Rinsing the choked mud, keeping the colours new.

EILÉAN NÍ CHUILLEANÁIN

1942–

The Second Voyage

Odysseus rested on his oar, and saw
The ruffled foreheads of the waves
Crocodiling and mincing past; he rammed
The oar between their jaws, and looked down
In the simmering sea, where scribbles of weed defined
Uncertain depth, and the slim fishes progressed
In fatal formation, and thought
       If there was a single
Streak of decency in those waves now, they'd be ridged,
Pocked and dented with the battering they've had
And we could name them as Adam named the beasts
Saluting a fresh one with dismay, or a notorious one
With admiration; they'd notice us passing
And rejoice at our destruction, but these
Have less character than sheep and need more patience.

I know what I'll do he said,
I'll park my ship in the crook of a long pier
(And I'll take you with me, he said to the oar)
I'll face the rising ground, and climb away
From tidal waters, up river-beds
Where herons parcel out the miles of stream,
Over the gaps in the hills, through warm
Silent valleys, and when I meet a farmer
Bold enough to look me in the eye
With 'where are you off to with that long
Winnowing fan over your shoulder?'
There I will stand still,
And I'll plant you as a gatepost or a hitching-post
And leave you for a tidemark. I can go back
And organise my house then.

But the profound
Unfenced valleys of the ocean still held him;
He had only the oar to make them keep their distance;
The sea was still frying under the ship's side.
He considered the water-lilies, and thought about fountains
Spraying as wide as willows in empty squares;
The sugarstick of water clattering into the kettle;
The flat lakes bisecting the rushes. He remembered spiders and
    frogs
Housekeeping at the wayside in brown trickles floored with
    mud,
Horsetroughs, the black canal with pale swans at dark;
His face grew damp with tears that tasted
Like his own sweat or the insults of the sea.

JOHN F. DEANE

1943–

Driving to Midnight Mass:
DUBLIN, CHRISTMAS EVE

Five thousand million years ago, this earth
lay heaving in a mass of rocks and fire, waste and
burdened with its emptiness. To-night –
when anthropods and worms and sponges
have given way to dinosaurs, and dinosaurs
to working, wondering apes, homo erectus
has given way to sapiens and he to homo
sapiens sapiens, alias Paddy Mac – look down
on Dublin from the hills around, the lights could be
a million Christmas trees, still forest standing,
while in the sky a glow as if of dawn.

> *This day a light shall shine on us,*
> *the Lord is born within our city.*

Look along the river towards O'Connell Bridge;
the lights, the neon signs all stream on water
like breathed-on strips of tinsel. All is still.
Eleven thirty, pubs begin to empty; men
stop to argue, sway and say the name of Jesus.

> *For those who have known darkness now have seen*
> *a wondrous light; those who have dwelt*
> *in unlit streets, to them the light has come.*

To-night few cars go by. The blocks of flats
with windowed plastic trees and fairy lights,
stand, watching for a miracle; here are no dells
where fairies might appear. Out from the dark
an ambulance comes speeding, sickly blue light searching,
siren still. The mystery of the night

ticks slowly on; it will pass and leave
memories of friends and small, half-welcomed things.

In him was life, in him
life was the light of men.

for neither prehistoric swamps, nor trilobites,
the mesozoic birds, neanderthal nor modern man

had ever dreamt or seen what was our God.

The shops are gay with lights and bright things, all
save funeral homes – they dare not advertise their presence.
As midnight peals and organs start to play
two cars meet headlong in a haze of drink; the crash
flicks into silence; pain crawls like slime
through blood and into limbs. God is revealed
a baby, naked, crying in a crib.

In the Church porches and out along the grounds
teenagers laugh and swear, smoking, watching girls.
So once more Christmas trails away, its meaning moves
back into the mist and marsh of time.

JOHN ENNIS

1944-

James

Last blue, blue hours, cousin, I hugged you in the flesh
Laughing, a Sunday you cycled February northerly for company.
Cold had slashed rusty scalpels across the sun's face for days.
Hurley strapped to the crossbar, you cycled to me.

Afternoon reinforced all-black ice in tanks. You helloed my parents
Blew indoors, ran out of the book-worm hearth-blazing house.
Back of it, James, in the hay-strewn bleached sandpit field
We hallowed off nine frozen cattle, two lean bleak dry cows.

You stood sentry one hundred-yards goal, I slope opposite,
We kept no track of scores. Shots echoed. Sounded axes
Sunken in wood. Laughter, till our two throats burnt sore,
Mimicked the once wintry courtships of the silver foxes.

Chairing in for supper, we thought words so beyond the beyond
My grey father across asking after health of yours. You said,
'Great, thanks!' Blue eyes met mine. You choke nowadays on
Mouthfuls browner than floury soda-bread or any wheaten bread.

Adolescents. We were same age. Ungovernable, a raw gaiety
Shook us. Last supper. The house was infectious,
Our mutual lean-to. A thin diluted sunset
Illuminated bread, plates, cups, knives, us.

Starlings flocked twilight in loose neap-dark waves across us.
We palmed rounds of handball against the southern gable
Breaths dawdling white, soft, gauzing the self-sharpening air.

Mad to get out we'd rushed, sprung free of the irrational
    table.

So caught up, engrossed in our twin scores, I forgot
A pond hollow thickly iced down our indigo forgefield.
Night in soundless little-glittering moonlight, I skated for us.
Five months later I huddled back from you. And still I am not
    steeled.

By August, killed and coffined, you rotted in Coralstown.
Cousin, hour you bled, I searched a cloud-stanched sky
Miles off. I did not know at all that you had died.
I felt savagely on edge. Loss I could not identify.

Hurley strapped fast, you got set to race dark home. 'So
Long,' waved back to me southward on Murtagh's Hill. Down
Hightown whistling under a snow-clad moon. You cut out on
    the Dublin–Galway
Arterial Road. Yes, we laughed a lot. Good-bye, James,
    Corbetstown.

PAUL DURCAN

1944–

Birth of a Coachman

His father and grandfather before him were coachmen:
How strange, then, to think that this small, bloody, lump of
    flesh,
This tiny moneybags of brains, veins, and intestines,
This zipped-up purse of most peculiar coin,
Will one day be coachman of the Cork to Dublin route,
In a great black greatcoat and white gauntlets,
In full command of one of our famous coaches
– *Wonder*, *Perseverance*, *Diligence*, or *Lightning* –
In charge of all our lives on foul winter nights,
Crackling his whip, whirling it, lashing it,
Driving on the hapless horses across the moors
Of the Kilworth hills, beating them on
Across rivers in spate, rounding sharp bends
On only two wheels, shrieking of axle-trees,
Rock-scrapes, rut-squeals, quagmire-squelches,
For ever in dread of the pitiless highwayman
Lurking in ambush with a brace of pistols;
Then cantering carefully in the lee of the Galtees,
Bowing his head to the stone gods of Cashel;
Then again thrusting through Urlingford;
Doing his bit, and his nut, past the Devilsbit;
Praising the breasts of the hills round Port Laoise;
Sailing full furrow through the Curragh of Kildare,
Through the thousand sea-daisies of a thousand white sheep;
Thrashing gaily the air at first glimpse of the Liffey;
Until stepping down from his high perch in Dublin
Into the sanctuary of a cobbled courtyard,
Into the arms of a crowd like a triumphant toreador
All sweat and tears: the man of the moment
Who now is but a small body of but some fleeting seconds
    old.

EAVAN BOLAND

1945–

New Territory

Several things announced the fact to us:
The captain's Spanish tears
Falling like doubloons in the headstrong light,
And then of course the fuss –
The crew jostling and interspersing cheers
With wagers. Overnight
As we went down to our cabins, nursing the last
Of the grog, talking as usual of conquest,
Land hove into sight.

Frail compasses and trenchant constellations
Brought us as far as this,
And now air and water, fire and earth
Stand at their given stations
Out there, and are ready to replace
This single desperate width
Of ocean. Why do we hesitate? Water and air
And fire and earth and therefore life are here,
And therefore death.

Out of the dark man comes to life and into it
He goes and loves and dies,
(His element being the dark and not the light of day)
So the ambitious wit
Of poets and exploring ships have been his eyes –
Riding the dark for joy –
And so Isaiah of the sacred text is eagle-eyed because
By peering down the unlit centuries
He glimpsed the holy boy.

HAYDEN MURPHY

1945–

Sword Swallower

For Seamus Heaney

There was a thorn in your foot
As a child before you caught it
In your mouth and sucked the blood
And bitter hue into your throat.

Your tongue, even with the honey
Round its edges blued by age,
Was ready to receive
Both rose thorn and blade's edge.

Sharp iron familiar to your throat
Came cleanly out, clear, distinct.
It might often in the future
Be a bayonet thrust –

Often a sword without
Its sheltering scabbard –
Or the knife tinged with your neighbour's
Fire-swallowing heat –

Sharp edges at your tongue ensure
You will never be unarmed

Or empty handed.

TOM McGURK

1946–

Big Ned

'A real horse of a man,' McTaggart
Called him, 'Nineteen hands high
With shoulders like a barn-door.'
Townland's champion, miser and horsedoctor,
Focus of all the neighbours' shallow gossip,
Uncle Eddey strode Brockagh's rushy acres,
Alone for eighty years, to outlive them all.
Unschooled and illiterate, a product of
Lean times, (he bought his first suit
With rabbits snared from the Lough shore)
He could guide a team of Clydesdales at ten,
At fifteen a man.

Rebuffed, a sullen parish admired his
Feats from a safe distance –
Fearing the hard honesty, the cold stare;
When he mowed all night in the 'Wet Meadow',
Lifted a trap across his bare shoulders,
Broke stallions, or drove a herd of
Bullocks to the Moy Fair, alone.
Well-able for pestering clergy, friendless
And woman-less all his life, he christened the
Great Bays 'Jack' and 'Jim', caring only that the
Lame collie 'Watch' shared his
Turf-piled heart, in the long winter nights.

'Laid out three police,' McTaggart marvelled,
'At Finnegans' Republican funeral.'
Finally, as lawyers and clergy prepared
To divide his money
The whole parish waited triumphantly for the
Last feat, when alone as ever, at the end,

He chased doctor and priest from his death-bed,
Wanting only the work-man
To bring the horses to the window,
So that he could see them.

RICHARD RYAN

1946–

God the Father

I will not travel tonight.
Towards dawn a star
In Andromeda will abruptly

Die, but the world
And his wife, shrouded in snow
Where they live, will see

Nothing of it and instead
Will marvel through glass
At a slow lace of snow slipping

Down the limbs of trees only
Or, if that bores them,
Will count as they drift

Towards sleep the thin skins
Of heat like leaves
Slipping from little hands

And little feet, feeling
Their houses with leaves
And snow filling, the rooms

Softly into dark drifts
Tilting, will take at dawn
Such comfort as they need

From the high spars
Of trees returning safely
Home on a grey tide and,

Under the trees, a few
Calm stars straying down
Over the rim of the world

Of the living, where each brain
In its pit stirs again for me
Only, I watch a planet

Recollect its purpose
And abroad I go once more,
Savouring my choices

As there and there life
Whistles from a clutch of thorn,
Spawns bone in the humming ponds.

HUGH MAXTON

Waking

(In memory of my father, died November, 1960)

Someone is breathing in the room
apart from me. It is my father;
I recognise the hiss of his nostrils
closing, closing ... It is late;
he is doing Milltown work,
we can use the extra money.
That stub in his hand is a rent book
high as a bible, thin as his widow.
Below that, in the shadow, I imagine
the soft metal of his heart
(a gold cog, slipping) finally burred,
refusing to bite. The angle
of his nose, the slight furrow
of moustache escape me. All I have
is that sound fathered in darkness
carrying a reek of tobacco-y linen,
the taste of his lip.
                      He rustles
like a curtain. Outside it is six a.m.
A sudden fleet of cars passes
drowning my breath for about the length
of a funeral. This has gone on ten years.

FRANK ORMSBY

1947–

Moving In

The first act of love in a new house
Is not private. Loving each other
We are half aware of door and mirror.
Our ecstasy includes the bedside chair,
The air from the landing.

Streetlamp and elm utter leaves on walls
As in no room ever. Theirs is the tongue
Our tongues join in translating. Their message
Is clear: tonight you cannot ignore
The world at the window.

So we love in the knowledge of a city
At a different angle. And sharing
Our bed with furniture and tree we claim
Their perspective, merging our lives here
In their established frame.

PETER FALLON

1951–

The Cardplayers

They're dealing in twos and threes
the corner-crumpled cards
that draw the pennies, half-pennies
to the board. It's evening,
Saturday, and their work's done.

That man has sheep beyond the mill,
and that works land his fathers owned,
a labourer. That man alone can boast
he made his tools, and that does anything
and is happiest at nothing.

It's this one says 'You know,
there's four Michaels that sat down
to this game.'
          The youngest
is circling his chair to change his luck
when in she comes;

She has followed her legend into the parish
to ruffle his hair and whisper wildly
'I'll be your luck. Let you win there
and later we'll together prize.'
The others laugh, ask who's to deal. He plays to win.

PAUL MULDOON

1951–

Duffy's Circus

Once Duffy's Circus had shaken out its tent
In the big field near the Moy
God may as well have left Ireland
And gone up a tree. My father had said so.

There was no such thing as the five-legged calf,
The God of Creation
Was the God of Love.
My father chose to share such Nuts of Wisdom.

Yet across the Alps of each other the elephants
Trooped. Nor did it matter
When Wild Bill's Rain Dance
Fell flat. Some clown emptied a bucket of stars

Over the swankiest part of the crowd.
I had lost my father in the rush and slipped
Out the back. Now I heard
For the first time that long-drawn-out cry.

It came from somewhere beyond the corral.
A dwarf on stilts. Another dwarf.
I sidled past some trucks. From under a freighter
I watched a man sawing a woman in half.

THOMAS McCARTHY

1954–

State Funeral

'Parnell will never come again, he said. He's there, all that was mortal
of him. Peace to his ashes.'

James Joyce, *Ulysses*

That August afternoon the family
Gathered. There was a native *déjà-vu*
Of Funeral when we settled against the couch
On our sunburnt knees. We gripped mugs of tea
Tightly and soaked the TV spectacle;
The boxed ritual in our living-room.

My father recited prayers of memory,
Of monster meetings, blazing tar-barrels
Planted outside Free-State homes, the Broy-
Harriers pushing through a crowd, Blueshirts;
And, after the war, De Valera's words
Making Churchill's imperial palette blur.

What I remember is one decade of darkness,
A mind-stifling boredom; long summers
For blackberry picking and churning cream,
Winters for saving timber or setting lines
And snares: none of the joys of here and now
With its instant jam, instant heat and cream:

It was a landscape for old men. Today
They lowered the tallest one, tidied him
Away while his people watched quietly.
In the end he had retreated to the first dream,
Caning truth. I think of his austere grandeur;
Taut sadness, like old heroes he had imagined.

AIDAN CARL MATHEWS

1956–

Woodniche

The dragonflies were here before us, friend:
Cupboard of branch and bramble, woodniche
Where the sun tumbles, foxgloves are gorgeous.
Children tore their knees among these thorns,

Fleshed their pullovers with raspberries.
Orange peel made ripples in the brown water,
Pebbles explored beyond our peering. I
Chewed dandelions and the sun brothered me.

Huge as policemen, sombre as soutanes,
The kind trees whispered in the long watch
And I used wonder in tremendous shadow
And be afraid of where the wonder led.

Summer was wealthy with a daze of suntraps,
Daffodil-spitting, sumptuous. Everywhere
Ours for the taking. Whoever has said
It is time to go home is an adult.

ACKNOWLEDGEMENTS

To all those who helped me in the compilation of this anthology, I offer sincere thanks. I am especially grateful to Robert Hutchison for his incessant help and encouragement, and to Deirdre McQuillan. And the assistance given to me by my wife, Peggy, was invaluable.

For permission to reprint the poems in this anthology, acknowledgement is made to the following:

For Samuel Beckett:	'I would like my love to die', from *Poems in English*, to Calder & Boyars Ltd, and to Grove Press Inc. © 1961 by Samuel Beckett.
For Eavan Boland:	'New Territory', from *New Territory*, to Allen Figgis & Co. Ltd.
For Timothy Brownlow:	'Portrait', to the author.
For Joseph Campbell:	'Days', from *Poems of Joseph Campbell*, Allen Figgis & Co. Ltd, to Mr Simon Campbell.
For Rivers Carew:	'Catching Trout', to the author.
For James Carney:	'The Questions of Ethne Alba', from *Medieval Irish Lyrics*, to The Dolmen Press Ltd.
For Austin Clarke:	'Martha Blake' and 'The Straying Student', from *Later Poems*, to The Dolmen Press Ltd.
For Sigerson Clifford:	'The Ballad of the Tinker's Wife', from *Ballads of a Bogman*, Macmillan & Co. Ltd, to the author.
For Padraic Colum:	'Plougher', from *The Poet's Circuits*, Oxford University Press Ltd, to The Devin-Adair Co.
For Anthony Cronin:	'For a Father', from *Poems*, to The Cresset Press.
For Eiléan ní Chuilleanáin:	'Odysseus', to the authoress.
For Cecil Day Lewis:	'Remembering Con Markievicz', from *The Whispering Roots*, to A. D. Peters & Co.
For John F. Deane:	'Driving to Midnight Mass', to the author.
For Seamus Deane:	'Derry', to the author.
For Denis Devlin:	'The Colours of Love' and 'Lough Derg', from *Collected Poems*, to The Dolmen Press Ltd.

ACKNOWLEDGEMENTS

For Paul Durcan: 'Birth of a Coachman', to the author.

For John Ennis: 'James', from *Dolmen Hill*, to The Gallery Press Ltd.

For Kevin Faller: 'Landscape', from *Island Lyrics*, Three Candles Press, to the author.

For Padraic Fallon: 'Field Observation', to The Dolmen Press Ltd.

For Peter Fallon: 'The Cardplayers', to the author.

For Robert Farren: 'The Mason', from *The First Exile*, Sheed & Ward Ltd, to the author.

For Padraic Fiacc: 'Alive, Alive O', to the Dolmen Press Ltd.

For Monk Gibbon: 'Salt', to the author.

For Oliver St John Gogarty: 'Ringsend', from *Collected Poems*, to The Devin-Adair Co.

For Bryan Guinness: 'Lough Etive', from *The Rose In The Tree*, to Heinemann Ltd.

For Michael Hartnett: 'I Love You', from *Anatomy of a Cliché*, to The Dolmen Press Ltd.

For Seamus Heaney: 'At a Potato Digging', from *Death of a Naturalist*, to Oxford University Press of America; to Faber & Faber Ltd.

For John Hewitt: 'The Glens', from *No Rebel Word*, to Frederick Muller Ltd.

For F. R. Higgins: 'Father and Son', from *The Gap of Brightness*, Macmillan & Co. Ltd.

For Rudi Holzapfel: 'The Employee', from *The Rebel Bloom*, to Peter Melander.

For Pearse Hutchinson: 'Look, No Hands', from *Tongue Without Hands*, to The Dolmen Press Ltd.

For Valentin Iremonger: 'Icarus', from *Reservations*, to the author.

For James Joyce: 'Gas from a Burner', from *Pomes Penyeach*, Faber & Faber, to the Society of Authors as the literary representatives of the Estate of James Joyce; from *The Portable James Joyce*, to The Viking Press, Inc. All rights reserved.

For Patrick Kavanagh: 'Shancoduff' and 'Prelude', from *Collected Poems*, to MacGibbon & Kee Ltd; to The Devin-Adair Co.; 'Lough Derg', to Dr Peter Kavanagh, The Goldsmith Press.

For J. B. Keane: 'Certainty', from *The Street and Other Poems*, to the author.

For Richard Kell: 'Spring Night', to the author.

For Brendan Kennelly: 'My Dark Fathers', from *Collection One*, to Allen Figgis & Co. Ltd, and to the author.

ACKNOWLEDGEMENTS

For Jerome Kiely:	'Lizard', from *The Griffon Sings*, to Geoffrey Chapman Ltd.
For Thomas Kinsella:	'Downstream II', from *Nightwalker and Other Poems*, to The Dolmen Press Ltd.
For James Liddy:	'To the Memory of Bernard Berenson', from *In A Blue Smoke*, to The Dolmen Press Ltd.
For Michael Longley:	'Leaving Inishmore', to the author.
For Seán Lucy:	'Senior Members', to the author.
For James McAuley:	'Stella', from *A New Address*, to The Dolmen Press Ltd.
For Thomas McCarthy:	'State Funeral', to the author.
For Donagh MacDonagh:	'The Hungry Grass', from *The Hungry Grass*, to Faber & Faber Ltd.
For Patrick MacDonogh:	'The Widow of Drynam', from *One Landscape Still*, Secker & Warburg Ltd, to Mrs G. M. MacDonogh.
For Roy McFadden:	'Saint Francis and the Birds', to the author.
For Tom McGurk:	'Big Ned', to the author.
For Louis MacNeice:	'Valediction', from *Collected Poems of Louis MacNeice*, to Faber & Faber Ltd, and to Oxford University Press, New York.
For Derek Mahon:	'In Carrowdore Churchyard', from *Night-crossing*, to Oxford University Press Ltd.
For Aidan Carl Mathews:	'Woodniche', from *Windfalls*, to the author and The Dolmen Press Ltd.
For Hugh Maxton:	'Waking', to W. J. McCormack.
For Ewart Milne:	'Ballad for an Orphan', from *A Garland For the Green*, to Hutchinson & Co. Ltd.
For John Montague:	'The Trout', from *A Chosen Light*, to MacGibbon & Kee Ltd; to A. D. Peters & Co.
For Paul Muldoon:	'Duffy's Circus', from *Mules*, to Faber & Faber Ltd.
For Hayden Murhpy:	'Sword Swallower', to the author.
For Richard Murphy:	'The Poet on the Island', from *Sailing to an Island*, to Faber & Faber Ltd.
For Ulick O'Connor:	'Oscar Wilde', to the author.
For Desmond O'Grady:	'Homecoming', from *The Dark Edge of Europe*, to MacGibbon & Kee Ltd.
For Sean O'Meara:	'The Lady of the Restaurant', to the author.
For Seamas O'Sullivan:	'Nelson Street', to Dr Michael Solomons.
For Frank Ormsby:	'Moving In', from *A Store of Candles*, to Oxford University Press Ltd.

ACKNOWLEDGEMENTS

For Basil Payne: 'Lines in Memory of My Father', from *Sunlight on a Square*, to John Augustine & Co., and to the author.

For W. R. Rodgers: 'The Net', from *Europa and the Bull*, to Secker & Warburg Ltd, to Farrar, Straus & Giroux, Inc., © 1952 by W. R. Rodgers.

For George Russell: 'On Behalf of Some Irishmen Not Followers of Tradition', from *Collected Poems*, Macmillan & Co. Ltd, to A. M. Heath & Co. Ltd, and to Mr Diarmuid Russell.

For Richard Ryan: 'God the Father', to the author.

For James Simmons: 'Art and Reality', to The Bodley Head Ltd.

For W. B. Stanford: 'Undertone', to the author.

For James Stephens: 'A Glass of Beer', from *Collected Poems*, to Mrs Iris Wise and Macmillan & Co. Ltd, and to The Macmillan Co. of New York, © 1918 by The Macmillan Company, renewed 1946 by James Stephens.

For Eugene R. Watters: *From The Week-End of Dermot and Grace*, to Allen Figgis & Co. Ltd.

For Richard Weber: 'Lady & Gentleman', from *Lady and Gentleman*, to The Dolmen Press Ltd.

For R. N. D. Wilson: 'Enemies'.

For W. B. Yeats: 'To Ireland in the Coming Times', from *Collected Poems of W. B. Yeats*, to Mr M. B. Yeats and Macmillan & Co. Ltd; to The Macmillan Company of New York © 1906 by The Macmillan Company, renewed 1934 by William Butler Yeats. 'September 1913', from *Collected Poems*, to Mr M. B. Yeats and Macmillan & Co Ltd, to The Macmillan Company of New York © 1916 by The Macmillan Company, renewed 1944 by Bertha Georgie Yeats. 'The Statues', from *Collected Poems*, to Mr M. B. Yeats and Macmillan & Co. Ltd, to The Macmillan Company of New York © 1940 by Georgie Yeats, renewed 1969 by Bertha Georgie Yeats, Michael Butler Yeats and Anne Yeats.

N.B. The notes to translations by Frank O'Connor are his own. Ed.

*

Since Irish mythological names vary greatly in spelling throughout this anthology I have retained the particular spelling of each individual author.—B.K.

INDEX OF POEM TITLES

INDEX OF FIRST LINES

READ MORE IN PENGUIN

In every corner of the world, on every subject under the sun, Penguin represents quality and variety – the very best in publishing today.

For complete information about books available from Penguin – including Puffins, Penguin Classics and Arkana – and how to order them, write to us at the appropriate address below. Please note that for copyright reasons the selection of books varies from country to country.

In the United Kingdom: Please write to *Dept. JC, Penguin Books Ltd, FREEPOST, West Drayton, Middlesex UB7 OBR*

If you have any difficulty in obtaining a title, please send your order with the correct money, plus ten per cent for postage and packaging, to *PO Box No. 11, West Drayton, Middlesex UB7 OBR*

In the United States: Please write to *Penguin USA Inc., 375 Hudson Street, New York, NY 10014*

In Canada: Please write to *Penguin Books Canada Ltd, 10 Alcorn Avenue, Suite 300, Toronto, Ontario M4V 3B2*

In Australia: Please write to *Penguin Books Australia Ltd, 487 Maroondah Highway, Ringwood, Victoria 3134*

In New Zealand: Please write to *Penguin Books (NZ) Ltd, 182–190 Wairau Road, Private Bag, Takapuna, Auckland 9*

In India: Please write to *Penguin Books India Pvt Ltd, 706 Eros Apartments, 56 Nehru Place, New Delhi 110 019*

In the Netherlands: Please write to *Penguin Books Netherlands B.V., Keizersgracht 231 NL–1016 DV Amsterdam*

In Germany: Please write to *Penguin Books Deutschland GmbH, Friedrichstrasse 10–12, W–6000 Frankfurt/Main 1*

In Spain: Please write to *Penguin Books S. A., C. San Bernardo 117–6° E–28015 Madrid*

In Italy: Please write to *Penguin Italia s.r.l., Via Felice Casati 20, I–20124 Milano*

In France: Please write to *Penguin France S. A., 17 rue Lejeune, F–31000 Toulouse*

In Japan: Please write to *Penguin Books Japan, Ishikiribashi Building, 2–5–4, Suido, Bunkyo-ku, Tokyo 112*

In Greece: Please write to *Penguin Hellas Ltd, Dimocritou 3, GR–106 71 Athens*

In South Africa: Please write to *Longman Penguin Southern Africa (Pty) Ltd, Private Bag X08, Bertsham 2013*

READ MORE IN PENGUIN

PENGUIN INTERNATIONAL WRITERS

Baotown Wang Anyi

One of China's foremost young writers draws on the stories and characters of the remote village where she was exiled during the Cultural Revolution, portraying peasant life with the vividness of a Chinese Gorky. 'This is an immemorial China of superstition, starvation and subsistence ... Here we have some of the same studied parochialism as in [Jane] Austen' – *Literary Review*

Marbles: A Play in Three Acts Joseph Brodsky

Imprisoned in a mighty steel tower, where yesterday is the same as today and tomorrow, Publius and Tullius consider freedom, the nature of reality and illusion and the permanence of literature versus the transience of politics. In a Platonic dialogue set 'two centuries after our era' in ancient Rome, Nobel prizewinner Joseph Brodsky takes us beyond the farthest reaches of the theatre of the absurd.

Scandal Shusaku Endo

'Spine-chilling, erotic, cruel ... it's very powerful' – *Sunday Telegraph*. '*Scandal* addresses the great questions of our age. How can we straddle the gulf between faith and modernity? How can humankind be so tender, and yet so cruel? Endo's superb novel offers only an unforgettable bafflement for an answer' – *Observer*

A Summer Affair Ivan Klíma

David Krempa, a biologist in Prague, and married, lives for his work. Iva, young and crazy, lives only for the moment. Their affair was madness, but once it had begun there was no going back. 'Short and sharp ... it leaves one breathless' – *Literary Review*

A Scrap of Time Ida Fink

'A powerful, terrifying story, an almost unbearable witness to unspeakable anguish,' wrote the *New Yorker* of the title story in Ida Fink's award-winning collection. Herself a survivor, she portrays Poland during the Holocaust, the lives of ordinary people in hiding as they resist, submit, hope, betray, remember. 'A masterpiece ... we are brought as close to the Holocaust as it is possible for literature to take us' – Alan Sillitoe

READ MORE IN PENGUIN

PENGUIN INTERNATIONAL WRITERS

On the Golden Porch and Other Stories Tatyana Tolstaya

'There are thirteen stories in this collection and every one's an absolute gem of emotion ... It's not hard to see why quite so much fuss is being made over Tatyana Tolstaya' – *Time Out*. 'With one collection ... she has established herself as a new and original force in Russian literature in her own right' – *Mail on Sunday*

A Song of Truth and Semblance Cees Nooteboom

Two writers meet in an Amsterdam arts club, drink wine, skirt nervously around any talk of their own work and argue about the nature of fiction. For one of them, a floating pair of epaulettes is on the point of fleshing into Georgiev, a nineteenth-century Bulgarian colonel. The banal and irritating phrase 'the colonel falls in love with the doctor's wife' itches at the back of his mind...

Half of Man is Woman Zhang Xianliang

'The gulag literature of the Soviet Union is world-famous, but China's equivalent is almost unknown. *Half of Man is Woman* is exceptional not only for belonging to this genre but also – in China – for daring to make sexuality its theme, together with politics, freedom and identity' – *Observer*

The Velvet Prison Artists Under State Socialism Miklós Haraszti

'A fascinating account of totalitarian aesthetics ... he describes a culture where the traditional antagonism between censor and artist has been replaced with a strange form of collusion. In this new relationship all censors and most artists are entangled in a mutual embrace. This is the "velvet prison"' – *Guardian*

Last Call Harry Mulisch

'Intricately rewarding ... Uli Bouwmeester, an obscure former vaudeville actor, wartime collaborator and member of a famous stage family, is unearthed to play Prospero in a version of *The Tempest* that is also a play-within-a-play about the swansong of a famous actor ... who nurses a guilty secret like the old man playing him...' – *Guardian*

READ MORE IN PENGUIN

PENGUIN BOOKS OF POETRY

American Verse
British Poetry Since 1945
Caribbean Verse in English
A Choice of Comic and Curious Verse
Contemporary American Poetry
Contemporary British Poetry
English Christian Verse
English Poetry 1918–60
English Romantic Verse
English Verse
First World War Poetry
Greek Verse
Irish Verse
Light Verse
Love Poetry
The Metaphysical Poets
Modern African Poetry
New Poetry
Poetry of the Thirties
Post-War Russian Poetry
Scottish Verse
Southern African Verse
Spanish Civil War Verse
Spanish Verse
Women Poets

READ MORE IN PENGUIN

PLAYS IN PENGUIN

READ MORE IN PENGUIN

PENGUIN INTERNATIONAL WRITERS

Gamal Al-Ghitany	**Zayni Barakat**
Wang Anyi	**Baotown**
Joseph Brodsky	**Marbles: A Play in Three Acts**
Shusaku Endo	**The Samurai**
	Scandal
	Wonderful Fool
Ida Fink	**A Scrap of Time**
Miklós Haraszti	**The Velvet Prison**
Ivan Klíma	**My First Loves**
	A Summer Affair
Jean Levi	**The Chinese Emperor**
Harry Mulisch	**Last Call**
Cees Nooteboom	**A Song of Truth and Semblance**
Luise Rinser	**Prison Journal**
Anton Shammas	**Arabesques**
Josef Škvorecký	**The Cowards**
Tatyana Tolstoya	**On the Golden Porch and Other Stories**
Elie Wiesel	**Twilight**
Zhang Xianliang	**Half of Man is Woman**

READ MORE IN PENGUIN

PENGUIN POETRY LIBRARY

Arnold Selected by Kenneth Allott
Blake Selected by W. H. Stevenson
Browning Selected by Daniel Karlin
Burns Selected by Angus Calder and William Donnelly
Byron Selected by A. S. B. Glover
Clare Selected by Geoffrey Summerfield
Coleridge Selected by Kathleen Raine
Donne Selected by John Hayward
Dryden Selected by Douglas Grant
Hardy Selected by David Wright
Herbert Selected by W. H. Auden
Keats Selected by John Barnard
Kipling Selected by James Cochrane
Lawrence Selected by Keith Sagar
Milton Selected by Laurence D. Lerner
Pope Selected by Douglas Grant
Rubáiyát of Omar Khayyám Translated by Edward FitzGerald
Shelley Selected by Isabel Quigley
Tennyson Selected by W. E. Williams
Wordsworth Selected by W. E. Williams

READ MORE IN PENGUIN

PENGUIN INTERNATIONAL POETS

Anna Akhmatova   Selected Poems   Translated by D. M. Thomas

Anna Akhmatova is not only Russia's finest woman poet but perhaps the finest in the history of western culture.

Fernando Pessoa   Selected Poems

'I have sought for his shade in those Edwardian cafés in Lisbon which he haunted, for he was Lisbon's Cavafy or Verlaine' – Cyril Connolly in the *Sunday Times*

Yehuda Amichai   Selected Poems
Translated by Chana Bloch and Stephen Mitchell

'A truly major poet ... there's a depth, breadth and weighty momentum in these subtle and delicate poems of his' – Ted Hughes

Czeslaw Milosz   Collected Poems 1931–1987
Winner of the 1980 Nobel Prize for Literature

'One of the greatest poets of our time, perhaps the greatest' – Joseph Brodsky

Joseph Brodsky   To Urania
Winner of the 1987 Nobel Prize for Literature

Exiled from the Soviet Union in 1972, Joseph Brodsky has been universally acclaimed as the most talented Russian poet of his generation.

and

Paul Celan	Selected Poems
Tony Harrison	Selected Poems *and* Theatre Works 1973–1985
Heine	Selected Verse
Geoffrey Hill	Collected Poems
Philippe Jaccottet	Selected Poems
Osip Mandelstam	Selected Poems
Pablo Neruda	Selected Poems
Peter Redgrove	Poems 1954–1987